MATHOS

JENNIE LYNN ROBERTS

Copyright © 2021 Jennie Lynn Roberts

First paperback edition July 2021

Editor: O. Ventura at Hot Tree Editing
Cover design by Damonza.com

ISBN 978-1-8383389-4-7 (paperback)
ISBN 978-1-8383389-5-4 (e-book)

www.jennielynnroberts.com

For Gill

"Believe in love. Believe in magic... Believe in your dreams."

Jon Bon Jovi

Acknowledgments

Thank you to all the amazing people in my life who have supported and encouraged me, especially Gill Harvard and Hannah Huffelmann.

A special thank you goes to Olivia Ventura at Hot Tree Editing for her insightful editing wizardry. Thanks also to Donna Pemberton for keeping such a close eye on my book-baby; to Ginny Gaylor, Casey Ford and Keeley Catarineau for their perceptive comments and eagle-sharp eyes; and to Charlotte Polland at Proof It Plus for her skilled proofreading and generous support.

Thank you to the awesome design team at Damonza.com for this gorgeous cover.

And most importantly, thank you to Mark, Alethea and Michael. I would be lost without you.

Prologue

FIFTEEN YEARS ago

MATHOS TIPPED his head up and watched the sky, clasping his hands behind his back as he considered it. It was a perfectly clear, unbroken blue. The kind of blue that a boy could lose himself in, floating away on his thoughts until the world around him no longer existed. There was a name for that particular shade of deep, vibrant blue. Azure, maybe. Or was it cerulean? One of his tutors would know... if he still had tutors.

The monk started speaking again, and Mathos brought his gaze back down to the slightly hunched older man with his rounded belly and shaved head. His singsong voice droned on—detailing the baron's illustrious noble heritage, his battlefield heroics, how beloved he was by the men he commanded. How honorably he'd died.

And with each further revelation, Mathos's mother's sighs grew more heartbroken and the monk more distracted.

Did any of it matter now?

The beast in his belly growled, twisting nauseatingly. Gods knew it hadn't settled since the messenger had arrived with the news. Father was dead on the northern battlefields. And they were left behind.

The father he had hardly seen over the last two years, except for brief weeks of home leave. The father who had taught him to fish and ride and play cards. Who had pulled him into a rough hug and whispered in a low voice, "Be a good boy, Mathos. I'll see you before midwinter."

That was the last thing he'd ever hear from the man who gave him life.

His throat burned, tightening around the tears he refused to shed. Mathos blinked, swallowing against the jumbled mess of grief and loss and rage and guilt. Clenching his fist against the roiling churn of his beast.

How could his father have done this to him? How could he have left him? Left them all?

His mother was resplendent in flowing black mourning robes that shimmered as the wind tugged at the hems. Sophisticated and stylish, despite standing in the wind beside her husband's grave. Her dark blond hair shone as it fell in artfully styled waves, while her face was a perfect alabaster streaked with elegant tears. She was being held up by her sister and one of her maids, somehow managing to look both beautiful and fragile.

The monk's speech moved on to the family left behind by the loss of the baron—the fatherless children and the grieving widow. Hearing her name, his mother gasped out a choked sob, and then, whimpering gently, sank helplessly to the ground despite the best efforts of the women around her to hold her up.

Gods, she loved drama. And Father had always indulged

her. He liked her soft and vulnerable and helpless, and she had played that role all her life.

And now what? Father was gone, and Mother was weeping on the cold ground.

Mathos's two older sisters had been encouraged to be the same way since the day they were born. They stood side by side, their silk handkerchiefs pressed gently against their faces as they wept. While Crissy, three years old and only just past babyhood, stood beside her nurse with her thumb in her mouth, watching in wide-eyed confusion.

Who was going to look after them all?

Mathos had a horrible idea that he already knew the answer.

If only he had a gold coin for every person who'd told him he was the man of the family now, he would be able to pay someone else to bloody do it.

Gods.

He knew he was an arrogant little shit—his tutors reminded him daily—but he was still only thirteen. Yvaine and Lunette were fifteen and sixteen respectively, and yet they were both currently crumpling to the ground behind their mother, none of them even noticing the tears springing to little Crissy's eyes, the way she burrowed into her nurse's skirts in distress.

What was he going to do? He honestly had no idea at all.

He wanted to howl for the father who was gone forever. Anguish and misery churned through him, and he wanted to scream in rage at the unfairness of it all. Or maybe just scream. Scream and cry and fall apart. But if he started, he didn't know that he could stop. And none of that was going to help now.

His aunt looked at him helplessly, his mother a porcelain

doll swathed in black silk at her feet. He stepped over to them and offered his hand to the sobbing woman on the ground. "Come now, Mother, you can't sit down there."

She sniffled pitifully and put her cold hand into his, but made no move to stand, even as the monk's voice trailed away unhappily.

A flicker of annoyance rose, but he immediately shoved it away. What was the point? Shouting at her would only make her cry more helplessly and leave him feeling like a brute.

After all, she had genuinely loved his father. And she was genuinely grieving. This was how she showed the depth of her pain.

He gave her an encouraging smile and lowered his voice. "Mother, it rained yesterday, and you look much too beautiful to sit in the mud. Let me help you up, and you can lean on me."

Her eyes widened; she obviously hadn't considered that she might have to walk around for the rest of the day with mud on the back of her dress. He gave her hand a small tug, and she allowed him to pull her back up, giving her skirts a surreptitious sweep with one hand while the other clutched an embroidered handkerchief to her eyes.

Thank the gods that his sisters followed her example and slowly stood, both still weeping loudly, as the monk cleared his throat and continued. The nurse picked Crissy up to rest on her hip, his sister's small blond head tucked under her chin.

Mathos wrapped his arm around his trembling mother and let her lean on him. He was already as tall as she was, sharing the same burgundy-and-gold scaling, the same thick, dark blond hair and hazel-brown eyes.

But that was where the similarity ended. His personality

was his father's—or so he'd been told. Usually when his tutors were accusing him of arrogance or stubbornness. Or when he was trying to charm his way out of trouble.

And now his father was dead.

"Thank you, Matty," Mother whispered through her gently falling tears. "I knew you'd take care of us."

He tightened his arm and willed her not to say it. *Please, gods, just don't let her say it. Please. Let me get through today first.*

The beast in his belly rumbled unhappily, but she didn't seem to notice as she dabbed delicately at her eyes.

"You're the man of the family now."

Chapter One

LUCILLA PICKED at her dinner and watched the staff around her. Something was definitely wrong.

One of the kitchen girls had gone into the village for market day and come back late, brimming with a strange kind of nervous excitement as she rushed through the house and into the scullery to gossip.

And now they were all looking at her. Not blatantly, no. Little glances that made her stomach clench. Speculative. Calculating, even. But they quickly turned their heads and looked away when she focused on them, whispering in corners and then suddenly falling silent.

They knew something. Something about her. Something bad.

She had asked her maid what was happening, only to be given a long, blank stare. They were Ballanor's people; they didn't answer to her.

There was only one thing she could think of that would make them behave so suspiciously. Ballanor's wife must be pregnant. Or perhaps the baby was already born?

Damn. That brought her life expectancy down dramatically.

While Ballanor had no heir, he could be expected to keep her around, just in case. But if he didn't need her anymore—if he had an heir of his own—what then? Then he would decide that the threat of her existence outweighed the benefit of keeping her around and finally act.

She had been locked away her entire life. Twenty-six years with no freedom, no friends and not one possession that was entirely hers. The last thing she wanted was more of the same. She had absolutely no desire to rule the kingdom; all she wanted was to be allowed to walk away and build something that was hers. Not the council's, not her family's, not her politically chosen husband's. Hers.

She wasn't a threat to anyone. But Ballanor would never see it that way. His mind was filled with plots and suspicions and hatred—he simply couldn't understand people who didn't want power at any cost—and he'd detested her since the moment she was born.

It was hardly surprising that Ballanor blamed her for the death of their mother; her father had felt exactly the same way. Geraint had sent her away to be brought up by strangers, rather than have to look at the little girl whose life had cost him his precious wife, and proceeded to do his best to forget she'd ever existed.

But her brother? Ballanor hadn't forgotten her. No, he hated her to the depth of his soul. If he even had one. And if he knew his line of succession was certain, he would love nothing more than to finally be rid of her.

For years it had hovered over her, that feeling of waiting

to die. Of wondering just what it would take for her father to forget her completely and her brother to finally act. And now that Geraint was gone and most likely there was an heir on the way, that moment had come.

When Geraint had died at Ravenstone, the need to run had become overwhelming. She hadn't bothered to mourn the father she'd hardly known—and never liked—she was too busy worrying about what his death meant for her. Ballanor was suddenly the man in charge of her fate, and it had filled her with horror.

She'd been determined to leave before she could find out what he'd do. And she'd almost done it. She'd been so very close... until she wasn't. That first attempt had been a disaster in every way, but she wasn't going to let that stop her. She had learned from those mistakes, and now she was really going to do it.

She ignored the whispering staff and schooled her face into the demure and slightly glazed look that had served her well through countless hours with governesses, tutors, and most especially Lieutenant Claudius, the man in charge of keeping her safely locked away.

It was the same look she wore when Geraint and Ballanor had made their rare visits to check on her, spending their few hours in the manor home talking with her guards, followed by finding fault with everything she did and said and thought. She was too stubborn. Too argumentative. Too unladylike. Too stupid. Too useless.

Slowly she had learned to keep all of her thoughts to herself—safely hidden behind her blank face and insipidly sweet smile—ranting in silence to avoid the threat of punishment. It was amazing just how cathartic a well-timed *fuck you* could be while delivered in the safety of her own head.

It served her well now too. The servants could whisper and stare, filled with their secrets. But they wouldn't guess that she had secrets of her own. Her own plans.

There was no more waiting for the perfect time to leave. There never would be a perfect time. There was only the danger she was in. And that meant she had to go.

Now.

She cast a resigned eye over the food spread out on the table. There was no way she could take any of it with her without rousing immediate suspicion, and she had no idea when she was going to get any more.

She pushed her chair back and dipped her chin. "You are all excused."

No one even blinked. These days, when she wasn't out riding Penelope, she stayed in her room. It felt like she spent more time lying on her bed looking out through the bars on her window than anything else.

She climbed the stairs, listening to the whispers starting up again, desperately straining to hear what they were saying. It was impossible, just a vague murmur beneath the clatter of dishes being cleared.

Lucilla closed her bedroom door, glad to finally be alone.

Thank the gods she'd already rid herself of having a personal maid months ago—the one and only good idea that Cerdic had ever had. He'd had an entirely different benefit in mind, but the maids had been only too glad to lessen their workload, and now it meant that no one was coming to check on her.

And that was the last time she was going to think about the sergeant. Cerdic had already taken too much from her. Even worse, she had given it to him freely. Never again. Now he was merely one of her jailors once more.

She opened her wardrobe and pulled out the leather satchel she had hidden at the back. Moving quickly, she filled it with two spare shirts, thick socks, an empty waterskin she'd taken from the kitchen, a pile of monthly rags, and her tiny hoard of treasure: a ring, a sapphire that had fallen from an ornate buckle, a few pearls, and several coins that she had stolen from Ballanor and Geraint—Grendel too, when her brother brought him. It was all she had. All her mother's jewelry was kept in the treasury at the Palace of Kaerlud, and no one had ever thought to give her any of her own.

She was already dressed for riding in knee-high boots over fitted breeches and a closely tailored, button-up jacket in deep forest green, her thick hair pulled back into a tight knot. She slung the satchel over her head, its strap lying sideways across her body, and slipped a heavy dark gray wool cloak over the top of everything. Finally, she added her only weapon, the jeweled letter opener glittering as she shoved it into her belt. It was too small and too blunt to do much good, but it was all she had.

She shoved a pile of clothes under her blankets in the hopes that the lumpy shape might pass as her in the darkness and then carefully tidied her room, hoping to avoid any suspicion if someone should check on her.

Was there anything else she should take? She cast her eye slowly over the room she had lived in all her life. It was beautiful and elegant, decorated in purple, cream, and silver. Luxurious and comfortable. She hated it.

Time to go. Before the house was too quiet. Before the guards settled in. While they were all still distracted.

She opened her door a crack and peered out into the corridor. Last time she'd gone out the window; now there were bars. Hopefully, they didn't expect her to simply walk out the door.

Her heart thudded heavily, her breath shallow and tight as she forced herself to stay still and focus. What was the worst that could happen? Someone could see her and bring her back. Punish her. Report her to Ballanor. Again.

And what would the punishment be if she stayed? Even if Ballanor miraculously forgot that she existed, how much longer could she live this hideous life of nothingness?

No family other than Ballanor, and he didn't count. No friends. No experiences. Never leaving. Nothing ever changing. Every day identical to the one before. She might as well have died already.

Lucilla forced herself to take a deep breath and then crept into the corridor, every cell in her body alert to the sounds of the staff moving around on the floor below. She clung to the wall, avoiding the squeaky central floorboards, placing her feet carefully, one after the other.

Her hands were damp where her palms pressed to the wall, and more than once she had to dry them on her cloak, working hard to keep her breaths even and slow.

She hovered at the top of the stairs, listening.

Cook shouted at someone in the distant kitchens. A guard called his rounds outside. Somewhere in the house a door closed heavily, and she flinched. Gods.

She couldn't stay on the landing. She had to move. Back or forward.

She had to decide who she was. The kind of woman who waited in her room for salvation that would never come, or the kind of woman who took her own life into her hands. The kind of woman who walked down the stairs and out the door. Who moved. Right. Now.

Yes. She was that woman. She was already halfway

down the stairs when her fear came back. The last time she had tried to escape, they beat the skin off her palms, then locked her in her room with her bleeding hands and no food, only water, for days. They hadn't even changed the pot or given her candles. They'd barred the windows and left her in the dark. What would they do this time?

She wasn't going to think like that. This time she was getting out.

Her hands were shaking by the time she reached the door, and it took her several tries to turn the key.

There was another clatter from the dining room, startling her just as she pulled open the door. She snuck a quick look behind her, letting out a shaky breath when she saw she was still alone, and then slipped through, still carrying the key, and shut the door behind her with a quiet click. The first thing she did was lock the door and push the key back through the gap under the wood. With luck, the guards would assume it had simply fallen out.

It was already dark, the air cold and damp as she sped away from the front of the house and darted onto the side path. Dead leaves, wet with autumn rain, littered the gravel, muffling her steps. Wispy clouds scudded across the crescent moon as she flitted into the darkest shadows; making her way into the small orchard that flanked the kitchen garden.

She paused for a moment, pressing herself against the hard trunk of a sprawling apple tree. Despite all the hours she'd spent imagining this moment, she still hadn't decided whether to run alone or to take Penelope. She would be found out much sooner if they realized the mare was gone. But she could travel further and faster on horseback.

In the end, it was an easy decision; she couldn't bear to leave her only friend behind.

When Penelope was born, the groom had taken one

look at the foal's rich red-copper coloring and told her that a bay mare would be difficult. Quick-tempered and hard to handle. Perhaps that was why Lucilla had fallen instantly in love with the gangly-legged filly—because everyone said the same things about her. But she had never had a problem with the mare; she gave Penelope all her love, and Penelope gave it back.

Lucilla stuck to the darkness under the trees until she was near enough to dash across the courtyard to the low eaves of the stables.

It was late, and the horses would have been settled in their stalls ready for the night... but was the stable boy with them? Or the groom? Or were they both sitting in the kitchen, flirting with the maids? Or getting drunk with the guards?

Lucilla crept closer. No light spilled around the stable door.

She tiptoed up to the door and pressed her ear against the heavy wood. She couldn't hear anything.

Did that mean anything? Probably not. But she either had to open the door or leave Penelope behind.

She pulled open the door and crept inside.

It was pitch-black as she leaned against the door, listening to the shuffling of hooves on straw, a soft horse's sigh from deeper in the building. Nothing else moved. No one called out in greeting or warning. If the stable boy was there, he was already asleep. Hopefully.

Holding her hand against the wall for guidance, she felt her way to the first stall on the left. A search of the wall with her hands led her to the hook holding Penelope's halter—she didn't have time to try and find, let alone fit, Penelope's bridle and saddle in the total dark, so the halter would have to do—and she snagged it before quickly letting herself into the stall.

Penelope whickered softly and nudged her shoulder. Lucilla wrapped her arms around the mare's neck and leaned her forehead against the warm solidity as the reassuring scent of horse and hay surrounded her. Gods, she'd needed that comfort so badly.

"I'm sorry, Penny, I know you're warm and happy," Lucilla whispered as she slipped the halter over her head. "We're going on an adventure. Just you and me."

She fumbled in her satchel for the rags and then knelt in the straw, lifting Penelope's legs one at a time to wrap her hooves. It wasn't perfect, but it was the best she could do.

As soon as she was done, she led the mare out of her stall, letting her hand drift along the wall to guide them. Penelope followed her trustingly through the darkness and out the stables.

Even with their bindings, Penelope's hooves seemed to ring against the cobbles, and Lucilla winced at the noise as she guided the mare slowly out of the courtyard and into the formal gardens that fronted the large manor house.

Her mother had planted them years ago, and her father had insisted they be maintained, even though he never saw them. Ballanor had simply ignored them. Now they were bare and bleak, flowers faded, roses trimmed, ready for winter. The symbol of the parents who had both abandoned her on the day she was born.

As soon as they reached the grass, she knelt to tug the bindings off Penelope's hooves and then shoved them back into her satchel. Gripping the halter, she pulled the mare past the formal beds and down to the iron gate set into a looming stone wall, just visible in the dim light.

Then she waited, running her fingers over Penelope's

velvety cheek and through her mane until, finally, she heard it. The thud of boots on the path.

She shrank back, pushing herself into the wall and rubbing Penelope's muzzle gently, praying that the gentle horse would stay silent. And then, as some dark, spiked plant scratched the side of her face, praying that there were no venomous spiders living between the stones.

Her imagination supplied her with images of fat bodies and hairy legs skittering over her shoulders and into her hair, and she shivered silently, chewing her lip.

The guard whistled and was quickly answered by another whistle from further ahead, and a less distinct reply from behind. The footsteps stopped, and she imagined him doing a slow turn, eyes raking over the dark fields and woods in the distance as she held her breath, her fingers clenched tight in the rough hair of Penelope's mane.

And then he started to walk once more. She counted to sixty under her breath and then let herself and Penelope out through the gate, closing it quietly behind them.

She used a stone flanking the path to help her scramble onto Penelope's back before leaning down to pat her flank and whisper encouragement.

She pushed Penelope into a trot as they cleared the manor's grounds and made their way along a sandy path and into the forest. She had ridden it hundreds of times. First with tutors, and later with... the sergeant. But she'd never been past the first stream before.

There was a sudden commotion behind her. A bell started clanging loudly. Shouts and whistles echoed in the distance. Gods. Did they already know she was missing? She'd hoped to have hours.

Penelope could see better than her in the thick darkness under the trees, and Lucilla let her take the lead, using the halter as best she could and guiding her to keep up a steady trot.

They splashed through the shallow stream and out the other side. Then, thinking better of it, Lucilla guided Penelope back into the stream and followed it south, staying in the water. The sounds of alarm faded behind them, but it wouldn't be long before someone realized she had Penelope. And then the true hunt would start.

Lucilla had never been outside the manor's farmlands before. She had never seen a map of the area, and she had no idea where she was. She had no food. She had no friends or family she could turn to. She had nowhere to go and no idea of what to do when she got there. And she had a house full of guards, and her brother, the king, with all his wealth and power, arrayed against her.

But for the first time in her entire life, she was free.

She chuckled, slightly hysterically, and pushed Penelope on as fast as she could go, into the night.

Chapter Two

"WE SHOULD GO and see her now." Tor thumped his tankard down on the dirty table with a belligerent scowl.

Mathos rocked back in his chair and fought for patience. Two weeks on the road together, and he was ready to kill the man. Tor was quiet and brooding at the best of times; now he was bloody miserable and looking for a fight, alternating between long glowering silences and terse complaints about everything from the weather, to the state of the road, to unreasonably high levels of taxation.

It was driving Mathos insane.

He put down his watery ale and linked his fingers behind his head in an attempt not to reach across the table and throttle the huge Apollyon. There were only three other men in the roadside tavern—all just about as ancient and unwashed as the tavern itself—and they'd all been ignoring each other perfectly well. Starting a brawl would not be a good way to stay inconspicuous.

"We've discussed this at least three times already today. If Lucilla is there—and she wasn't in the hunting lodge, the stately homes, or the castle that we checked already—she won't want visitors turning up in the dark."

Tor cracked his knuckles, one after the other. A move that was no doubt intended to be intimidating. All it succeeded in achieving was to scrape painfully along Mathos's one last remaining nerve.

Mathos barely restrained the eye roll that would probably push Tor over the edge. "She's a queen who doesn't even know it yet. A girl who's been kept away from court. Coddled, spoiled, and protected her entire life. Two big armed men turning up out of the blue and frightening her won't help. We want her on our side, remember?"

Tor looked down into his empty mug and muttered something just too low to hear.

"We can't go tonight," Mathos repeated.

Tor looked up through narrowed eyes. "She's there. I'm telling you. This is the only manor house on the list with a garden designed by her mother."

Mathos was beginning to see why Tristan never bothered to respond with more than a grunt. "The fact that we think this is the one, is exactly why we can't go now. A queen doesn't get out of bed in the middle of the night for mercenaries. Especially not mercenaries who watched both her father and her brother die."

Tor cocked his head. "So let's get in there and explain it all to her. This is the last place on our list. If we go tonight, we can get this stupid mission over and done with."

"For fuck's sake, Tor, if we'd wanted to terrify the girl, or better yet, start a war, we could have simply swept down here with a regiment of Nephilim. We're trying to do this quietly."

Mathos sighed pointedly. "You know, same as me, that Dornar's out there looking for her. Looking for us. What do you think will happen if we stir up a pile of trouble? He'll have our heads on pikes before the sun comes up, and Queen Lucilla will be standing next to him when he does it."

Tor grumbled loudly, and Mathos sighed again, rubbing a tired hand down his face. "I honestly don't understand why you even came with me."

"Garet and Jos went east, Jeremiel and Rafe went north. We are going south."

Mathos gave in and rolled his eyes. Trust Tor to say something both blatantly obvious and completely useless. They both knew how the Hawks had spread out while Alanna, Val, Nim, and Tristan stayed at the temple. The work at the temple was important; not only were they urgently sending messengers back and forth to Alanna's mother, trying to undo the damage Ballanor had done to the treaty, but they were also gathering evidence to prove Lucilla's birthright so that they could get her onto the throne as quickly as possible once they'd found her.

The only Hawk not helping was Reece. Damn the hardheaded stubbornness of the man. He had left his squad. Left his brothers. Determined to go back to Kaerlud alone, and nothing Mathos had said would change his mind.

All because of one selfish, betraying ex-lover. A good example of why, in Mathos's opinion, it was better to never get too involved with anyone who wanted a relationship of any kind. On those rare occasions when his need for human contact was too great to ignore, he made sure that the women he spent time with had no real interest in him. Far safer for everyone that way.

And sitting across from him, staring morosely into his

empty mug as if it held the answers of the Abyss, was an even better example.

Keely had chosen to stay and help at the Temple. And why wouldn't she? Her friends were there. It was comfortable there. No one had expected her to sign up for a tour of the kingdom looking for a lost, and possibly no longer even living, woman.

What he didn't understand was why Tor hadn't stayed with her and resolved whatever drama was going down between them. Personally, Mathos would have walked away, no problem. If there was one thing he hated, it was drama. But it was eating at his friend. He should have stayed and sorted things out. It was bloody obvious to everyone except Tor.

He gave his friend a long look. "Why didn't you stay with Keely?"

Tor wrapped his hand around the back of his neck, accentuating the swirling black-and-red tattoos that sleeved both his arms. "I'm needed here."

"I can look for some pampered little girl without you holding my hand, you know."

Tor looked away. "She doesn't want me there."

"Keely said that?"

"No, but…."

Gods save him. Mathos took a long sip of his ale. "Fine. You decided, without talking to her, that she didn't want you to stay. But what did *you* want to do?"

Tor grunted, still looking away. As far as Mathos could tell, his friend had wanted to get away from the woman and whatever had happened between them but had then instantly regretted the decision and was now desperate to get back to her. Hence the surly glowers and the fight about finishing their mission immediately.

Mathos contained a groan. How did he always land up in the role of nursemaid? "Did you tell her how you feel? Did you say anything to suggest to her that you might be interested in... I don't know, gods... whatever it is you're interested in?"

The big Apollyon stared into his cup for a moment before muttering a rough, "No. I... No. I hurt her."

"You *hurt* Keely?" Mathos growled, his beast unfurling in his belly.

Tor scowled darkly before clarifying, "Her feelings. I hurt her feelings."

His beast settled slightly. "And did you apologize?"

"No." Tor's reply was so quiet, he almost didn't hear it.

"And then you left? Just like that?"

Tor blinked, saying nothing. Then he turned his face to the smudged window and the darkness outside.

"You didn't fight for her at all?" Mathos asked, slightly shocked.

He'd lived his entire life avoiding exactly the kind of turmoil that Tor and Keely had created for themselves, but Tor didn't have the same kind of horror of relationships that he did. And he obviously cared for Keely. The bond that they'd formed had been clear to everyone. What the hell had happened?

Before Tor could reply, the ancient tavern door crashed open, and a heavily armed Apollyon guard stepped in. A guard wearing palace blue and the insignia of a lieutenant. Bloody hell.

Was this one of Dornar's? Mathos looked at him as closely as he could without drawing attention. He didn't seem familiar, but there had been so many changes at the palace that it was hard to be certain. And in the days they'd spent in Eshcol desperately combing through temple records and then on the road, anything could have happened.

His beast twitched, preparing for danger with a ripple of hardening scales. Mathos leaned back slowly, further from the light, while Tor did the same beside him.

The lieutenant ran a considering eye over the tavern's occupants, lingering for a moment on their table, and then strode forward to the door that led to the kitchen and banged loudly. The scrawny landlord ripped open the door with a scowl, only to quickly reassess his attitude and dip his chin politely.

The lieutenant pulled out a small, framed picture, murmuring something too low to hear, and showed it to the man, who shook his head firmly. The Blue Guard lifted the picture closer, his heavy gauntleted hand coming to rest on the landlord's shoulder in a way that made the man wince, but he shook his head again.

Then the landlord looked up and pointed directly at Mathos and Tor. Fuck. He could feel his scales sliding through his skin, rippling up his arms and neck. He glanced at Tor and groaned at the small smile twisting his friend's lips up at the sides—this was not the time to beat out frustrations.

The guard marched across the room and glared down at them. Before Tor could ensure that every Blue Guard in fifty miles knew exactly who they were, Mathos spoke, "If you've been sent over here for a review of the ale, I can tell you now, it tastes like piss."

The guard didn't look amused. He pulled off his gloves and tapped them against his thigh. "Tavern keeper says you took the only two rooms."

Mathos raised an eyebrow. "Would you like to buy them off us?"

"I need to search them."

"Why?" Mathos asked before Tor could refuse out of hand.

The lieutenant leaned forward, eyebrows pulled down in a tight scowl. "Do you know what this tunic means?"

Thank the gods, the lieutenant didn't recognize them. Not someone from the palace then, and almost certainly not one of Dornar's men. Mathos hid his relief behind a smirk. "Well—"

The guard cut him off. "It means you fucking do as you're told."

Mathos thrust his hand out to hold Tor in his seat. "My friend and I don't respond well to threats. How about you sit down, drink some shitty ale, and tell us what you really want?"

The lieutenant's nostrils flared as his face darkened, neither of which bothered Mathos. He rocked his chair back onto two legs and raised an eyebrow as he spoke. "We're in the business of helping people. Maybe we could help you?"

Before he could reply, two new guards walked in, both also Apollyon, both unfamiliar. They made their way to stand beside their leader with a quick shake of their heads. Clearly whoever, or whatever, they were looking for hadn't been found outside.

"Show us the picture," Mathos nudged, doing his best to look helpfully contrite and not overly mocking. It was a look he had perfected on commanding officers over many years. "Maybe we've seen your... wife? Brother? Great-aunt Camilla?"

The guard gave him a look rich in frustration and Mathos kept his eyes wide and clear. Gods he loved this game. Tristan didn't take his shit, if anything, he expected him to be the responsible one in the squad, and he hardly ever had a chance to stir up trouble just for fun anymore.

With a sigh of annoyance, the lieutenant handed over the painting. It was a small oil in an ornate gilded frame, like something from the mantelpiece of a wealthy home. The kind of home Mathos did his best to stay far away from.

The subject of the painting was a young woman wearing rich velvet robes of deep forest green, sitting on an elegantly carved chair, and holding a large leather-bound book in her lap. She was prim and demure looking—her face set in a small, lopsided smile—but the artist had captured a twinkle in her eyes that suggested that her thoughts were far less meek than her modest pose might suggest.

Mathos's first reaction was relief; it wasn't a picture of Nim or Alanna or even any of the Hawks. The last time a Blue Guard had handed over a picture, a great deal of pain had followed close behind, and he hadn't been looking forward to a repeat.

But his next emotion was far more complicated.

He didn't know the woman in the picture. He had never seen her heart-shaped face, framed by waves of thick ebony hair, her dark eyes, or her seductively plump lips, curled up on one side as if she knew something she wasn't sharing. But he knew exactly who she looked like. Ballanor. And if the fact that Lucilla looked just like her brother wasn't enough, he would recognize the barbed black-and-red family tattoos entwining her arms anywhere.

The palace women had always considered Ballanor handsome, but Mathos had never been able to see it. Now, looking down on the feminine version, he finally understood. She was breathtaking.

And she was missing. Bollocks.

Not safe at home waiting for them to find. No. He stifled a rough groan. Why was nothing ever easy? Instead of a short ride in the morning to cover the last few miles down to the manor house, followed by a civilized conversation, an easy win—who wouldn't want to be queen?—and a rapid return to his squad, now the woman they needed was gone.

The amount of effort this was going to take had just increased exponentially. Gods, he hadn't even met her yet, and she was already more annoying than he'd imagined. And he'd imagined that Ballanor's cosseted little sister would be fucking annoying.

And yet… there was something about those huge eyes. That almost-smile. Something that lit a tiny flame of concern deep in his belly. Knowing that a pampered, vulnerable woman was out all alone in the darkness brought to life the protective instincts he had spent decades working hard to erase.

He was grateful for the jerkin he was wearing; its collar was high enough to hide the scales now flickering up his throat as his beast turned and twisted in his belly.

Who was this lieutenant? His gut said this was a guard from the manor house, Queen Lucilla's home. And his instinct was generally pretty bloody good.

Mathos shrugged, winking at the guards with as much of a leer as he could manage as he passed the sketch to Tor. "Sorry, haven't seen her… I'd remember."

The lieutenant snatched the painting back from Tor with a stony glare and shoved it inside his coat, the gloves in his other hand slapping against his thigh as his irritation rose.

"You're welcome to check our rooms if you like," Mathos added as he reached into his pocket and pulled out a key. They hadn't been into them yet, so there was nothing to see.

The lieutenant snatched the key and handed it to one of the dark-haired sergeants standing impatiently behind him. "Sergeant Cerdic, take a look around."

The sergeant stepped forward, his face twisted into a deep scowl, saluted, and hurried away.

They all stared at each other as the lieutenant slapped his gloves and watched them with undisguised irritation. Mathos took another swallow of his increasingly tepid ale.

Finally, Cerdic came back with a sharp shake of his head and dropped the key onto the table. "Nothing there, Lieutenant Claudius, sir."

Lieutenant Claudius grunted in annoyance and pulled on his gloves, his men falling in behind him.

"Hey, we really could help," Mathos urged as the guards turned to go. "Why don't you tell us how she became… lost? We'll help you find her. Our rates are very reasonable."

Claudius gave them a long look over his shoulder, his lip twisted up in a sneer. "The Blue Guards don't need mercenaries to find one bloody disobedient woman. She'll be secured by morning, I assure you."

Fuck. Mathos had not expected that at all. This was not a man speaking out of care and concern for his overprotected charge. Claudius had no respect for the queen whatsoever; if anything, he sounded like a warder looking for his prisoner.

His beast gave a menacing growl, too low for anyone else to hear. His primal side did not approve of holding an innocent woman captive.

Mathos gave the man a lazy two-fingered salute, as if he genuinely didn't care, and took another long slow sip of his ale. He hadn't been lying—it did taste like piss, and now it was warm and flat—but he kept his face neutral as he settled back into his seat and watched the Blue Guards march out the door and back into the night.

Gods. They had found Lucilla's home. But she wasn't safely waiting in her luxurious manor. Nope, she was gone. Lost somewhere in the miles of woods around them. Infinitely more difficult to find.

And worse than that, she had three separate sets of armed men after her—the Hawks, Dornar's men, and the guards from the manor. Fuck it all.

Tor raised a mocking eyebrow and smirked. "I told you we should go earlier."

Chapter Three

LUCILLA SAT ON THE GROUND, her back against a tree, head resting on her knees. Her body ached from hours of riding bareback. She was dirty. She stank. She was exhausted. She was so thirsty that her lips had cracked to the point of bleeding.

And she felt deeply, deeply sorry for herself.

She had been alone in the woods for three days. At first, she had been terrified, fleeing on adrenaline and fear. But slowly, as the hours passed, her fear diminished, replaced with an ever-growing sense of isolation. The sense of how truly small she was, surrounded by the vastness of the world.

All through the first night and for most of the first day, she had heard men in the woods behind her, whistles blowing and trumpets blaring. At one point she thought she might have heard dogs baying far away. She had paused only once—to fill her waterskin and let Penny drink before they left the stream—and had pushed on solidly hour after hour, until they were both trembling with exhaustion and, finally, had to stop.

She had slept brokenly that night, constantly waking to listen, trying to gauge whether the guards were any closer. But the sounds continued to fade.

By the afternoon of the second day, there were occasional noises that she couldn't quite decipher. Perhaps trumpets, perhaps birds. But mostly just the noise of the woods, alive with the activities of a myriad of small creatures around her.

The third day was free of any human noise. Birds sang, magpies chattered and screeched, and Penelope's hooves thudded along the rough animal tracks they followed. Otherwise, it was silent. No cook clattered and banged pans in the kitchen, no maids cleaned and gossiped while the stable hands whistled, no guards chortled at rough jokes and flirted with the staff.

She was completely, utterly alone.

Then she had started to get hungry. Hungrier than she had ever dreamed possible. By the end of the second day, her stomach ached constantly and she was starting to feel lightheaded.

But now, on the third day, she'd stopped wanting food. And it worried her. For the first time, she was starting to suspect that she was genuinely in trouble.

Penelope seemed happy enough eating the autumn grasses of the small glades they'd passed through. And, thank the gods, they'd found another stream yesterday— although that water was now gone. But there hadn't been any food for her.

Around mid-afternoon, she had found a huge bush weighed down with vivid red berries and been highly tempted. Birds danced between the branches, feasting, and she had almost convinced herself to try a handful. But then thoughts of dying in agony all alone in the woods filled her head, and she'd lost her nerve.

How many hours had she spent learning the history of Brythoria? Or the legends of how the Apollyon people had descended from the angel-become-goddess Muriel? Or how to play the harp? What use was the harp to anyone when they needed to eat?

Why couldn't she have spent time in the woods learning about which berries were poisonous and which safe? Or how to set traps. How to hunt. How to make clothes. Where she was, or even what direction the nearest town was in. There were a million and one helpful things for a person to know, and she didn't know any of them.

Everything she'd been taught was useless. "*Fucking* useless," she added aloud.

She would have been sent to her room for swearing— even now, having left her childhood behind years ago. But out here, there was no one to punish her.

She gave a rough snort against her knees. No one cared whether she starved to death, but at least she could curse as much as she wanted. Not that she felt like it; what she really felt like was curling up in a ball and wallowing in how sorry she felt for herself.

But she wouldn't.

She wouldn't curl up in a ball of misery. And she wouldn't cry. After Cerdic, she had decided that crying didn't change anything. He didn't deserve that honor, to have her weeping after him. None of them did. She could feel miserable and lost and alone, but she wouldn't cry.

She had tried to keep the sun so that it always set to her right shoulder, in the hopes that she wouldn't get turned around and start heading back to the house. So far, it seemed to be working. But she still had no idea where she was. The woods were just one endless array of almost bare autumn trees, muddy paths, and cold winds.

She could be five miles from a village, or fifty. Maybe every day she traveled she went further from any kind of settlement? She had no way of knowing.

Now the sun was setting once more and the wind was picking up, tugging disconsolately at the damp leaves on the ground around her. In the dim light, she could see that the spiders were out, their massive webs winding between the leaves and branches. A bird hopped through the undergrowth beside her, shuffling and fussing as it hunted for its dinner.

She had tied Penelope's halter to a tree branch before sitting down to rest so the mare wouldn't wander off into the night, and soon it would be time for her to try to sleep. But first she wanted to see if there was anyone nearby, or if there were any villages she could aim for. It was her habit, now, to climb the tallest tree she could find each night and try to look for lights.

She waited until the sun was completely set and then stood, turning to face the tree. She had chosen it for its massive height and its wide-spreading branches. She tried to remember the route she'd decided on in the last rays of daylight and slowly lifted herself, carefully feeling her way and checking her handholds. It was painfully slow and nerve-wracking; if she fell and hurt herself, there would be no one to help her. By the time she was high enough to look out over the forest, she was breathing hard with exertion and anxiety.

The woods spread out in front of her, black and brooding under the milky sheen of the cosmos. The moon was not yet up, and the streaks of high silver-white clouds were too fine to block the light of the multitudes of stars that lit the world around her with a pale glow. It was beautiful and haunting, like a dream.

Something in the corner of her vision snagged her attention, and she carefully turned on the branch.

She saw it again and shuffled further along the branch to get a better view.

Her breath caught. It was the flickering orange glow of a fire. A small campsite—tiny, but vivid against the reds and oranges of the last remaining autumn leaves—a couple of miles from where she was, maybe closer.

Could they be hunters? It didn't make sense for travelers to be so deep in the woods. Claudius and his men? No, she didn't think so. She would have heard them during the day, wouldn't she? And there would be more fires, or at least a much bigger one for the whole squad, surely?

Lucilla climbed slowly down the tree, carefully testing each foothold until she was safely back down on the ground.

What should she do? Should she run? Or should she investigate?

She leaned on the tree, muttering to herself while she tried to decide. The sensible thing was almost certainly to run. But what good would that do her? Would it simply prolong the inevitable until she died in the woods, as unloved and unnoticed as she'd been her entire life?

Or she could sneak up on the campfire and have a look. Maybe they would have some food—to steal, if not to share or buy.

She snorted ruefully. It had finally come down to this, planning her life as a thief.

In the end, it was the idea that she might be able to follow the campers back out of the woods that decided her. She would take a quick look and then hide half a mile back and follow them out. Part of her thought it was probably an epically bad plan, but it was overruled by the fact that it was the only plan she had.

She wiped her dusty hands down her tunic and went to check on Penelope. The big mare bumped her with her nose, snuffling her pockets hopefully.

"Sorry, beautiful, there's nothing there." Penelope huffed as Lucilla patted her gently. "Come on, let's go see what that fire is all about."

Penelope whickered softly as Lucilla untied her and led her carefully through the dark in the direction she'd memorized.

She picked her way down narrow paths, trying not to stumble into roots and hollows. Time seemed to move especially slowly in the dark, and it felt like they'd been walking for ages when she started to hear voices. Men. Talking and laughing.

She slunk closer, until she could almost make out their words, and then tied Penelope to a tree, leaving her satchel slung over a low branch. She wanted the mare far enough away that the men wouldn't hear her but close enough to reach easily.

Dropping down into a crouch, she crept silently through the woods.

A campsite slowly came into view and she quietly lowered herself onto her knees behind a large, twining bramble, making sure to stay well in the shadows. Carefully avoiding the thorns, she peered around it.

Two canvas tents were pitched in a small clearing, horses hobbled nearby. Between them a small fire crackled and hissed, throwing warm, amber light up onto the surrounding trees.

Two men, dressed in leathers and carrying an array of weapons strapped to their backs and legs, sat on logs beside the fire. Neither wore the blue tunics of her guards or any other military uniform that she recognized. There were no skins or carcasses, so probably not hunters. And they were too well armed anyway. Mercenaries, maybe?

One of the men was a huge Apollyon, marked with their people's swirling red-and-black tattoos. The other was less brawny but seemed no less powerful. He was leaning forward, resting his elbows on his long legs, his shirt stretched tight across his broad back, while his rolled-up sleeves showed heavily muscled forearms circled in bands of glittering burgundy-and-gold scales. His hair was a dark blond that gleamed almost caramel in the flickering light, and when he turned his head, she could see a firm, unshaven jaw.

She had never seen anyone like him.

Oh, she knew she was looking at a Tarasque warrior. One of the ancient and most primal races, deeply connected to his inner beast. Prone to bloodlust in battle, savage when riled. But she had never met one before—her brother, like her father, surrounded himself with Apollyon only—and he was magnificent.

Something was roasting over the fire, and it smelled rich and delicious. Her hunger roared back to life in a wave of desperation, fierce enough to distract her from the Tarasque warrior she had been staring at, and her stomach rumbled painfully as she dragged her attention back to focus on the conversation.

"I'm telling you, she's near here," the Tarasque man was saying. "Those assholes have no idea what they're doing."

Lucilla cringed back. They were looking for someone. A woman. Gods.

The big Apollyon gave a rough snort. "I agree. But just because they're bloody useless doesn't mean she's here."

"It makes sense to look here," the first man argued. "Remember when I bet you that I knew exactly where we would find Nim? You still owe me ten groats for that, because I was right. And I'm right again."

The Apollyon laughed. "You bet us you could catch her, but as far as I remember, that was all Tristan."

Lucilla felt a wave of icy dread rippling up her spine. Gods, these men hunted women and then joked about it.

The Tarasque was still speaking. "I scouted down from the manor. If she went out the back, then she would have hit the stream first. She's rich, so she's got a horse, right, and she knows they've got dogs, so she would have kept the horse in the river as long as possible. Then, when they hit the rapids, she was already going south. Wouldn't make sense to turn around. Let's assume she's pushing pretty hard for a woman who's never done anything for herself in her life, but she's taking breaks for rests and when it's dark." He looked across to the Apollyon. "Double or nothing on the ten groats you owe me, she's around here. Somewhere close."

They were talking about *her*. Hunting *her*.

Cold sweat broke out down her back as she started to crawl over the mud and leaves of the forest floor, back toward Penelope. She should have run the second she'd seen their fire.

Fuck.

"Hey, Tor, I think it's time for us to check the horses," she heard the Tarasque man say somewhere behind her. Thank the gods, he was going in the opposite direction.

The Apollyon didn't reply, or if he did, she couldn't hear him over the pounding of her heart, the rough gasp of her frantic breaths. She pushed herself into a crouch and started to run over the uneven ground.

She was nearly there. She just had to reach Penelope.

Brambles caught in her cloak, and she tugged at them, ripping her hands on the thorns as she fought to free herself in the darkness. She whimpered under her breath in desperation as she gave a last brutal tug and ripped her cloak free.

She stumbled on a tree root and almost fell, but righted herself and kept going, heart in her mouth, acid burning in her throat.

And then she was there. Thank the gods. Penelope was waiting for her quietly in the murky shadows.

She reached for the halter, her fingers shaking so badly that she almost couldn't undo the knots.

She took a breath and tugged again, working her finger in between the leather. At last, it opened. Penelope was free.

She took a step forward, about to fling herself onto Penelope's back. They would make a noise, but there was no alternative; speed meant everything now.

But before she could even fully process what was happening, the Tarasque man stepped out of the shadows and grabbed Penelope's halter.

"Going somewhere, darlin'?" he asked in a deep, rumbling voice.

She whirled, ready to run the other way, and stopped dead. The Apollyon was standing right behind her.

"Fuck it all." The big Apollyon glared at the Tarasque. "Now you'll be bloody insufferable."

Lucilla shrank back against Penelope, turning her head between them. There was nowhere to run, no escape. She'd heard horrendous stories of mercenaries. And even more horrific rumors about the savagery of the beast-like Tarasque.

And now she was their prisoner. Out here in the

darkness. Far from any kind of help. Gods. What would they do to her? She didn't even want to imagine.

She pulled the letter opener out of her belt and held it up defensively, trying—but failing—to get the trembling in her hands under control. The small blade wavered in front of her hopelessly as she prepared herself to fight.

"Hell." The Tarasque slowly lifted his hands, as if to show that he held no weapons.

Lucilla pushed herself back into Penelope's warm flank, blade still high, not trusting him for a moment.

"Tor, show her you're unarmed."

The Apollyon grunted in response, but he took a step back and also lifted his empty hands.

"Here, darlin', sorry, we didn't mean to frighten you," the Tarasque said, easing back a small step, but, tellingly, keeping a tight grip on Penelope's halter. "My name's Mathos, and that great big ugly brute is Tor."

Tor rolled his eyes but didn't reply. Nor did Lucilla.

Mathos gave her a lopsided grin. "We won't hurt you. I promise. You look thirsty... maybe hungry too? We can help."

Finally, Lucilla found her voice. "Just let me go. Please."

"Ah, I'm sorry, but we can't do that. I know we look frightening, but we're on your side. We've spent weeks looking for Queen Lucilla, and I think we might have found her in the nick of time."

Lucilla wiped the back of her free hand across her damp forehead. Nothing that he said made any sense. Why would anyone other than the Blue Guards be looking for her? How had they even heard of her? Especially since whatever they'd heard was wrong—she was a princess, not a queen. And what would they do with her if they knew who she really was?

Lucilla cleared her throat and tried to keep her voice from shaking as badly as her hands. "Please. I'm no one important, and I don't have anything for you to steal. I just want to be allowed to go."

Mathos chuckled, although she noticed he didn't sound amused. "Come on, darlin', we can see that isn't true. And now I know you're royalty—only a woman who has always had everything would think that a beautiful, purebred mare and thick cloak aren't worth stealing. Never mind that satchel you were about to leave behind."

Lucilla felt her cheeks flush, but she kept her chin up, working hard to keep her face set and unreadable. Striving for the "demure princess" look that would hide her thoughts. She didn't want them to know how terrified she was. Or how desperate she was to escape. Or how much she hated being called darlin'.

His eyes ran slowly down her face. "You look just like the portrait we saw, you're exactly where I expected you to be, and you speak like the women at court. How about we stop this little game of pretend. Your lips are dry, which tells me you're thirsty, and after three days out here, I'm sure you're hungry. Come and have something to eat and drink and we'll explain why we're looking for you... Your Majesty."

He stepped back and waved an arm forward, as if to lead her back to the camp. It was her opportunity. Lucilla took off as fast as she could.

She made it about three steps before a heavy arm circled her waist and she was dragged back into his hard chest. The Tarasque had her. Mathos. Gods.

She threw her head back, screaming and thrashing in a frenzy, trying desperately to stab him in the thigh. But the letter opener glanced off the heavy leather of his breeches.

He grunted, clearly annoyed, and a second later he had her wrist gripped tightly in his free hand.

He used his arm around her waist to lift her fully, her body pulled tight in against his chest while her legs dangled uselessly. He held her easily, most of his attention on the letter opener as he extended her knife arm out, away from them both. "Tor, do me a favor and take that nasty little blade."

Tor laughed. "You're on your own, my friend. I remember how well getting involved worked out for me with Nim." The Apollyon turned away and started walking back toward the fire.

What was he doing? The only familiar person was walking away. Leaving her with a man driven by the primal voice of his inner animal.

The terror that had been bubbling through her suddenly overwhelmed her. "No!" Lucilla screamed, hating how high her voice sounded, twisting frantically as she tried to get herself free. "Don't leave me with him! Not with a... a...."

Tor stopped walking and turned slowly to face her. The grim look on his face was enough to make her stop struggling and hang limp.

"What are you saying?" Tor asked softly.

Lucilla didn't know what to say. Why was he looking at her like that? These men had kidnapped her. She was the one fighting for her life. "I don't... I... the beast...," she stuttered eventually.

"Fuck it all to hell." The snarled curse behind her vibrated through her back.

And then Mathos simply opened his arms and let her fall.

She stumbled, going to her knees, and then she stayed there, bruised and shaken, not sure whether to move as she looked up at the two men. The tight look on Mathos's face was easy to see, even in the dim light.

"You know what," Mathos said, his voice deep and rumbling as he looked over to his friend, completely ignoring her. "I'm out. I've had enough spoilt little girls for one lifetime. You explain how we're trying to save her life."

And then he walked away into the night without even looking back.

It was what she wanted. Wasn't it? They were kidnappers. Men who hunted women. And there was only one of them now. The civilized one. One of her own people. She had a better chance of surviving with Mathos gone.

So why did she feel like she had just done something awful?

Chapter Four

MATHOS STALKED into the darkness cursing princesses, queens, the world, Tor, Tristan for sending him on this gods-forsaken mission, darkness, princesses again, horses, and, mostly, himself.

What had induced him to take her into his arms like that? You'd think he knew better.

The beast in his belly snorted in wry amusement. Mathos kicked a tree and ignored it.

She had pressed herself back into her horse, mud streaks across her face, eyes wide, her dry lips and the dark rings under her eyes clearly showing that she wasn't drinking enough or sleeping enough. And he had been filled with an overwhelming need to keep her safe.

Then she'd tried to run, and he'd known that she wouldn't last more than a day or two in the woods alone, and without stopping to think, he'd pulled her up against him, so soft and warm and vulnerable. His beast had howled to protect her, and he had fully agreed—even when she tried to stab his leg with that ridiculous letter opener—right up until she'd called him an animal.

Gods. Lesson learned. That woman was trouble.

But you like trouble. Especially trouble with big eyes and delectable curves. Beautiful, luscious trouble.

"Shut up," he told himself with a growl. And then winced, hoping Tor and Lucilla were too far away to hear him talking back to the primal voice inside him. He'd done it most of his life, but he generally tried to do it far away from anyone else. Especially people already prejudiced and filled with hatred toward *beasts*.

Gods, that had stung. Which was ridiculous. She was a pampered and bigoted soon-to-be-queen. He had watched as she pulled on her haughty mask, every inch the blank and unfeeling royal. Exactly what he would have expected from Ballanor's sister.

He tried not to think about how terrified she had been—or how she had looked up from the ground, those huge eyes glistening with unshed tears—before she pulled her face into that closed-off mask.

His beast growled, wanting to go back, and he curved his path back toward the fire instinctively without really thinking about what he was doing.

And then he did think about it and he stopped. Bollocks. If she could rile him up so badly with so little effort, the only sensible thing was to walk away and leave Tor to handle this.

He told himself that he didn't care whether she had been hurt when he dropped her. He didn't care that she was alone and frightened. He was absolutely not going to check on her.

Whatever you say. If his beast had eyes, it would have

rolled them. *But you have to get back there and… not… check on her.*

Gods. His beast was right; he had to go back. He needed to hear what was being said between Lucilla and Tor. He was in charge of the mission, after all. More importantly, he was an adult, not a little boy hiding in the woods nursing his hurt feelings. It was his duty to go back and deal with this shitshow.

His beast twitched, but he ignored it.

It only took a few minutes to get back to Lucilla's mare. He grabbed the abandoned satchel and slung it over his shoulder, then led the mare closer to the camp. Once the horse was safely hobbled, he found a tree to lean on and lurked in the darkness just outside the reach of the firelight.

Lucilla was sitting on the log opposite Tor, taking long sips out of their spare waterskin. "Thank you," she said eventually in a soft voice, passing it back to Tor.

Tor grunted and cut a leg off the wild duck they'd shot that morning. They'd been lucky to stumble on a small pond teeming with mallard. It was rich, fatty meat, and the roasting scent was making his stomach rumble, even though he'd eaten two decent-sized meals already that day.

Tor dropped it onto a wooden trencher and passed it to Lucilla, who said thank you politely enough but then stared at the meat in confusion for a few moments. Mathos rolled his eyes. No doubt she was hoping for silver cutlery. Eventually, she lifted the duck in her hands and blew on it before taking a delicate bite.

She gave a soft moan of appreciation as she chewed, which Mathos did his level best to pretend he didn't hear. She swallowed and then looked up at Tor with a small smile. "That's delicious. Thank you."

"Mathos shot it," Tor replied. "You should thank him, Your Majesty."

Lucilla tipped up her chin. "I'm not... I mean, you've got the wrong person."

Tor shrugged without responding. They all knew she was the queen.

Lucilla ducked her head for a moment, but then seemed to gather her courage and lifted it again. "I will thank him, then. You're friends?"

"Brothers," Tor corrected firmly.

Mathos leaned against a tree and crossed his arms, his beast finally settling. Because Tor had his back, of course, not because he could see Lucilla safe and well. Obviously.

"But...."

Mathos could see Lucilla frowning as she thought through her question. Tor merely watched her, his arms crossed over his chest.

"Do you have the same father?" she asked uncertainly. At least someone had explained that the mother's line determined the child's characteristics.

"No. We were in the army together. We served together in the north as part of the Hawks squadron in the war against Verturia."

Lucilla stayed silent, watching him quizzically, as if wondering how they'd gone from the war in the north to this lonely southern woodland. Or, perhaps, why that faraway war had bonded two such different men, with vastly different backgrounds, so deeply. That was the problem with princesses—they'd never had to fight those wars themselves.

Tor sighed and added, "When we returned, we were stationed at the palace. We were Blues together."

"Palace Blues!" Lucilla stood, her duck leg clasped in

her fist like a sword as she looked around frantically. As if she might try running again.

Gods.

Mathos gave an annoyed sigh and pushed off his tree to step into the light. "As much as we'd like to be rid of you, we haven't finished our conversation yet. And you have to realize that a reaction like that suggests at least some working experience of the Royal Guards."

She took a big step away from him, her mouth gaping open in shocked surprise at seeing him so close. Gods, he would like to put something in it.

Yes. Your tongue.

He snarled at himself, trying to get his insane beast under control, and then grimaced in frustration at the newly terrified look on her face.

He let out a long, slow breath and counted to ten, something he hadn't had to do in years. He finished counting and started again from the beginning, just to be sure. Finally, he felt calm enough to deal with her.

"Sit down, darlin' and finish your food. We're not Blues anymore." There, that was polite.

She lifted her chin, her face a mask of haughty indifference even while she was still waving that bloody duck leg. "I'm not your darling."

Mathos ran his hands through his hair instead of throttling her and gentled his tone. Just like he'd done so many times, long ago. "Please sit down, Your Majesty."

"Don't call me that." She stayed standing, her head tilted to one side as she considered him. "If you're not Blues, what are you?"

"We're mercenaries."

She flinched but didn't run like he'd thought she would.

Slowly, trying to reassure her, he dropped her satchel at

her feet and then sat on the ground a few feet away and held his hands up. "No one here is going to hurt you. Please, eat your food, and I'll explain."

She looked at him for a long moment, but then she sat.

Tor passed Mathos a plate of duck and then added a handful of blackberries they'd found growing on the brambles nearby before reaching over to heap some onto Lucilla's trencher too and then helping himself to a plate.

As he lowered himself to the ground, Tor observed quietly, "If we were going to hurt you, we would have done it by now."

Mathos glared at him. "Thanks for that. Another true but extremely unhelpful comment."

Lucilla narrowed her eyes at him. "How is that unhelpful?"

Mathos turned his glare to her. "Well, the last thing we need is you getting it into your head that we are planning to hurt you, dar— Your Maj—" Fuck it all. What was he supposed to call her?

Lucilla put her duck down on her plate and leaned forward, her eyes flicking to Tor. "It is helpful. You haven't really hurt me—other than kidnapping me and threatening me—so maybe it is true that we can have a vaguely civilized dinner together."

Fuck. They were threatening kidnappers now; this just got better and better. Never mind the hot flare of resentment from his beast that she was so blatantly supporting Tor over him. Again.

It was irrational that he found her preference for Tor annoying. And that made him even more irritated. "I very much doubt that we can have a *civilized* dinner," Mathos sneered. "I am a beast, after all."

Lucilla settled back onto the log, a bright red flush

climbing her neck. "I'm sorry I insulted you," she said quietly a few moments later, not quite meeting his eyes. "I've never met anyone who wasn't Apollyon before. And I'd been taught.... Anyway, it was rude, and I'm sorry."

Mathos hmphed, completely taken aback that she had apologized and suddenly not sure what to say next.

"Why not?" Tor asked bluntly.

Lucilla stared quietly at Tor, her face so impassive that Mathos wondered if she would reply until she surprised him by admitting, "My father filled the house with only his own trusted servants. They were all Apollyon."

Tor wrapped a big hand around the back of his neck, a sure sign he was unsettled. "What about your friends? Or when you went out? Surely someone must have given you some idea of how to avoid insulting your own subjects?"

Lucilla gazed at him silently for a long moment, and then looked away; obviously she didn't plan to comment on that.

Gods. A horrible idea occurred to him—maybe she had never had friends? They knew she'd been hidden away since she was born, but maybe she'd been kept isolated too?

Mathos pushed away the sudden burst of pity. He was probably imagining the sad downward tilt to her lips. And anyway, she would have plenty of friends once she was established as the queen.

He took a bite of duck and chewed slowly while he tried to get his thoughts in order. She was determined to keep pretending not to be Ballanor's sister, which didn't make this any easier.

"Whatever. I'm confident that you are Lucilla, Geraint's daughter. And if I'm right, which I am, then we've been looking all over for you."

She watched him with wide eyes as he continued. "King

Ballanor is dead, which makes Lucilla the Queen of Brythoria."

"What?" Her hand flew to her throat as she stared at him, her fingers trembling slightly against her pale skin.

Mathos leaned over to take the dangerously tilted trencher from her lap and settle it beside her before it could fall. Hell. She hadn't known. Maybe he should have tried to soften the blow a little—what a way to tell her that her only brother had died. Just being around this woman was turning him into the brute she thought he was.

His beast rattled deep inside him, and he fought to keep his voice smooth. "Gods. Sorry, I didn't realize no one had told you. I should have found a better way."

"I… um… it's not, I mean, I'm not…" She took a slow breath and seemed to get her thoughts together. "And the baby?"

Mathos blinked. "What baby?"

"His wife, what's her name? Something with an *A*?"

"Alanna?" Mathos asked, still lost.

"They've been married long enough…." She moved her hand from her throat to clasp it tightly in her lap. "It would make sense for mercenaries to be hunting her, Lucilla, I mean, if Alanna had a baby. Ballanor might have seen her as a threat to the baby, don't you think? And now Alanna might feel the same, especially with Ballanor gone."

Lucilla hunched forward over her clasped hands, and Mathos began to have a horrible suspicion about why Lucilla had run. And why she was so terrified. She thought she was going to die. And, despite how annoyed he was with her, he hated how vulnerable she looked.

Moving slowly and carefully, doing his best not to startle her, he raised himself onto the log beside her and gently laid a hand on her shoulder. For all her bravado, she felt very delicate to him.

And he remembered just how much she'd gone through. Alone and lost and hungry. It was no wonder she was overwhelmed.

She had no reason to trust them at all. Why would she? If one of his sisters had been lost in the woods and strange men accosted her, terrified her, and then just blurted out that her only brother was dead, he would have no hesitation in killing the lot of them. Whatever good excuse they thought they had.

He rubbed his free hand down his face, trying to clear his muddle of swirling thoughts and feelings. Given everything she'd been through and how much he'd just thrown at her, she was handling it all very well.

"I'm sorry, I'm doing this all wrong." He let out a huff of almost laughter. "You know, some people even think I'm charming."

She turned to look at him, her head giving a tiny, involuntary shake of disbelief.

"Not you, obviously. Which is fair enough," he admitted with a rueful smile. He squeezed her shoulder gently and then let his hand drop. "There is no baby. And Alanna certainly doesn't want you, Lucilla, dead."

She watched him carefully as he continued, "Ballanor died in trial by combat a few weeks ago." He couldn't bring himself to say that he was sorry for the loss, and he continued with the facts instead. "The trial was held at the Temple of the Nephilim at Eshcol and overseen by the Supreme Justice. You've heard of the Nephilim?"

She dipped her chin a few millimeters.

Of course she had. She had almost certainly been taught that the Nephilim and the Apollyon were both descendants of the angels—with rightful dominion over the *animals* of the earth. Suddenly Ballanor's complete blind spot toward having any Mabin in his personal guard was making so much more sense. Fuck it all.

He swallowed down his confused irritation and continued. "So you understand the trial was legal?"

Her face was blank, but she was still watching him closely.

"After Ballanor died, his wife, Alanna, chose not to return to the palace with his advisors. Instead, she let everyone know that you are the rightful queen. She asked us to find you, and we've been looking for you ever since."

"Why would she do that?" Lucilla whispered, perhaps not realizing that she was giving herself away.

Mathos looked across to Tor, who merely shrugged. How the hell was he going to explain this?

His beast rumbled. *With the truth—tell her everything so she understands.*

Mathos had spent his life listening to his primal beast. He was as close to it as any Tarasque he knew—although he was still waiting for it to finally provide him with some lovely lethal claws like Tristan had developed—but he would not be listening to it this time. Telling her everything all at once, when she was tired and suspicious already, was a horrible idea. He'd already been much too blunt and upset her. It would be far better to ease her in gently.

He would tell her the truth, yes, but in bite-size pieces. Start with the most important facts, and then let her get used to him and Tor and eventually get to know the others. Then it would all make sense to her when they told her everything.

He chose his words carefully. "The man who fought against Ballanor in the trial was one of the Hawks. Lanval. He was Alanna's personal guard. They grew… close. Afterward, she chose to stay with him rather than return to the palace."

"And this man, Lanval, he killed Ballanor?" Lucilla asked in a low voice.

Mathos shook his head. "They fought in front of witnesses, but Val didn't kill your brother." He hesitated. Gods. How did you tell someone that their brother was a lying, cheating, abusive asshole? In as few words as possible, that was how. "Ballanor dipped his sword in a fast-acting poison. During the fight, the tip broke off and cut him on the cheek. He died by his own hand."

"He cheated? And tried to kill someone? In front of the Supreme Justice?"

"Yes."

Lucilla closed her eyes for a long moment, and he wondered if she was about to cry. Hell, he hoped not; his beast was in turmoil as it was. But when she opened them again, her eyes were surprisingly clear.

"No. It doesn't make sense. If Ballanor died, then the Lord High Chancellor would simply go and get this Princess Lucilla."

Mathos shook his head. "The previous Lord High Chancellor—Grendel—died a few days before Ballanor. There's a new Lord High Chancellor now. And he was just as surprised as the rest of us to learn that Ballanor had a sister. But he's looking for her, I assure you. In fact—"

"Ballanor and Grendel are both dead?" she interrupted.

"Yes." He winced as he admitted it, hoping that he wasn't going to have to admit that not only had the Hawks been inadvertently responsible for the death of her brother, but they'd been directly responsible for the death of the Lord High Chancellor. Bollocks.

"They're really dead." She seemed to be talking to herself. She pressed her hands to her mouth, and Mathos braced himself for the tearful breakdown he was sure was coming this time.

Which never happened. Instead, she laughed. It was shaky and quiet, almost hysterical, but it was definitely laughter. "I'm free," she said softly, her eyes suspiciously bright. "Gods."

"Yes," Mathos agreed, flooded with relief at how well she was taking this. And the fact that she wasn't pushing for any more details. "You're free to come out of hiding and take your rightful place as queen."

She dropped her hands and frowned. "I'm not the queen. I told you that already."

Mathos frowned back. "You thought you were the princess. Now you know that you're the queen."

She pursed her lips and then shrugged. "No. I'm just a normal person. I'm not this Lucilla person, my name is… ah… Claudia."

Mathos could feel his blood pressure rising, and he fought the very strong desire to roll his eyes. The guard in the tavern leading the squad that was looking for her had been a Lieutenant Claudius…. Had she seriously just named herself after him? "There's no point in denying it. We all know that you are Lucilla. And now you know that we're not here to hurt you, you can admit it."

She shook her head more forcefully. "I'm not the queen, and nor do I want to be the queen."

Mathos narrowed his eyes. "Of course you want to be the queen. Once you're the queen, you can do anything you want. Everybody wants that."

"Alanna didn't want to be queen," she said slowly.

His beast twitched as his irritation grew. "Alanna was never really the queen. You are."

She gave a small shrug, as if the subject meant nothing to her. "Thank you for this, ah, lovely dinner. And for telling me all of this news, of course. But I'm not the queen. I'm —" Her eyes darted to the side and back again. "—Claudia."

She smiled encouragingly, and he imagined it was a look that she was used to using to get her way. "I don't want to be involved in any of this. If you can maybe help me find my way out of these woods, I'd be very grateful, and then we can go our separate ways."

It had been so long since Tor spoke that the deep rumble of his voice startled them both as he declared firmly, "You must go back and do your duty."

Lucilla frowned, biting her lip. Then she seemed to realize how much she was giving away and schooled her features back into the haughty princess look that was starting to really get on Mathos's nerves. "I'm not this person you're looking for, and I don't want to be. I want to be free. I want to travel and see things. Meet people, maybe make some friends. I'm tired of constantly being watched and told what to do by my father's staff. I'm sure it's even worse for queens."

Hell. Just when he was starting to feel sorry for her, she had to pull out the spoiled princess card and make him want to throttle her. "We have been searching for you for weeks. As we speak, we have people, including Alanna, working to prove your birthright, to make sure you can take your throne the second we get back. There is no one else. The kingdom needs you."

She shook her head slowly, denying his words. "You need to find this... Lucilla woman. Or otherwise, find someone else. I'm sure there are lots of people who'd like to be the queen. Or king. Ask one of them."

His scales flickered up his arms in a slow wave. Gods, she sounded just like his mother. A million and one things she wanted and didn't want; meanwhile, he was the one working like a dog to hold everything together.

And, when it came down to it, what had all that hard work meant? Nothing. He had still failed. But he wasn't going to fail at this.

He stood up, not caring that he was looming over Lucilla, fully scaled. "We are trying to save the kingdom from civil war. Do you know how many people will die? What it would mean to have our people fighting each other?" Mathos snarled. "I know that you're too spoiled—"

A heavy hand clamped down on his shoulder, and he swallowed the nasty observation he was about to make, allowing Tor to continue for them both.

"I don't think you understand," the Apollyon rumbled in his deep voice. "We're looking for you because your kingdom needs you, but we're not the only people hunting for you. Lieutenant Claudius and his men are also looking for you. And Dornar—the new Lord High Chancellor—he's looking for you too, and I wouldn't wish that conniving bastard on my worst enemy."

It was one of the longest speeches Mathos had ever heard Tor make, but his friend wasn't done. "We could have walked away and left that asshole Dornar to take the throne. We could have allowed the inevitable civil war that followed when the council and the nobles split into factions, all trying to take power for themselves. But we didn't, because we are guards of Brythoria and we will always protect her people."

Tor gave Lucilla a stern look. "We want you to be queen. The others... well, I can guarantee that Dornar has no intention of letting you make your own decisions; he'll have you married to him and under his control so fast, you won't even have taken a breath. Now, you can come back with us, sit safely on the throne where you belong, and protect your people at the same time. Or you can take your chances out in the woods until one of the others finds you and makes the decision for you."

Mathos glared at Tor. "After all this, you're just letting her go?"

"Yes. And if you weren't being so irrational right now, you'd do the same."

Mathos looked at Tor and then back at Lucilla. Then he stared up at the canopy of trees over their heads in silent contemplation as his beast churned unhappily. Fuck it all, Tor was right. They couldn't kidnap her, however bloody unreasonable she was being. But it didn't mean he had to pander to her either.

Finally, he sighed, met her eyes, and swept one arm out toward the dark woods. "He's right. You're free to go."

Lucilla peered over her shoulder to the cold, dark woods, her eyes widening.

"But then we're leaving without you," he added firmly.

Chapter Five

Lucilla sank back down onto the log.

She'd been about to stand up, hand them back their plate, and walk away. Back to the dark woods on her own. Back to being hungry and thirsty and cold and lonely. Back to having no idea where to go or even how to get out of the forest.

But she knew she wouldn't last more than a week. Damn them.

"Or you can stay here, and we'll figure it out in the morning," Tor said with a conciliatory smile.

She dipped her chin in agreement and turned back to her food, filled with a riot of confused and uncomfortable emotions.

Should she leave? Should she stay? She watched the two men uncertainly as they ignored her to concentrate on their food.

Who were they, these self-proclaimed mercenaries? And what right did they have to judge her? They didn't know what her life had been like. While they had been out in the world, living their lives, she had been locked away to slowly suffocate. None of *them* wanted to take the throne—Alanna herself had refused it—but they didn't see the hypocrisy of trying to force it on her.

And yet... and yet... they were helping her, weren't they? Or at least, they seemed to think they were. And what if there genuinely was a war? What if lots of people got hurt? *Her* people.

Should she feel responsible for a kingdom full of people she had never known and who had never cared for her? She thought back on the casual disrespect and downright nastiness of the staff who had surrounded her at the manor. Should she sacrifice her life for them? For Cerdic and Claudius?

She sighed, wishing she hadn't given herself the lieutenant's name. The man whose job it was to imprison her. Who watched her as if she was an errant child and didn't hesitate to discipline her like one. She could have kicked herself for that. Hard. But she had been under pressure to come up with something quickly, and it was the first thing that came into her mind. Which was pretty damn sad, when she thought about it.

And now they wanted her to go to live in a palace she had never even seen, to rule over people she had never met, without ever once doing one single thing she'd chosen for herself.

If they were even telling the truth.

When Mathos had been telling her about how her brother had died, she'd been so focused on the idea that she might finally be free that she hadn't thought to ask who these Hawks were or how one of them came to be in trial by combat with her brother in the first place.

If Alanna had truly known she was alive and genuinely

wished her well, then why, in all these months, had she never bothered to come and see her?

And what had happened to Grendel? She had loathed her brother's best friend, but it was quite suspicious that he was also conveniently dead.

She wanted to ask all those questions, but she couldn't. Showing that kind of interest, knowing the things she knew, would only confirm that she was Lucilla, and she'd already given away too much.

Everything would be so much better if they had just believed her when she told them she was Claudia. They could have helped her find the nearest road, and she would have disappeared into the countryside, none the wiser, not having to deal with this newly woken feeling of responsibility.

Damn them. And especially damn Mathos with his too-big arms and his too cocky smile and his too arrogant, too grumpy, too annoying attitude.

She glanced across at him as he scowled at his food. His scales were rippling and flickering up his wrists and onto the heavy muscles of his forearms in a rich burgundy sheen, jewel-like with their gold rims. Fascinating and beautiful, with an air of danger.

He must have felt her gaze, because he looked up and caught her eye, and she quickly looked away to concentrate on her plate while she worked to get her face back to the serene façade—the indifferent mask that allowed her to think her thoughts and make her plans without being punished for them.

When she finished eating, Mathos took her empty plate and added it to his and Tor's, his lip curling ever so slightly with disdain.

It was only after he'd wiped them down with handfuls of

long grass and then polished them on a cleaning cloth that she realized that he and Tor had done all the work while she had sat and watched them. Gods.

She was trying to decide whether an apology would make it even worse when Mathos grunted and gestured toward one of the tents. "You can sleep in my tent tonight."

"What about you?" she asked uncertainly, suddenly nervous again. They hadn't hurt her, had even given her the choice to leave, but that didn't mean she wanted to share a bedroll.

She couldn't deny that he was attractive, with his long muscles flexing as he worked, deep voice, and intense hazel-brown eyes enhanced by fine crinkles that showed he laughed often. But she didn't trust him, not at all. And there was no way she was sleeping beside him.

She stood up and took a step toward the woods.

Mathos narrowed his eyes for a moment, but then seemed to reconsider and soften slightly. "I didn't mean... bollocks. The tent is all yours. Tor and I will take the other one; we need to take turns on watch anyway."

He rubbed his hand over his face tiredly, seeming to reach some kind of conclusion. "You know what, Tor's right. Go wherever you like. Here, take a waterskin and the berries. I'll give you some blankets, and you can just go."

She glanced at the tent and back again. Sleeping there would make her vulnerable... but would she be any more vulnerable than she had been sleeping in the woods?

The woods were dark and cold; here there was a warm tent and a fire and two armed men looking out for danger. Two men who had sworn up and down that she was safe with them and so far had been true to their word.

Two men who could find her just as easily in the woods. And she'd have to sleep sometime.

She let out a long breath, accepting that she couldn't see any reason not to take the tent. Tor was right; if they wanted to hurt her, they could have done so many times already. And she was utterly exhausted.

She felt full and warm for the first time in days, and the slow flicker of the flames was making her impossibly tired. Either she accepted their offer or she would pass out next to the fire.

She mumbled her thanks, picked up her satchel, and staggered into the soft darkness of the tent, closing the flap behind her.

As soon as she was safely inside, she unbuttoned her cloak and pulled it off with her jacket, followed by her boots. She searched around in her satchel and found a clean shirt to change into, leaving her breeches on. Finally, she was able to crawl into the soft bedroll, pulling blankets and her cloak over herself until she was snug and hidden.

The bedding held a slightly spicy male scent of fresh-cut wood and something warmer, nutmeg perhaps. She nestled deeper into the den she'd made, breathing deeply as her aching muscles relaxed in the warmth, letting the feeling of safety surround her as she drifted to sleep within moments.

Lucilla woke to deep voices talking outside—Tor and Mathos. It sounded as if Mathos had just returned from doing a sweep of the woods, and now they were packing up the camp.

A dim gray light filtered into the tent, and birds sang cheerfully in the woods. She stretched luxuriously, feeling comfortable and rested. It was the best sleep she'd had in days. Longer, even. She couldn't remember when last she'd slept so soundly.

"We need to get her up," Mathos was saying. "We've got to move. Right now."

"Yes," Tor agreed, "I feel it too. Dornar, maybe?"

"Maybe. I don't know... all these days of searching, first the homes and then the woods, and we haven't seen him? I don't like it. We've found the queen. Now we need to get our asses out of here while we still can."

Tor snorted. "We'll go north then? Get her back to Alanna so she can decide what to do with her?"

Lucilla stifled a gasp. Decide what to do with her? Yesterday they'd promised Alanna was on her side— Lucilla's side, anyway. And that she could leave if she wanted to. They didn't sound nearly so convincing when they didn't know she was listening.

"Yeah. I think that's best. After last night..." They lowered their voices, and Lucilla couldn't hear what they said next, despite straining her ears desperately.

All her questions from the night before swirled through her brain like angry bees, reminding her that she could not trust these men. No matter how well she'd slept under their watch.

The low murmur continued softly until Mathos barked out a humorless laugh. "How will she know? Just tell her we're going wherever she wants, and we'll figure it out later."

Lucilla stifled a gasp of outrage as Tor muttered something angrily and then there was a short silence.

"Fine. Gods. It was a joke." Mathos growled, and she could imagine him rolling his eyes as he continued, "But seriously, we need to decide what to do if Dornar finds us."

"We should run," Tor said firmly.

"Agreed. But we need a plan. See, here on the map, there's a port town, Darant. That'll be a good place to pick up a merchant ship. We should split up. You go north and get help, and I'll stay with the queen and take her south and west, make for the sea."

There was a quiet rumble of disagreement from Tor before Mathos spoke again. "No. I'm not going to argue about this. You go back to the temple, explain everything. Get help. Maybe see Keely and apologize for whatever you did. Someone needs to stay with the queen, and this mission is my responsibility."

Damn it all. They were planning to take her north no matter what. They didn't believe that she was Claudia, and they weren't going to let her go off by herself when they reached the road. Their whole go wherever you want speech had been a lie to keep her quiet.

If she went north, she would be sucked deeper and deeper into their plans until it was impossible to escape. And if she saw the Truth Seekers at the temple, there would be no way she could keep calling herself Claudia—not that they believed her as it was, but at least they couldn't prove that she was lying. The north was not a good option for her.

Well, she would go along with them, keep up the sweet and insipid act, eat their food and drink their water, and as soon as she was clear of the never-ending bloody forest, she'd make a run for it.

A few seconds later, someone cleared their throat right outside the tent. She immediately closed her eyes and forced herself to breathe softly and steadily. She didn't dare let them know that she was awake and had been listening.

"Ahem." The voice was louder. She ignored it.

"Ah… Claudia," Tor boomed. "Wake up."

"Wha-What?" Lucilla called back, as sleepily as she could.

"Wake up. It's time to go."

She gave a loud yawn. "Okay."

She got dressed quickly and then swung her satchel over her shoulders before leaving the tent. The day was cool and misty with low gray clouds blocking the sun, and she was glad of her warm clothes.

She made a quick trip into the woods to relieve herself, and then made her way to the log she'd sat on the night before. Tor passed her a lump of bread with dried beef and a waterskin, and she ate ravenously despite the stale dryness of the bread and the tough beef.

While she ate, the men took down the tents and rolled everything into neat bundles attached behind their saddles.

Damn, they'd done all the work again. Should she have done it? Or offered to help at least? No. Since they were abducting her and forcing her to go north, there was no reason why she should have to help them.

Mathos had a particularly grumpy look on his face, his hair standing up in spikes as if he'd run his hands through it too many times. He also hadn't shaved, which was a pity. The rough beard made him look even more attractive than he had the night before, and thinking he was remotely good-looking was the last thing she needed.

He also had his sleeves rolled up again, and the way the light glinted off his scales as his muscles flexed was really quite distracting. He moved around the campsite with a fluid, predatory grace that she couldn't help noticing.

If only he wasn't a lying, kidnapping bastard.

By the time she was finished eating, there was nothing to show that they had camped there the night before.

"Why are we leaving in such a rush?" she asked Tor as he tightened the last pack behind his stallion's saddle.

"We told you last night. You have the Blues from the manor out looking for you—Lucilla, I mean—as well as the new Lord High Chancellor. We can't take the risk that they find us. We need to get away from here as quickly as we can."

"Okay." She nodded slowly. "And where is it exactly that we are going?"

Tor turned to face her properly. "We think you should come north with us to Eshcol and see Alanna and the rest of the Hawks. Then we can all sit down and talk about the best way forward."

Well. She hadn't expected him to admit it. "Why?"

"We need to plan for you to take the throne, or at the very least figure out what to do if you refuse."

She shook her head. "No, I'm—"

"Claudia," Mathos said with a disbelieving snort from behind her, startling her. Ass.

She turned and gave him her best death glare. "I don't want to go north. There's nothing for me there."

"I thought you wanted to see the kingdom?" Mathos said with a mocking glint in his eyes. "What's wrong with starting in the north?"

There was no way she could explain it to him. She cast around for another option instead. "I want to go to… Kaerlud." There. That made sense. Not that she had any plans to go to Kaerlud. Not with the palace there and however many hundreds of Blue Guards. But that might throw them off the scent.

"We're not going to Kaerlud," Mathos said, folding his arms and narrowing his eyes.

"That's okay." She ignored Mathos and smiled at Tor instead. "Please can you just drop me at the nearest village, and I'll find my way there."

Mathos replied, despite the fact that she was obviously speaking to Tor. "It's not safe."

"Why not?" she demanded.

"We don't know where Dornar is, and there'll be men looking for you."

"Looking for Lucilla," Lucilla corrected.

Mathos rolled his eyes without bothering to reply.

It was true; Claudius might well have guards looking in the villages, and possibly this Dornar person too. But she wasn't actually planning to stay in the village. All she needed was to buy some supplies, get hold of a map, and then she'd be gone. "I'm not going north. Either you can take me to the nearest village or you can leave me here."

Mathos shrugged. "Or we can stop listening to this idiocy and simply take you to where you should be."

Lucilla glared at him in outrage, but before she could think of a sensible reply, Tor frowned at his friend. "We talked about this."

Mathos shrugged and raised his eyebrows innocently.

"We're not kidnapping the queen," Tor said casually.

"Then what are we supposed to do?" Mathos snarled, ignoring her completely. "Going to a village is the stupidest idea I've ever heard."

"Yes, it's a stupid idea," Tor agreed with Mathos, also ignoring her. "But since we can't kidnap her and she won't come willingly, what else do you suggest? Leave her here until she dies of starvation?"

Lucilla let her rage flow and stamped her foot, something she didn't think she'd done since she was eight. It was strangely exhilarating. "I'm standing right here!"

Mathos glared at them both until he finally sighed loudly. And then gave another even longer and more pained sigh just to prove his point. "This is a bad idea."

Lucilla looked between the two men. They looked deadly serious, which was putting a real dampener on her plans. She turned to Tor. "Would it really be dangerous?"

"Yes!" both men replied with equal levels of exasperation.

Damn.

"Okay, fine. We don't have to go to the village." She cut off their sighs of relief by saying, "But then you need to tell me how I can get a map and some supplies."

Mathos ran his hands through his hair, pulling it into spikes. "What do you need a map for?"

"I need to know the way to Kaerlud." Actually, she needed to know how to go in the opposite direction to Kaerlud, but they didn't need to know that. With a bit of luck, the map would show her the way to the sea; that was where she really wanted to start. She'd read about the ocean, and she wanted to see it for herself.

Mathos tilted his head back and stared up at the sky, muttering to himself under his breath. She could have sworn he was counting to ten.

Eventually, he looked back at her, his voice strained as he replied, "There won't be a map shop in any of these villages."

Lucilla blinked. She had never been to a village, and she'd never been to a shop. She'd somehow assumed that the villages around them would have shops that sold what she needed. Which, now that she thought about it, was a pretty massive assumption—one that showed that Mathos was right about how little she knew about how most people lived, as well as being damn depressing, all at the same time. It also made her feel stupid, and she hated feeling stupid.

Mathos gave her a look that she imagined was meant to be reassuring. "How about we all go north together and you meet with Alanna to start with. Afterward, if you still want to leave, then I will personally give you my map and even take you wherever you want to go."

She dipped her chin slowly. She really needed a map, and, if she was being brutally honest, she needed help. This might make sense. She could go along with the plan to go north and learn a bit more about how to look after herself and get the things she needed. Then, when they got to a big enough town, she could take off. "Okay."

"Good." Tor clapped Mathos heavily on the back. "I told you that you could have a reasonable discussion."

Mathos merely grunted in reply.

Tor grinned as he turned toward Lucilla. "We don't have any tack for you. And the destriers' saddles will be too wide for your mare. The best we can come up with is for you to ride Mathos's stallion, Heracles, and he can ride your mare, if that works for you?"

"No." She shook her head firmly. She was not going to be separated from her mare, not even for the chance of a comfortable seat. "Thank you, but I would rather ride Penelope. I've been riding bareback all this time. It'll be fine."

"Fine," Mathos repeated from right behind her, startling her into a flinch again. The reassuring look faded from Mathos's face, and he glared at her in irritation. "That's it, enough of this time wasting. We need to go."

He led her to Penelope and then lowered his hands, fingers linked together like a step. Lucilla glared back at him, but she put her foot into his hands anyway, all while thinking of sarcastic replies about how Mathos was the only real waste of time.

Soon they were on their way—Mathos first, her in the middle, and Tor following behind—at a steady, ground-eating trot. Occasionally Mathos would turn back, as if to check on her, and she glared back at him every time. Grumpy ass. Speaking to her like that. Telling Tor that they should just lie to her to make her go where they wanted. Damn him to the Abyss.

Anyway, she far preferred the view when he faced the front. His breeches were tight enough to wrap around his powerful thighs, but even better than that, his sleeves were still rolled up, so she kept getting glimpses of his arm muscles flexing as he held his reins. The glitter of scales over tanned skin as he moved was almost mesmerizing. Gods. What was it about his arms? She had never had such a ridiculous problem before. Not even with....

She shook her head and forced her eyes away.

The morning stayed cool and gray as they followed Mathos. By her judgment, they were traveling north and slightly west, angling away from the manor house she'd lived in for all her life.

"How long will it take to get there?" she asked his back after about an hour of riding in silence.

He didn't even turn around as he replied. "A couple of days."

"A couple, like two, or a couple meaning a few?"

"I don't know. Two or three." Mathos grunted. "Depends on how fast we can go."

"And will we see anything interesting?" she asked, determined to make the most of this enforced detour. "Do you think we could—"

"No. We're going straight there. But you can see the temple of the Nephilim at Eshcol; that's interesting," Mathos interrupted, sounding distracted.

The temple did sound interesting. It was a pity that she probably wouldn't ever see it. "And what happens at the temple?"

That made him turn around. "You'll have to ask the Nephilim after you speak to Alanna and the rest of the

Hawks and we decide what to do, *Claudia*. Now keep quiet; I'm trying to listen."

Lucilla leaned forward, trying to hear whatever it was Mathos was listening to. But all she could hear was the thudding of the horses' hooves on the muddy paths and the muted song of birds she couldn't see. Stupid ass.

A few long minutes later, he turned and looked at Tor, neither of them saying anything. Then Mathos shrugged and settled back into his saddle, and they continued in silence once more, the two men listening and watching carefully as they rode.

Several hours passed without any variation. The trees all started to look the same. The paths all looked the same. The sun presumably climbed overhead behind the gray blanket of clouds. And Lucilla became more and more bored, and more and more uncomfortable.

Long, detailed fantasies of what she was going to do with her life, based entirely on the books she'd read, had kept her amused for some time. She was going to travel, swim in the sea, visit famous market towns and go shopping. She was going to try different foods and meet different people. Make friends. Maybe even fall in love and, for the first time in her life, someone would love her back.

But there was only so long a person could daydream about things they've never seen or done. With every passing minute, her body ached more and her thirst grew. Planning adventures stopped distracting her and started annoying her. She had never done any of those things. Couldn't imagine how she was going to achieve them. And she started to worry that she would make more silly mistakes, like with the map.

The whole idea was making her exhausted. And irritable. She wanted to stop and have a break. She wanted to have someone talk to her, not be stuck in silence yet again. She wanted food. And a drink.

But the last thing she wanted to do was seem weak—weaker—than they already thought she was. Than Mathos already thought she was. For some ridiculous reason, his opinion mattered.

Tor seemed to be prepared to forgive her just about anything, and everyone else she'd ever met dismissed her outright. But not Mathos. Mathos was interested in her and annoyed by her. He wanted more from her, and somehow she found herself wanting him to like her. Wanting him to stop looking at her like she was spoiled. Gods, that comment had hit her right where it hurt. And that made her even more cranky.

She squirmed and stretched, all while muttering nasty names for Mathos in her head. It was his fault that she was going north. His fault they couldn't go to a village. His fault that she was so uncomfortable. He was the leader of this little mercenary gang, so all her discomfort was his responsibility.

"Time for a break," Tor called from behind her, breaking into a particularly creative rant she was busy having in her head.

"What?" Mathos turned with a confused frown. "Why?"

Tor shrugged without replying, and Mathos gave him a frustrated look of disbelief.

She could have hugged Tor at that moment. Instead, she turned back to face him and gave him a huge, grateful smile.

"Definitely not," Mathos said from the front, surprising them both.

She whipped back around. "Why not?"

Mathos looked between her and Tor, his face settling

into an annoyed glower. "Because we're close to the track that cuts through this forest, and who knows what we'll find when we get there."

"Surely a few minutes' break to have a drink wouldn't make much difference?" she demanded. "Tor wouldn't have suggested it if he thought it was dangerous."

"Is it Tor who wants the break, *Claudia*, or is it you?" Mathos asked belligerently. "Because Tor's a soldier. He's gone many, many hours without needing a break before, and I'm guessing he'll survive again today. But if it's you who wants the break, all you have to do is say the word. Give us the command, and we can all stop and have a rest."

She narrowed her eyes. Damn, she hated the way he called her Claudia. And she really hated the way he kept emphasizing it, like she didn't know her own damn made-up name. She also hated his condescending tone.

She blanked her face and stared at him, wishing they could take a break, but accepting that nothing could make her say so now.

When she didn't reply, Mathos passed her a waterskin, waited for her to take a long drink, and then grunted and turned back. Leading them onward once more.

Lucilla stared at his back and imagined all the nasty things she was going to say to him when she was finally able to be rid of the patronizing bastard.

They reached a dirt track cutting through the woods a short while later, and the smug air that rolled off Mathos made her want to throw something at the back of his head. She turned to look at Tor, who gave her a small smile of commiseration.

She didn't bother saying anything, simply added another curse to the list she was keeping in her mind.

They stopped where they were, hidden in the darkness

of the trees, for long moments, as the men carefully scanned the road and its surrounding woodland.

"Is it safe on the road?" she whispered to Tor.

"No. We can't stay on it long, but the Derrow River lies to the north and west of us. It's deep and fast; the horses would have to swim. If we can stay on this road for ten minutes, we can go over the old bridge and then branch off as quickly as we can. Overall, it's less risky than the river, particularly since we haven't seen anyone looking for us in all this time."

"Wouldn't it be better to just go the other way?"

"Maybe, but it would take us a couple of days out of our way. Every day out here is a risk."

Mathos gave them a stern look, and Lucilla swallowed her next question. The men were wound up tight enough as it was.

They made even better time on the road. Mathos and Tor flanked her, both seeming to be on high alert, constantly scanning the road, the woods on either side of them, even the sky.

By the time they reached the open fields that suggested they were nearing the village, she was exhausted and irritable. The tension in the two men had rubbed off on her, and she was jumpy and anxious as well as feeling well and truly battered.

Farmland rolled away in front of them, barren after the autumn harvest, the soil dug into deep furrows of dark earth, giving a clear view to the far distance where she could see tiny rows of what seemed to be cottages, with a small building on top of one of the hills overlooking the village. But the main change she noticed was how the fresh, clean scent of the woods was slowly overpowered by something that smelled truly hideous.

With every mile they covered the smell grew, burning the back of her throat until her eyes watered and she wished she could cover her face.

"I'm guessing we're downwind from a pig farm," Tor muttered beside her as she wrinkled her nose and did her best to breathe through her mouth.

"Where are the pigs?" she asked.

"They'll have pens closer to the farm, but this time of year, the farmer will have taken them into the woods to look for acorns," Tor replied.

"So why does it smell so bad?"

"They most likely spread the manure on the fields," Tor explained.

She turned to look at him. "Does it always smell like this?"

Mathos snorted loudly. "What do you think, Princess?"

She ignored Tor's conciliatory look and turned to face Mathos, her aching body and the hours of tension combining with her well-nurtured irritation toward the man. "I told you already that I'm not the princess."

"Yes, yes, *Claudia*, we all know what you said." Mathos turned in his saddle to look directly at her even though they were riding around a sharp turn in the road. "And I couldn't agree more, you're not a princess... you're the queen. But since we're all going along with this ridiculous story of yours, and since you've ruled out darlin' and your majesty, princess it is."

Lucilla felt her jaw drop. She had never been spoken to so rudely in her entire life. Even Claudius had never spoken to her like that.

"Listen to me, you arrogant piece of—" Her voice broke into a frightened scream as Penelope startled and suddenly sidestepped, the mare snorting and tossing her mane wildly as she spooked, crashing them into Tor and his massive destrier. Penelope neighed loudly, rearing up as Lucilla fought to grip her with her knees and cling on.

The sudden commotion made both the warhorses toss their heads angrily, although they were too experienced to do more, as Mathos and Tor quickly brought them to a controlled stop. Mathos reached across and grabbed Penelope's halter, holding her firmly as she twitched and snorted and slowly settled.

"Take the lead rope," Mathos commanded tersely, passing it across to Tor as he slid off Heracles and stalked to the side of the road.

He walked slowly back the way they'd come, peering intently into the bramble-filled ditch that marked the border of a farm. A short while later, he called loudly, "I can see you. You might as well come out."

There was a scuffling noise, and Lucilla winced. She did not envy anyone planning to go through those brambles. Her nights in the woods had taught her that.

Mathos sighed. "You can't go that way, you'll get stuck. Come out here. I promise we won't hurt you."

"Yeah, right," a child's voice replied.

Mathos lowered himself to one knee on the side of the dusty road and held up his hands, just as he'd done for her the night before. "Look, no weapons."

"No weapons *yet*," said the voice, dripping cynicism despite its youth.

"Gods." Mathos dropped his forehead to his bent knee and rested for a moment before trying again. "How about this. I'm sure you didn't spook the horse on purpose, I'm guessing you fell into that ditch trying to get away. I just want to check that you're okay."

"Was an accident!"

"Yes, it was an accident," Mathos agreed calmly. "Come on; we're in a hurry. I need you to climb up here so we can make sure you haven't broken anything."

"No fanks," said the child.

"Look." Mathos's voice dropped to a growl. "If I wanted to hurt you, I could just shoot you with my crossbow from here."

There was a small scream and more scuffling, which made Tor laugh. "What?" Mathos demanded, turning back to look up at them. "That's what you said yesterday!"

Tor laughed harder and shook his head, not bothering to reply.

"Fine," Mathos said, standing up and dusting his hands on his legs. "You stay there, and we'll just give the dried beef and apples to someone else."

He walked back toward Heracles just as a small blond head appeared above the ditch. "Beef and apples?"

"No, no." Mathos waved his hand airily, not turning around. "You don't want any. Fair enough. Carry on about your day."

The rest of the child emerged, scrambling up the bank onto the side of the road. She was wearing a brown homespun hemp shirt that was far too big and dirty breeches that were far too short. Her face was thin and dusty, her feet were bare, and her long blond hair was tied back in a scraggly braid. Lucilla had never met a child, but she couldn't imagine that this one was older than about nine or ten or that food was something she had much of.

The girl took a small step forward and then hesitated, her face riveted on the three horses and their intimidating riders.

Mathos ignored her and made his way to Heracles to rifle through his saddlebags. From where Lucilla was sitting, transfixed, she saw him pull out an old apple and a big piece of dried beef.

He turned slowly and faced the girl, before taking a massive bite of the apple and chewing loudly. "Mmm," he said as he swallowed and wiped his mouth with the back of his hand. "Delicious."

The child took an uncertain step forward and then froze when Mathos took his own big step toward her.

He stopped immediately and they both stood, a few feet apart, staring at each other.

The girl watched him chew and swallow and took another step forward.

Mathos held out the apple, not saying anything, and after a few more seconds, she darted closer, snatched the apple, and darted back again, already shoveling it into her mouth.

Mathos smiled and asked gently, "What's your name, darlin'?"

The girl was immediately defensive. "What's it to ya?"

"Nothing," he replied with a shrug. "Just wondering. Would you like some beef?" He held it out for her, and she stepped forward to snatch it before cradling it against her chest like a treasure.

"Eat it," Mathos commanded. But the child shook her head and stepped back.

"Eat it, and I'll give you more."

The girl's face fell as she looked between him and the beef.

"What's wrong, apple pip?" Mathos asked in a gentle voice that made Lucilla try and remember if anyone had ever spoken to her with so much kindness. She didn't think so.

The girl's lips quirked up at the sides. "Apple pip?"

"Yeah, you look like an apple pip to me."

The girl shrugged, as if adults did things she didn't understand all the time.

"If you tell me the problem, maybe I can help you," Mathos pointed out. Lucilla could see that his shoulders were tense, and she knew he was concerned about the delay on the road, but he kept his voice gentle and kind.

"Can't eat it quick enough," the girl admitted sadly. "S'posed to be back already. There's work to do. That's why I was rabbiting when...."

"When you fell into the road and frightened the horse?"

She gave a small nod. "Sorry." She flicked a glance across to the three horses, her face softening. "Gods, I wish I could have a go."

Mathos grinned at her as if she'd impressed him. "Tell you what, if you promise to eat it yourself, I'll give you the other piece."

The girl nodded frantically. "Promise."

"Cross your heart and hope to die?"

"Cross my heart and hope to die." A dirty finger dutifully crossed her heart.

Mathos pulled out another piece of dried beef, and a handful of small coins, which he handed over slowly. "Now, apple pip, you be more careful on the road, okay?"

"Okay. Fank you, mister." The girl gave him a small smile as she backed away. "It's Alis."

"Nice to meet you, Alis," Mathos replied sincerely, although Lucilla noticed that he didn't offer their names in return.

And she was relieved. For some insane reason, she didn't want to be introduced as Claudia.

The whole interaction was unsettling her. Was this how Mathos had been treating her? Like a feral child in need of soothing? Purchasing her compliance with food and soft words. Or was he genuinely trying his best to help them both? How could she possibly tell?

The girl turned and ran down the road ahead of them, and Lucilla stifled a gasp. She had wings! Gods. Hidden behind that big shirt, she was a Mabin.

Mathos turned toward her, his nostrils flaring as he bit out, "Don't. Say. Anything."

Lucilla blinked and kept her mouth shut, deeply insulted. But, at the same time, she realized that he had heard her sudden breath and was trying to stop her from hurting the child.

Oh, that realization burned. She wanted to tell him that she would never, could never hurt a child. But then it occurred to her that, for all his strength and confidence, she had hurt *him*, and the words died in her mouth.

Mathos stalked toward them and flung himself back onto Heracles with a grunt, but as he turned to watch the young girl disappear into the distance, she saw his face soften into a smile, his skin crinkling at the corners of his eyes.

It was the first real smile he'd given since she met him. A smile of real warmth. With no agenda, no points to score, just a genuine reflection of his feelings. And it did something strange to her.

It made her wish he would look at her like that.

Chapter Six

MATHOS WATCHED ALIS "RABBITING" down the road with a bittersweet ache in his chest. She was a bright little thing. Too young to be out scurrying, half-starved, through the hedgerows. She should be in school. Or learning from her mama at the very least. But he knew from too many years as a soldier traveling through the kingdom how many children lacked even that. Especially with the way that Geraint, and those in power before him, had been pouring the kingdom's resources—especially the lives of the young men—year after year into the campaigns in the north.

He watched until she was safely off the road and running down a dirt track between the fields, then nudged Heracles into a fast trot, with Lucilla once again flanked by him and Tor.

They had spent too long on the road, and he was anxious to get off it. The bridge was less than a mile away, but he wanted them over it and back in the safety of the surrounding forest. Ideally, they needed an animal path that would take them away from any kind of habitation or other people.

Still, he didn't regret stopping to check on the girl. Nor did he regret making sure she had something to eat. All in, it had probably only cost them three or four minutes, and he would have worried about her forever if they hadn't stopped. It would have been horrendous if she had lain, hurt and helpless, by the side of the road, unable to get home, no one knowing where she was.

And, although he would have done the same for anyone, Alis had reminded him of Crissy.

She'd been about the same age when he left; nine years old and full of life and cheek. Gods, he missed her. He'd written regularly and sent small gifts when he could, but over the years she'd replied less and less. Eventually, she'd stopped altogether, and after two more years of trying, he'd admitted defeat. But it never stopped hurting.

She'd be eighteen now. Almost a woman. Someone who might not even recognize him on the street, even though he had raised her almost single-handedly from when she was three years old.

In the end, their mother's new husband had been the one who separated them. He hadn't wanted Mathos around. Mathos was too young, too cocky, too used to being the head of the household. Too much of a failure, if they were all being honest. And Baul had given them an ultimatum. If Baul was going to marry Mother, Mathos had to go.

Mother had wept and begged her new fiancé to allow him to stay. Well, she'd begged for a few days at least. Maybe two. And then she'd dried her eyes and asked her son to leave.

After years of taking care of them all. After working night and day to keep the household running. After eking out their dwindling resources as his mother's and older sisters' frivolous spending brought them to the edge of ruin. After battling against his own inabilities and lack of experience, day after day, desperate not to fail them all. After being almost a father to Crissy, despite being little more than a child himself.

In the end, he'd lost it all. And then Mother had told him to go… and he had.

He'd walked away the next day and enlisted. Signed up to the army at nineteen and was immediately posted to some of the worst hellholes imaginable. And yet, in so many ways, he had still felt freer than when he'd been struggling under the impossible responsibility he had tried to shoulder all alone.

He still missed Crissy, though, and he probably always would. What was she like? Had her time with him helped her to grow into a strong, independent woman? Or had she become more like their mother in the years since he had gone?

He cast a glance at Lucilla. What would she have been like if she'd ever been allowed to experience life outside the house she was born in? Would she still have been so unaware of the needs of her people? So completely helpless?

She's not helpless.

True, she had surprised him several times. Her quick apology when she felt she'd been in the wrong; the way she had survived alone and lost for so long; even now, how she hadn't insisted on taking a break. He had to admit a growing respect for her stoicism. She was clearly tired and hungry and sore, but she didn't whine or complain or expect any kind of special treatment.

She got grumpy, sure, but he couldn't really blame her for that. Nope, he could only blame himself.

Gods. She had been so excited to see new things, her face truly coming alive for the first time as her mask of indifference finally slipped away. He'd felt terrible when he told her to keep quiet and saw the flush of embarrassment climbing up her neck.

He'd made her feel bad… but what could he do? He couldn't take her off on a holiday when they urgently needed to get her to safety. They had to find their squad and make some decisions about what the hell they were going to do if she truly refused to take her place as queen. And he had to concentrate, to listen for danger and keep them safe.

Keep telling yourself that, rumbled his beast. *We all know why you told her to keep quiet.*

Mathos sighed. He had needed to listen for danger, but the truth was that he also didn't want to spend the entire journey having her chattering and asking questions. Sooner or later, she would start asking questions he wasn't ready to answer. It would be far better to wait until they were safe and she could meet Alanna for herself. Then they could tell her everything in detail without running the risk that she'd bolt at the first opportunity.

And now she was riding, curious but silent, her throat still mottled pink from her outrage when he'd told her not to speak to the little Mabin.

Bollocks, that was the second time he'd told her to keep quiet.

She had that look on her face, the slight smile that didn't reach her eyes, her face set into some kind of insipid perfection with no real expression. The look she had, he was coming to realize, when she was keeping herself in check. Hiding her thoughts and feelings.

Despite everything, she still hadn't cried. Not even once. His mother and sisters would have collapsed into a heap of weeping and demanded hours of coddling in the first hour of what Lucilla had gone through. It was so much more than he'd expected, and it made him like her despite himself.

Of course you like her. She's vibrant and curious. And very brave. Not forgetting beautiful. Doing her best in a completely foreign world.

His beast was right. But it was a feeling that was challenged every time she smiled cheerfully at Tor and then turned to frown at him. Or flinched when he spoke to her.

It riled him, even while he knew it was ridiculous. Any other woman, and he wouldn't have minded that she liked his usually taciturn friend more than him. But for some inexplicable reason, not this one. Despite the myriad of reasons that he should want nothing at all to do with her, he wanted her to smile at *him*. Not bloody Tor.

Not that he could blame her for giving his friend all her attention. Tor had been kind to her, while he had been behaving exactly like the brute she thought he was.

As soon as they were in the woods, he would make sure she had a good long break.

And tell her the rest.

Yeah... that.

He brought his attention back to his surroundings; taking another long, slow look, checking for possible danger.

Which was when he saw it. A flash of light, and then another, coming from the roof of the small building on the hill ahead of them. A shrine probably, based on its location.

Whatever it was, it had no business having lights flashing on the roof. Shit. Someone was sending a message. And out here, surrounded by pig farms, there was only one message they might be sending.

Mathos's body armored in thick scales as his beast roared forward. They were less than two minutes from the bridge. All they had to do was get over it and away.

To the south were several miles of open farmland before they could turn into the woods, and the lookout would be able to watch them the whole time. Ahead was the bridge and the woods, and with every mile they passed, they got closer to safety at Eshcol.

They had to get over that bridge.

"Run!" He pushed Heracles into a tearing gallop, roaring at Tor and Lucilla to follow. Thank the gods they did.

In a swirling thunder of hooves, they all fled along the dusty track.

The world narrowed to the creaking of the saddles, the snorting breath of the horses, their drumming hooves, and the wind howling across his ears.

He glanced sideways to check, and Tor and Lucilla were with him, leaning forward and riding hard. He had a sudden horror that Lucilla was riding without a saddle, but she and Penelope moved smoothly together, a graceful, coordinated unit—woman and horse together—despite their neck-breaking speed.

And then they were there, clattering heavily over the old wooden bridge, the Derrow churning and thundering below them.

Mathos immediately began hunting for a path or track into the woods. Anything that would allow them to disappear into the murky depths beneath the trees.

Up ahead, just a hundred yards away, he could see a dark opening, and he urged them forward with a shout.

They were almost there.

But then, seconds before they reached the path, a tall,

mounted officer wearing the black of the cavalry urged his massive gray stallion forward, emerging from the exact opening that Mathos had been aiming at.

Gods. He pulled back viciously, forcing Heracles into a brutal stop as Tor and Lucilla did the same beside him, the horses whinnying and snorting in the cloud of dust.

Mathos whirled to Tor. "Go! Now!"

Tor didn't hesitate, he simply took off, splitting them up and hopefully ensuring at least one of them would get away to go for help.

More riders flooded from the woods, half a dozen speeding off after Tor.

Mathos turned Heracles, impressed to see Lucilla do the same, and the two of them fled back the way they had come. Pushing the sweating horses once more, desperate to make it back onto the open road.

They clattered over the ancient wooden bridge with horns blowing and hooves thundering behind them. They bent low and pushed the horses harder.

They hurtled around the corner where they'd met Alis, desperate to see an open escape route ahead, only to meet the worst sight imaginable. Arrayed across the road were more cavalry troops, walking their horses in formation, three deep.

They pulled to a stop, Heracles and Penelope stepping anxiously and breathing hard as Lucilla leaned down and soothed her mare with quiet words and gentle pats. Gods, she was a magnificent horsewoman.

More men flooded the road behind them. Fuck it all. They'd been trapped. Soldiers ahead and behind.

Mathos could feel his scales settling in a wave, up his arms and over his face. Beside him, Lucilla sat straight-backed, chin up, looking entirely regal. But, perhaps because he'd been watching her all day, he imagined he also saw a hint of uncertainty, vulnerability even, beneath her serene composure.

He gave her a quick smile, hoping it was reassuring, and whispered, "Well, Princess, it looks like our plans for an afternoon of hard riding, no breaks, and occasional sniping at each other are about to fall through."

She gave a slight shake of her head, ignoring his joke to nervously watch the ranks of soldiers forming.

Gods. He had let her down in so many ways. His beast turned unhappily, desperate to make her feel even a little better.

He leaned closer. "My father used to tell me that the best thing to do is to imagine them all naked. That might help." Finally, the side of her mouth twitched ever so slightly, and his beast rumbled in relief.

Her eyes flicked to his and then back to the soldiers, and he noticed that, despite his being fully battle-scaled, she didn't seem bothered by his beast at all.

She nudged Penelope closer to him—away from the array of Apollyon—and his beast grumbled even louder in a surge of protective watchfulness.

He angled himself so that Lucilla was behind his shoulder, then turned to the soldiers and raised his voice. "What is the meaning of this?"

A burly Apollyon wearing the marks of sergeant stepped forward. "I'll be asking the questions. What are you doing with Queen Lucilla?"

Mathos opened his mouth, fully intending to explain that the woman beside him was called Claudia and they could all fuck off. But a look at her white-knuckled grip on Penelope's mane had him swallowing the words. Everyone there knew exactly who she was. Insisting on maintaining the farce that she was Claudia would only humiliate her. He closed his mouth again and shook his head.

He was still trying to think of a sensible, and ideally amusing, explanation when they were interrupted by a voice calling loudly from behind them, in the direction of the bridge. They both turned to see the lieutenant from the tavern pushing his horse past the ranks of cavalry.

Beside him, Mathos felt Lucilla go absolutely still. Her spine went, if possible, even straighter, and her chin went up another notch as her face drained of all expression.

The day before he'd thought it was haughty and condescending—her spoiled princess look—but from his position right next to her, seeing her heavy swallow, the pulse beating frantically in her neck, he realized what it really was. It was fear.

No. It was bravery. It was the look she got when she felt threatened and was trying to stay calm and not give herself away.

Fuck. How could he only be realizing that now?

"Thank the gods," Claudius stated grumpily. "We've been looking everywhere for you."

Mathos blinked. Claudius sounded like he was rebuking a child. And by the mottled red creeping up Lucilla's neck, she thought so too.

Something about the way she sat, disheveled, tired and hungry, but still facing down multiple soldiers without flinching, spine straight and elegant—despite not even having a saddle—made him want to lay waste to these rows of unfeeling soldiers. Starting with the man who had the nerve to treat her with so little respect in front of everyone.

Ah… like all the respect you've shown her.

Mathos swallowed. He hadn't been at his best. Still, it was one thing for him to call her princess in private when she was denying everything about herself. It was another thing entirely from this man who should know better. Especially in front of the troops.

Mathos opened his mouth to respond, but Lucilla beat him to it. "Actually, Lieutenant Claudius, I don't believe I requested your assistance." Her voice was resolute, but he noticed that her hands were shaking where they tangled in Penelope's mane, gripping it like a lifeline.

"Lieutenant Claudius"—the troops parted, and another rider trotted forward, his smooth voice ringing across the assembled troops as he pressed forward—"you are addressing your queen, and you will do so with a great deal more respect."

Fucking hell. Mathos sighed loudly, not even bothering to be subtle. Dornar had arrived. The fact that he was saying exactly the right thing was not even remotely reassuring.

Dornar slipped off his horse and sank to one knee in the middle of the road, his crisp blue uniform bright against the dust. He looked fresh and rested, and he was wearing the heavy gold chains of the Lord High Chancellor.

Almost as one, the men around him followed his lead and sank to their knees in a slow wave of obeisance. Mathos was almost impressed—discipline had certainly improved in the short time since Dornar had taken charge—but his beast had gone insane the minute he realized Dornar was there, and most of his focus had to be on keeping Heracles calm.

Lucilla looked slightly stunned as she stared down at them all, and Mathos felt like an idiot as he sat beside her wondering if he should dismount and kneel with everyone else.

After a few moments of respectful silence, Dornar stood gracefully and stepped forward to reach up and take Lucilla's hand in his. "Your Majesty, I can't tell you how delighted we are to have found you unharmed. Rest assured that we have been doing our utmost to see to your safe return. Please allow me to introduce myself. I am Dornar, your Lord High Chancellor."

Finally, Lucilla's eyes flicked across to Mathos. Looking for advice? Reassurance? He had no idea.

What should he say? How could he explain the horror that was Dornar? All while the man himself and an array of troops looked on.

Bollocks. He already regretted his surly behavior. Now he sincerely wished that he had spent the long hours of silence explaining everything to Lucilla.

He dragged a hand down his dusty face, regretting just about everything he'd done over the last day. And he had the horrible suspicion he was going to regret it a lot more before the day was over.

He had no immediate answer for Lucilla, so he fell back on what he knew. Insolence. "Imagine seeing you here, Lord Chancellor. You were so quick to leave us last time we saw you, after all."

Dornar smirked as he pulled himself lightly back into his saddle. "It's not at all a surprise to see you here, however."

"No?" Mathos asked, enjoying Dornar's flicker of resentment.

"No. We've been waiting for you to turn north."

"You waited for us on this particular road?" Mathos snorted disbelievingly.

"Not at all." Dornar gave him a smug smile. "We've had troops on *all* the roads north. I relaxed in my comfortable base near the village and as soon as you were seen they signaled for me."

Mathos stared at him, trying not to snarl. "Why would you set up your base near here?"

"Court records showed that there were only two manor homes with gardens planted by the previous queen that still had visits from Geraint and Ballanor. I was certain that with a little patience, we'd find Queen Lucilla at one of them."

Dornar made it sound like he and his men had been actively looking for Lucilla in those homes, but he couldn't have, or Lucilla would have met him earlier. And then she would never have run away. More than that, none of Dornar's men had been hunting them in the woods; Mathos was sure of it.

Bollocks.

It occurred to him that Dornar had narrowed down his targets and then simply watched both homes. He didn't need to storm in and upset the delicate princess, who might react poorly to a stranger. He didn't need to tell her that both her brother and Grendel had died while under his guard, or that he snatched power and was now consolidating it. No… he had avoided every uncomfortable conversation they might have had and simply waited for Mathos to arrive first and fuck it all up.

Then, when Mathos had delivered the bad news, riled up the new queen, taken her from her home and put her completely on the defensive, Dornar could sweep in as the charming rescuer.

Which was bloody insulting.

Worse, it was completely mortifying because it was so accurate. Mathos had done everything Dornar had predicted.

On the bright side, Lucilla running away must have given Dornar a few gray hairs. Completely unsettled his nice little plan. Or maybe not… Here they all were, exactly where Dornar wanted them to be. And the next step would be to make certain that Lucilla knew Mathos was the villain. Gods.

Dornar nodded to a red-faced Claudius and then pointing straight at Mathos, ordered loudly, "Lieutenant, arrest this man."

"What for?" Mathos challenged, despite knowing it was coming. His beast flickered angrily, rumbling loud enough that the soldiers must have been able to hear it and causing Heracles to toss his head uncertainly.

Dornar gave him a slow smile, his copper scales flashing brilliantly in the sun. "Kidnapping the queen. Obviously."

"I didn't kidnap her. I rescued her," Mathos snarled as Claudius pressed his horse forward and lifted his dagger.

Dornar tilted his head to one side as he turned to Lucilla. "Are you traveling with this man willingly?"

"Sort of," Lucilla admitted.

Dornar gave her a politely expectant look. "And where is he taking you, Your Majesty?"

"To the north, to the Nephilim Temple. To meet with Alanna," she answered slowly.

"Mm-hmm." Dornar's look was positively smug. "And did he mention that Alanna is working with Lanval, the man who killed your brother?"

Lucilla frowned. "He said that Ballanor had died in trial by combat from poison on his own sword. And that Alanna chose to stay with Lanval rather than take the throne...." Her eyes flickered toward Mathos. "It sounded like, I mean, I thought they were... ah...."

Dornar shook his head sadly. "Did he also tell you that Lanval admitted publicly that he was having an affair with Alanna's maid? It really doesn't make any sense that Alanna would choose him over her throne when he already loved someone else. I'm sorry to have to tell you this but Alanna didn't choose Lanval, or anyone else, instead of the throne, no, she is still very much hoping to rule this kingdom."

"No! That's—" Mathos's exclamation was cut off by Claudius waving a hand to the nearest archer, who pulled up a crossbow and aimed it at his head. Fuck, Dornar was twisting everything.

"And," Dornar continued, "I'm guessing that he forgot to mention that Lanval also confessed to arranging the massacre at Ravenstone. The attack that resulted in the death of your father."

Lucilla spun to stare at him wide-eyed, her face slowly draining of color, and he shook his head frantically.

But Dornar was still speaking. "Lanval's sister murdered the previous Lord High Chancellor and she did it with a poisoned blade. Think for a moment, how did the poison get on Ballanor's blade, if not put there by someone who knew exactly what they were doing? Someone who'd done it before. Someone working with Lanval, Alanna and the Hawks."

Dornar gave Lucilla a sorrowful look. "Mathos and his friends have wiped out your entire family and are currently colluding with the nation that killed many thousands of Brythorians. They're actively conspiring with the Verturians —Alanna's people—to take control of Brythoria, and now they've come for you."

Fuck it all. Put like that, it really didn't sound good. He had to fix this somehow.

The archer held his crossbow steadily, but it didn't stop Mathos from trying to explain. "Don't listen to him. He's twisting what happened to suit him. I promise I told you the truth... Alanna and Lanval are married, and the rest... sounds bad, but when you meet the—"

"Shut up Mathos," Dornar interrupted, "or we will shoot you right here."

Lucilla closed her eyes for a moment, seeming to center herself, before opening them to look right at him. Her face was pale, framed by escaped tendrils of thick black hair, her big eyes filled with betrayal.

He reached out a hand toward her, trying to think of the best way to explain, but she simply turned her mare away and began to ride toward the village.

Soldiers scrambled out of her way while, behind her, Dornar smirked at Mathos.

The new Lord High Chancellor gave a brisk nod to Claudius. "Lieutenant, arrest this man."

Chapter Seven

DORNAR HELD the door open for Lucilla as she made her way into the small, empty tavern.

A quad of guards had been sent ahead to ensure everything was ready for her. Penelope had been taken to be cared for in the stables. A corporal was carrying her satchel. Another had arrived with a cool, damp cloth for her hands. Everyone was bowing and smiling, polite and respectful.

It was surreal.

Dornar was treating her like she was valuable. Like what she wanted was the most important thing in the world. When she commented that she was thirsty, within a minute she had a corporal at her elbow holding flagons of water, ale, and wine for her to choose from, and the entire company had paused in the road while she drank it.

When she mentioned that she had been riding all morning, Dornar immediately sent men to prepare the tavern for her to rest in.

He made eye contact. He always called her "Your Majesty." He asked for her opinions. He insisted that his men treat her with absolute respect. She had never experienced anything like it.

At first, she had been deeply suspicious of him. And she still had moments where she felt that something was too good to be true about the entire situation. But what did she know? Geraint and Ballanor's staff had always spoken to them with the utmost courtesy; maybe this was how she should have been treated all along.

Should she compare him to Mathos? Ha. Bastard. Arrogant, idiotic, asshole. He had lied to her. Manipulated her. Was planning... who knew what?

He deserved to be punished.

He did.

Didn't he?

In the half hour since she'd ridden away from him, she'd started to doubt herself. And a nasty feeling of guilt had started to climb through her belly. He had given her their food, his tent, led her safely out the woods, stood up for her against the soldiers... damn. Was it all a manipulation?

She thought about how he'd checked on little Alis, insisting that she take some food and coins and stay safe. That hadn't been of any personal benefit to him. He hadn't told Alis his name. Was that a lie? Or had he done it to keep them all safe?

Gah. There was no way to know. And now she was genuinely worried about whether she'd done the right thing in turning away and leaving him to be arrested.

She took a deep breath and forced her shoulders down, hoping to ease the pressure building behind her eyes, and tried to sort through her thoughts.

What would she have done if Mathos had told her everything? She would have run for sure. Did Mathos's care for her excuse that he had manipulated her into staying by leaving out a load of important information?

Did he do it because he genuinely wanted to help, like he did with Alis, or was it all part of some greater, more sinister plan?

Almost certainly the latter; Mathos and Tor were working with Alanna, and she was Verturian. They had betrayed their kingdom for the enemy, and now Alanna was planning to take control of—hang on, that didn't make any sense. Why would Alanna need to take over a kingdom she could have been the queen of had she wanted it?

She paused in the middle of the taproom and narrowed her eyes at Dornar. "Why would Alanna go through all these complicated machinations to take over a kingdom that she was already the queen of?"

He gave her a sincere look. "Unfortunately, Alanna was deeply hated by everyone in the palace. You can ask anyone. In fact—" He motioned to one of the guards at the door, a young Apollyon, to come closer. "What did the courtiers call Alanna? Please tell the queen."

The young man looked between them nervously until Dornar waved for him to continue. "Princess Peevish, Your Majesty."

Lucilla stared at the guard, shocked. Her own guards thought nothing of treating her with disdain, but even Claudius would never have been so rude.

"Please tell her Majesty how Alanna got that name," Dornar commanded.

The guard blinked nervously, but Dornar gave a "carry on" gesture, and he continued, "She was selfish and difficult. Refused to ever join the court. Refused a wedding party, so the whole of Kaerlud missed out on a celebration, the food and coin the palace would have provided. Always throwing tantrums when she didn't get her way." He lowered his voice. "And they say she was responsible for the death of King Geraint. That it was Verturian arrows they pulled out of him when—"

He stopped suddenly, his face growing pale as he realized it was her father that he was discussing, and Dornar dismissed him with a curt wave.

"But why would she stay with Lanval if he loved someone else?"

The new Lord Chancellor shook his head, his mouth turned down with sadness as he took her hand and led her to a table. "Alanna was only ever interested in what she could get out of Brythoria: power and wealth for herself. When her constant demands weren't met, she rid herself of your father and then King Ballanor. Lanval helped her do it and is being rewarded handsomely. Their partnership is one of mutual benefit."

He gave her an apologetic look. "Now she's turned her eye to ruling over the kingdom. She knows that, without an heir, she would never control the Royal Council, who already mistrust and dislike her, so she's hunting you instead. With you as her pawn, she can control you, and through you, the riches of Brythoria."

Gods. She felt sick. She had fled one form of prison only to almost fall into another.

Except.... The thought reminded her of Tor's words the night before. He had said that Dornar would want to marry her and rule through her. Almost exactly what Dornar said Alanna wanted, without the wedding.

One of them was lying—maybe both—but she had no way of judging who. All she knew was that for a brief moment, she had been free, and now she was back exactly where she didn't want to be. And just as alone as she had always been.

Dornar pulled a chair out for her, and she sank into it gratefully, body aching. A tired-looking serving woman arrived and set a plate of floury rolls, cold ham, and slightly overripe tomatoes on the table for her.

"Can I get you anything more, Your Majesty?" Dornar asked softly.

"No, thank you, Lord High Chancellor."

He smiled gently. "Please call me Dornar."

She nodded agreement as she picked up a bread roll, watching him.

He was tall and strong with long, lean muscles. His light brown hair was cropped military short, highlighting the pale blue of his eyes. Scales circled his wrists in bands of burnished copper that caught the light when he moved.

He gave her another charming grin as he passed her a plate of apple slices, and she imagined he could be considered handsome. He was attentive and polite. And he had an answer for everything.

But now that she'd thought of them, Tor's words kept circling through her head… *The new Lord High Chancellor … I wouldn't wish that conniving bastard on my worst enemy.*

It made it difficult to trust him. Even though he'd saved her.

Hadn't he?

She nibbled on a bread roll, wondering where they'd taken Mathos. She'd glanced back once to see that he'd been pulled from his horse, his arms bound behind him. His scales had covered his arms, neck, and face, all the way to his eyes. He had looked grim and somber, his eyes meeting hers for just a moment, but he hadn't fought at all or tried to escape. He hadn't even made a sound. Nothing like the savage animal she'd been taught to expect.

And he had never once mentioned that she had named herself Claudia. Or that she had spent the night in his tent. He could have embarrassed her terribly, but he hadn't.

She remembered him telling Tor that someone had to stay with her and keep her safe. Had he allowed himself to be arrested on purpose, in an effort to stay close?

Gods, she was so confused. And utterly, completely exhausted.

She could only act on the evidence she had. And so far, all she had were two parties each accusing the other of similar crimes. Mathos and Tor had clearly been sneaking through the forest and openly admitted to supporting Alanna of Verturia, while Dornar had the full weight of the Blue Guards and the Cavalry supporting his claims.

Not that any of her experiences with the Blues had left her with much faith in them. And if Dornar had been searching for her so frantically, why hadn't he been looking in the woods?

Gods. What a mess.

She realized that she had been silent for too long and dipped her chin, reaching for politeness. "Thank you, Dornar. I appreciate all of your assistance."

He smiled back. "You're welcome, Your Majesty."

She took several long sips of her water as she tried to gather her thoughts. "What has been done with Mathos?"

Dornar gave a slight flick of his fingers. "He will be kept imprisoned while we interrogate him regarding his plans with Alanna, and Verturia of course, and then returned to Kaerlud for his execution."

Lucilla's stomach lurched, and she had to put down her cup before it slipped from her suddenly damp fingers.

Interrogate. Execute. Gods. Why hadn't she realized that was what would happen?

"No." She shook her head, struggling to keep her face impassive. "I didn't agree to an interrogation or execution. I would like to question him, of course, and imprisonment would be sensible, but I'd like to understand the details of what happened more clearly before we discuss his trial."

Dornar steepled his fingers on the table, speaking slowly. "With all due respect, Your Majesty, he kidnapped you. The penalty is death."

She almost rubbed her fingers down her pounding forehead but managed to clasp them in her lap instead. Damn, she was tired of being treated like a child. "I never said that he kidnapped me."

Dornar lifted his hand as if to pat her shoulder, but then seemed to decide against it and folded his arms instead. "Your Majesty, you didn't need to. Your silence when we arrested him was sufficient."

Gods. She had tacitly accused Mathos of kidnapping, and now he was going to die. Even though he had given her the chance to leave. Twice.

How the hell had arresting him gone so far? Was this what Mathos had meant when he said that she was spoiled? That she was too inexperienced, too naïve, and that people could be hurt because of it. *Too stubborn... too argumentative... too stupid...* the dark voice in the back of her head whispered as cold fingers of guilt twined in her belly.

Dornar must have seen something of her horror on her face despite her attempt to stay blankly stoic, and he gave her a reassuring look. "You have been shielded from men like Mathos all your life—untrustworthy people with no morality. You couldn't possibly know that he was scheming with Alanna. As your Lord High Chancellor, it is my honor to protect you."

She frowned. Gods, she'd been surrounded by untrustworthy people since the day she'd been born.

Dornar gave her a soft look, misreading her expression. "Don't worry about Mathos. He's been taken care of. You concentrate on looking after yourself after your horrible time in the woods. You're safe here with me, and I'll make sure that you always have everything you need."

Lucilla held her hands clasped tightly in her lap to avoid crossing her arms over her chest like she wanted to. The way Dornar was speaking, so soothingly and reassuringly, was unreasonably annoying. She didn't want someone to coddle her and treat her like a child. She wanted the truth.

She wanted to know why Mathos had lied. What his true intentions were. Then, when she understood his guilt, she would make a decision. If he truly had betrayed her, manipulated her to control her for Alanna, then she would hand him over to Dornar to be imprisoned with a clear conscience.

"I want your promise that you will not torture him or hurt him in any way. Not until I've had a chance to speak with him. And execution is off the table."

"Your Majesty—"

She firmed her voice. "Your promise, please, Lord Chancellor."

Dornar looked her straight in the eye. "If that is your command, then I promise."

Okay. That gave her some time to try and understand what had happened. "Good. I'd like to finish my food, and then you can take me to see him."

This time he didn't even begin to argue. "Of course, Your Majesty."

That had been easier than she expected. Maybe she and Dornar would be able to work together after all. He didn't seem dangerous or anything like the controlling asshole Tor had described. If anything, he had been overly solicitous, bordering on condescending.

She tried to think of something else to say and simply couldn't. Instead, she concentrated on eating while Dornar filled the silence.

He had secured a room in the tavern for the night, in respect of her having been out in the woods for several days. He was mixing his personal guards with the Blues from her manor home so that she would have a well-trained honor guard of men that both knew her well and were recently decorated in the field. They would make their way to Kaerlud, stopping at a selection of hand-picked estates on the way and giving the Blues time to prepare the palace for her arrival in a few days. Her coronation would be held the day after they returned to Kaerlud….

Wait. What? His voice had been drifting over her as she ate, nodding and occasionally agreeing. But now he was talking about being in the palace before the end of the week. And saying that she would be crowned the next day.

She took another sip of her water while she collected her thoughts. She had learned from Mathos and Tor's reaction that straight out saying she didn't want to be the queen didn't work well. "I'm not ready to go to the palace."

Dornar blinked, his face neutral but his gaze assessing. "When do you think you will be ready?"

"I want to see some of the kingdom. Get an understanding of my people." There, that sounded reasonable.

He dipped his head briefly, considering. "I understand, and I think it's a very good idea."

Lucilla felt a surge of relief, which quickly faded with his next words. "As soon as you're officially recognized and crowned, I'll take you on a tour. It will be good for you to see your kingdom and for your people to meet their queen."

Damn. That wasn't what she meant. "Is all of this urgency necessary?"

"Yes." Dornar was emphatic. "If you want to avoid a civil war, then you need to take the throne."

"A civil war?" she repeated softly, reluctantly recognizing that Mathos and Tor had said the same thing.

Dornar grimaced. "Indeed. There will be distant cousins many times removed and young peers of Ballanor who were close to him, all of whom think that a vacant throne is an opportunity they can't ignore. Some might feel that military rule would be a good idea. Even your kidnapper, Mathos, could make a claim—his father was a baron who fought directly under King Geraint in the northern wars, after all."

He folded his arms, leaning back in his chair. "Any one of those people might bid for the crown, and if one tries, they all will. The result will be conflict and destruction that leaves the entire country poor and defenseless. The economy would suffer terribly, and we might open ourselves to an invasion from Verturia that we have no hope of winning."

"But surely you would prevent that?" she asked weakly.

"Ah, my queen, thank you for your faith in me." He gave her another soft smile, his eyes wrinkling in the corners. "Unfortunately, they would most certainly challenge me, try to remove me from my position as Lord High Chancellor, and it would take me years to fight them all. No, you must take the throne as soon as possible."

Lucilla kept her face serene while her thoughts tumbled

over themselves. Dornar was making the same point Mathos and Tor had.

How might things have turned out if she hadn't begun their relationship by mortally insulting the Tarasque and then repeatedly lying to them about who she was, all while insisting that she was never even going to consider being queen? Would Mathos have felt comfortable telling her everything? Would she still be sitting here with Dornar? Would Mathos be under arrest, facing his execution?

Had she been as much in the wrong as they were? Even more, maybe. Had she just caused a man to be sentenced to death because he'd pissed her off?

Gods. It was the sort of thing Ballanor would do. The thought made her feel ill, and she pushed her plate away unfinished.

Dornar waved a guard over to clear her place. "Your Majesty, you have suffered a terrible ordeal, and you must be exhausted. We have a room prepared if you would like to rest?"

As appealing as it sounded, that wasn't an option. Not until she had a clearer understanding of what was going on. "No thank you, Lord High Chancellor—Dornar—I'd like to see Mathos now."

"Of course. Give me a moment." He stood and walked across to the soldiers guarding the door before speaking to them softly. One of the men saluted and then rushed outside, the door swinging closed behind him.

Dornar folded his hands behind his back and waited patiently.

A few minutes later, the soldier was back. He murmured something to Dornar, who clapped him on the shoulder and then motioned him back into his position at the door.

He returned to the table, his face grim, but his eyes were

clear and direct as they met hers. "I'm sorry, Your Majesty, but there was no suitable cell in this small village. As a result, Mathos has already been sent ahead to Kaerlud. They are on the road as we speak. I will send a note ahead to ensure that Mathos is treated with"—he paused ever so slightly before continuing—"all the respect due to him. You can question him when we arrive in Kaerlud."

She shook her head slowly. "No, I want to see him today. If we leave now, we can easily catch up."

Dornar dipped his head graciously. "I will make arrangements. I believe you need a saddle; is that correct? In the meantime, would you like to freshen up in the room that was prepared for you?"

Lucilla considered for a moment before agreeing. It would take a little while to find the right tack and bring Penelope to the tavern. It made sense to wash her face and rest for a few minutes while she waited. And she could do with some time by herself.

Dornar led her up to a small room that smelled strongly of wax and lemons. There was a narrow bed against the wall that someone had covered with a green velvet throw, beside it was a small table with a drawer, and a second table in the corner holding a basin and a jug. A tiny window let in a beam of pale afternoon sunlight that fell across a wooden chair piled with colorful cushions. Someone had clearly been in and tried to make it suitable for her. For their queen.

She gave him a quick smile. "Please thank the men responsible for the room."

Dornar promised he would and bowed slightly before leaving her alone.

She found the water in the jug was still warm and splashed her face before drying it with a small cotton towel. It was heavenly to have a clean face.

She was combing her fingers through her hair when there was a soft tap on the door, and she opened it to see a young sergeant carrying a tray with wine and autumn berries. He dipped his head courteously and then, at her gesture, stepped inside to place the tray on the table. "Your Majesty, the Lord Chancellor said that as you'd only had water at lunch, you might like this while you're waiting."

She murmured her thanks as he left and then bolted the door behind him.

She poured a glass of the wine, so dark that the red was almost black, and took some berries with her to sit on the chair beside the window while she waited. The idea of sitting in that small square of sunshine for a few moments was irresistible.

The wine was rich and sweet, and she found herself taking another deep sip as her muscles relaxed. And then another.

Days of stress and hunger and too little sleep combined with the soft sunshine to send the syrupy wine straight to her head. Her ears buzzed and her lips tingled as she licked them.

Gods. How strong was that wine? Perhaps she should have stuck with water if she was going to concentrate when she saw Mathos?

The world started to spin disconcertingly, and she set the crystal glass down, worried she might spill. Everything tilted hazily, and she grumbled at her own stupidity. What an idiot to get drunk on a few sips of wine.

She had to rest. Had to take a moment for the world to stop spinning.

She wiped a damp palm down her face and stumbled from the chair to the bed and collapsed. She would just close her eyes for ten minutes and then she would be able to face the world again. That was a plan. A good plan.

She lifted her head to look down at her boots. Too far. Too difficult. They had to stay on.

She curled into a ball on top of the covers and closed her eyes.

Chapter Eight

MATHOS LEANED back against the icy stone and earth wall, stretched his legs out in front of him, and closed his eyes. His left eye was so swollen that it was almost closed. And it was pitch-fucking-dark anyway.

Heavy iron chains clanked as he shifted his hands and prodded his side gently. Prodding was completely unnecessary—every aching breath told him he had at least one broken rib—but somehow irresistible. His whole body felt bruised, and he could smell the coppery tang of blood above the musty earthiness.

The asshole lieutenant and his sidekick, Cerdic, had decided to let him know exactly how they felt about him. His lip twitched—they must have felt bloody stupid when he found their princess for them, especially after their derogatory comments the first time they met. Well, they probably felt better about it now that they'd kicked the shit out of him.

They'd also taken his jerkin, leaving him in his cotton

undershirt, but thank the gods they'd left his leather breeches and his boots.

Mathos forced his eyes open a millimeter and then closed them again. What was the point? He couldn't see his own legs.

In a way, it was good that it was dark. It meant he didn't have to see the other occupants of his prison.

His beast snorted to itself in amusement, but he was going to keep telling himself that it was good that it was dark. For as long as he had to, until he believed it. It was better all round. Definitely.

When Claudius and Cerdic, together with a couple of other Blues from the manor house, had dragged him through the village instead of to Dornar's encampment, he'd been certain they were going to take him to the nearest local magistrat, or perhaps throw him in the local prison or sturdy basement.

The villagers—men and women, even children— had stared at him, wide-eyed and silent. Watching with the tired resignation of people who'd seen it all before as the Blues shoved and kicked him, the soldiers laughing and joking among themselves. He'd kept his eyes down, not wanting to inadvertently involve anyone else, and concentrated on protecting himself when he could.

Then they'd turned up the hill that he'd seen from the road. Only it wasn't a hill, it was a series of burial mounds and, as he'd expected, an ancient shrine.

Not one of the airy flower-filled temples dedicated to the archangels by the Nephilim, or the opulent courts favored by the Apollyon. This was darker, deeper, more primal. A shrine dedicated to the gods and goddesses of the earth, wind, fire, and water. The progeny of the dragons and the first rough clans who had ruled the land and the air before the angels came.

Hundreds of generations of Mabin and Tarasque would have worshiped between the rough stones over the centuries. Praying for good harvests and safe births. Praying that their soldiers would return and that their dead would rest easy.

And, of course, they'd also buried their long-dead priests and priestesses inside the mounds.

Which, because that was the kind of day he was having, was exactly where they'd taken Mathos. Deep into the crypt-like center of a mound. Down the smooth steps, into the heavy, earthen darkness. Past the stone recesses holding ancient bones and into a small space where acolytes would hold rituals and special services.

Mathos had tried suggesting that he would be just as uncomfortable in a cellar or an abandoned hut and that they would be able to reach him far more easily, but the Blues had ignored his suggestions completely. Assholes.

They'd knotted a heavy iron chain around his wrists and then climbed a ladder to secure the end over a hoop high up on the wall, giving him just enough slack that he could sink to the ground. And then they'd left, taking the ladder they'd used with them. And their lamps. Bloody stinking bastards.

So now he sat in the pungent, moldy darkness. Alone with his beast and his thoughts.

He wished he'd done things differently. He'd felt the constant itching awareness that Dornar would be hunting them, but he'd allowed himself to be lulled into a false sense of security because they hadn't seen any sign of him. Had convinced himself that Dornar would be actively searching, as they were. It had never occurred to him that the new Lord High Chancellor would simply spread out and wait, like a fisherman with a net.

Fucking stupid, in hindsight.

Overconfidence in his ability to predict where a person might be, mixed up with all the narrow-minded egotism of a schoolboy so busy focusing his attention on the prettiest girl in class that he didn't notice the teacher standing right behind him. A bad combination. Possibly, in this case, a fatal one.

Hopefully Tor was away and free. He hadn't been thrown into the darkness with Mathos, which could mean that he had made it. Hopefully. He'd had a good head start and no one to look out for except himself.

Or maybe he was in the next mound along and this was all some complicated mind fuckery by Dornar.

Note to self. Stop underestimating Dornar.

And what was Dornar, even now, saying to Lucilla? Was he treating her well? Given the way he'd treated Alanna, not bloody likely. And wasn't that a truly horrific thought?

She had managed to press every single one of his buttons, but she had also been brave and determined, trying her best to escape the prison she'd lived in her entire life. And now he'd seen how Claudius treated her, he could only imagine that it had been pure, unadulterated hell.

Bollocks. When he thought about it like that, he felt even guiltier than before.

The thought of fighting his way out and leaving Lucilla with Dornar hadn't even crossed his mind. Of course, he hadn't expected to find himself at the bottom of a burial mound. Why couldn't the guards have locked him up somewhere easier to escape from? And less creepy.

Time passed slowly down in the darkness with the dead while his head churned with fantastical ideas of escape.

He tried standing and using the chain like a rope to lean back and climb the wall. It was aching, sweating progress, but he made it up several feet of the slippery stone. But then, no matter how he squirmed or threw himself upward, he couldn't release the knot, held tight against the hook by his own body weight.

The third time he crashed back to the ground in an agonizing heap of screaming ribs and pounding head, he gave up and sank back down to sit.

Gods, it was dark and close and musty, with strange smells of decay and ancient earth.

Is it essential for you to call the gods from down here?

"That's enough sarcasm from you, thank you," Mathos muttered at his internal running commentary, letting his head fall back against the numbingly cold wall. And then froze—he'd heard something.

The wooden door creaked open, and light flared in the doorway. It moved closer, throwing wavering shadows up the walls and stone arches and flickering across the stone niches and the slumbering skeletons.

Yup, he'd been right. The darkness was better than those undulating corpses. Mathos pushed himself to his feet with a pained groan and opened his good eye.

"Afternoon, Lord High Chancellor." Mathos ignored his screaming side to give a mocking bow and his best dealing-with-authority grin. "So nice of you to drop in. I would love to offer you a cup of tea. Or perhaps ale? No… you've always looked more like a glass of rancid goat milk kind of a man…."

"Shut the fuck up, Mathos."

Mathos forced himself not to laugh. It was always a win if you could get a superior officer annoyed in under two minutes. And annoying Dornar was even more fulfilling than most. He leaned back against the wall and crossed one leg over the other, as if they were standing in a nice warm barracks having a pleasant conversation.

They stared at each other in the pool of lamplight as long moments ticked past.

Eventually, Dornar propped the lamp into a stone niche and clasped his hands behind his back in a meticulous parade ground rest. "Let's get to the point. I know exactly where the Hawks are and what they're all doing, and none of them are a threat to me. I don't need any information from you—I know it all already."

Mathos shrugged. After the events of the day, none of that surprised him.

"I know, and a handful of Ballanor's courtiers know," Dornar continued, "that Alanna had no desire to be queen." He gave a slow, satisfied smile. "But it turns out that they are most appreciative of strong leadership. And promises of land. And will swear to anyone who asks that Alanna declared her intention to take control of Brythoria. Everyone else at court, including the council, is more than happy to believe that she's trying to take power. That she plans to sweep in and punish them for their treatment of her. That the murders of Geraint and Ballanor were just a warmup for the bloodbath that's coming."

Dornar smiled. "They're waiting for Lucilla to save them as we speak, and they know that I'm the only one that can bring her to them."

Mathos snorted. "Yeah... and what do you think the Nephilim will say?"

"Doesn't matter," Dornar replied confidently. "The Nephilim aren't here, they're staying safely in their temples like they always do. And even if they did decide to break with years of tradition and ride on Kaerlud, all they'll find is the queen they have chosen to support already on the throne."

Gods.

"And Lucilla? What does she believe?" Mathos couldn't help asking.

"She believes what I tell her."

Mathos almost rolled his eyes, but it hurt too much. "Which is?"

"That Alanna was planning to use her as a puppet, a nice easy means of taking control of the throne."

Bollocks. Dornar had played directly on Lucilla's worst fear.

Dornar pulled a wicked-looking dagger from its scabbard. It curved upward with a vicious serrated edge, the spines catching the light as Dornar spun it slowly in his hand.

Mathos kept quiet and tried not to watch the gleaming blade while his scales rippled in waves up his arms and neck.

"You're going to confess to Lucilla that Alanna is planning to consolidate the two kingdoms, taking the power and wealth for herself, and that she plans to make Lucilla her pawn, holding the throne in name only as she serves Verturia's bidding. She's almost convinced; she just needs a tiny nudge in the right direction."

Mathos snorted. "Let me guess: if I tell Lucilla what you want, you'll give me a nice clean death in exchange."

Dornar chuckled. "Certainly not. There's no way I'm letting you speak to the queen. You're going to die a bloody and painful death, and several witnesses are going to tell her all about your earlier, heartfelt confession."

Mathos could feel the deep rumbling of his beast thrumming through his veins. "What in the kingdom for?"

Dornar gave a mocking shrug, an exact copy of the

movement Mathos himself had used. But he didn't bother to reply.

Mathos had to give him some grudging respect for that. Ballanor would have shared his entire plan by now, and Grendel would have grown bored and gone back to the luxury of Kaerlud.

And honestly, Dornar didn't need to tell him. Mathos could imagine his plan without any help. It made perfect sense to keep him away from Lucilla. Alone, she was far more vulnerable, and if she believed that Mathos and Tor had lied about everything, she would be unsettled, unsure of herself. A corroborated confession would do just the trick. She would be very likely to turn to the closest protector. She would endorse Dornar. And let him guide her. Or at least, that was almost certainly what Dornar expected.

Thankfully, Lucilla was unlikely to follow along meekly however sweetly she smiled and nodded. But Dornar didn't know that about her.

Dornar flicked the dagger into a smooth rolling spin, until it blurred in the lamplight.

"What are you telling me this for?" Mathos asked in a rough voice. "I can't bargain for anything or change anything, so why tell me how badly I'm going to die?"

"Because," Dornar replied slowly, "I knew you'd be sitting here alone in the dark." He smiled. "And I thought you'd like to know."

"Really?" Mathos asked, surprised as much as disgusted. Dornar was many things, but he hadn't seen him as an outright sadist, not like Ballanor.

"It's a hobby of mine… taking things apart to see how they work." Dornar tapped his temple. "The mind is like a machine. Change one small connection, undo one vital link, and everything around it starts to fail. The interesting part is determining which piece to loosen."

I told you he was broken.

Mathos's beast thrashed in his belly, his scales spreading to fully battle-ready, as Dornar continued. "Let's see which of your components is the most responsive, shall we?"

The blade left Dornar's hand so fast that Mathos might not have escaped it even if he hadn't been chained to a hook. As it was, it pierced through his scales all the way into the heavy muscle along his left shoulder. Two inches to the side, and it would have hit his jugular.

He grunted at the agony of severed sinew and gored flesh, his beast frothing inside him in a frenzy of impotent rage and pain.

Dornar stepped forward, his face blank, and pulled out the blade.

Hot blood rushed down Mathos's arm, and he leaned back heavily against the wall, desperately trying to use his bound hands to staunch the flow.

Dornar took a step back and then another. "Don't worry, the artery is intact. You'll still be alive tomorrow… more or less."

"What's happening tomorrow?" Mathos ground out through his clenched teeth.

"You leave for Kaerlud. You have an appointment there with the queen. Such a pity you'll try to escape and be injured in the attempt." He clucked his tongue sadly. "I expect that you'll be very nearly dead when you get there. In fact, with the herbs you're going to consume tomorrow, I can guarantee it. I think it will work well for you to take your last few breaths at her feet, don't you?"

Mathos grunted, trying to keep his voice steady. "I won't confess to anything."

"Of course not. I thought we'd already clarified that your role will be to frighten our vulnerable young queen while providing a nice reminder to everyone else that there are consequences to interfering with my plans."

Pain radiated from his shoulder as he glared back at the man he was coming to hate more than he had ever imagined possible.

"Goodnight, Sergeant. Sleep well." Dornar laughed.

Mathos groaned as he slid slowly down the wall onto the cold earthen floor and watched Dornar walk away with the light.

At least he didn't go for the jugular. That's one good thing.

Being alive in the morning was definitely better than the alternative. But other than that, he was pretty sure Dornar had, in fact, gone for the jugular. And, for the first time in his life, he had absolutely no idea what he was going to do.

Chapter Nine

LUCILLA OPENED HER HEAVY EYES. Hair was stuck to her cheek, and her mouth was dry and sour. She slowly pushed herself up to sitting, feeling disoriented and slightly nauseous as the world spun slowly before settling.

For some reason she was fully dressed; she even had her boots on. She had gone to sleep in the middle of the afternoon, but now the room was dark and cold, and she shivered as her head started to clear.

The last time she could remember feeling so awful, she had spent the night drinking the cook's cider. And had then spent the early hours of the morning being thoroughly sick before waking up disoriented and fuzzy with a throbbing head.

She hadn't drunk that much, had she?

She scrabbled in the drawer beside her bed until she found a flint and a candle, which she managed to light after several fumbling attempts. It was a relief when the wick caught and a circle of golden light fell around her. Somehow the room felt warmer and less ominous.

The small clock on the mantelpiece read nearly seven o'clock; she'd slept deeply for several hours, but it hadn't left her refreshed. If anything, she felt significantly worse.

She forced herself to stand, still feeling as if she was wading through mud, and took several deep breaths, then she stumbled to the small table and lifted the wineglass. It was half full.

Gods. She wiped a shaky hand down her face, trying to think. She hadn't drunk enough to pass out. And although she'd been exhausted, she wouldn't have simply gone to sleep like that.

The nasty suspicion that someone had added a sleeping drug to her wine curled through her, and she shivered again.

Who would do something like that? The sergeant who had brought the tray? Why?

Presumably they didn't want to kill her, or she would be dead. Kidnap her, maybe? Someone else wanting to take her north? Were there more guards working with Alanna?

She wrapped her arms around her belly, swallowing against the acid taste in her throat. Thank the gods she'd locked her door.

She was trying to imagine who could have corrupted one of her guards when a firm tap startled her. Her heart hammered in her ears as she tried to convince herself that she was safe. That no one who meant her harm would have knocked.

There was another firm tap on the door.

She really didn't want to deal with anyone while her head was still so foggy and unsettled, but another knock on the door suggested whoever was out there wasn't going anywhere. She cleared her throat while trying to smooth some of the knots from her hair. "Who is it?"

After a long, silent pause, there was a rough sigh from

outside her door and then a low voice spoke. "It's me, Lucilla, open the door."

Oh, hell no.

She didn't bother to answer, simply folded her arms and waited for him to leave.

The knocking started again, reverberating in her head until she wanted to scream. She swallowed away the urge and muttered, "Go away."

"I can't. I have a trunk full of clothes and your things from the manor for you."

"Why do *you* have my clothes?" Lucilla asked, her voice sharp with annoyance.

"The Lord High Chancellor sent a quad to fetch whatever the housemaids thought you might need. And since you don't have a personal maid, they just packed everything."

She could feel her blood pressure rising. "Yes, I very clearly remember you suggesting that I should get rid of my maid, Cerdic, thank you."

"Don't be like that, Lucilla—"

She interrupted, growling through the door, "That's 'Your Majesty' to you, Sergeant."

"I've always called you Lucilla. Surely you don't—"

She stopped him by striding forward, slamming the bolt to the side, and ripping the door open. "Put my things in my room and leave. And don't ever speak to me again, Sergeant."

She waited impatiently as he shuffled in carrying a massive trunk and several large satchels looped over his shoulder and laid it all beside the bed. But he didn't leave. Instead, he moved to stand in front of her, his mouth turned down, eyes soft. Damn, it was his cajoling face. "You used to like it when I called you Lucilla."

In a strange, painful way, it was interesting to stand there looking at him for the first time in so long.

He was tall, well built. He had short dark hair and the dark Apollyon eyes, a strong jaw and full mouth. By far the best-looking of all the guards. The maids had flocked around him. But he had wanted *her*.

She had loved it when he paid her attention. He'd taken her riding around the estate, complimenting her on everything from her riding skills to the color of her lips. He'd brought her presents from the village. Left meadow flowers on her pillow. She remembered how he would wrap a lock of her hair around his fingers and pull her closer. How he'd slipped her dress from her shoulders. How she'd let him. How she'd wanted him to do it.

How she'd thought she'd loved him.

No, that wasn't entirely honest—in hindsight, she knew the truth. She'd thought *he* had loved her.

Damn, it had hurt to find out she was wrong. That had been the last time she'd cried. It was what had finally, after so many years alone, made her realize that crying changed nothing.

But somehow, the last few days alone in the woods had changed her. She had escaped and survived and grown. And, even in the short time she'd been alone, she had learned enough about herself to recognize that the bond between her and Cerdic had only ever been real in her imagination.

She had been the lonely, lost girl. Unwanted. Desperate for attention. And he had wanted to claim a princess.

He had wanted her enough to take everything she offered. But not enough to keep her. Not enough to stand up for her. His attention had only lasted until there was something that he wanted more. The gratitude from Prince

Ballanor when he had told them all that he had discovered her plans to run away. The promotion. The reward, paid in gold.

Of course, when he took her brother aside and told his tale, he'd entirely neglected to mention that Lucilla had thought that they would be running away together.

And yet now he was standing in front of her, all soft-eyed and tender. Apparently, now that she was the queen, he wanted her again.

She took a step back and lifted her chin. She didn't love him. She didn't even like him. And she trusted him less than she liked him. "You may call me 'Your Majesty.'"

She waved toward the door. "You can go."

He gave a sad shake of his head, his hand clasped to his heart as if her words were truly wounding him. "Your Majesty, I've been assigned as your guard by the new Lord High Chancellor."

"What?" The question exploded out, her shoulders tensing painfully.

"Lord Dornar asked Lieutenant Claudius if there was anyone who knew you well who would make a good addition to your own personal guard… and he recommended me."

He stepped forward, closing the distance she'd created. "Claudius remembered how close we've always been and thought that it would be reassuring for you to have someone you know nearby."

Lucilla narrowed her eyes. She hadn't even spoken to Cerdic for months. Not since that terrible night. No, Claudius didn't care about that. But he would have remembered that it was Cerdic who prevented her escape the first time.

"I'll speak to Dornar and get that changed immediately."

"Surely you'd rather be guarded by someone who knows you?" he asked softly. "Someone who cares about you?"

He reached out a hand as if to wrap a lock of hair around his fingers, as he'd done so many times before, and she flinched.

His jaw tightened, but he pulled his hand back. And as he did so, she noticed that his knuckles were bruised, the skin torn in places. "What did you do to your hand?"

He shifted his hands to clasp them behind his back. "My hand?"

"Yes. How did you tear your knuckles?"

He cocked his head to one side. "I, uh, banged them on the wall."

No. She knew those kinds of bruises from when the guards practiced fist fighting. It looked as if Cerdic had been punching something—or someone. Perhaps someone in armor.

She watched him skeptically. Dornar didn't seem like the kind of commander to allow brawling among the men, but there was no point in asking Cerdic; he would never give her a straight answer. And she would never trust anything he said ever again anyway.

She forced her shoulders back down and strode from the room. At least her annoyance at Cerdic had helped to clear her head.

She needed to see Dornar. She was going to find out what was going on, and she was going to get rid of Cerdic at the same time.

Lucilla found the Lord High Chancellor in the main dining hall of the tavern, speaking softly to a small group of meticulously dressed officers. They were all standing with their hands clasped behind their backs, hair trimmed, boots gleaming, watching him respectfully.

As soon as he saw her, he smiled and hurried to meet her. He stopped a few steps away and gave her a short bow before turning to scowl at Cerdic standing behind her. "Did you not give Her Majesty her things?"

Before Cerdic could reply, she answered for him. "He did, thank you."

Dornar turned to look at her curiously, his gaze flitting briefly up her body. "Was none of it suitable? I assumed that you would want to freshen up."

Lucilla looked down at herself. She was still wearing the breeches and riding jacket that she'd fled in several days before. They were creased and stained and definitely on the wrong side of well used. Embarrassment twisted in her gut. She probably should have changed before coming downstairs for dinner. Damn.

And now that it occurred to her, she wasn't at all sure how she was going to get rid of Cerdic. It wasn't as if she could tell Dornar why she didn't like the bastard.

She folded her hands in front of her and composed herself, striving for the blank serenity that had always appeased Claudius.

Dornar gave her a reassuring look that somehow made her feel even more unsettled, even more unsure of herself. As if she had done something wrong, and now he was fixing it for her.

She took a breath, determined not to lose momentum. "I was hoping to talk to you about my personal guard. I would like to choose my own men."

"Yes, of course, Your Majesty." Dornar smiled. "That's a very good idea. We can hold a tournament as part of your coronation celebrations."

"I'd like to choose them now."

Dornar frowned slightly. "In the dark?"

She felt a tendril of heat creeping up the back of her neck. "Not in the dark, obviously, but perhaps in the morning."

"If that's what you want, Your Majesty, we certainly can arrange a parade or something similar, but I'd understood that you wanted to get on the road as soon as possible and catch up to Mathos?"

Damn. "That's true," she admitted slowly.

Dornar smiled down at her, his frown gone. "Perfect; so it's agreed. We'll ride for Kaerlud first thing in the morning and we'll hold a tournament as soon as possible."

Lucilla blinked. Had she agreed to that? Or had Dornar somehow manipulated her into doing exactly what he wanted while encouraging her to think it was her idea? And she hadn't forgotten about the wine either. She'd get to that next.

She hated having Cerdic standing behind her back, a heavy presence behind her, and she stepped to the side so that she could see both men more clearly while she spoke to Dornar.

She dipped her chin, not agreeing, but not disagreeing outright either. "And then when we're in Kaerlud, I can interview Mathos?"

"Of course, Your Majesty," Dornar replied smoothly, his expression warm as he focused on her. "Since you were asleep when we were due to leave earlier, I've sent a message ahead to meet the squad guarding him on the road. I've confirmed that he should be kept safely in the Constable's Tower at the palace until you wish to see him."

His pale blue eyes watched her with perfect sincerity as

he spoke. And she would have believed him—if he hadn't been standing next to Cerdic.

The moment Dornar mentioned Mathos being ahead of her on the road, Cerdic's head tipped, ever so slightly, to the side.

Dornar and Cerdic standing side by side, both dressed in their Blues, hands behind their backs, buttons gleaming, hit her with a sudden powerful sense of déjà vu. A memory that she had tried so hard to block permanently from her mind…. The memory of standing in the front room of the manor house. The soft light of the fire and the lamps falling on Claudius and Cerdic where they stood in front of her, immaculately dressed in their Blues, the burnished copper of their buttons glowing softly in the flickering light.

Open on the floor between them were the saddlebags she'd filled with food and spare clothes, the small cache of jewels she'd planned to surprise Cerdic with still wrapped in her rags. She could still feel the horrified shock crawling up her spine as the man she had planned to escape with, who she had thought she would marry and grow old with, told the Captain of the Guards how he had caught her trying to sneak out.

His hands had been behind his back and his head cocked slightly to the side.

He'd done the exact same thing, standing in her room, when he said he'd hit his knuckles on a wall. Gods. How had she never noticed that before?

And in that moment, she began to doubt everything Dornar had said and done.

Her mind ran with a riot of questions. If Mathos wasn't on the road to Kaerlud, then where was he? And how was Cerdic involved? Could the tears on his knuckles be caused by punching someone? Maybe someone who had scales? Gods.

She let her breath out slowly, concentrating on keeping her face blank, desperately hoping that they wouldn't realize that she didn't believe them.

And there was something she still wanted to resolve. She turned to Dornar. "Thank you for the wine you sent up, Lord High Chancellor."

He raised his eyebrows curiously. "What wine?"

She kept her voice even as she replied, "The wine and berries that the sergeant brought for me."

"I never sent any." Dornar gave a small shrug. "Your Majesty, you've been overwhelmed and exhausted. It's perfectly understandable that you're confused. But I never sent anything. You went up to your room and didn't come back down. I simply assigned guards and left you to rest—as I imagined you wanted."

She shook her head vehemently. "No, I'm not confused. It's in my room right now."

Dornar's frown returned. "We have to investigate this immediately. If someone was able to reach you…." He turned and marched up the stairs with Lucilla and Cerdic following behind him, the other soldiers watching curiously from their place near the fire.

Within a minute they were back in her room. It was exactly as she'd left it—the single candle burning on the side table, curtains open to the small, dark window, her trunks and satchels lying beside the bed. But no tray. No wine. No half-empty crystal glass.

She reached out and ran her hand over the empty table. "It was right here."

"If you say so, Your Majesty." The disbelief dripped from his voice.

She firmed her spine. "It was. I know it was. Someone must have come in and taken it."

Dornar nodded slowly. "In that case, I think we had better assign more guards. From now on, you will have a quad with you at all times. Sergeant Cerdic, you may lead, but you report directly to me."

Gods. The last thing she wanted was four guards with her, watching her, at all times, especially guards led by Cerdic. She gave as gracious a smile as she could manage. "Thank you for your concern, but that won't be necessary."

"Your Majesty, I must insist. As Lord High Chancellor, I am also the Commander of the Blues, and it is my duty and my honor to deploy the guards. I simply have no alternative but to take any necessary steps to ensure your safety."

"But I don't want a quad of guards following me everywhere."

Dornar reached out to pat her shoulder. "Of course you do. How do you think your guards would feel if something happened to you because they didn't have enough men to keep you safe? How would you feel if your guards were hurt, or even killed, because they were outnumbered?"

"I… uh…."

"There, you see. This is for the best." Dornar looked down at her and smiled. His smile was warm, understanding even, and she imagined he thought it was reassuring. But it didn't reassure her at all.

Chapter Ten

MATHOS SHIVERED RELENTLESSLY in the darkness of the freezing burial mound. Even his scales couldn't keep the chill from settling deep in his bones.

The bleeding from his shoulder seemed to have slowed, but it was still oozing, and his fingers were tingling and aching as the initial agony settled into a relentless, inescapable torment.

This was what it felt like to be an insect pinned to a card. An interesting specimen to investigate and then discard.

Don't fucking think about insects.

It was too late. His skin crawled as he imagined scuttling feet and slithering bodies churning around him in the total darkness. Nasty crawling beetles with little skittering legs and eggs to lay. Spiders with clinging webs and vicious bites…. He heard a quiet scrape.

His head filled with images of ancient bones in tattered rags scratching their way free of their stony niches. Their claw-like hands reaching—

Fucking stop it!

He took a deep breath and let it out slowly. At least his beast had a grip on things.

When was the last time he'd prayed? Was it standing beside his father's grave? He remembered the blue of the sky, his mother's dress floating in the soft breeze….

Something scraped again, and he pushed himself up the wall, determined to stand.

Something rattled—the bolt that locked the crypt door perhaps—echoing in the silent tomb, and then a sudden draft of fresh air raised the hair on the back of his neck.

He was already fully battle scaled, but for some reason, his beast only flickered as a small pool of light appeared in the doorway. And then a quiet voice whispered, "Who's there?"

Mathos let out a soft breath of surprise. He couldn't be certain, but he thought he knew that voice. "Apple pip?" he asked softly, not wanting to get an innocent child in trouble if he was wrong.

There was a moment of silence, and then the young girl stepped into the crypt, bringing her candle with her.

The rush of relief and hope flooding through him nearly brought Mathos to his knees. Quickly followed by an even greater terror. This was the worst place in the kingdom for Alis to be found.

He tried to grin, hoping that his battered face wouldn't terrify her too much. "What are you doing here? It's not safe for you."

She took a few steps closer, focused on him. "I saw those men, the soldiers. They were hurting you…."

Damn, she'd seen him on the road. He had always hated Dornar, but knowing she had been watching the soldiers bully him filled him with an even deeper loathing. The Blues used to be heroes. They had protected the innocent. Not terrified small children.

Ballanor had destroyed so much. In less than a year, he'd overturned everything they had stood for. And Dornar was the same. He cared nothing for the people who were hurt in his relentless scheming.

And now he has Lucilla.

Gods.

"I'm sorry, apple pip. You shouldn't have had to see that."

She shrugged her thin shoulder. "Seen worse."

As if that didn't break his heart.

He smiled, desperately hoping she wouldn't take it into her head to start looking in the hollows filled with bones and add them to her list of worse things. "Alis, coming here was incredibly brave and kind, but you shouldn't be here. It's not safe."

She gave him a small, sweet grin. "You shouldn't be here neither."

Mathos chuckled. "Well, that depends on who you ask."

She giggled, a breathy sound of fear and relief, and he was blown away by how much courage it must have taken to walk into the dark shrine, come down the stairs, and open the door to the burial chamber.

And now it was up to him to get her out safely. "Where are the guards?" he asked gently.

"Playing cards outside. They were too scared to stay inside the shrine. They're even doing their rounds in pairs." She lifted her eyebrows in derision at the cowardice of adults.

"And you weren't? Scared, I mean."

She shook her head slightly, her fist clenched around the candle in a way that spoke to him, all the way down to his soul. She had been scared, but she wasn't going to show it. She had stood up and done what she felt needed to be done. "No one dead ever bothered me before. No one alive ever tried to help me before. Other than you."

Gods. "Where's your mam and dad?"

"Dad's dead. Mam's… busy." She shrugged again. "I look after myself."

He liked this feisty little girl. And admired her more than nearly all the adults he'd ever met. He dipped his chin toward her. "Thank you, Alis. And now we need to get out as quick as we can."

He lifted his hands so that she could see the chain and pointed up to the ring high on the wall. "Do you think you can unhook it?"

"Yup." She put the candle down on the ground and unfurled her wings before jumping up to the hoop.

She pulled and tugged, hanging heavily from the chain despite holding herself aloft with rapid beats of her wings, each jerk traveling through the chain and painfully jarring his ribs and shoulder.

The chains clanked and shifted, but she didn't seem to quite have the strength to hold herself in the air and pull the heavy chains. She tried again, with no success, before finally flying back down, wings low and dejected.

Mathos looked up, considering. There was another option, but it was going to hurt. A lot. "If you stand on my shoulders, do you think you can unhook it?"

She gave him a quick nod and stepped forward trustingly.

He bent down to let her clamber up him, balancing herself with her wings, and gritted his teeth against the howl of agony that tried to escape. His ribs, his shoulder, even his swollen eye seemed directly in the path of her small feet.

A cold sweat broke out down his back as he concentrated on breathing evenly and not flinching or groaning.

Long, excruciating moments passed as the chain clanked and she dug her feet in, wings beating slowly to help her balance. The wound in his left shoulder reopened, and blood trickled down his arm, along with hellish waves of fresh agony.

Then, with a small crow of success, she jumped backward and floated down, carrying the chain. Within a minute, she had tugged and pulled the coiled chain away from his wrists and his arms were truly free.

A slow wave of woozy lightheadedness gripped him, and he leaned against the wall for a moment, trying to get his breath, while Alis picked up the candle.

Long before he was ready, he pushed away from the cold stone and held out his good hand. She slipped her small hand into his, and they picked their way across the floor to the open door.

Maybe it was the trust she gave him. Or perhaps her bravery. Or maybe it was the loss of blood. Or the lightheaded gratitude he felt for his sudden reprieve. But, for the first time in over a decade, he felt responsible for someone else, and it didn't make him want to run. If anything, it made him want to stay and take care of her.

They tiptoed through the door and pushed it closed, sliding the bolts across to seal it. Alis blew out her candle and tucked it into her pocket, and then they stepped silently up the narrow earthen stairs into the fresh air and more gentle darkness of the shrine.

It was a circular building of rough stone and carved images, with a huge altar standing in the center, smooth and worn from hundreds of years of sacrifices and offerings.

Above it, the oculus in the domed roof let in the rain, the sunshine, and, at that moment, the fresh nighttime air.

He looked up to the circle of star-strewn sky and let out a slow breath. There was something about looking up into the sky, that wide, free space, that settled him. Even that small circle of stars above him in the shrine gave him hope.

He could hear men's voices laughing and joking just a few yards from the entrance to the shrine, but Alis tugged on his hand and they turned in the opposite direction. She led him to the back wall where a row of window-like openings in the stones would serve as ventilation and to bring in light during the day. Usually, they would be covered by thick leather hangings during the night, but they were still rolled up and tied to the side, no doubt left that way when the local priest or priestess was sent away by Dornar.

Mathos and Alis stopped against the wall, listening.

Slow minutes passed. And then the rough tread of two pairs of booted feet echoed outside.

They shrank back in the darkness and waited until the path was silent. As soon as he could hear the guards welcoming back their comrades, he squeezed Alis's hand and pointed up.

She immediately flew up and through the opening, pausing on the ledge to carefully look around before flying down and out of sight.

It was significantly more difficult for Mathos. He heaved himself up onto the ledge, jaw clamped tight against the screaming agony.

He paused for a moment to check that no one was waiting, and then turned to lower himself out the other side as far as he could. He had to let go and allow himself to fall the last two feet, but he somehow managed to do it silently enough despite the grinding pain.

He crept forward into the low scrub on the side of the burial mound and stopped next to the small blond girl who had saved him.

The relaxed voices of the guards still murmured from the other side of the shrine. And why wouldn't they game and chat and relax? Who could ever free themselves from heavy chains and open a bolted door from the wrong side? Fuck, he was lucky. And deeply grateful.

Alis guided him down the small hillock and into a copse of birch and spiny buckthorn, following a narrow trail that led to a small pond.

"Is it safe?" he asked, almost under his breath, looking longingly at the water.

"The priestess uses it," Alis replied just as quietly.

Thank the gods.

Mathos dipped his hands into the cold water and took deep, glorious gulps and then splashed his face, biting back a gasp as the icy drops ran down his neck. He was desperate to clean and bandage the wound on his shoulder and bind his ribs, but there was no time.

They walked quietly together to the edge of the stand of trees, where the village came into view, and paused. "Do you know where they're keeping her?" he asked, looking down the small path.

"In the tavern. Fixed the room special, I heard."

He nodded slowly. "I don't know how to thank you for what you did, apple pip," he admitted in a whisper. "You saved my life, and probably the queen's too."

She flashed him a cheeky grin. "Pay me back in beef. Or even better, teach me to ride that big horse." Her small face grew wistful. "I wish that I could ride away."

"I'll do my best." If he lived, he would come back. With beef and riding lessons. "If you can ever get yourself north, go to the temple of the Nephilim. Tell them that Mathos of the Hawks sent you. They'll keep you safe."

He held out his hand, and she slipped her small one into his to shake. "You need to get away home now. Don't let anyone see you."

She took a step away, her face so young and yet so tired. "No one ever does…."

"I do, apple pip," he replied quietly. "And the soldiers might too, so don't take any chances, okay?"

She rolled her eyes, but she muttered a soft "Okay." It was the best he could do. So little in exchange for the huge gift she'd given him.

She turned on to the path toward the village and started to run. Within a few seconds, she was lost in the darkness, and he whispered a final thank you into the night.

Mathos counted to three hundred, and then, when nothing else moved, he quietly took off his cotton shirt and tried to rip a strip from the bottom. It was ridiculously difficult. He glared at his hands, wishing for claws and silently nudging his beast to help.

It ignored him. Typical.

In the end, he was able to bite a hole in the cotton and then use that weakness in the fabric to tear off a long piece. He wrapped it around his shoulder and then used his teeth to help knot the ends, hoping that it would be enough to stop the bleeding. It restricted his movement as he pulled his shirt back on, and it hurt like hell, but it was the best he could do. His ribs, his eye, and the rest of his bruises would have to wait.

He followed the path toward the village, staying silent and trying to force his tired brain to come up with some kind of useful plan. The night wasn't over, and he had a princess to find. Then, all he had to do was convince her that he was on her side and she should not immediately turn him over to Dornar.

His beast groaned, but he ignored it, there was no way he could simply walk away and leave Lucilla with Dornar. He had to try to fix things.

Chapter Eleven

THE FIRELIGHT on the ceiling flickered unevenly, as if a chilly breeze was somehow still making its way into the room, and Lucilla pulled the blanket closer, wrapping it over her shoulders and holding it tight. She was freezing despite the fire burning in the grate and the heavy drapes pulled shut against the night.

She was sitting on the bed with her back to the wall, her legs pulled up, head resting on her knees, contemplating just exactly how angry she was. And, damn it all, she was cold and hungry. Yet again.

Dornar had offered to take her to dinner, but she had told him that she wasn't hungry. In reality, she couldn't bear the idea of eating or drinking anything he gave her, and she'd retired to her room instead. Accompanied by four bloody guards. Two of whom now stood outside her door while the other two rested. Damn them to the Abyss.

Now that the wine was completely out of her system, and the adrenaline and shock had worn off, she was able to think. She had gone over everything that had happened again and again in her mind. Whether he intended it or not, everything Dornar had said had merely confirmed what Mathos and Tor had said.

And they had said not to trust Dornar.

Dornar had manipulated her so skillfully, making her feel young and in need of guidance, stupid even. He made her feel bad about her clothes and question herself about the wine. Somehow, he seemed to always agree with what she wanted and then convince her to do something else entirely.

It made her think that, whatever else they may have omitted, Mathos and Tor had been right about Dornar. And, if she was being honest, the only time she'd been warm, full, and safe, had been with them.

It was a truly appalling realization, but she should never have trusted the new Lord High Chancellor.

She shifted in her bed, too filled with nervous energy to sleep. Too worried about what Dornar would do next. She had been lying there for hours, listening to the noises of people moving around downstairs and finally leaving with loud farewells and slamming doors. The tavern keeper and his family cleaning, then closing up for the night.

But she still couldn't sleep. Couldn't even close her eyes. She wasn't safe, and she had no idea what to do with the two guards standing outside her door.

She watched the firelight playing across the ceiling. What had happened to Mathos? Was he even going to Kaerlud? How badly had they hurt him? The last one was a stupid question. She knew they would have wanted to punish him. All those soldiers against one man. One man who had stayed behind for her.

She groaned and let her head fall back against the wall as her thoughts flittered in an endless, anxious loop.

She had to do something. The certainty grew bigger and bigger. She couldn't stay in that cell-like room, allowing herself to become a prisoner again—she had to know the truth. Who had lied, and who was manipulating her to make her do what they wanted?

It was her life, damn it. Her kingdom too. The one thing everyone had agreed on, and presumably the only thing she could believe, was that her kingdom was in danger of being ripped apart.

It was terrifying to think that she could be personally responsible for so many lives. But did her fear give her the right to hide in her room, ceding control to a man who had drugged her and made her feel stupid? Wasn't it worse for her kingdom to be under the control of a liar who only cared for himself than under the control of an inexperienced queen with no idea what she was doing?

She had to figure out who she could trust and start taking control back. Starting now.

She threw off the bedding and climbed out of the bed to pull on her boots as well as the jacket and the thick cloak she'd run away in. She rifled around in her satchel and found the jewels she'd hidden, tucking them into a small pocket sewn on the inside of her jacket, just in case.

Lucilla stamped over to the door—there was no point in being quiet with two guards outside—slid open the bolts, and flung it open.

She didn't know the men standing neatly at attention, and she hesitated. She opened her mouth to ask to go to the kitchen and then closed it again. She was the queen, wasn't she? That's what everyone kept telling her. So that meant she could bloody go downstairs if she chose.

She raised her chin and marched down the narrow stairs, through the dimly lit main taproom to the back of the tavern, and into the kitchen, her guards following her closely, casting concerned looks at each other that she pretended not to see.

She had no idea what she was doing, and since getting something to eat seemed like the most pressing problem, she decided to start there.

The kitchen glowed with a soft red light from the banked fire, illuminating a large wooden table and pungent rows of herbs hanging from the rafters. A narrow doorway at the back of the kitchen opened into a shadowy larder where she found a wrapped loaf of bread and a crock of butter in amongst rounds of cheese and preserves, smoked fish, and dried meats.

The two guards had a worried, whispered conversation before one of them let himself out the back door and rushed into the night, while the other trailed after her, watching suspiciously as she dropped the loaf of bread onto the table and started cutting.

She was still spooning honey-preserved berries from a heavy clay jar onto the slightly stale slice of bread when Cerdic arrived, uniform half-untucked, breathing hard, and looking as if he'd just woken up.

She raised an eyebrow at him. "I expected Dornar."

Cerdic grimaced at the other guard without replying.

Ah. They wanted to handle her without speaking to Dornar. No doubt their commander would hold them responsible if she wasn't where he expected. He'd sent her to bed, and he intended for her to stay there. Clearly, her guards thought they would be blamed along with her if Dornar didn't get what he wanted.

Lucilla took a bite and chewed slowly before swallowing deliberately and then glared at Cerdic. "Go away."

He folded his arms. "I'm in charge of your security."

Gods she was sick of this. "I'm your queen. I decide what I want, and I want you to go away."

Cerdic gave a brief wave to send the other guards back into the main taproom, waiting until the door closed behind him to take a step closer to her, and then another.

He spoke softly as he closed the distance between them. "Lucilla, please, stop with all this. I know we disagreed, but I was only trying to protect you. All I ever wanted was to keep you safe. You must know that I love you."

She was so stunned by his outrageous statement that it took her a moment to realize that he had tilted his head to one side. And that he had wrapped a lock of her hair around his finger.

She slapped his hand away, the hurt and betrayal that she had carried so long morphing into a white-hot rage. "Get your hands off me!"

"But Lucilla—" His next words were lost in the loud squeak of the back door as it opened, and they both spun.

Lucilla's brain couldn't quite encompass what she was seeing, and she stood frozen trying to understand. Mathos's face was chalky beneath his rough beard. One of his eyes was swollen shut, he had dark bruises over his cheek, his lip was split, and his shirt was torn and covered in blood, with tattered strips wrapped around his shoulder. But he acted as if everything was completely normal as he dipped his chin toward her. "Hello, Princess."

Cerdic went rigid, and then he drew his sword. Slowly and deliberately. The heavy steel rasping viciously over the scabbard.

Mathos didn't flinch. He simply lifted his dagger toward Cerdic and widened his stance, his lips twisting up in a mocking grin.

Gods. Mathos had been beaten to within an inch of his

existence, and yet he'd come back. She had heard him saying that he would stay with her, whatever happened. And here he was.

And he was about to die.

Cerdic would kill Mathos. Or, at the very least, hurt him even more than he already had. And by the look on the sergeant's face, he would relish doing it.

In the frozen second, as no one moved, it occurred to her that it was the only reason that Cerdic hadn't called for the rest of his team; he thought killing Mathos would be easy. He wanted to do it himself and take all the credit. Just as he'd done when he betrayed her.

She looked between the two men—one whom she had thought she'd spend her life with, the other whom she'd done nothing but argue with, whose beast had terrified her —and realized that it was an easy choice.

Mathos had promised not to leave her, and despite whatever brutality had been done to him, here he was. And she wasn't about to let Cerdic hurt him.

Without even thinking about what she was doing, she hoisted the heavy jar off the table, as high as she could, and then smashed it directly onto the back of Cerdic's head.

Cerdic collapsed forward in a crumpled heap and lay still. Leaving her still holding the miraculously intact clay jar.

She took a deep breath and then another, looking down at Cerdic unconscious on the floor. She let out a slightly hysterical giggle and then had the horrible idea that she might have killed him. Her giggles choked in her throat on a rush of bile.

Slowly and carefully, she placed the jar back onto the table, her hands shaking so badly that it rattled.

She looked up at Mathos, still brandishing his dagger.

His eyes were wide, but his lips quirked up at the sides as if he was trying not to laugh. Was he laughing at her? She wiped her shaking hand over her eyes, reminding herself that she did not cry.

He lowered the knife and whispered, "Remind me not to piss you off."

Ha. She straightened her shoulders and glared. How dare he laugh at her? And then make sarcastic comments when he'd been pissing her off since the moment she met him. She lifted her chin so that she could look down her nose at him. "Too bloody late."

He gave her a quick nod, and she almost imagined it was one of respect, as he replied, "There she is."

"Who is?" she demanded, still glaring.

"The woman with the backbone."

Oh. Damn. It was the nicest thing anyone had ever said to her.

"Do you want to go?" he asked quietly.

She almost took a step forward, but she stopped herself. "Why should I trust you?"

He looked up toward the ceiling for a few seconds, then met her eyes. "I'm sorry that I didn't tell you everything, but I promise that everything I did say was true. Dornar made everything sound a lot worse than it was. I really am trying to do the best thing for the kingdom… but, in the end, it's your choice."

He lowered his dagger and watched her. Wary, but without judgment.

She stared at him, realizing that he genuinely would walk away if that was what she decided. And that made her trust him more than anything else he could have said.

"Yes, I want to go." She looked down at Cerdic, still lying inert on the floor. "Is he going to be okay?"

Mathos glanced down, his face unreadable. "Your boyfriend is breathing."

She gave him a withering look. "Cerdic is not *my* anything."

"Whatever you say, Princess. But we have to get out of here. We can hang around to see if he's going to wake up, or we can take this chance."

Mathos stepped over Cerdic and into the larder as he spoke. She heard him scratching through the contents until he reappeared a minute later carrying a large ham and a full waterskin.

He passed her the waterskin and motioned her forward, but she hesitated. "What will Dornar do to him?"

Mathos glanced over his shoulder as he quietly opened the back door. "Hard to say. Dornar does whatever will give him the most power. He will certainly punish him for letting you escape, but I reckon how bad it will be depends on whether he still has a use for the man." He stopped in the doorway and gave her a slow look. "If you love him, you should stay. Otherwise, I can break his neck now, and you won't have to worry about it."

He was joking. At least, she hoped he was joking.

She didn't love Cerdic. She didn't even like him. If he had dropped off the edge of the world and she had never had to see him again, she would have been more than happy. But she didn't want him hurt because of her either. It was a horrible feeling—to have such power over someone. To know that they could be hurt because of her. Hurt like Mathos had been.

She closed her eyes and tried to think. Should she try to save the man who had betrayed her? Or should she save herself? Would Mathos be able to get away more easily if she wasn't with him? Did that change anything?

She stood, frozen. "I don't know what to do. I don't love him, but I don't want him hurt because of me. I don't know if you'd be better off going without me."

Mathos gave her a steady look, only the burgundy scales flickering up his arms and neck and onto his face betraying how on edge he was. "If you stay here with Dornar, he'll be ruling the kingdom within the month. There are many thousands of people who could suffer with him as their king. I believe you'll do far more good if you walk out of the door with me now. But you have to accept that Cerdic could suffer."

She closed her eyes, taking a long, slow breath. This was exactly the kind of responsibility she hadn't wanted. Hadn't been prepared for in any way. And damn it all, now she was realizing that walking away from the throne was the same kind of decision. Because of the accident of her birth, people would live or die based on the decisions she made. What the hell was she supposed to do?

"Princess, the man I killed outside—the one whose knife this is—isn't going to be responding when the guards call their checks. Someone is going to notice, or a patrol will see his body, most likely very soon. Our options are for you to go back inside and me to leave, or for us to leave together right now. You need to make a decision and make it fast."

She opened her eyes and looked at him. "What would you do?"

"Not my decision. You'll only hate me later when you start to second-guess it. You have to choose."

Gods.

Mathos stood watching her, not prompting or demanding, simply ceding the decision to her and waiting. His face was badly swollen, the bruises stark in the candlelight, and he was holding his left arm awkwardly.

That was what decided her—she had to get him away before they were discovered. If he was recaptured, Dornar would never let him live.

"Let's go. We can get Penelope and—"

"No."

Damn it all. Just when she was starting to like the ass. "What do you mean, 'no'?" she hissed.

He didn't budge. "The stables will be heavily guarded. Trying to get in there is a death wish. We leave right now, as we are, or we don't go."

Leave Penelope? She didn't want to even imagine leaving her best friend behind. Of all the awful things that had happened to her that day, this was the most painful. What would happen to Penelope without her? How would she know that she was okay?

Mathos's eyes flickered over her face, his expression softening. "I am sorry. If it helps, the last thing I want to do is leave Heracles. But we can't help them if we're dead."

She rubbed her hands down her arms, wishing that he wasn't right. That there was something, anything, that they could do to bring Penelope with them. And Heracles.

"This is our only chance," Mathos said in a low voice, "but if you'd rather stay here with your… Cerdic and Penelope, tell me now."

No. She'd already decided to go. She didn't bother to answer, she simply stepped over her former lover's prone body and toward the door.

Mathos slipped through it ahead of her with a grim look as he whispered, "Don't look right."

Of course she immediately looked right and instantly regretted it when she saw a gloomy shape pulled into the bushes, only slightly illuminated by the glow from the window, his head bent at a horrible, unnatural angle. She realized it must be the guard who had been stationed at the door, and immediately looked away, swallowing hard.

Ahead of her, Mathos sighed, but he didn't say anything other than, "Stay close."

She huddled up to his back, glad to have his big body in front of hers as they crept down a small path through the kitchen garden. Within seconds they had reached a low stone wall with an open wooden gate, and Mathos paused, listening.

He must have been reassured by whatever her heard, because he quickly sliced a few large pieces off the ham he'd stolen and then sprinkled them around all over the path and the base of the gate. Noticing her raised eyebrows, he whispered, "Hopefully it'll confuse the dogs."

He sliced more pieces off the ham and then threw them, increasing the distance each time, onto the path outside the gate, leading away from the tavern. Finally, he took the ham itself and threw it as far as he could in the same direction.

Once the decoy was done, Mathos clambered up onto the wall with a muttered curse and a groan she was sure she wasn't supposed to hear. He put out his hand, and she grasped it to be pulled up onto the wall.

He took a few careful steps, testing the stones for stability, and then pointed to a large oak with branches spreading high above the wall. "Can you climb it?" he murmured.

"Yes." She had climbed exactly three trees in her life, all of them extremely slowly and cautiously during her time in the woods, but she wasn't about to tell him that.

He gave her a doubting look. "Are you sure?"

Damn, whatever had happened to him hadn't cured him of his ability to make her want to punch him in the face. She narrowed her eyes. "I will climb it."

"Good." Without another word, he leaped up, catching the branch with a low grunt, and hauled himself into the branches.

He turned, straddled the thick branch, and then leaned down and lowered his hand to her. She reached up and took it without hesitating. "I'm going to count to three, then you jump. One, two, three——"

She jumped, and he swung her up at the same time. It was awkward and painful, her shoulder screaming at the strain, but he managed to drag her up enough that her belly lay over the branch. He immediately shifted his grip, off her hand and onto the meaty part of her upper arm where he could hold her more firmly, while she lay like an ungainly sack of grain over the branch.

She lifted her foot, scrabbling to reach the branch, breathing hard. At first, it felt as if she wouldn't make it however far she stretched, and she felt a moment of helpless panic.

But then her toe found a hold and she worked her way up until she found a branch that she could press her foot into, and, with a rough grunt, she pushed herself up, higher into the tree.

Mathos waited until she was steady, his hands ready to catch her, and then urged her on into the dark branches. They circled the trunk and then followed the next branch to an adjoining tree, leading further away from the tavern and the village, deeper into the band of trees that bordered the farmland.

Heading south, away from the bridge and the road to Mathos's friends, back in the direction they'd come from.

It was exhaustingly difficult. The branches blocked the faint starlight, and she struggled to find handholds in the darkness. Her arms and legs scraped on the rough bark of the trees, while her heart thudded in her chest at the constant fear of falling as they moved rapidly, relentlessly forward.

Mathos found them a path from tree to tree, always there to support her, hold her hand, and urge her forward, and she slowly grew in confidence. But as she settled into a rhythm, she noticed that he seemed to lose his. The panther-like grace that she associated with him seemed to be failing. He took longer and longer to choose their path, and once he almost lost his hold.

By the time the row of trees ended, she was sweating and trembling and deeply grateful that neither of them had fallen.

They reached the fields and dropped down from the final tree in silence. They stood there, panting from exertion for a few moments, Mathos a few steps ahead, his body turned toward the open fields ahead of them.

The furrowed earth flowed away in silvery starlit funnels that would have been beautiful if not for the overwhelming stench of pig manure making her eyes water.

She'd thought she'd grown used to the vague background smell in the village, but the prevailing wind had been to the south and the band of trees had blocked the worst of it. Now, back on the fields, it was strong enough to make her throat burn.

Mathos was still turned away, carefully scanning the fields. "Hopefully it'll confuse the dogs."

He stamped his boots in a particularly large wedge of disgustingly moist manure and gestured for her to do the same. Then with their boots well drenched, he waved for her to follow him and started to jog down the narrow path through the fields.

They ran in silence, watching the path carefully to avoid

turning an ankle on the uneven ground. Occasionally a nightjar called, its whistling and churring loud in the quiet of very late night. Or perhaps it was very early morning?

She could happily spend all day on horseback, but running was a new kind of torture. Her muscles quivered and ached, and her side burned, but she sure as hell wasn't going to complain.

Instead, she counted in time with her steps. Counting to three breathing in, to four breathing out. Daydreaming that if she could just count to three one more time, they would stop. And then counting to three again. And again.

It felt like forever before they reached the edge of the fields and the beginning of the woods. Finally, they slipped between the looming trees, following a narrow dirt path that she could barely see. Mathos seemed to have much better night vision than her, but even he had to slow to a walk on the rutted path.

Finally, she could catch her breath. She pressed her fist into her side as she dragged in ragged lungfuls of rank, manure-laden air.

"Where are we going?" she asked the dark shape of his back when she could speak again.

"We're looking for somewhere to hide."

"But we're going south?" she prompted as they walked.

Mathos grunted. "Dornar will look north first. Maybe. Didn't have any other option though; we couldn't risk going through the village. If we can avoid the Blues long enough, we'll turn west. We're going to try and make it to the nearest port."

He walked quietly for a moment before continuing. "If we get split up, for any reason, try and get to Darant. Tor and the others will look for you there."

He fell silent again, and she didn't press him. She didn't

want to imagine the situation where the man who had come back for her, looking beaten to the Abyss and back, couldn't be with her.

They walked on as the sky lightened. She kept listening for dogs or horns but heard neither. Surely Dornar would have already discovered that she was missing?

"Why aren't they chasing us?" she asked quietly.

Mathos picked his footing carefully down the twisted, rutted path. "I guess that it took a while for Cerdic to confess. He would have tried to find you himself first. Quietly. No dogs, minimum number of men. He'll hope to get you back before anyone notices. When that fails, then he'll go to Dornar. That's when they'll find I'm gone. And that's when all hell will start raining down around us."

All hell. Damn. That would be bad. But she was too tired to think about it. All her remaining energy was focused on putting one foot in front of the other and following where Mathos led.

The air around them began to soften into a misty silver, and slowly the trees emerged from the darkness. Thank the gods, she could actually see where she was stepping. She let out a small groan of relief.

Mathos turned to face her, giving her a quick appraising look. "You okay, Princess?"

The words caught in her throat. She wanted to say that she was sore and tired and thirsty. That she'd had no sleep and that everything about the last day had been hideous. And could he please stop calling her princess.

But he looked so dreadful that she couldn't bring herself to do it. He had been pale before; now he looked gray, lines of pain and exhaustion forming harsh grooves down his face, visible between the mottled bruises even with his three-day beard and the dim light. The cotton of his tattered shirt was stained deep red all down the front of his left shoulder and she wondered if he had been bleeding the entire time.

"Gods, Mathos." She reached out a hand, not sure what to do to help.

His lip quirked. "Just a scratch. Ignore it."

"I can't. I—"

"Shush," he whispered roughly, cutting her off. His eyes darting back to the path that they had just traveled.

She would have argued, but she heard it too. Horns, in the distance. Gods, they would find them, and what would they do to them? It would be bad, whatever it was. Claudius had beaten her hands until they bled. What would Dornar do? Would he really hurt her, the queen?

No, the real danger was to Mathos. They would kill him. Painfully.

She took a step away, looking back the way they'd come. Maybe it would be better if she gave herself up and let Mathos go. She could—

"Stop it." Mathos's rough voice interrupted her thoughts at the same time as he reached forward, grabbed her hand, and started pulling her off the path and into the deep part of the woods.

She gasped. And then scowled, but before she could come up with a suitably acerbic reply, he was whispering forcefully, "I'm not leaving you. So, whatever that thought was, you can forget it."

Her jaw dropped open, and she immediately shut it again. He'd done it again. Somehow managed to annoy the living shit out of her, and then, almost in the same breath, say the nicest thing she could imagine.

Never in her life before had anyone promised to stay with her and meant it. And she didn't know how to respond.

They jogged as quickly as they could through the thick

undergrowth, taking care not to disturb the dense layer of leaves that spread out over the forest floor.

The horns sounded again. Closer.

"Here." Mathos pulled her toward a huge fallen tree trunk. It looked like it had lain for years, gradually decaying, slowly developing a thick covering of moss and leaves, even a cluster of flat, cream-colored mushrooms.

Mathos gave it a good kick, and then another, working his way down its length, watching it carefully. He gave her a lopsided smile. "Just checking for anything that bites."

Damn. She quickly moved forward and helped. Something small landed in the leaves and scurried away, probably a mouse, but other than that, just a few woodlice and one big daddy longlegs spider fleeing on wobbly legs. She found a big leaf and scooped it up to deposit far away.

Mathos grinned at her spider rescue and then turned his attention to the earth running along the side of the trunk furthest away from the direction of the path, digging into the soft, muddy ground with his hands.

She knelt beside him, helping to form a hollow down the side of the trunk and partially under it. Her hands were completely caked in mud by the time they'd finished, and she wiped them as best she could on her cloak.

The mud was icy, and the hollow they'd made looked horribly like a shallow grave. She tried very hard to keep her voice steady as she whispered, "I don't want to go in there."

Mathos looked down at her, his expression exhausted and grim, but kind. The swelling around his bad eye meant that it was only slightly open, but he was still looking directly at her. She had never noticed his eyes before. A deep green-brown hazel flecked with gold. The same gold as the rims around his scales. She could so easily lose herself in that reassuring warmth.

He lifted his hand and cupped her cheek. "I know, Princess, and I'm sorry. But it's the best I can do."

Without thinking, she leaned into his hand as he continued. "I need you to promise me something."

"What?"

"If they find us, you must tell them that I kidnapped you. That I brought you here against your will."

Chapter Twelve

SHE BIT HER LIP, looking up at him, her soft cheek still pressed into his hand, and he could see that she wanted to refuse.

"It's the only way," Mathos explained. "I'll take the blame for this, and you'll be safe. And free. You can choose what you want to do with that freedom." He chuckled dryly. "Maybe even meet up with Alanna. But you have to get through this first. I need you to promise."

She blinked, slowly, considering. And then finally gave a tiny nod of agreement. Thank the gods.

Everything in him had focused on the need to know that she would be safe. When he'd looked through the window and seen that guard wrap her hair around his finger, he'd been filled with an unreasoning, inexplicable, tidal wave of jealousy.

And then—when he'd heard her voice, so outraged and yet sounding so hurt, so betrayed, telling Cerdic to get his hands off her—it had turned to a fierce need to protect her.

He would have gladly ripped Cerdic's hands completely

off his body. Honestly, he'd only been half joking; he would have happily broken the man's neck.

But then Lucilla had chosen to go with him. Had chosen *him*.

She had followed him out that door and trusted him to lead her. She had put her hands in his and climbed those trees. Never complaining, never protesting or grumbling. With every step they took, his respect for her grew. And some other feeling, something complicated and primal and protective, grew alongside it. Something that terrified him.

He wanted to lean forward and rest his forehead on hers. He wanted to suck that plump, rosy lip into his mouth and kiss away that look of loss and fear. But he knew better.

Sure you do. You "know" it would be better not to slide your fingers into her hair and tilt her head just enough that—

He ignored the beast, dropped his hand, and stepped back. It cost him, but he did it. Because he did know better.

He'd always known she was beautiful, but it had taken time for him to see past his blinkers, to appreciate how brave and clever she was. How kind. She would be a magnificent queen.

And he was a Tarasque mercenary with almost certainly a very short future; who had lost the only home he'd ever had through his own incompetence. There was nothing he could offer her. And he wouldn't know how to offer it, even if he had anything. She needed someone who would be with her forever, and that was never going to be him.

He pulled her cloak together and closed the buttons under her chin while she watched him with big eyes, then he gestured for her to lie down along the side and slightly underneath of the fallen log.

He didn't have a coat, but he could feel his scales forming a thick armor to keep him warm, and he glanced down at Lucilla as she burrowed into the hole they'd made, worried that she would be nervous about the beast.

She lay still, watching him with dark eyes, but she didn't seem bothered. His beast turned over with a strangely relieved grunt.

"Can I join you, Princess?"

She rolled her eyes in response, and he sat down beside her, used the pile of leaves and dirt they'd created to spread a covering over both of their legs and torsos, and then lay down, pulling the last few handfuls of leaves with him.

If they were lucky, the Blues would keep to the paths, and anyone who wandered off at exactly the right place would see nothing more than a fallen log.

If they were really lucky, the dogs would have lost their scent, or never had it in the first place, or be completely confused by the stink of pig manure all around.

The soldiers would be coming through the fields covered in it too, hopefully their tracks would blend together… except where he and Lucilla had turned off the path. That was their weak spot. Gods.

He twisted his face until he could see a small patch of sky through the dense branches above them. It was gray with clouds, but it was still the sky. It was enough to allow him to take a long, slow breath and force his body to relax. There was nothing they could do now except wait.

He hurt more than he could remember ever hurting before. Now that they weren't moving, simply lying on the cold, wet ground, he could feel every one of his injuries, and the aftereffects of so many hours without sleep.

He had always healed quickly—all Tarasque did—and the swelling was already starting to go down around his eye. His ribs still ached, but perhaps a few hours of forced rest would help. But his shoulder was a concern. The whole area felt hot. The rough bandage he'd made from his shirt felt as if it was cutting into the wound, and it was a struggle to use his hand effectively. He'd almost fallen from the trees when he'd tried to put his weight on it.

If he was able to get it clean and properly bandaged and then sleep for the day, it would be fine. But none of that was going to happen. His priority was the queen.

The horns blew across the field, and now they could hear the hooves thundering in the distance. Commands were called, and a whistle blew.

Dornar would want them to search in a grid, calling out as they cleared each area. The Lord High Chancellor knew that they were on foot and injured; he would aim to get ahead of them and then form a net to drag them back in.

Mathos glanced sideways at Lucilla and found her watching him with those big, dark eyes. He had tried to avoid crowding against her, but now he could see that she was shivering, her body trembling as she pressed her lips together in silence.

"What is it?" he asked in a low whisper. "What do you need?"

"I'm afraid."

He stared at her for a moment. He hadn't expected her to admit it, to be so open with him, and he hated that she was afraid. "You're going to be okay. Whatever happens, the Hawks will find you."

She didn't answer for a long moment. "Will you hold me?" she asked eventually, so quietly that he almost missed it.

He shuffled closer, thankful he'd positioned them with his good arm against her, and wiggled his hand through the tight space under her shoulder. She rolled slightly and settled her head onto his chest, letting him hold her against him, and breathed out a long, slow sigh.

Hooves thundered closer. The guards were in the woods, storming down the paths that he and Lucilla had been on just a short while before. They would overshoot and then work their way back. That's what he would do, anyway.

Lucilla tensed, and then slowly softened as the minutes passed. They could hear the men calling out their search patterns several miles past where they were hidden. Dogs bayed from the direction of the fields.

They were in the eye of the storm now. Couldn't go forward, couldn't go back.

Lucilla pushed herself even closer to him, clinging to his side, and he couldn't help himself; he pressed a soft kiss to the top of her head.

A minute passed, and he thought he'd gotten away with it. Until she raised her eyes to his.

"Mathos?" she murmured.

"Yes, Princess?"

"I'm really sorry that I was so rude to you the first time we met. I didn't understand...."

Gods. She was killing him.

He squeezed her side and tried not to think about how softly curved she was under that thick cloak. "And I'm sorry that I was such a grumpy ass who left out a pile of information you needed to know. But let's wait until we're out of here to talk about all of this, yes?"

"I just wanted...." She let her whisper fade away. But he knew. She was terrified that they would be caught, and she wanted to make things right.

He tightened his grip around her waist and forced himself to grin. "We're not quite ready for deathbed apologies yet. We have to be quiet now, but you can use this time wisely. Compose something truly heart-wrenching for later, okay?"

She snorted against his chest but relaxed slightly.

Inside him, his beast huffed and settled in his belly. The beast only wanted one thing—Lucilla safe. No, if he was honest, there was a second thing—her in his arms. But he wasn't going to think about that.

The minutes passed slowly. The clouds grew heavy and low, and then a steady rain started to fall.

It tapped a rhythm on the bare trees above them and the thick carpet of leaves around them. Lucilla was mostly covered by the tree trunk and his body, but Mathos could feel the cold drops sliding down his exposed arm and quietly soaking his dirty breeches and tattered shirt.

It was as uncomfortable as hell, but it was a godsend. He would gladly stay cold and wet while the rain washed away their trail.

Eventually, the rain stopped, but the clouds stayed dark and ominous. A deep chill penetrated his bones as the hours crept past.

All through the day, they heard soldiers. Sometimes on horseback, sometimes on foot. Twice, soldiers went off the path, beating the bushes and calling for the queen. One even came within a few feet of their tree trunk. But thankfully, after a long, terrifying pause, he walked away, calling out to his squad.

Lucilla fell asleep soon after that, the intense fear and exhaustion suddenly too much for her. He held her as she snored gently, her chest rising and falling against him, as he kept watch.

By the time the sun began to set, Mathos was freezing everywhere except in his shoulder, which felt like it was on fire. His whole body had stiffened during the long day of holding himself still, but they had to get moving.

He gave her a small shake and murmured, "Wake up, Princess."

She half-opened her eyes and turned her face to look blearily up at him.

"You've had enough beauty sleep. The soldiers are gone for now, and it's time to go."

She blinked a few times and then looked him up and down before replying in a rough voice, "And you look like you haven't had any at all."

Mathos's chuckle turned into a groan as he rolled out of their small hollow. His shoulder throbbed, but there was nothing he could do about it other than press on.

He forced himself onto his feet and gave the gloomy woods around them a long, slow sweep.

Walking as quietly as they could, they went back through the trees to the path, now a muddy, churned-up mess, but instead of following it, he cut across the forest, traveling as near to due west as he could guess in the dark.

It was hard going. Slogging through the heavy carpet of leaves and mud from the earlier rain, constantly having to avoid fallen branches that were almost impossible to see in the increasing darkness—even with his beast's help—while brambles snagged their clothes and scratched their skin.

It was a relief to reach the road, even though it was by far the most dangerous part of their journey. They paused under the trees, and Mathos strained to listen to every noise, every crackle of leaves, every beat of wings as owls and bats hunted and night birds called.

He didn't hear or see anything out of place, but then he hadn't realized that Dornar had blocked every road north before, either.

Eventually, he decided they should risk moving, and he led Lucilla along the edge of the forest, staying deep in the shadows until he found a shallow dip in the road. The kind of dip that would be very difficult to see from a distance, particularly in the dark, but one that gave them some slight hope of not having their silhouettes stand out against the sky like two huge arrows directing Dornar straight to them.

He tilted his head toward the dip. "We have to crawl. I suggest lying down on your belly, as flat as you can, and using your toes and elbows to help you wriggle across."

She looked at him and then back at the road, her shoulders hunched and her hands gripped tightly at her waist. "It's time to cross?" she asked uncertainly.

He knew her now. This was not a woman behaving like a spoiled princess or refusing to crawl—she had saved a spider and then spent the day lying in the mud without complaining—but it was dangerous standing around on the road, and he wanted to get across. He raised a questioning eyebrow. "Is there a problem?"

Lucilla took a slow breath and then turned to face him properly as she murmured, "I'm sorry, I know we have to leave Penelope and Heracles, but this is the first time it's felt real. She's the only friend I've had, and this is the moment that I truly leave her behind." She gave him a small half-smile. "I'm ready now."

Gods. He really had been an ass. So much of what she did was driven by her lifetime of loneliness, and yet she was still brave and loyal. She was amazing.

Exactly what I've been saying all along.

He took her small hand in his. "I'm sorry, Lucilla. I know you love your horse." There didn't seem to be anything else he could say.

She nodded slowly. "So, I'm Lucilla now?"

His lip quirked as he fought a smile. "Unless you prefer Claudia?"

"Gods, no."

"Your Majesty?"

She gave a mocking shudder. "Definitely not."

"Then Lucilla it is."

She gave him a slightly wider smile, and he couldn't help but smile back.

She gave the road a skeptical look and then faced him again. "We go across on our bellies?"

Mathos nodded.

Her smile grew. "Wanna race?"

Gods. He almost did, just to keep that happy look on her face. But making her smile wasn't his job, no matter how much he might wish otherwise. His job was keeping her safe and getting her to the Hawks.

"Next time. This time, I'll go first. If anything happens to me, go back the way we came and hand yourself in. Remember, I kidnapped you—"

"Yes, yes." She gave a mocking sigh, and he couldn't help his quiet bark of laughter before they turned to the road and grew serious once more.

Chapter Thirteen

LUCILLA STAYED IN THE SHADOWS, watching Mathos crawl across the road and then disappear into the trees on the other side. She knew he wouldn't leave her—she had no doubts about that at all—but it was still difficult to stand there, completely alone, in the darkness.

She wondered what he was thinking as he scoured the trees and paths on the other side. No backup, no squad, just Mathos, by himself, already hurt, hunting for danger.

He wanted her to blame everything on him, and she had agreed to it, thinking that unless she was the queen, she had no way to save him. But standing there, surrounded by the night noises of the forest as he went alone to check for soldiers, she knew that he didn't expect to survive being recaptured.

Seeing him reappear among the trees and gesture for her to join him made her want to run across the road and fling herself at him; to reassure herself that he was truly safe. But she didn't, she lowered herself to her belly and squirmed across like an extremely inelegant worm.

Her thoughts of how graceless she might look were quickly overwhelmed by the thought that if anyone saw her, everything would be over. Or, worse, if anyone rode down that narrow track, they would plow straight into her. Gods. The last thing she wanted was to find herself under galloping hooves.

She lowered her head and crawled faster, desperate to reach the safety of the other side.

She reached the trees and pushed herself up to her knees under their cover, breathing hard with relief and exertion. Before she could even think, Mathos hauled her to her feet and wrapped his big arms around her as he pulled her against his chest. She wound her arms around his body, feeling the hard muscles shifting beneath her cheek.

"Fuck. I didn't like leaving you alone." The words were so quiet, murmured into her hair, that she wondered if he even knew that he had said them.

Had he been thinking about her as he scoured the woods? Did he know how terrified she was that he might be hurt again trying to help her?

She didn't have time to reply before he was gently setting her away, not meeting her eyes as he spoke quietly. "Let's go."

Mathos picked his way along narrow animal tracks, finding them a path, and she followed, trying to step where he did, to avoid the small snapping twigs and crackling leaves that he seemed to spot so easily.

They walked in silence for at least an hour before Mathos began to talk in hushed whispers.

He told her about how he had been a soldier on the northern campaign but came back with the Hawks to take up the Blue. How glad the Hawks had been when they'd been promoted to such comfortable, prestigious positions;

Tristan leading their squad as Captain of the Blues, and Val quickly promoted to queen's guard.

She felt his grief and loss as he explained how everything had fallen apart, the horror of Ravenstone, and how they had found themselves demoted and exiled. And she couldn't help but smile as Mathos described how Tristan had fallen in love with Nim, much to his shock and the amusement of his men.

But then he started to explain about Val. And Alanna. And she wanted to vomit.

What kind of a person tortured his wife? Hung men from his walls? She had never liked Ballanor—she had feared and distrusted him—but she hadn't realized just how bad it was. How bad *he* was. And he was her brother.

Mathos stopped on the path ahead of her, a shadowy shape in the darkness.

"I'm sorry, Lucilla, but there's something else I have to tell you." His voice was deep and quiet. Somber even. Gods. She wiped her suddenly damp palms down her legs, trying to read his face in the low light and failing.

"We think that Ballanor was responsible for the massacre at Ravenstone."

"You think… what?" Her voice came out as a rough whisper.

"Ballanor. He was responsible for Ravenstone. He…." Mathos's voice faded away, but she already knew.

"He killed my father?" She phrased it as a question, but it wasn't. Not really. She had been afraid that Ballanor would see her as a threat and get rid of her. Something deep inside her had known that he had it in him. But somehow, it had never occurred to her that Ballanor would kill their father, the man who had given him life.

Mathos nodded, the movement only just visible.

Gods. She didn't know how she felt. She'd hardly known Geraint, but he had still been her father.

He had spent her whole life ignoring her, hiding her away, criticizing everything about her on those rare occasions he bothered to remember she existed, but she had understood—she was the living embodiment of everything he had lost.

She didn't like him, but she still felt the need for a father. The need that all children felt, however horrendously their parents behaved. And Ballanor had killed him. It was unexpectedly painful.

"Why?" She knew the word sounded strangled, and she lifted her chin, holding her composure.

Mathos took a step closer. Close enough that she could feel the heat from his body, the concern radiating out from him.

"They hated each other. Your father never trusted Ballanor, and he refused to give him any power at court. In the end, we think that Ballanor decided that if it wasn't given to him, he would simply take it. He also wanted the war in the north to continue—he believed he could win where Geraint had failed—and victory would come with power and riches far greater than your father had ever enjoyed."

She forced herself to ask the next question. "And Alanna? How did she fit in with… Ravenstone?"

"She never wanted war. All she wanted was to save her people. She stayed with Ballanor, despite everything he did to her, to uphold the treaty. In fact, she was also attacked at Ravenstone. She and Val fled the massacre, but they returned to the palace to defend their innocence. That was when they were both captured. Val confessed, under torture, to planning the massacre, but only because he thought his confession would save Alanna."

"And his relationship with her maid?"

"There never was one. They claimed to be having an affair to try and save Alanna from execution." Mathos gave her a wry look. "Actually, Keely and Tor... well, there's something between them."

Lucilla wrapped her arms around her belly, feeling a cold shiver work its way up her spine. "Did Dornar know all of this?"

"Absolutely." Mathos's reply was instant and unequivocal.

Gods. Dornar had looked her in the eye and lied to her about everything. He would have used her, manipulated her, hurt her. Just like Cerdic had. And he would have done it with a completely straight face.

What was it about her that made people treat her like this? Even her own father had hated her.

A warm hand landed on her shoulder and squeezed while his other hand cupped her cheek, his thumb under her chin, tilting her face up. "Don't do that."

She blinked. "Do what?"

"Whatever that was, that look on your face. None of this is your fault."

She opened her mouth to argue, to tell him how tired she was of being treated like dirt by people who should have loved her, to ask if he could tell her what was wrong with her that they did it to her again and again. But he shifted his fingers over her lips, and she swallowed the words.

"No, Lucilla. Those men were all assholes, and Dornar is just as bad as any of them. You can't blame yourself for the actions of people like that. If you feel responsible every time the selfish people around you do bad things, you'll go insane. You can only be responsible for your own actions, your own mistakes, not theirs."

Something about the look on his face, the way his eyes tipped down at the sides as a muscle jumped in his jaw, made her realize that this was personal to him. That he was sharing something that he normally kept hidden behind his jokes and mocking grins.

"Is that what happened to you?" she asked softly.

His fingers tightened on her face, and she heard a deep unhappy rumble that he didn't seem to notice. But then he shook his head slightly and gave her his usual lopsided smile. "Nah. Who would make me responsible for anything?"

He dropped his hands and turned to walk away, but she knew the truth. Someone had hurt him, badly. So badly that he couldn't even see that he was responsible—deeply so—to her, to the Hawks, to the people of Brythoria.

She walked quietly beside him, giving him the space that he needed.

A low sound began to grow in the distance. At first, it was a soothing whisper, just on the edge of her hearing, but as it grew louder around them, she realized that it was the rush of fast-flowing water. They were getting close to the river that Mathos had told her about that first day. Gods, that felt a long time ago.

"Are we going to cross it?" she asked.

Mathos looked back over his shoulder. "Not unless we have to. My plan is for us to follow it south. Darant, the port town I told you about, grew up around where the river meets the sea. With a bit of luck, we can find a trading ship that will take us up the western coast toward Glevum. We can buy horses and make our way to—"

He stopped midsentence, holding his hand out toward

her as if to stop her or push her back, and she froze. His Tarasque hearing was much better than hers.

They stood silently together as slow moments ticked past. But nothing happened.

Eventually, she leaned forward to murmur beside his ear, "What is it?"

He gave a slight shake of his head, his eyes slowly scanning the dark woods around them.

After another long sweep, he gestured for them to move forward once more. This time in total silence.

The muted roar of the water grew steadily, filling the air as their tiny path met a much more defined track running parallel to the river. White foam glowed as the Derrow churned against the rocks, and she could feel the cold spray on her face.

The track was wide enough that they could walk side by side, but Mathos signaled for her to stay just behind his shoulder, always in the darkest part of the path.

They moved quickly, and every drop of her concentration was focused on avoiding the rutted holes and twisted roots of trees trying to reach the water. They left the rapids behind and the roar softened to a constant murmur as the water ran fast and deep beside them.

She was looking down, and not in front of her, when Mathos suddenly stopped. She didn't have enough time to stop, would have fallen, but he reached behind his back and grabbed her, holding her safely, close to his side.

There was a thump behind her, and Mathos spun, keeping her tucked under his arm.

A Blue stood on the path behind them, busy straightening from a crouch, sword in hand. As if he had just leaped from one of the nearby trees.

There was another thump, this time from the path

ahead, and Mathos spun again. It was another Blue Guard, and he was slowly raising his crossbow. He looked young, too young to be standing there with their lives in his hands, but he held the crossbow in a firm grip as he watched them.

Mathos immediately pushed her toward the dense bush beside them. "Run. Run now."

But she couldn't do it. The only thing stopping Mathos from being shot was the risk that she would get caught in the middle. She dug her heels in, refusing to budge.

"Lucilla." His voice was a deep rumble. Almost a growl.

She ignored it and stepped in front of him, pushing her back against his chest. "If you shoot," she called loudly against the rushing burble of the river, "you'll kill us both."

The first man whistled loudly, the sound piercing behind them. A whistle answered, maybe a mile away. And then another. Gods, there were soldiers up and down the track and spread out through the forest.

She felt Mathos grow completely still behind her. They both knew that running was not an option.

He leaned down, his lips against her ear. "Can you swim?"

She dipped her head a fraction. She had learned to swim in the pond outside the manor house, but the last time she'd tried was more than a decade ago.

"Do you trust me?"

That was easier. She nodded more firmly. And immediately found herself being lifted into his arms.

He cradled her against his chest, and for the first time in her life, there in the darkness, surrounded by men with weapons, she felt protected.

Until he called out in a clear voice, "How much will you give me for her?"

She stiffened. What?

Mathos tightened his grip on her as he walked slowly toward the soldier with the crossbow. "I'm sure we can come to some arrangement. Think how much Dornar will reward you if you're the man that brings her back. Surely you don't want to share with that idiot?"

The young Blue's eyes flicked toward the guard closing in behind them as a horn blew in the distance.

"I'll give her to you, just for you, but you'll have to lose your partner."

She started to squirm, but he held her ruthlessly tight as he stepped to the side of the path.

"Shut the fuck up," the soldier behind them said loudly, but she could see the crossbow wavering, as if the guard in front of them couldn't quite decide where to point it.

Mathos looked down at her, his face serious. "Sorry, darlin'."

"Don't you dare call me——" Her words cut off into a shriek as he spun and threw her. She sailed through the air and into the river with a loud splash. The freezing water closed over the top of her head in icy darkness and her chest burned with cold and frantic panic. She kicked desperately, purely on instinct, and suddenly found herself above the water.

She heard a rough scream from the shore, but then the water filled her ears. Her heavy woolen cloak dragged her down as fast as the rushing water pulled her forward, and she fought to get it off her shoulders. Soaked, it was lethally tight, the buttons slippery and almost impossible to open.

She hung, suspended below the swirling water for a moment, working the buttons, and then, suddenly, she was free.

She kicked furiously back up until she reached the surface, gasping in huge lungfuls of precious air.

The river hauled her relentlessly forward, and it was all she could do to relax her body, to concentrate on staying afloat.

Gods. Was he already dying? Shot through by a crossbow bolt after saving her and sacrificing himself? Would the last thing he knew be the realization that she had not trusted him as she said she did?

Or, if he lived, would he take that knowledge with him as they dragged him back to Dornar?

Chapter Fourteen

MATHOS USED the momentum from throwing Lucilla to launch himself at the shocked guard and grab the crossbow, forcing it to the side.

They wrestled viciously, but Mathos had years of campaign experience that this young Blue didn't come close to. Mathos spun to face the way they'd come, jabbed a brutal elbow back into the man's face, shattering his nose, and then lifted the crossbow still gripped in the soldier's hands and pulled the trigger.

The guard with the sword fell with a gurgling scream, the bolt through his throat.

Mathos stepped away, and the young guard staggered back, whimpering, with his hands over his face.

He ignored him. The boy was no threat, and he was out of time. He threw the crossbow into the raging Derrow and then took a running leap into the water himself.

The cold punched the air out of his lungs as he kicked hard, looking for Lucilla.

Fuck. It was too dark, the river too fast, and he couldn't see her.

His beast howled in rage and horror as scales settled over his skin all the way to his eyes. His shoulder throbbed in agony, but he forced himself to pull against the water, again and again, constantly searching.

She had said she could swim. But then, she'd also said she could climb trees, which had been a stretch of the truth at best. Gods.

He found a rhythm and kicked hard, allowing the water to push him forward as he scanned for Lucilla. His scales helped him to conserve heat, but Lucilla didn't have that advantage. He had to find her. Had to get her out of there… if it wasn't already too late.

The clouds parted, and the river was suddenly drenched in pale light. But it didn't help. There were strange shapes, rocks and logs and old tree roots, everywhere.

Everything looked like a body. A log half in and half out of the water caught his attention, but it wasn't her.

Gods.

The appalling thought that he'd killed her began to build in his chest. Had he done the wrong thing? Maybe he could have protected her better on land?

Are you fucking insane? How long would they have let you live to protect her?

He didn't have an answer. All he knew was that he was getting tired. More tired than he'd ever been before. And his wounded shoulder was in agony. If he didn't find her soon, he would have to get out of the water and the leeching cold.

There!

Where? His belly rumbled with frustrated growls as he swept his eyes over the dark water once more, not seeing what the beast had sensed.

And then he saw her, a dark shadow around a pale oval. Lying back in the water, arms and legs spread so that her face was in the air, floating.

He shut down all other thoughts and focused everything on pulling through the water to reach her.

"Lucilla!"

She didn't answer. Her face so white in the moonlight, eyes closed.

But then she kicked her legs, and he could breathe again. She was alive.

He reached her, still shouting her name, and she rolled in the water, eyes wide and startled.

He grabbed her hand and towed her to the far bank as she kicked and swam beside him, trying to help as they slowly crossed the river together.

A gnarled old willow tree hung low over the water and he reached up with his spare hand to grab hold of it as the water pulled them past. The rough bark scraped his water-softened hands, and his damaged shoulder howled with the pain of keeping Lucilla held tight, but he was able to cling to it and then slowly haul them both into its shelter as she reached up and gripped the branch beside him.

The water was quieter there, smoothed by the tree and its roots, and he was able to let go of Lucilla while she clung to the slick branch. He heaved himself out of the river and onto the muddy bank, and then he turned and pulled her out of the water. She was shivering in teeth-chattering waves as he forced himself to his feet, dragging her up with him.

He found a dead branch and swept it over the muddy bank, doing his best to disguise the marks from their bodies. Lucilla quickly understood and swept up armfuls of leaves from beneath the bushes to scatter over the bank.

When he was confident that it would take an

experienced tracker to find where they'd left the river, he tucked her under his good arm, and they stumbled into the forest, following a tiny deer track away from the water.

The brutal cold of the water and the harsh abuse of the swim seemed to have strangely helped the stab wound in his left shoulder. He rotated it gingerly as they walked, testing the limits of the pain. It throbbed in relentless tormenting waves, but it felt less swollen and much cooler, as if the rough scouring it got in the river had purged out the gathering poison.

He pushed branches out of the way, guiding Lucilla through the woods, helping her where his better night vision showed obstacles she couldn't see. The moon was high enough now that it would have been easy going on a path, but he wanted to avoid any unnecessary exposure, and the trees were dense and thick as he led them south.

Lucilla didn't complain. In fact, she didn't say anything at all.

Now that he thought about it, she hadn't said anything since he pulled her out of the river.

At first, he'd thought she was in shock from the cold, but it had gone on for too long. Had he hurt her when he threw her in the river? Was there something more seriously wrong? Did she resent him for what he'd done?

Gods, maybe she'd actually wanted to go back with the guards. He could understand that she was tired of being hungry, cold, and scared. He could completely understand wanting a warm bed and a safe place to sleep. Wasn't that what people did? They chose safety. And he hadn't been able to give that to her.

Eventually, he couldn't take it anymore. He stopped in the path, watching her until she lifted her face and met his eyes. "Did I hurt you?"

She blinked. "What?"

"I'm sorry, Lucilla, I couldn't think of anything else to do and—"

Freezing fingers settled on his lips, and he stopped speaking.

She stared up at him, her eyes wide and shocked. "I'm not hurt. I'm very grateful."

His beast flipped over with a quiet rumble. Thank the gods she wasn't hurt. But then what was going on? He had never met a woman who confused him so much.

His beast let out a mocking snort. *You've never spent this much time with a woman you didn't think of as a sister before.*

Maybe. Bloody know-it-all. But he still hated the feeling that he was missing something. "Then why are you so quiet?"

Her lips twitched. "You keep telling me to be quiet so you can listen for danger. And it seems to me that there's a lot of danger around here."

Bollocks. He had said that.

"Also," her voice was low, "I was worried you might think I didn't trust you...."

Gods. That hadn't occurred to him. Although it should have after the way she'd frozen in his arms.

"Do you trust me?" he asked, regretting the words as soon as they were out. The answer was important. Too important. He desperately wanted her to trust him. And that need unsettled him. Made him wish he'd just avoided the subject entirely. And he truly did not want to know what it would feel like if she said no. "You don't need to—"

"Yes, I trust you. Absolutely."

Gods. She never did, or said, what he expected. And this, her trust, meant so much to him. She didn't trust easily, but she had given it to him. And more than anything, he wanted to be worthy of it.

He pulled her closer to his side and started moving them forward once more, avoiding thinking about the feelings swirling through him by concentrating on finding them somewhere safe to warm up.

It took about an hour for him to find what he was looking for. A huge spreading oak tree with thick, twining roots, standing a few feet in from the tiny deer path. He quickly dug out the leaves and twigs that had fallen into the hollow formed between the roots and trunk while Lucilla helped as best she could with her shaking fingers, her body shivering and teeth chattering.

And then came the difficult part. He had to get her warm. And there was only one way to do it.

He cleared his throat. "You need to take off your clothes."

Smooth. His beast chuckled, and he wished he could take a swipe at it. He hurried to explain, "I will too… ah… we have to get you warm."

"What about you?"

"My beast, scales… ah, I'm warm enough."

"O-kay," she replied slowly.

Well. She hadn't run screaming.

"We have a couple of hours before dawn. We can rest here, try to warm you up, and then get moving again. If you stay like that, you'll get sick."

"Okay," she said again. But she didn't move.

It occurred to him that this was probably the first time she'd ever taken her clothes off in front of a man, and he wanted to kick himself for how blunt he was being. He was the charming one, damn it.

Well, partly he wanted to kick himself. Mostly, he

wanted to start taking her clothes off for her. Ever since he'd seen her floating in the water like that, he'd had a potent need to touch her. To feel his skin on hers. To know that she was alive and safe.

Oh, please. You've wanted to touch her since the moment you first saw her.

Several different ideas for touching her as he helped her to warm up immediately played through his mind, but he forced them away.

"Sorry, I'll turn around." He faced away into the dark forest and peeled off the damp, shredded, and bloody remains of what used to be a decent shirt. He laid it over a branch to dry and pulled off his boots.

Behind him, he could hear the soft rustle of clothes being stripped off and hung over the branches, and it took everything he had not to turn around and watch.

Not that he needed to. His imagination went mad supplying him with a detailed vision of exactly how those soft curves would glow in the moonlit darkness. How her hips would flare out and then taper into her narrow waist. How the bindings would fall away from her heavy breasts, nipples hard in the night air. How her pulse would speed up as he ran his hands over that silky skin.

Fuck it all. He ripped off his breeches, desperately wishing the cold would ease the massive erection he could feel growing with every passing second.

He lowered himself across the front of the hollow, facing the tree, and then looked back at her over his shoulder, keeping his eyes resolutely focused on her face.

He studiously ignored the way she wrapped her tattooed arms around herself, red-and-black ink contrasting with pale skin. Pushing her soft breasts even higher. He wouldn't look down.

Wouldn't. Look. Down.

"You want me in there with you? Between you and the tree?" she asked. It was too dark to be sure, but he thought he could see a hint of red creeping up her cheeks.

"Yes." It was all he could manage. And it was true. Sort of. He wanted her in many, many ways. But he would settle for holding her against him while she warmed up.

She let out a slow breath and then stepped over him into the hollow he'd made and curled on her side.

He wrapped his arms around her, his chest to her back, her head resting on his bicep, the oak protecting her front. The dark spikes and waves of the tattoos up her arms contrasted with her pale skin in the dim light, and he longed to run his fingers along them, tracing those harsh, vibrant patterns.

He tucked his legs into the back of hers and let his scales cover his back until he surrounded her cold body with heat. All while quietly praying that she wouldn't know enough to recognize what she was feeling pressed against her backside.

She froze.

Fuck.

"Sorry," he whispered into the back of her neck. "Ignore it, and it will go away."

She lay still for a moment and then turned her head to look at him over her shoulder, those huge, dark eyes staring into his.

She raised an eyebrow. "Really? Just like that? I would have expected it would take a bit more than that."

He couldn't help but laugh. "Why? How much do you know about men?"

He felt her whole body go stiff, and he wondered if she was about to throw off his arm. Why would she...?

Bollocks. She did know about men.... The fucking Blue.

Cerdic. Lucilla's voice tight with hurt and betrayal as she told him to get his hands off her. A powerful surge of pain spiked through his chest. He knew he should have killed the bastard when he had the chance.

His beast growled a long, low rumble, and she started to pull away.

Mathos tightened his arm. "Did he hurt you?"

She was still staring at him, her eyes deep and sad. But she shook her head. "Not like you think."

"What happened?" He had no right to ask. But he fucking needed to know.

She let out a long, slow sigh, and he wondered if she was going to answer. But then she rolled to face him more fully and started speaking softly. "I thought that he loved me. We were going to run away together, but instead, he told Claudius."

The beast was snarling now, a low rumble of unhappiness as Lucilla continued, "I was punished...." Her pause made him think the punishment had not been an easy one. "Bars were put on my windows. And he got a promotion and a reward."

Gods. No wonder she struggled with trust. Wanted to get away from everything. From all the people who had abused her all her life. Not one man, not one *person*, had ever treated her with any kind of loyalty or compassion.

Not even the man who she had loved.

No, his beast murmured, *she didn't love Cerdic. She thought that* he *loved her.*

"You didn't love him?" The words fell out before he could stop himself.

"No." She shook her head, her damp hair trailing in a black wave over his arm as she moved. "I was lonely and stupid. And I wanted someone to care, just a little."

Fuck it all.

Mathos looked down at her as he ran his fingers across her soft cheek to cradle her face. How could the asshole have betrayed her like that? How could he have made this strong, intelligent woman feel so small? To describe herself as lonely and stupid. If he had the chance that Cerdic had thrown away, he would….

No. Absolutely no way was he going to think about that.

But he could do something about this. "Lucilla, you're beautiful, brave, and smart. He was so far below you that he might as well have been in a different kingdom. You deserve so much more than him."

She rolled fully onto her back and pressed her cheek against his hand, her gaze fixed on his face despite the darkness. "What do I deserve, Mathos?" she asked, her voice so quiet that he felt the words almost as much as he heard them.

"You deserve someone who sees your true worth. A man who is strong enough in himself that he can support you when you need it and the rest of the time stand behind you and let you shine."

"Someone like you?" She asked the question with genuine curiosity. No sarcasm or coyness. Just those dark eyes watching him as if she could see all the way into his soul.

Yes!

Gods. He wanted it to be yes.

"No." He forced the word out.

His beast rumbled unhappily, but he had to tell her the truth. He couldn't live with himself if he misled her or she felt that he had lied. "Not me. I'm not built for relationships. I'll get you to Alanna, or to wherever you want to go, safely. And then I'll leave with the Hawks."

"You'll leave?"

"Yes. The Hawks won't stay at Eshcol forever, when they go, I'll be with them."

You're a fucking idiot. You're pushing her away, and now she'll go, just when you finally have her in your arms.

He ignored the beast. Pushing her away was the best thing he could do.

"Okay." She whispered the word, but he felt the warmth of her breath against his skin. He felt it through his whole body.

"Okay?" he repeated, not sure he understood.

She nodded slowly. And then she wrapped her hand around his neck, pulled him closer, and kissed him.

It surprised him so much that, at first, he didn't respond. The soft pressure of those full lips, her body nestled against his, the glide of her long hair over his arm.... It was overwhelming. Captivating. The world seemed to pause in its movement, and even the nighttime sounds of the forest fell away.

And then he kissed her back, and it all spun back up. So much sensation, so much feeling. Gods. He had never been so aware of a woman.

He licked slowly across the seam of her lips, and she opened, softening further into him. Her head relaxing back to rest on his arm.

Her mouth was hot under his, and he lost himself in the slow tangle of their tongues as they tasted each other. He gently scraped her bottom lip with his teeth, that gorgeous full lip that he had been desperate to taste for days, and felt her breath hitch as he ran his hand slowly up, over the curve of her hip, and onto her belly, letting his fingers trail slowly along the bottom of her full breasts, back and forth; still kissing her. She arched her back, lifting her breasts, and he took her offering, running his palm up over her velvety skin, his calluses catching on her taut nipple as he circled softly, again and again.

She whimpered, and he took that as his cue to pluck the tight bud between his fingers until it stood hard and puckered, and then moved his attention to the other side, as their kiss deepened.

Lucilla panted against his mouth, her hand tangling in his hair as she turned onto her side, facing him, and slid her leg over his, and then shifted closer, pressing herself against him until he could feel the entire length of her body against his.

Their kiss grew desperate, his cock aching and weeping in the heated crush against her belly.

Gods, he wanted her. In a way that would have terrified him if he'd been able to think about it. But he couldn't think of anything other than how perfect she felt.

Her leg slid further over his hip, opening her, and he throbbed with the need to haul her even closer. To pour himself into her.

He broke their kiss to lean back slightly. "Do you want this? Are you sure?"

"Yes." Her voice was as rough as his, her head thrown back against his arm, eyes closed.

It wasn't enough. He needed her to see him. To know him.

His beast was riding him hard, and he knew that scales glittered all the way to his cheekbones. They gilded his forearms, gleaming in the dim light as he ran his fingers languidly over her thigh and up the length of her body, over her shoulder, along her neck and up, to rest on her cheek once more. "Open your eyes."

She opened. Looking up at him with those big, dark eyes.

"Tell me again. Tell me you want this, with me."

Her lips were red and swollen as she smiled, her eyes clear, not even hesitating. "Don't stop."

Gods.

He ran his hand back down sliding into the tight heat between them, and paused, almost touching her, but not quite.

Her eyelids fluttered closed as she spread her leg even wider, stretching over his hips. "Gods. Mathos, I told you, don't stop."

His beast growled agreement as he slipped his fingers through her folds, dipping into her wetness and then back to her swollen clit. She was so wet that he slid easily, spreading her open. Circling that throbbing bud, and then returning to glide two fingers inside her, deeper and deeper, driven on by her husky moans and by the powerful surge of need streaming through him.

He curled his fingers inside her, pressing his thumb against her clit as she shuddered in his arms, gasping and whimpering softly. And then she pushed her hand down next to his, circled his cock with her slim fingers and gripped him hard, and he nearly lost his mind.

He rolled onto his back, bringing her with him, helping her to straddle him, and she paused for a moment, her dark hair falling damply around her shoulders as she looked down at him—glancing appreciatively at the scales covering his face—and then, still watching him, she sank down, guiding him inside her.

It was almost too much. She saw him. She saw his beast. And she still wanted him. Still chose him.

She was so tight, surrounding him, her skin like a

furnace against his as she leaned back, her legs splayed wide, and he ran his hands down her body, one to find her clit, adding pressure in tight circles, so close to where they were joined, the other to rest on her hip, supporting her.

She groaned, and her walls tightened around his cock like a searing glove as they both trembled.

Then he began to move, thrusting up as she pushed down, again and again in a frenzy of slick skin and grunted breaths as his beast began to growl relentlessly. She gave a long, shuddering moan and collapsed forward to lie her weight on top of his body, her mouth open against his throat.

The glide of flesh at the new, sharper angle, ratcheted him higher, into a feverish blur of mind-blowing pleasure and his balls drew up tight against his body as she ground down. Gods. He had never imagined something so perfect.

Mine. Ours.

He gave in and curled up, holding her tight against him and clamped his teeth down over her shoulder, just hard enough to appease the beast's need to claim her.

His beast roared triumphantly, vibrating deep inside him, deep inside her, and she flew apart. Her body clenching as she writhed and whimpered, and he lost his rhythm, pumping up into her in rough thrusts, holding until the last possible moment, and then lifting her off and rolling them to the side so that he could come all over her belly in heavy, shuddering spurts.

He pulled her into him, wrapping his arms around her, his seed slick between them, and then found her mouth to kiss her, needing to taste her as they came back down together.

He could feel his beast still rumbling in his belly, deeply satisfied, urging him to hold her for eternity.

He had never felt anything like it. Never had his beast been so close to the surface when he'd been with a woman. Never had both parts of him been so totally focused, so intent on everything about a woman. How she looked, how she felt, how she tasted. Never had he been driven to this incandescent high, completely lost in one person.

Lucilla.

Chapter Fifteen

LUCILLA LAY QUIETLY on her side, savoring the warm heaviness that filled her body. Mathos had gotten up and come back with his damp shirt to wipe her clean, and then he'd lain back down behind her, curling around her, his heavy arm draped over her waist, his hand resting over her breasts.

He was half asleep. But she knew he was still aware—birds had begun to sing in the dawn, and she felt his body twitch with their rising cacophony—and she knew, deep in her soul, that he would never fully relax while he was her guard.

She could hear a deep rumbling sound, almost a purr, behind her, and it made her smile softly to herself. He didn't seem to realize that he was doing it, but she liked it, a lot.

Gods. She'd kissed him. Kissed him and then… she could feel an unfamiliar heat rising through her body as she thought about everything that came after the kiss. She had wanted him. If want was the right word for that depth of hunger.

She'd lusted after him for days, even when she thought he was an arrogant asshole. And then he'd kept his promise not to leave. He'd fought for her, again and again. Proved himself to be honorable and good. And then he'd wrapped her in his arms, looked her in the eye, and told her that she was beautiful, brave, and smart.

If she could go back in time and hear his rumbling voice, full of sincerity, genuinely telling her that he saw her, that he admired her, she would do the exact same thing and kiss him again.

Not that it was anything like any kind of kiss she'd ever experienced before. None of what they'd done was like anything she'd experienced before. That rolling wave of ecstasy. The way she'd lost all sense of anything in the world other than him. And how he had held her so tightly, and yet so carefully, as if she was precious to him. How he was still holding her now, hours later.

Never in her life had her pleasure been of any consequence. And no one, ever, had been content to simply hold her. More than content; the rumbling purr was one of quiet pleasure.

A heavy flood of emotion rose through her, and it took everything she had to keep her body relaxed. To hold in the tears that wanted to slide down her face, despite her decision never to cry again.

If she cried, he would know. He would worry and want an explanation. And what could she say? That she had waited her whole life for someone to make her feel like he had? Someone who would look her in the eye and tell her the truth, even when things were bad. Who would expect her to make her own decisions, but would support her once she'd made them.

Someone who saw all of her—not her position, nor her

wealth, not what she could give them or how she might threaten them—her. And want her anyway. Someone brave and strong and honorable who sincerely thought that she was brave and smart too. Someone who would wrap his arms around her and make her feel alive.

It wouldn't change anything if she told him how much his words had meant to her. He would still leave, maybe even sooner. He had told her that he didn't want a relationship, and she wasn't going to chase him off by telling him how badly she wanted him to stay.

She would allow herself this time to simply be. And to memorize it all for later.

The sun rose, and Mathos stirred behind her. His voice was deep, rough almost, as he lifted himself on one elbow to look down at her. "Lucy?"

She felt her grin stretch her face as she twisted round to look up at him. "Lucy?"

He nuzzled into her neck, making her squirm. "Do you mind?"

She loved it. "Not at all, I like it… Matt."

He laughed, and she watched the burgundy scales ripple over his wrist where his hand lay on her hip. "No one's called me Matt for a long time."

She lowered her voice and copied him. "Do you mind?"

He lifted his head from the crook of her neck to look at her, his usual half grin turned into a full, relaxed smile. The swelling was almost completely gone from his eye, although there was still a pale green bruise, and she lifted her hand to run her fingers down his face, into his rough beard. A bright ring of gold sparkled around the green-brown of his irises, and she wanted to stare into them forever.

He shook his head gently against her palm. "No, I like it

too." He sat up, bringing her with him, his face growing somber. "We have to go."

She let out a slow breath, knowing he was right. As much as she would have liked to stay wrapped up in him like that forever, they had to go.

She stood up and pulled her shirt down from the branch she'd hung it on. It was cold and damp, but at least it wasn't dripping anymore.

She turned it inside out to find the seams and then picked at the join between the sleeve and the shoulder, biting at it with her teeth until she was able to rip the sleeve off and then turn her attention to the other side.

She bound her breasts, put on her now sleeveless shirt, and struggled to pull on her wet breeches and boots, trying not to shiver as the chilly fabric tugged at her skin. She finally added her damp riding jacket, its rough wool scratching her bare arms, before turning to see Matt leaning against the tree, one leg crossed over the other. Watching her with his eyebrows raised.

To cover her embarrassment—no one had ever watched her get dressed before, and certainly not with such a hot, speculative look—she held up a sleeve. "Here, let me see your shoulder."

He looked surprised, but he stepped closer and pulled off the rags that were all that was left of his shirt.

Gods. Those arms. And now she could see his chest too. In the dark, she'd been able to feel the hard muscles; now she could see his lean pecs and the ripple as his stomach flexed.

He had a dusting of dark blond chest hair that grew thicker in an enticing trail down past the waist of his leather breeches, and she licked her lips, imagining what it might be like to follow it down, not with her eyes but with her mouth.

She'd never done anything like that before. But damn, she wanted to.

Mathos cleared his throat, and she looked up, a fiery blush spreading up her neck and onto her face. By the look in his eyes, the way the gold leaked almost all the way across his irises, he knew exactly what she'd been thinking.

His voice was deep and smooth. "If you keep looking at me like that, we won't be going anywhere."

She stepped forward, almost unaware she was moving until she was right in front of him and reaching out her hand to rest it on his warm chest, running her fingers through the rough curls.

His hand came over hers, pinning it against his heart as he leaned down to speak into her ear. "Don't tempt me."

Oh, but she wanted to.

"Not now." His voice rumbled. "You're…. You make me lose myself. I can't do that here where I can't keep you safe."

Damn. How did he know exactly what to say to her to make her want to melt into him forever?

He must have sensed how unbalanced she was, because he wrapped his arms around her and held her, her cheek pressed against the steady thudding of his heart.

They stood like that for a moment as the world came back into focus.

Then she pulled away to look at the cruel wound in his shoulder. She pressed her fingers lightly into the bruised flesh; it was warm and slightly swollen, but not as bad as she'd expected.

"The swim helped clean it out." His lips twitched up. "And then you took my mind off it."

"And that helped, did it?"

"Absolutely. You're enchanting… didn't I tell you that already?"

Lucilla rolled her eyes. Clearly, this was what he'd meant when he said he was usually charming.

"Well, I don't know much about healing, other than horses, but I can bandage it for you if that'll help?"

He held out his arm in agreement. "Thank you."

"How did it happen? You never said."

"Dornar stabbed me."

Her hands faltered, the sleeve held halfway under his arm. Gods, how had she so badly misread the man? She hated that she had listened to him, eaten with him, and all the time he'd been torturing Mathos and lying to her about it. "Dornar stabbed you? Why?"

Mathos ran a knuckle down her cheek before answering quietly. "He was planning on killing me. The idea was for me to die at your feet moments after confessing Alanna's evil plans, I believe. Experimenting with blades was merely a side benefit."

Lucilla swallowed. And then swallowed again, trying to get her voice to work. "Why would he do that?"

Scales flickered up Matt's arms as he replied, his pupils rimmed with gold. "He's the coldest man I've ever met. He doesn't care about anyone or anything except himself. Never forget that he can lie with a straight face as he manipulates, cheats, and steals. Whatever happens, Lucy, you need to protect yourself from him."

Gods.

"I know I promised," she said quietly, "but I don't think I can tell him that you kidnapped me."

His huge hand stilled on her cheek. "Don't let him catch you. Run, and keep running to the nearest Nephilim Temple."

"And what will you do?"

"I'll give you time to get away."

She leaned into his hand, not replying. There was no way she would leave him like that, no matter what he said. "And if he captures us both?"

His scales flickered up his arms all the way to his neck, but his voice was calm as he replied. "There's only one option, no matter how you might feel about it. You have to scream and cry and tell them that I'm responsible for everything."

"And what would that mean for you?"

He didn't look away. "It would mean that I have fulfilled my promise. That I have lived with honor, and that the only woman that I could ever—"

He didn't finish the sentence. Instead, he let his hand drop. Then he pulled on his shirt, gestured to the path, and started walking.

She didn't ask him what he'd been going to say; she didn't need to. She knew that he cared for her. It had been right there in his face. But she also knew that he didn't want to. That he wanted his life free of complications. And damn, was she a complication.

But that didn't change the way she felt about him. And with every moment that passed, with every touch and smile, her feelings grew.

As they walked, he slowly relaxed and started showing her which berries they could eat. There were late autumn brambles still with a few blackberries, and a crab apple tree with small, round, incredibly tart fruits that made her gasp as she bit into them. He pointed out the fiery red rowan berries, and she recognized the fruit that she had been so tempted to try when she'd been on her own. Mathos snorted when she told him and assured her that she'd made a good decision; they were bitter and completely inedible unless they were cooked.

Mathos was a good teacher, and the time passed easily as he taught her woodcraft and told her stories about the Hawks. She soon felt that she would recognize them immediately from all his funny anecdotes and insightful observations. Whatever he might say, there was no doubt that they were his family.

She never heard anyone else in the woods, no sounds of dogs or horns in the distance, although Mathos never lost his vigilance, constantly checking around them and occasionally stopping to listen. He was moving more easily than he had the day before, but she could see that his shoulder still bothered him.

"How did you get away? From Dornar and the Blues?"

"Alis saw me being dragged through the village. She snuck into the shrine, through the darkness, past all the dead bodies, and let me out. She was amazing."

His face changed as he spoke of the young girl. His eyes softened as he grinned, impressed and proud, and Lucilla couldn't help smiling back. "She's special."

"Yes." He reached out his hand to help her jump over a particularly high log. "She's why I joined the army."

"You know that doesn't make any sense, right?"

He chuckled. "Not Alis personally. Girls and boys like Alis. People who should be protected. Who should be able to live their lives in safety, knowing that strong men and women are standing between them and danger."

Lucilla felt the words pierce into her heart, and she faltered, but Mathos had moved slightly ahead of her on the path and didn't see how deeply affected she was.

This was what he wanted from her. Why he had argued so hard that she should be queen. To stand up for the boys and girls like Alis, to protect them from the danger of men like Dornar, and the rampant destruction of more war.

She caught up to him, quietly letting the knowledge settle. She had never really felt much purpose in her life. Everything—all her thoughts, all her plans—had been focused on running away. Perhaps now, for the first time, there was something she should run toward.

But she still hesitated. How could she be the queen they needed? What if she agreed to take the crown but only ended up making things worse? What if her inexperience, her lack of skills, meant that she made terrible mistakes? The kinds of mistakes that resulted in people being hurt.

The thoughts and worries churned through her mind until the quiet of the walk finally eased them.

Whenever he found something edible, Mathos pointed it out, and they either stopped to eat or collected what they could. It was heavy going, following the tiny animal tracks, constantly being scratched and tugged back by brambles and bushes, occasionally leaping over small streams and having to detour around large thickets.

Gradually the day passed and the forest changed around them, the trees starting to thin and grasses growing higher, and she knew they must have covered a good distance.

The sun was low in the sky when Matt pointed out a large fallen log. He asked her to pick up the other end, and together they carried it to a gnarled and wind-swept pine where they balanced it between two low branches.

She saw immediately what he was trying to do and helped him gather armfuls of long, dry branches to prop against the frame he'd made, then together they covered the shelter with leaves and long grasses that they wove roughly together.

The sun had fallen behind the trees some time before they finished, and it was fully dark by the time they crawled inside the rough shelter.

Mathos lay down and immediately lifted his good arm for her to crawl under so that she could rest her head on his shoulder.

There was only just enough space for the two of them, pressed hard up against each other's bodies. His breathing mingled with hers, and the sound of his heart beating thudded in her ear.

He had said that he didn't have relationships... but he had also almost said something more. Something about how he felt about her. Maybe even admitting that he cared for her.

Lying there in the dark, feeling him holding her so protectively, she wanted him to care for her. Wanted him to feel as attracted to her as she was to him. To respect her as much as she was coming to respect him.

Her life stretched out ahead of her, as lonely as it had been in the past. Or maybe this was the turning point? Maybe this was where she started to take control of her life and her body.

Now she understood him so much better. She admired him. Genuinely liked him. What she felt was so much more than lust. And maybe this could be a turning point for him too?

She pushed herself up his body, feeling his rough beard tug at her hair, his hands settling loosely on her hips until she could lean her forehead against his. "Matt?"

"Mm-hmm," he rumbled.

"Will you kiss me?"

He stilled. "Is this what you want, Lucy? Knowing... what you know about me."

"Yes." It was. Did she hope that maybe he would find something in her to make him want more? Of course. But she would take his kisses in the meantime.

His hands came up to her face as he pulled her down, meeting her mouth with his.

At first, he kissed her slowly. Small sips and tastes. She ran her tongue along his lower lip, loving how he groaned in response, his hand fisting in her hair and pulling her closer.

His beast rumbled loudly, a vibrating purr that reached down to her belly and lower as she slanted her mouth and sank deeper into him.

Their kiss grew harder, moving from hot and sultry to frantic and breathless as her whole body came alive.

He pushed her shirt up and over her head, and she quickly unwound her bindings, thrilled by the way his breath caught as his hands wrapped around her ribs, his thumbs rasping over her puckered nipples.

He pulled her back down for another heated kiss, his hands scorching on her cold flesh, a deep ache growing in her core. She reached down to unbutton his breeches, squirming in the tight space until she released him and could feel his heavy length against her belly as they pushed themselves together, panting and aching and trying to get closer.

She shoved her boots off with her toes and then lifted her hips to help him pull her breeches down, and she shivered in the cool air until he ran his scorching hands back up the length of her legs.

She expected him to pull her forward, but instead he guided her to lie back onto his body facing up, her legs spread on either side of his hips, her head resting on his shoulder.

His voice was rough, and she shivered as he whispered, "I want to touch you so much... Do you know how beautiful you are? What you do to me?"

Gods. She had never imagined this position. She

sprawled, spread open above him in wanton abandonment, as his hands moved reverently over her; sweeping down her sides and over her hip bones, finding the hollows at the creases of her legs; over her belly, lingering at her naval, and onto her breasts, cradling and shaping, his thumbs rasping against her tight nipples, all while his shaft pulsed at the apex of her legs, a rigid length against her core.

One of his hands played with her nipple, pinching and tugging, and the other slid down to find her clit, teasing and rubbing with torturous precision. Dipping inside her, and then finding that swollen bud once more, as his beast rumbled continuously at her back.

"Ah, fuck, Matt!" The curse fell out of her mouth, and he groaned as his fingers worked harder, driving her mad.

She had never had so much attention paid to her body, never felt as if every nerve ending was slowly catching fire, but it wasn't enough. She wanted her mouth on his. His body inside hers.

"Matt, please. I want to see you."

"Gods, Lucy. That...." His words faded as he rolled them, guiding her onto her back and settling between her thighs while the sound of his beast's rumbling purr rose all around them.

She lifted her head and pressed her mouth to his. He slid his hands into her hair and held her, his mouth taking hers in deep sliding pulls as he poured himself into her. Then, shuddering, as if he was barely holding onto his last shred of control, he notched his heavy cock at her entrance and paused, waiting.

She wrapped her legs around him, digging her heels into his clenching buttocks, and drew him closer, sliding her hand between them to guide his cock into her, as his hard body tensed above her, and they both groaned.

He lowered his head into her neck, kissing and sucking her skin as his hips began to move. A slow, sultry grind as she melted beneath him.

She lifted her hips, meeting his as he pumped harder, and wrapped her arms around his body, using him as an anchor. Holding him deep inside her.

"Lucilla. I… fuck." His teeth scraped along the tendons of her neck and her body tightened, clamping onto his.

She clung to him as he thrust harder, surrounding her with heat and pleasure. Her body shuddered and a frantic whimper escaped. "Matt. Please. I need…." She gasped for breath, trying to find the words.

"Do it, Lucy. Come. Now." His voice was more a growl than anything human, his entire body vibrating with the rumble of his beast, and it pushed her over the edge into a powerful, rolling orgasm as blazing waves of ecstasy crashed over her.

A second later, he pulled out and then came in pulsing surges over her belly and onto her breasts, his eyes glowing gold as he looked down into hers.

He collapsed at her side and pulled her into his arms, and they lay together, skin against skin, his heartbeat thudding in her ear. Gods. She had never felt anything like what she felt with him.

Eventually, he wiped her clean as best he could in the confined darkness and helped her get into her breeches and shirt before pulling her back under his arm.

She lay against his side, her head on his good shoulder while he ran his fingers down her back in light strokes. She felt warm and safe, deliciously relaxed, and languorous in a way that she never had before.

She rolled further onto his chest, cupping her chin on her fist so that she could look at him, even if it was too dark to really see him. "I love hearing your stories about the Hawks," she told him quietly.

The bands of gold in his eyes gleamed in the darkness, and she felt his smile, even though she couldn't see it. "They're like brothers," he admitted.

"And what about your family? Dornar said that your father was a baron."

She felt him stiffen under her, and she rolled herself to lie fully on top of him, pinning him down. He could move her, of course, but she didn't think he would. She hoped he wouldn't.

"Yes, he was a baron." It was a rough admission, and she wondered how many people knew the truth.

"Doesn't that make you a baron then? Shouldn't you be at court or managing your estates?"

He let out a humorless laugh. "There are no estates. No lands. Nothing left to manage."

Something in his voice made her hesitate, but she wanted to know it all. "What happened to your lands?"

"I lost them." The words were clipped. Final. And she didn't believe them for one second.

"Lost them how?"

"I couldn't manage the estate—we lost too much money —and I had to sell them to a neighbor. I lost everything my father left me."

She could feel the tension thrumming through him, the way that his beast growled, low in his belly, and knew, without doubt, that there was more to this story. She turned it in her head, considering, thinking about everything he'd told her. About how long he'd been a soldier. And then realized the truth.

"How old were you when your father died?"

There was a long pause before he answered. "Thirteen."

"And when you sold the land?"

This pause was even longer. "Eighteen."

"Gods. You were a child." She couldn't keep the shock from her voice. "Where was your mother?"

He grunted unhappily. "She also went to the neighbor. He married her and took in my sisters a year later. His only requirement was that I leave. She chose him... and I joined the army. I've been a soldier ever since, and that is what I'll always be. I'm happier on my own."

Damn. He'd been little more than a baby. Left to take responsibility for the adults who should have been protecting him.

She wished she could meet his mother one day and tell her what she thought of her selfishness. And she wanted to tell him that she would never leave him. Would never choose status and wealth over him. Would never choose anyone else.

But she knew he didn't want to hear it. And she also knew that—while he would never intentionally lie to her again—he was lying to himself. He said that he wanted to spend his life moving. That all he wanted was to be a soldier. But the way he spoke of the Hawks and the grief in his voice when he talked about how his family had rejected him told her that it wasn't true. Deep inside him, he wanted to be loved, but having been hurt so badly, he wouldn't take the risk.

It made her want to weep for him. To tell him that she would prove herself to him so that he would know he was safe with her. But she held the words in. Instead, she tried to give a truth that he could accept. "Gods, Matt, you are so much more than you think. I wish you could see what I see. A good, capable man who takes far more than his fair share of responsibility. You didn't let your family down—they let you down."

She leaned down to press a gentle kiss to his chest and then another, letting her mouth trail down his chest and then up to his neck. He shivered, and some of the tension left him, encouraging her.

She ran her tongue along his collarbone and up his neck, then sank her teeth gently into his earlobe and tugged.

His hands clamped down on her hips as the tension surrounding him coalesced into a predatory focus on every move she made.

She shifted to look down on him in the darkness—his eyes were almost completely gold—and then he pulled her down and took her mouth once more.

Chapter Sixteen

DAYS PASSED FAR MORE PLEASANTLY than should have been possible—on the run from Dornar, no horses, no shelter, having to forage for their food—but he had Lucy's smile, and it was enough.

They woke early every morning and spent the day walking hard as the landscape changed around them from dense forest, through increasingly sparse woodland, and eventually to open heath.

She learned fast. By the second day, she was gathering far more of their food than he was and was increasingly aware of potential dangers around them.

She was bright and interesting. He loved talking to her, hearing her opinions. Or, even better, her rare, husky laugh. Her eyes would widen as she laughed, as if she was surprised by her own amusement. As if she had never laughed before.

And damn it, he wished he could make her laugh every day.

Each night they built a shelter together and then spent

the hours between sunset and sleep in each other's arms, learning each other's bodies.

It was a surreal fantasy. As if he'd found himself catapulted through the stars and onto a strange, uninhabited planet. Somewhere in the distant heavens, with no past and no future. No demands and no responsibilities. Just Matt and Lucy.

She was the only woman he had ever spent more than one night with. The only woman he'd ever told about his family. She was the only woman he'd ever deeply cared about in anything other than a brotherly way.

He'd almost told her how he felt. Fuck, that had nearly been a disaster. But, strangely, it had helped. It was a warning that he couldn't ignore. After that, he'd been far more careful with what he said.

Except at night. Alone in their tiny shelter each night, surrounded by her, by her scent, by the slow glide of her skin on his. Then, he couldn't help himself. He told her how beautiful she was, how much he admired her. How he loved the way she tasted, the feeling of her in his arms, the look on her face as she fell apart. How much he needed her.

All of it true.

But however magical it was, however enchanting the fantasy, he knew that was all it was. And that their time together would be ending soon.

The slight tang in the air, the whip of sea breeze and salt in the air told him that their journey was nearly done.

He gave another long look around, checking for danger. They were in the open, out on the grassy heath beneath a darkly clouded sky.

She walked beside him, quietly holding his hand, and he wanted to commit the picture to his mind forever. Her fine shirt was stained and torn, loosely tucked into those sinful leather breeches, her close-fitting riding jacket was ruined beyond any redemption, and her high boots were muddy and cracked. Her cloak was long gone at the bottom of the Derrow.

She had braided her heavy black hair, but tendrils flew around her face where they had slipped free. It was cold, the wind constant, and her cheeks were flushed, her nose pink and her eyes shining.

They were going to reach the sea within the hour, and she had been excited since they'd woken up. This was how she should be, free and happy. Glowing with joy.

He was going to take that from her. He was going to deliver her to a lifetime of responsibility and constraint. Rules and laws and people constantly demanding her time and attention. And however bad he felt about it, he was going to do it. Because it was the right thing to do.

Would she ever forgive him? For making love to her like she was the only woman in existence and then walking away while she faced the commitments she hadn't wanted all alone?

Don't walk away, you idiot. Stay with her.

He shook his head roughly. He could never be what she needed.

When he first met her, he'd resented the thought of having to look after someone else. Now, after these days with her, remembering his family, he saw the truth. The reality was not that he hated being expected to take care of someone else, it was that he knew he couldn't do it.

Lucy needed someone who could succeed at court, and gods knew, it wasn't him. Better to walk away early than to watch her resentment slowly build. To see the sparkle in her eyes turn to bitterness as she realized he had cost her her freedom and given her nothing in return. Until she finally lost whatever regard she'd had for him and sent him away.

"I can see it!" Her voice was bright with joy, pulling him out of his dark thoughts.

He looked where she was pointing. There was a hazy, dark gray line nestling between the curves of the distant hills, beneath the sky full of heavy clouds that had followed them all day.

She spun in a circle, dragging him with her as she laughed, and he forgot his worries, all his dire predictions, in the sparkling delight of her happiness.

She grinned. "Let's run!" And he laughed with her as she pulled him along for the last mile and then up the steep grassy slope of the massive headland.

They arrived, breathless and windswept, to stand at the top of the chalk cliffs. The moody sea filled the horizon, dark and gray. Whitecaps danced as far as the eye could see, and a lone ship tossed outside the harbor, tiny in the distance.

"It's beautiful," she murmured.

He couldn't help wrapping his arms around her and pulling her close to reply, "You're beautiful."

He kissed her, standing there on the headland as the wind pulled at them. Their clothes and hair whipped wildly in the cold gusts, but all he could feel was her warm body. Her mouth on his. Her hands in his hair. Her.

Everything. She is everything.

He didn't argue. Somehow, it was true.

She leaned against him, resting her head against his chest, her arms wrapped around his waist as they looked out.

About a half a mile to the east lay the wide, gray-brown river Derrow that they had followed faithfully for the last four days. No longer churning and frothing, here it ran deep and still through the valley the water had hollowed out on its way to the sea.

Below them, beside the huge river mouth, nestled against the rolling grass-covered hills, was the town of Darant, beyond it the tall masts of the ships at harbor in the sheltered bay.

Surely one of them could be convinced to sail west and up the coast to the town of Glevum? He would promise them payment on arriving at the Nephilim Temple. Or he could work the voyage. They'd made good time traveling south, and they couldn't wait to see if Tor had made it back to Eshcol and then all the way back down to the harbor town.

Somehow, they had avoided Dornar and his men on their flight south, but the town was sure to be crawling with his men. Why rip the woods apart looking for a needle in a haystack when he could find somewhere comfortable to sit and simply wait them out? That was Dornar's way, after all.

Lucy ran her free hand over his forehead, rubbing away the scowl lines with a smile. "What's wrong?"

Gods. She had crawled all the way into his mind. "Dornar will be down there. And somehow we have to convince a ship to sail with us."

"Oh." She grinned. "I keep forgetting…." She pulled a rag from the inside pocket of her jacket and unfolded it. "Maybe I can help. Hold out your hand."

He stepped back slightly and held his hand out, palm up as she shook the rag into it. A gold ring, heavy with emeralds, fell into his hand, along with a bright sapphire, a set of luminous pearls, and a couple of gold coins.

He stared at the small treasure blankly. "What's this?"

"That's my running-away fund." She laughed sweetly,

and he wondered how long it had taken for her to gather her stash of jewels and coins. How dangerous it had been to pilfer from Ballanor and her father. How little she'd ever truly had, that this sad handful was her entire running-away fund. Gods.

It was everything she owned, the tangible symbol of her dream. And she had given it to him.

He didn't know what to say. Having funds to purchase passage on a ship would be a huge help. But taking her treasure from her felt wrong. Especially since he had every intention of stealing her dream of freedom from her, and then leaving her to face that destiny on her own.

He lifted her hand and gently put it all back into the rag that it had come from, folding up the sides to keep it safe and curling her fingers over the top. Scowling at the reminder of just how small her treasure was.

Her face fell, and for the first time in days, he saw the vulnerability that she worked so hard to hide. She had smiled and laughed so openly with him. She had shared her fears and grief. She had trusted him enough to let him into her body. And now she was about to get that look again. The cool mask that she used to hide behind. And he couldn't bear it.

He lifted her hand and dropped a slow kiss onto her fingers. "Thank you, Lucy. This means more than I can tell you."

"Really? You don't think it's silly?" Her voice dropped to a murmur; her eyes riveted on their clasped hands. "Spoiled?"

"Gods, no. Absolutely not." Where had she even got that idea?

You know exactly where she got it. From you.

"But you didn't like it?" she asked in an even softer voice before he could follow the thought.

He kissed her again and then wrapped his hands over her closed fist, holding her safely. "I was… overwhelmed… for a moment, that's all."

She still didn't look at him. "Then why don't you want it?"

"I… want you to take care of it for us. I don't want to take away your chance of escape, especially not with Dornar and who knows how many of his men down there."

She nodded slowly, finally lifting her eyes to his. He didn't know what she was looking for, but he didn't flinch; what he'd said was true. It wasn't everything, but it was true.

"Okay." She gave a small nod and tucked it back into her jacket's inner pocket.

He'd set two fingers under her chin and tilted it up, needing those plump lips on his, when he heard the whistle.

He didn't even think, he simply reacted. He flung her to the ground and covered her with his body, surrounded by the long, damp, swaying grasses. Only once he felt her, soft and safe beneath him, did he fully register what he'd heard. Not just any whistle. The high, piercing whistle of a hunting bird.

He rolled to the side, keeping her body covered, brought his fingers to his lips, and whistled back.

He was immediately answered by a series of high blasts followed by two low. No one else knew that signal. And none of them would share the code, not even under torture. It was definitely them.

"Come on." He rolled to his feet and then put a hand down to lift her. "Help is here."

"Help?" She clasped his hand uncertainly. "What kind of help?"

"The Hawks." Gods. A huge weight lifted from his shoulders. His brothers had made it. Together they could keep Lucy safe. They would have plans and money and resources that would get them through the town and somewhere that she could regroup. He didn't have to worry that she would be captured in that trap of a town.

He grabbed her hand, grinning madly, and pulled her down the grassy slope, down toward the tree-filled gorge that led toward the town.

There they were, emerging from the shadows. Tall men on horseback; Tristan in the lead, then Tor, Jeremiel, Rafe, Jos, and Garet close behind. Everyone except Val and Reece.

Salvation.

A shaft of blinding pain struck him. They were her salvation, but they were his ruin. They were the end of his fantasy. They were there to take her away.

Tristan leaped from Altair's back and sank to one knee, his voice deep and resonant. "Your Majesty." The others followed behind him, sinking to their knees in a long row.

Beside him, he felt Lucy stiffen and then take a long, slow breath, as if she was gathering herself. Mathos turned to her and smiled. "They're my friends. You can trust them."

She let out the breath, and then stepped forward and smiled, a true smile. "It's so lovely to meet you. I've heard so much about you."

She turned to Tor. "I can't tell you how glad I am to see you safe."

Tor gave her a soft look. "My only concern was for you. Are you well? Has Mathos been looking after you?"

Lucy glanced at him out the corner of her eye, a deep

blush climbing up the back of her neck, but she didn't falter as she agreed warmly, "Yes. He saved me."

The men all turned to stare at him, and he realized that he was still holding her hand. Like lovers out for a walk.

You are lovers, you idiot.

He dropped her hand, pretending that he didn't see the flash of surprised hurt cross her face, and stepped back. He forced himself to grin at Tristan and changed the subject. "I'm hoping there's a plan, Captain?"

Tristan rose from his knees, his face grim. "The town is riddled with Blues. We need to get through it before they realize you're here and get the queen onto the *Star of the Sea*."

"The *Star of the Sea*?"

"A Nephilim warship," Tristan replied. "As soon as Tor reached us at the temple and told us what had happened, we knew it was too late for any kind of diplomatic solution. The Nephilim have supplied two regiments. One marched south to keep Dornar occupied; the other sailed here as quickly as we could."

Tristan grunted before continuing. "Tor guaranteed us that you would escape and head toward the port—and that the first place you would come is the headland, to get a look at what was happening in the town. We were planning to set up camp out here, but you beat us to it."

Mathos shuddered. He couldn't get his head around how much faith they'd had in him. Especially when he'd almost lost her to Dornar.

"We're going back to the temple, then?" he asked, his voice gruffer than he'd hoped.

Tristan looked from him to Lucy standing uncertainly beside him and back again. "Maybe. Let's get back to the ship safely and then we can talk about it."

That made sense. No point in standing around in the open. Before he could even say a word in agreement, Tristan had wrapped Lucy in a heavy black cloak from his saddlebags, offered her his hand, and boosted her up onto Jos's horse.

"Won't he need—" she started, but Jos simply chuckled and launched himself into the air.

Lucy stood up in her stirrups, watching as Jos beat his heavy wings, her face rapt, and the bastard loved it. He spun himself over in a lazy tumble and then bowed with a flourish, still a yard off the ground.

"That was beautiful!" All of Lucy's tension fell away as she laughed. That gorgeous laugh he thought of as his.

How could he have ever been so blind to her natural joy and kindness? She had genuinely never meant anything hurtful by her first response to his beast. She had been a woman alone in the dark, constrained by two big, well-armed men. She had been afraid, and he had punished her for it.

And yet she had asked for his forgiveness more than once. Had freely given him her trust. And he knew, instinctively, that she would love him if he gave her half a chance. Maybe already did.

Gods. He would never deserve her.

Jos gave another aerial tumble and then smiled and winked at her, basking in her approval. Then looked straight at Mathos with a smirk.

Fuck. Was this what Tristan and Val had felt when he had flirted with Nim and Alanna? It was a miracle they hadn't killed him.

"Can you do it again?" Lucy was still gushing. "Can you fly next to me and tell me what it feels like?"

Jos lowered himself to the ground and walked beside her

as the stallion started to move. "Of course, Your Majesty. What do you want to know?"

Garet rolled his eyes heavily as he handed over his reins to Mathos along with another heavy black cloak and launched himself into the sky. At least one of those idiots could be trusted to do his job as a lookout.

Garet's stallion skittered beneath him, and Mathos realized that his beast was grumbling loud enough to disturb the horse as he watched Jos banter with Lucy, Tor riding up to flank her on the other side.

She turned her head to look at him over her shoulder, her smile as wide and as beautiful as he'd ever seen. Lucy, looking at him like he had given her the world.

Not Lucy. Lucilla. The fucking queen.

And he wasn't giving her the world, he was taking it from her.

Chapter Seventeen

Lucilla hesitated at the entrance.

She was going in. She was. She just needed a moment.

Captain Cassiel's cabin was far smaller and darker than she would have imagined, filled with trunks and books and heavy wooden furniture.

But that wasn't what made her pause; it was the three pairs of eyes watching her so intently. The three serious faces that belonged to people she had never met before but felt as if she already knew.

Gods. Did it have to be these three people?

The ride down the chalky paths from the headland into the town had passed in a blur. The Hawks had flanked her, Mathos at her rear, two men in the skies at all times, directing their path away from danger.

Everyone was cloaked, hoods up, tense and vigilant, making her heart beat hard in her throat in a way that had nothing to do with the speed with which they were riding or the treacherous rock-strewn paths they sped down to reach the town.

They had stormed down the narrow ravine and onto cobbled roads, past rows of whitewashed cottages and beguiling market squares that she barely registered before they had passed. She kept her head down and her focus on the road ahead, even as she promised herself that one day she would come back and see them properly.

She didn't even have a chance to stop when they reached the quay and she finally, for the first time, stood beside the sea.

Within minutes, she had been bundled onto a small boat and rowed out into the harbor. The sea spray on her face was salty and cold, and she had been very glad of the thick wool of the cloak they'd given her.

The men rowed them with rapid dips and pulls to a tall-masted ship with furled sails anchored near the harbor entrance. There was no figurehead, no flags flew, and the crew wore nondescript loose brown breeches and clean white shirts, with scarves tied around their sun-browned necks.

To a distant observer the ship would be unidentifiable, but up close, Lucilla had noticed the orderly discipline of the crew and the cleanly scrubbed deck, the speedy attention to commands, and the bristling array of weapons the impeccably tidy sailors carried.

Tristan had bustled her along the deck, briefly introducing her to Captain Cassiel, and then down a short flight of wooden stairs as the ship creaked and groaned, rocking on the swells.

He had taken the heavy woolen cloak she'd borrowed and hung it on a peg and then opened the door into a world of dark wood and gleaming bronze, compasses, and huge maps secured in rolls behind the captain's desk.

What would it be like to have the freedom those maps

suggested? To plot a course by the stars as you sailed over open seas toward new lands?

Or maybe it wasn't like that at all—maybe it was weeks of being cold and lost and hungry? Certainly, that's what her adventure had been like… until Matt. He had made everything different. Better. And he had started to make her want to be the queen that he believed in. That these people expected.

She looked behind her, wanting his reassurance, his comforting presence. But she didn't see him, only Tristan, and behind him Tor, gently urging her inside.

She forced her shoulders down and lifted her chin, knowing that she couldn't hang around in the doorway ignoring the people sitting in the room ahead. She took a step forward and then another, striving for her perfect mask of serenity.

One of the women caught her eye and gave her a reassuring smile. Her loose chocolate-colored braid hung over her shoulder, and silver-gray wings lay softly at her sides. The other was tall and slim with short golden-blond hair tucked behind her ears. Beside her, his fingers laced through hers, was a dark-haired man with a heavy beard and lines down his forehead that suggested a lifetime of frowning.

Nim, Alanna, and Val.

Lanval leaned closer to Alanna, as if to protect her, and with that, her mask faltered. Damn it all. She knew them from Matt's stories. She knew all the horrendous things her brother had done to them. Knew how difficult it must be for them to see her standing there, looking just like Ballanor.

She looked behind her again, desperately wanting Matt to be there, but Tristan and Tor were blocking the door. She was alone. But she had never been a coward before, and she wasn't about to start. She took in a breath, let it out. Faced forward. And did what she had to do.

She walked across the slowly tilting floor and dropped the most perfect curtsey of her life. She knew it looked ridiculous in her stained leathers and dirty shirt, but she had to do something. "I'm so, so sorry."

Before she could even start to rise, both the women were up and moving. And by the time she was ready to meet their eyes, Nim had grabbed her hands and Alanna had wrapped an arm around her shoulders.

"Nope." Alanna grinned. "What did you say, Nim? None of that."

What? Lucilla blinked. She had no idea what was happening. She tried again. "I can't begin—"

Nim cut her off with a kind laugh. "Lanni, you forgot the rest!"

"Oh, yes," Alanna agreed with a smirk. "This is all on Grendel and that asshole I married." Then she turned, her face lit up with a magnificent smile, and looked back at the scowling man. "Not you, Val, obviously."

And then they all laughed.

Laughed.

It was almost too much. The beautiful, golden woman had cursed and then laughed, and everyone had joined her. And she was a queen. Could have been a queen.

Lucilla was totally lost. She was alone and intimidated, and she was standing next to the woman who, by rights, should have been her queen. Ballanor had stolen everything from Alanna while torturing the man she loved. And Lucilla felt responsible for the crimes her family had committed.

She felt her face fall, despite her best attempt to keep the blank look that had worked so well to keep her safe in the past.

"Oh Bard, I'm so sorry." Alanna's arm tightened around her shoulders. "Of course, he was your brother."

"No. No...." Lucilla shook her head, trying to explain. "I hardly knew him, and I was very frightened of him. I can't imagine...." She let the sentence fade away. Gods, now she was reminding the poor woman of what had happened to her.

And yet Alanna didn't flinch. Lucilla couldn't imagine this smiling, open woman ever hiding behind a blank face and demurely clasped hands. Instead, she seemed so confident, so noble. Straight-backed and elegant. She was everything Lucilla imagined a queen should be.

"Are you sure you don't want to be queen?" The words slipped out. And then she instantly regretted them. How could she ask something like that of someone who had already endured so much?

Alanna gave her a gentle look as she led her to a wooden seat next to the captain's desk. "That ship has sailed, as it were," Alanna said, throwing a massive, cheeky grin toward Val, "and I'm very glad."

"Tor mentioned that you don't want to be queen," Nim added.

Damn. Matt had said that Nim was direct, but she hadn't expected to get there quite so quickly.

She sank onto the hard chair, glancing helplessly around the room. Tristan had gone to stand beside Nim, one hand on her shoulder. Val sat next to Alanna, their hands entwined once more, and Tor had followed them in. But Matt had still not arrived. It was like being on trial with no friendly witnesses.

What could she say? That she'd been in prison her entire life, and that the idea of being queen had always felt like more of the same slow death? How could she admit that to these people, people who actually had been imprisoned?

Should she tell them that she'd spent hours every day since she'd learned the truth riddled with guilt for what her brother had done and was prepared to take on almost any burden to make it right, including the throne, if that would help?

Or should she admit that it was Dornar, who they all hated, who had convinced her that the kingdom would be torn apart unless she took the crown?

Should she tell them that she wanted Matt's respect? That he had made her see that she could genuinely make a difference, that she could help the people of her kingdom to find the peace and prosperity that they deserved.

Or more personally, that something in her would die if he called her spoiled ever again. That she wanted him to look at her and see a strong woman, loyal to her people. A woman he could love enough to stay with.

She didn't want to explain all of that, but neither did she want to lie to these people. Her family owed them too much. She personally owed them too much.

She took a deep breath and told them the truth, or a part of it anyway. "I think I've begun to understand why the kingdom needs me. And I want to do the right thing. But I'm afraid."

The room was silent for a moment, until Nim asked, "What of?"

Gods. Part of her wished she'd never opened her mouth, but she had, and she would finish. "At first, I was afraid of never living. Of having other people direct my entire life until I die. Now, I realize how much is at stake, and I want to help. But I don't want to get it all wrong. I don't want to be the"—damn, she'd nearly said spoiled; she cast around for a better word—"the naïve princess everyone takes advantage of, or who makes mistakes just because she doesn't know any better."

Too stubborn. Too argumentative. Too unladylike. Too useless. And more recently she'd been forced to add too spoiled, too naïve, too unaware. How could she ever do what they were asking for?

She sighed, and quietly admitted the fear that had dogged her ever since her escape from the tavern. "I don't know enough of this world. I've made mistakes...." Trusting Cerdic and Dornar. Not trusting Mathos. Calling him a beast. Not even knowing that her kingdom was on the brink of another war. "I'm terrified of making that kind of mistake again. Making bad choices that could get people killed."

Lucilla looked down. She could feel her heart thumping heavily against her ribs, her mouth so dry she'd struggled to get the words out. She felt completely exposed, and she didn't want to see their disapproval.

"Yeah, I get that," Nim said quietly beside her.

"Me too," Alanna agreed.

She lifted her head to stare at them. "Really?"

"Why do you sound so surprised?" Nim asked.

"Well, Tor and Matt, they said... they...." She let her sentence fade. They had made it sound like Nim and Alanna were brave and strong and perfect. So different from her. Only one person, Matt, had ever thought anything genuinely good about her, and even he had disliked her when they first met.

Tristan and Val turned their formidable scowls on Tor, who scratched his chin guiltily. But Nim rolled her eyes and laughed. "Don't listen to them. What do they know?"

"Agreed." Alanna folded her arms and scowled, her

expression a perfect mirror of Val's beside her. "They've done whatever they wanted for their whole lives. All of them have. They don't know what it is to have other people making all your decisions and taking away your choices."

Tristan merely grunted, but Val's frown deepened as he spoke. "I was in the army, sweetheart. I did exactly what I was told every day of my life."

Nim elbowed her brother in the side. "You don't get it, Val. You chose to go into the army in the first place, and you could have left if you'd really wanted. I was never given a choice. You decided to become a soldier and off you went, while I stayed home and cared for Papa. Don't you think I might have wanted to do other things with my life? You never even asked me."

She looked over toward Alanna. "How many choices was Lanni given about where she had to go and what she had to do?"

Val's look got even darker as he turned to his wife. "You don't feel that now, do you? Gods. That you don't have choices?"

Alanna kissed him gently on his cheek, running her fingers down his forehead until his face softened. "No, of course not. But that's the whole point."

Alanna faced Lucilla with a smile. "This is what I learned when I was almost the queen: make your own choices and own them. Whatever you decide, be the person who you want to be. If you decide to take the throne, then you can be the kind of queen you want to be. Or choose to walk away. But either way, don't let anyone else take that power from you."

Nim nodded slowly. "And most importantly, you don't have to do this alone. Choose the people you want around you. I understand why you're worried, especially after spending time with Dornar, but that man is truly not right. There's something broken inside him." Her face was deadly serious as she admitted, "I was terrified of Grendel, but I'm even more frightened of Dornar."

Gods. It hadn't occurred to her that Dornar was the problem, not her. Even when Mathos had told her not to take the blame for other people's actions, she still hadn't quite believed it. But now, she finally could see that he was right.

Even more stunningly, she could ask for help. She could find people who she could trust, who would genuinely, honestly support her.

Matt had promised to protect her, and he had. Tor had promised to come back with help, and he had. They had promised to let her choose whether to be queen or not, and here were Alanna and Nim, offering her that choice. For the first time, she started to see how she could realistically take the crown.

Perhaps the Hawks could stay with her and help. Give her advice. They wouldn't expect her to know everything on the first day. And then Matt could stay too. That would be enough. That would be the adventure that she always wanted. And the kingdom would avoid another war.

Nim smiled. "It'll be okay."

She let out a slightly hysterical snort as the thought settled. It would be okay. Gods. It would be okay.

She suddenly felt shaky, as if she'd run a long race and now had nothing left. Too many days with little or no food, on the run, always anxious and looking for Dornar and his men. Not enough sleep. The joy and thrill of being with Matt, now followed by the anxiety of this strange inquisition by his friends. Facing them alone and admitting her fears.

The door opened, and two tall, fiery-haired men strode

into the small cabin, both straight-backed and intimidating. Tristan stood and gestured toward them. "Your Majesty, these are Haniel and Rafael, the Nephilim Master Healer and Supreme Justice of the Truth from the Temple at Eshcol. They very kindly provided us with this ship."

She gave them her practiced smile and thanked them politely. But she wasn't concentrating on them, she was concentrating on Mathos striding in behind them, finally. Thank the gods.

Without thinking, she stood, planning to go to him. Wanting to be near him. Wanting his support and belief in her.

But she stood too quickly, just as the ship rocked beneath her, and the blood rushed from her head. Her vision went fuzzy as her palms grew damp, and she put out a hand, reaching blindly for the desk. Someone took it and helped her back into her seat, guiding her to lean forward.

"What the fuck is happening here?" Matt sounded outraged.

She held her hand over her eyes as her vision slowly cleared, utterly mortified. "Don't worry, Matt, I just felt dizzy for a moment. I think I stood up too fast."

"Not you, Lucy." There was a rumbling growl beneath his words. "I'm talking to Tristan."

Lucilla lifted her hand to see Matt fold his arms across his chest, his scales flickering belligerently as he faced his captain. "We've spent days on the run. Can't you see that she's exhausted? Why are you interrogating her before you've even given her any food? You were supposed to look after her, for fuck's sake."

Tristan rumbled next to her, and it occurred to Lucilla that she was caught between two Tarasque warriors. Both with powerful, primal beasts.

Just a few weeks before, she would have been terrified. But not anymore. Now she knew that they were strong, honorable men. That being a monster had nothing to do with having a beast. Her brother was proof of that. And she knew that Matt would never hurt her, no matter what.

"This was not an interrogation—" Tristan started.

Lucilla snorted. It had damn well felt like an interrogation. And then immediately regretted her response when Matt's glare grew even icier.

Nim stood up and put a hand on each man's shoulder, forcing them to look at her. "This is not an interrogation. Although"—she shot a conciliatory grin back at Lucilla—"it probably felt that way. I'm sorry. And I agree, the queen needs to rest. But first, we need to know which direction to sail in—east or west?"

"What do you mean?" Lucilla asked, hoping to help Nim defuse the situation.

"We need to leave as soon as the tide changes. We took all the back routes and avoided the soldiers stationed in the town, but they've seen the ship…. We've already had a boatload of Blues trying to board," Tristan answered. "Cassiel sent them away, but as soon as they report to Dornar, he'll know it's us. You need to make a decision. We can go west, follow the river up to Glevum and from there overland to the Nephilim Temple at Eshcol, where you can spend some time thinking about what you want to do—"

"Or?" She looked at Mathos, hoping for a clue, but he was watching Tristan as closely as she was.

"Or we can turn east. We can follow the coastline, pass Brichtelmas and continue around the eastern cape, then north to the Tamasa river estuary. We can be in Kaerlud by the day after tomorrow."

"Why Kaerlud?" she asked slowly, fairly sure she wasn't ready for the answer.

"Dornar is looking for you, but he's made a mistake—he's told the council that you're coming." Tristan's lip twitched. Given how stern he seemed, it was almost gleeful. "If you get there first, you can walk in and simply take the throne."

Lucilla blinked. "What do you mean?"

"Everything we've done so far has been focused on avoiding a war." He gestured toward Mathos and Tor. "We hoped to find you before anyone else could and then spirit you away to consolidate our plans. We knew that if we marched down with the might of the Nephilim Clibanarii behind us, it could force the council's hand and, in the worst case, trigger the exact kind of brutal civil war we are trying to prevent. A civil war, not just between different noble houses, but between the council, made up mostly of Apollyon, and the Nephilim—between the crown and the courts—with the rest of the kingdom caught in the middle."

He gave her a long look. "But, while we were lying low, Dornar went the other way. He assembled an army with the backing of the council, and he did it under your name."

"In my name? What does that mean?" Lucilla asked weakly.

"Garet and Jos came back from their search for you via Kaerlud," Tristan explained, "and the city is buzzing with the news that the queen will soon return. Dornar has built his credibility on the back of your legitimate claim. He has convinced the council to support him on the grounds that he is the only one that can bring back their rightful queen. And now they're all expecting you."

Mathos nodded slowly. "Yes, he admitted something like that, but where does that leave Lucilla?"

Tristan dipped his chin, his eyes crinkling at the sides with an almost smile. "That leaves her with all the power." He focused directly on her. "You have this chance to use all the groundwork Dornar's already done. You can take the initiative back and simply walk in like you own it—because you do, and everyone already knows it."

Lucilla gripped her hands in her lap to stop them shaking. Damn wasn't a strong enough word. This was definitely a "fuck" situation.

Fuck.

Everything they said made sense. If she was going to be the queen, this was her best chance. They could slip in and steal control from Dornar while he was looking the wrong way. Use the plans he'd made but do it without him. Completely avoid any head-to-head confrontation or military battle for power.

But that meant she had to choose. Right now. West up to Eshcol to regroup. Or east straight to Kaerlud. Run and hide or stand up and take the crown.

She looked up at Matt, still hovering angrily at the door. "What do you think?"

He leaned against the doorframe, one leg crossed over the other. He would have seemed relaxed if she didn't know him so well. If she couldn't see the way his shoulders were bunched with tension and his scales flickered on his jaw as he folded his arms over his chest. "I think this is your best chance to take your crown back."

She gave him a half-hearted smile. "I agree. But do you think I'm the right person to be the queen at all?"

He gave her a long look and then looked briefly up to the low ceiling, as if the answer was somehow there among the creaking wooden beams. And then he looked back, held her eyes, and nodded decisively. "Yes. I think you'll be an excellent queen. You are strong and smart and quick to learn. You have a good heart. And I think your kingdom needs you."

The kingdom needed her. And Mathos thought she could do it. He believed in her.

In a way, it was a relief. She didn't have to think about it anymore. She didn't have to worry, or wonder, or second-guess. She didn't have to run, always looking over her shoulder. Or hide, always wondering if lives were being lost because of her. She could accept the inevitable and focus on making the very best of it that she could.

She looked slowly around the room and lifted her voice. "Okay, let's go east."

Chapter Eighteen

WHY DID she have to ask what he thought?

He didn't want to be the one to tell her that she had to take on the responsibilities she'd been running from. He didn't want her to blame him for the loss of her dreams of freedom and adventure. And she would—not immediately, maybe, but eventually.

She would realize that she had lost the very things she wanted most, and that he was responsible for that loss. And he knew from bitter experience what would happen after that.

And even worse, he was asking her to do something he knew he couldn't do. He hadn't been able to manage one small barony, but he expected her to rule an entire bloody kingdom.

But he'd had to tell her the truth: she would be an excellent queen. Strong and thoughtful. Generous to her people. Quick to learn and resolute when she needed to be. And she would save the kingdom from years of war.

It was the right thing to do, even if it cost her all her dreams.

He only half heard her voice. She made her decision, and she chose to go east. To the palace that she had never seen, in the capital city that she had never visited, and which would now be her home. The place where she sacrificed her life for everybody else's. And he was responsible. If she had never met him, she would still be free.

Lucy sank back into her chair and ran her hand over her mouth, her fingers trembling against her dry lips as if she was suddenly truly appreciating what she'd just done.

All his earlier anger came back to him in a hot rush of outraged indignation. "Couldn't you idiots at least have gotten her a drink before you started badgering her?"

"I've asked the galley—" Nim started, but it was too little, too late. Lucilla was crashing, and if there was one last thing he could do for her, it was to get her somewhere she could take a moment.

"That's enough. We're done here." He found himself at her side, reaching down to help her stand, pulling her up and then dragging her through the crowd of Hawks and Nephilim and out of the cabin.

If he had stopped to think, he would have realized how possessive he looked, how protective, his scales flickering angrily. How relieved Lucy had looked when he'd arrived, and how gladly she'd put her hand in his. And how the Hawks stepped back and let him pass without comment.

But he wasn't thinking about that. He was thinking about Lucy and the choice she made. How she was still smiling at him—prepared to follow him—as if she trusted him.

Gods knew she should not. He had already failed her.

He should have been in there with her, not pulling Rafe

aside and asking him to take a look at his shoulder. He had thought it would be better to give her a little space, let her get used to the idea of being with the Hawks without him… but it was a mistake. All he'd achieved was to leave her exhausted, dehydrated, and completely overwhelmed, alone, to be grilled by half the squad.

That was done now. He couldn't change what he'd done, but he could fix this. He could make sure she was comfortable, fed, rested….

For how long exactly? Until she's in the palace, and then what? Who'll put her first once she's at the mercy of the entire kingdom?

No. Staying with her would only make things worse.

For whom?

"Matt?"

He pushed the snarling disagreement of his beast resolutely to the back of his mind. He wasn't going to think about it. Wasn't going to think about how soon their time would be over. They were going east. He had a day and a half left. Two more nights. And he was going to give her everything he could in that time.

If he'd had it in him, she would have been the woman he would have loved for the rest of his life.

Fuck. She was already the woman he would love for the rest of his life.

The realization had him gripping her hand too tight, as if he could somehow hold her close forever.

"Are you okay?"

He loosened his grip and forced a smile. They only had this time, and he was going to use it to show her how it felt to be someone's priority. To be cared for. For the rest of her life, she would know.

It should be you. You should be the one who loves her.

Gods. His whole being pulsed with the wish that he

could be that man. It took everything in him not to fall to his knees and beg her to forgive him for robbing her of her dream. To make her promise him that she would never grow to realize how much she resented him. That she would never send him away. But he knew that was impossible.

She turned her face up to look at him as he pushed open the cabin door. "Matt, you're worrying me."

How could he answer? There was no sensible reply. Instead, he wrapped his arms around her and leaned his forehead down on hers. "I'm sorry you had to face that alone."

She gave him a tired smile, rubbing her nose along his before stepping back and into the cabin. "Where did you go?"

"Rafe was checking on my shoulder." He circled it forward and back, appreciating how good it was to have the achy stiffness healed. Rafe had spent some time on his ribs too, and he felt better than he had in days.

And so much worse.

"Good." She watched him rotate his shoulder with soft eyes. "I'm glad."

He looked around the first mate's cabin, rather than at her, not wanting to face her easy forgiveness. It was tiny, cluttered with barrels and wooden chests, a small desk pushed into the corner, and imbued with a strong smell of salt and rum. A hammock was strung between two large timbers, only just clearing the crates beneath it.

She stepped over the barrels to the small porthole, her face pale, but relaxed as she looked out over the tossing waves of the harbor. "Isn't it beautiful? I imagined it as big, but I never realized quite how vast."

His heart kicked in his chest. Or maybe that was his beast turning. He didn't know anymore.

The view through the porthole was, indeed, beautiful, in a cold, dangerous way. A vast gray expanse of white-capped seas and low, ominous clouds.

He had seen storms raging over the sea as lightning forked and flashed and had sat on sandy beaches under blue skies. But none of those experiences had ever made him feel the depths of what he felt when he looked at her—the power, or the beauty, or the danger.

There was a tap at the door, and a tall sailor with deep auburn hair and dark skin let himself in to set down a waterskin and wooden cups with two plates of hard biscuits, salted meat, and pickled radishes.

Lucy thanked him, and the sailor turned to open the door just in time to let Nim in.

Mathos leaned back against the wall and scowled at her. Nim hadn't thought to offer any food or drink before, and she could fuck off now.

"Good," Nim said, "I'm glad your food arrived." She held out a bundle. "Here. We have some clean clothes for you. Keely is probably the best fit, and she was glad for you to have them."

"Keely?" Lucy asked. "Matt mentioned her, but I assumed she wasn't on board."

Nim grunted, a disturbingly Tristan-like sound. "She's been staying on the deck. Poor woman. I have never seen such bad seasickness."

Lucilla made a sympathetic noise. "And you're sure she's happy for me to have these?"

"Absolutely. And Eloa said that there is a barrel of water under her desk that you can use to wash with, although it's a bit chilly."

Lucilla looked at him with raised eyebrows, and he

answered, "She's the first mate, a Nephilim naval warrior. This is her cabin."

"Oh…."

He could see the thoughts flickering across Lucy's face. "Don't worry. I asked her if you could use it, and she said it was fine." He grinned. "Actually, she said, 'Of course the queen can use my shitty hammock. Just make sure she knows where the rum is!'"

"My kind of woman," Nim agreed, turning to go. "Let me know if you need anything else."

"Thank you, Nim, I appreciate it," Lucilla said softly before Mathos pushed the door closed and locked it. Everyone needed to go away.

"We're going to have to sit on the hammock to eat. Or the floor."

"I vote hammock," Lucy said as she picked her way across from the porthole. "I'm so tired of sitting on the ground."

She turned and plopped herself into the hammock, only to have it swing drunkenly away, and she collapsed backward with a surprised huff. "Oh, damn. So elegant."

Her eyes were shining, a hint of color returning to her cheeks, her hair escaping from her braid in wild tangles.

Gods. He could feel his heart thudding, as if it was starting to tear all the way out of his chest.

"I don't know much about elegance" he admitted quietly, "but I do know that you're the most captivating woman I've ever seen."

Her face was completely serious as she replied, "And you're the most captivating man."

He had no idea how to answer her. Instead, he gestured toward the food. "Are you hungry?"

"I'm not hungry yet; too much has happened. Thirsty, maybe."

He passed her a cup of water, and then took it from her when she'd finished drinking, before leaning over to tuck those curling black tendrils behind her ear.

She tilted her head, closing her eyes as he dragged his rough fingers over the creamy softness of her cheek and down her neck to the sharp ridges of her clavicle, and then, so slowly that he could feel the heat of her breath, he slanted his head and melded his mouth over hers.

He felt her soft sigh echo through him as her mouth opened and she met his kiss. Slow and soft and warm. Their tongues barely touching as they breathed each other in.

And then, in a long, sensuous slide, she pushed forward and deepened the kiss, their mouths moving against each other in a rhythmic dance of wet heat and yearning as he stood over her.

The ship tossed on the waves, creaking and groaning, alive beneath them as he lost himself in everything about her. Their kiss growing hotter and faster as they sipped and nipped at each other.

The ship gave a lurch, and he pulled back, breathing hard as his whole body thrummed with the pressure of his aching cock against his breeches.

She followed him up, sitting with her feet splayed on the wooden deck as the hammock swayed. Her dark eyes met his, and then, very slowly, she unbuttoned her ruined riding jacket. She shrugged her way out of it and then began to unbutton the frayed and dirty shirt she'd worn for so many days.

He watched, transfixed, as she pushed it off her shoulders—revealing her pale arms with their sinuously spiked red-and-black tattoos—and slowly unbound her breasts.

Gods. It was the first time he'd seen her properly. The cabin was small, cluttered, and dimly lit. But compared to a shelter made of branches huddled up against a tree, it was incredibly luxurious.

And the most precious part was her.

Dimly, at the back of his mind, he thought he should stop this. It was too much. Too intense. For both of them. His entire being was completely overwhelmed with a depth and array of feelings unlike anything he'd allowed himself to experience for years, and he couldn't cope with any of it. He had spent his entire life making jokes to avoid dealing with emotion, and now he was like a man who couldn't swim, suddenly thrown into the deep ocean.

And then she pulled off her boots and wiggled out of her breeches, leaning back in the hammock, completely naked, her nipples pebbling in the cold air. He was drowning, and it was all he'd ever wanted.

"Kiss me again, Matt."

Gods. He was going to kiss her. Everywhere. "Spread your legs."

She whimpered, a hot flush burning up her throat. But she opened her legs as the ship tossed beneath them and the hammock swayed.

She was magnificent. Hard muscles under soft curves. Her heavy breasts tipped by darkly budded nipples. He dropped to his knees between her spread legs, like a man falling at the altar of a goddess, lifted her breasts in his hands and took one pebbled bud in his mouth, running his tongue in circles and then biting gently. She gasped with pleasure as he trailed his tongue down the valley between her breasts, over her belly, all the way down. She was perfect. Pink and plump, with dark curls. A feast.

He dragged his hands down her body to her inner thighs and groin, using his thumbs to hold her open as he ran his nose through her slick folds and inhaled her, loving how her hands trembled as they came to rest on his head.

"Matt?" Her voice shook, and he pressed a soft kiss directly on her clit. She arched back, pushing the hammock into a slow rock, and he grinned against her soft skin.

He ran his tongue, hot and slow, down her outer folds, tasting and spreading, and then in toward her hot core, rewarding her with each rock of the hammock by spearing his tongue inside her and then back up to circle her clit as she gasped breathlessly.

"Matt, I…."

He growled, letting the beast have control in a wave of possessive want. Gods, how much he wanted it. "Shh. I love this. I love how you taste." He looked up over her body and met her dark eyes. "I love how you feel. Swollen and hot and needy. Do you need me, Lucy? Tell me."

She let her head drop back, her eyes fluttering closed. "Yes. Gods. You already know…."

He circled her clit once more with his finger before dipping it inside her, searching, curling, until he found the place that made her shudder, and then he lowered his tongue, flat onto her clit, feeling it swell as she groaned and twisted beneath him.

Then he started to move. Small flicks and twists of his tongue, a second finger, curling and rubbing against her rough inner wall. Breathing in the heavy, musky sweetness of her arousal as her hands crept onto her breasts and she whimpered, arching closer.

He lifted his head for a moment, letting his breath flow

over her hot flesh. "Pinch your nipples. Pull them. I want to see."

Her fingers closed, tugging, and he timed his fingers with hers, plunging inside her as he lowered his face and sucked her clit between his lips, enveloping that swollen pearl, thrusting harder with his fingers as the hammock rocked her against his mouth.

"Gods… Matt…."

He growled, letting the beast rumble through him, and she exploded in a rush of moisture, a hot flush spreading over her chest as she moaned, pushing herself down against his mouth, shuddering, her inner walls clamping down on his fingers as he milked out every last flutter. Every last shaky whimper.

He slipped from her body and licked his fingers clean before quickly stripping away his clothes, never taking his eyes off her. She lay, spread out and soft, breasts still heaving as he stepped between her legs.

He took his cock in one hand, wrapped the other under her buttock to pull her closer, and paused, waiting for her.

She opened her eyes a fraction and looked at him from under heavy lids. Smiled. "Yes, Matt. Please." And then she added, "Matt, I want you to know, I lo—"

He didn't let her finish. He slid inside her in a powerful thrust, and she gasped, her hands reaching back to grasp the top edge of the hammock and hold on. The position pushed her breasts up toward him, and she licked her lips, looking like the fulfillment of every dream he'd ever had.

The *Star of the Sea* rolled, and the hammock swung, pushing them together, adding to the surging motion of his thrusts. He kept them shallow, building her up once more as he glided his free hand down her body and then back up to massage her perfect breasts and pluck softly at her peaked nipples.

Her breathing picked up, and her eyes closed once more as she moaned, arching into him.

He skimmed his fingers down her soft skin, mapping it, tracing it. She surrounded him, hot and wet and tight. And he fitted. Gods. How he fitted.

He thrust harder, sweat trickling down his back, but he held on, kept his eyes open. He wanted to remember. Remember her head thrown back, mouth slightly open. Her hands clutching the hammock. Her soft skin glowing in the dim light as her body gripped him, holding him inside her.

The ship pitched and swayed, and she undulated closer and deeper, then farther away, and then back again. She moaned again.

"Do you want more, Lucy? Tell me."

"Yes, more. Gods," she whispered as she pulled her legs up, opening herself even further, trusting him to support her.

It was too much. The beast took over, and he plunged into her, plundering her. He settled his thumb over her clit and rubbed in tight circles as he pumped his hips. Everything was her. And then she came, her whole body quivering as she gasped out his name again and again.

He kept thrusting, kept his rhythm, right until the end, and then he pulled out, against every instinct in his body.

He was desperate to pour himself into her. Desperate to stay inside her. But he pulled out and clenched his fist around his cock while his body shuddered, and he sprayed his hot seed all over her belly.

He caught his breath, head bowed, as he fought for some kind of stability. He ran his hands over her hips, up her arms, petting her, soothing her and himself. Grounding them both.

And then he stepped away.

He found his shirt and dipped it in the barrel, trying to warm the cool fabric with his hands, and then gently bathed her body.

She seemed dazed as he pulled her to sitting and helped her into the clean shirt that Nim had brought, but she smiled tiredly. He handed her one of the plates of food and she ate quietly while he pulled on his breeches and then sat beside her with his meal.

He had never felt closer to a woman, or more overwhelmed. Somewhere along their journey, he had realized how very far above him she was. And would always be. How extraordinarily lucky he was to have had this time with her.

He felt her soft body leaning heavily against his, and he wanted to tell her what he felt. How incredible he thought she was. Wanted to find the words to thank her for the precious gift that she had given him.

And, as much as it hurt him, would hurt them both, he had to remind her that they only had until they reached Kaerlud. That when they reached the city, she would go to her new life as the queen. And he would go back to his old life as a mercenary with the Hawks.

The future stretched out, gray and lonely ahead of him. He had no idea where Tristan would take them next. Perhaps they would offer their services to the Nephilim. Or become true mercenaries and work for pay.

Actually, I think the Hawks will stay with—

He forced the beast back down. Either way, it would be far away. And that would be for the best.

He couldn't be near her and not touch her. It would

destroy him to watch her from a distance. And it would destroy them both when she realized that he had stolen her dreams and she sent him away.

When his mother had sent him away, it had hurt his soul. When Lucy sent him away, it would obliterate him.

It was better to take these last hours as the gift that they were. To relish every one of these last moments. And then to make a clean break. Before they got closer. Before she made the mistake of saying the words that had almost pierced his heart.

He turned to look at her so he could see her face while he explained. But she was asleep.

Her head rested on his arm, her plate still on her lap. She twitched against his side, and her plate started to slide. He caught it with one hand and stood to put it safely on the deck.

Gods. He hadn't imagined she would go to sleep. But he couldn't bring himself to wake her.

He gently lifted her legs so that she was lying fully in the hammock and pulled a thick blanket off a nearby peg to lay over her.

She sighed and stretched a leg to the side, settling into a deeper slumber. Sated. Safe and warm and fed for the first time in weeks. And, for that one last moment, his.

He pulled a lock of hair out of her face and kissed her gently on the forehead. This was how he would always remember her.

Chapter Nineteen

THERE WAS A LOUD BANGING. A pause. And then the banging started again.

Lucilla groaned and tried to sit up, only to find herself rocking out of control. It was pitch-black, and she was swamped in a heavy wool blanket. She breathed hard, trying to orient herself as she slowly realized where she was. On the *Star of the Sea*. Sailing toward Kaerlud. With Mathos... or maybe not? Where was he?

The banging started again. Gods. It was someone at the door. She tried to speak and managed a croak. Clearing her throat, she tried again. "Who's there?"

"Nim."

Lucilla pushed herself up and tried to swing her legs over the side, becoming aware of the loud groaning of the ship around her. Its deep pitch and roll. "Come in."

Nim slipped inside carrying a small lantern, and the room was filled with warm light. Around her, the furniture, the boxes and crates, all lay as she'd seen them last. But otherwise, the small cabin was empty.

"Good, you're awake." Nim stepped forward and started gathering up her breeches and boots and handing them to her.

Lucilla ran her hands down her face and stifled a yawn. Gods, it was noisy. Feet clattered on the deck, voices shouted, and occasionally something thumped. How in the kingdom had she managed to sleep through all of that?

She stood on wobbly legs and started pulling on her breeches. "What's happening?"

Nim seemed to consider for a moment. "Do you want the good news or the bad news?"

"The bad news first. Always the bad news."

Nim chuckled and then looked serious once more. "There's a ship following us. The lookouts spotted them a couple of hours after we left port, and they've been catching up. We're certain it's Dornar... they're flying the Royal Standard."

"He's flying my flag?"

Nim nodded, frowning heavily.

Lucilla tucked in her shirt and sat on a trunk to pull on her boots while the rest of what Nim had said sank in. "A couple of hours? How long have I been asleep?"

Nim shrugged lightly. "Just over a day."

"Over a day!" Her voice sounded suspiciously like a shriek. How was that even possible? How could she have lost a whole day?

"You were exhausted. Mathos said we should let you sleep, and he was right." She handed Lucilla a full waterskin. "Here."

Lucilla took several long swallows, glad not only of the water but also for the time to formulate her next question. "Where is Mathos?"

There. She was quite proud of that. She hadn't called

him Matt. She hadn't asked why he wasn't with her, or why
he would have left her, or why he'd sent Nim in his place.
Even though, as her head cleared, she was growing
increasingly desperate to know.

"He's on deck with the Hawks. We've been working on a
plan."

"What kind of plan?"

"Well, that's the good news—we're close to Kaerlud
now, almost at the estuary. If Dornar's going to board us,
he'll do it on the open sea, where there are no witnesses. We
plan to send you ashore with a small squad while the crew
of the *Star* keeps him busy here. The Nephilim have a
temple with a hostel near the river mouth. They'll have
horses and clothes for you so that you can get to the palace
as fast as possible."

Lucilla let her booted foot fall with a thunk. "I'm not
sure that's a good idea. Doesn't that put everyone left on the
ship in danger?"

Nim gave her a slightly bloodthirsty grin. "Well, some.
But honestly, many of the warriors on board saw how
Dornar tried to manipulate Alanna, and they've been
looking forward to spending some time explaining their
views on honor."

Lucilla pulled her hair into a tight braid. "And if Dornar
boards the *Star* and arrests everyone? Or immediately
decides to execute you all?"

Nim rolled her eyes. "You're assuming we're going to
lose."

Gods. How could she explain? She had total faith in the
Hawks and their Nephilim allies. She'd slept better on the
Star than she ever had in her entire life, because she was
with them. But she couldn't just abandon them. Surely a

captain went down with her ship. And a queen stood at the front of her army?

"It's not that. I'm completely confident in the *Star* and the Hawks. But I couldn't let you get hurt in my place; that would just be wrong. If you're fighting for me, then I should be with you."

Nim stepped forward and took hold of her hand, clasping it in a firm, capable grip, her eyes serious. "We don't think it'll come to that. But if it does, this is our choice. We all choose to support you, whether by coming with you or staying on board and distracting Dornar, because we know that it's the right thing to do. We need you to live—no matter what happens to the ship, her crew, or the warriors fighting for you—to take that throne and own it. Because that is the right thing for *you* to do, for everyone in the kingdom."

Damn. Damn it all to hell.

Lucilla held in a groan. This was the beginning of a lifetime of making tough decisions. Decisions that could get people hurt. But now she knew that not making those decisions meant people got hurt anyway.

She had decided on the night she ran away that she was not the kind of woman that waited in her room for salvation. She was the woman who had walked down the stairs and through the door. And if there was anything the last few weeks had shown her, it was that she was tough. She could make difficult decisions and then act on them.

She could do this. She would do it. Lucilla raised her chin and stared at Nim, and Nim stared back.

They stayed like that for a few long seconds, and then Nim's lips twitched. Lucilla could feel her own trying to force themselves up into a smile. To accept how ridiculous this all was. She was only a person. Just like everyone else. A snort escaped. Which only made Nim's lips twitch more. And then they both laughed. A deep, freeing, full-bellied laugh.

Nim wiped her eyes with her free hand. "Gods, I hate making serious speeches."

"Why? You were great. I'm thinking of making you my speechwriter for the future."

"Please don't do that to me. Or to anyone else." Nim opened the door. "Come on, the sun will be rising soon. We have to go."

They sped past the middle decks, teeming with men and women no longer wearing browns and grays, but gleaming in their white Nephilim armor, up to the main deck, to a hive of orderly activity. Warriors worked in the lantern light, climbing rigging, trimming sails, and belaying ropes.

It occurred to Lucilla that she had never seen a female Blue Guard—and yet here male and female Nephilim warriors worked together with impressively efficient coordination. Another thing she could change when she was queen.

A tall woman dressed in breeches and a neat white tunic stood at the helm, occasionally calling orders, keeping a close eye on the commotion around her. Eloa gave a small salute and waved them toward a longboat that was being lowered into the choppy black sea, then turned to Cassiel standing beside her. He gave a matching salute and a small bow as Lucilla saluted back and then dropped a curtsey, thanking them both as best she could.

She turned to see Val and Alanna standing at the ship's rail, as well as Tristan, Tor, Jos, and Rafe, who were busy lowering a rowboat over the side. Watching them were the two Nephilim, Haniel and Ramiel, as well as a striking red-haired woman who was leaning over the rail clutching her belly.

But no Matt. Where was he? Didn't he know that they were leaving?

The boat hit the water with a splash. Tristan raised his chin and grunted as Val handed her the thick cloak she'd worn before, and she pulled it on while the others called out their greetings.

Tor led the way over the rail and down a narrow ladder to the lurching boat as the others began to follow.

Alanna stepped forward and pushed a heavy folded cloth into her hands. "This is for you."

"What is it?" Lucilla moved to open it and look, but Alanna covered her hand with her own and smiled.

"It's a gift. Something I made for you. Keep it folded until you're at the temple."

"Aren't you coming?" Somehow, she'd thought Alanna would be with them, safely away from the ship.

"No. I don't want to do anything that might hurt your claim. We'll join you later; I promise." She turned and winked at Val, who was frowning next to her. "Anyway, this is fun."

Gods. She didn't know what to say. She couldn't think of one single thing. How could she possibly leave these people to fight for her?

Alanna reached over and wrapped her arms around Lucilla's shoulders to whisper in her ear. "You can do this."

"Thank you." It wasn't enough, but it was all she could think of.

She ran her gaze across the deck again. Where the hell was Matt?

"Okay, bye, Lanni. See you soon," Nim said to Alanna

before turning to Lucilla. "You climb down, and then Tristan and I will follow."

She took a step forward and then stopped. This was all happening too quickly. And they couldn't go yet anyway.

"Coming around!" a male voice boomed from the helm.

"We need to go, Your Majesty. Right now," Tristan ordered in a rough voice.

"But… I…."

"Right now."

She knew that they had to go. She did. But surely…. She looked at Tristan, confused. "What about Matt?"

It was hard to tell in the dim light, with the ship lurching beneath her feet, but she would have sworn that Tristan's gaze softened even as emerald-green scales flickered up his neck.

Tristan opened his mouth to reply, but then closed it again as a gleaming figure swathed in white armor strode forward from the forecastle deck, his arms rippling in burgundy-and-gold scales. "I'm here."

"Thank the gods." She let out a relieved breath. "I was getting worried."

Mathos gave her a small smile, but she noticed it didn't reach his eyes. And his beast was rumbling again—but this was no contented purr. It was a half-feral growl, only just audible above the crash of the waves and the groaning of the ship.

"Matt?" she asked uncertainly.

He stayed just too far back to reach as he bowed his head and then slowly lifted it to meet her eyes. "Goodbye, Queen Lucilla."

What? That didn't make sense. It couldn't even be possible. He had told her he would be with her as she took her throne. And if he wasn't coming, he would have been the one to wake her. Said goodbye properly, in private, not here on the deck in front of the entire ship.

Wouldn't he?

"I don't understand. You... I...." Lucilla stumbled as the ship swayed, and Tristan put out a strong hand to hold her. Tristan, not Mathos.

Mathos stared down at her, not speaking, as the grumble of his beast grew even louder.

Eventually Tristan grunted. "Mathos is joining the warriors on board," he explained in a low voice. Tristan's expression was stern, angry even, but his eyes were kind. "The plan is to ensure that Dornar sees him, which should keep him focused on the *Star* and not on you."

"No, I don't want that." Lucilla stepped closer to Mathos, close enough to see that his eyes were almost entirely gold.

"I promised to protect you, and this is the best way to do it," he said firmly. And then he lowered his voice to a whisper, too low for anyone else to hear. "I wanted...." He swallowed heavily. "Goodbye, Lucy."

"No, Matt—" She reached out to hold him back, but he had already spun and walked away.

Gods. What was she supposed to do? Should she run after him?

Tristan gave her a gentle nudge toward the ladder. "Let's get you to the palace, and you can speak to him when he meets us there. I'll make certain of it."

"No." She didn't want to wait; she wanted Matt at her side. "I—"

Nim came forward and clasped her arm gently. "I'm sorry, Lucilla. He's not coming back. And we're out of time. If we don't move now, you'll be caught on the *Star* and all of this will be for nothing. Concentrate on one thing at a time. Get to the palace and then you can—"

"Hard-a-port! Evasive maneuvers!" Captain Cassiel bellowed, and the crew leaped to respond.

There was no more time. They had to go. Nim's voice echoed in her mind. *One thing at a time.*

She took a deep breath. Let it out again. And then turned and climbed down the ladder, the deck—and Mathos—soon lost from view.

Strong hands lifted her into the longboat and settled her onto a wooden bench as Nim and Tristan jumped down behind her. *One thing at a time.*

"Cast off," Tor rumbled, and suddenly they were loose. Oars dipped and pulled, and the boat moved steadily away from the ship. They had no lanterns, no light of any kind, the sound of the oars lost in the rush of water around them.

Spray from the waves and the oars ran down her face, and she wiped it away, tasting the salt, trying to breathe through the ache in her throat. Mathos had left her. That's what Nim and Tristan were trying to tell her. That was the reason for the soft looks and gentle kindness. That's what they meant when they said he wasn't coming back.

He had said he didn't have relationships. Not with anyone. He had told her. But she hadn't believed he would leave her like this.

If she was being honest with herself, she hadn't believed he would leave her at all.

He'd promised, hadn't he? Not to leave her. Gods.

She'd felt so connected to him. The way he looked at her. The way he'd made love to her. It had felt like something real. Something lasting. It had made her hope.

She had been about to tell him that she loved him.

And he'd stopped her. She hadn't realized at the time,

but looking back, she wondered. Had he done that on purpose?

What was she going to do without him? Every time she'd imagined being queen, she'd imagined him with her. He was her new dream. Her new adventure.

Except he wasn't. It had never been more than a fantasy. She stared out to the dark waves and wiped her face again, breathing hard against the sob caught in her throat, forcing it down.

A warm hand slipped into hers, and she turned in surprise to see Nim watching her, her eyes understanding. Nim leaned closer and whispered, too low for anyone else to hear, "Men make mistakes, just like the rest of us."

"What do you mean?" Lucilla whispered back, fighting the tremble in her voice.

Nim's forehead furrowed. "I've never seen Mathos behave in the way he's been acting. He's angry and sullen, picking fights. See that bruise on Jos's cheek—that's from Mathos."

Lucilla squinted in the darkness across to Jos. He did have a deep purple bruise underneath his eye.

"Mathos is the man who has a joke for everything. Who never takes anything seriously. And then he did that because Jos made some crack about how Mathos kept checking on you."

"He checked on me? Really?"

"All the time. But I'll tell you what surprised me the most." Nim squeezed her hand. "He hasn't called anyone darlin', not even Keely"—she gestured to the pale woman staring resolutely out into the darkness—"and he normally loves flirting with her just to get a reaction out of Tor."

Matt had checked on her all day. But then he'd left her

alone when it was time to leave. She swallowed. "What does it all mean?"

"It means that whatever stupid decision he's busy making is the wrong one. He's hurting, and he's lashing out to try and make himself feel better." Nim gave her a kind smile. "He's being an ass. But if you think you can forgive him for hurting you, if you want him enough, despite the way he's behaving, then speak to him and force him to listen. If you feel the way that I think you feel about him, you're going to have to fight for him."

Fight for him. Yes. She could fight for him. His mother had made him believe that no one could want him. But she could show him that she would never want anyone, or anything, else.

"And," Nim continued softly, "if you can't forgive him or he doesn't fix this, just remember that we are all with you. Whatever happens with Mathos, you are not alone."

Gods. She wasn't alone. The knowledge settled lightly into her heart, and as it did, so did a sudden understanding —she had *never* been alone. She had always been surrounded by her people.

Yes, she had been lonely, and likely would be again. But she had always had a purpose, she had only needed to realize it. She could do this. She could be the queen she was meant to be.

She straightened her spine and watched the first golden tendrils on the horizon slowly spreading into a magnificent peach-and-honey-colored dawn.

Gray light filtered over the sea, and in the distance behind them, she picked out two ships. One just ahead of the other as they danced forward, racing for the estuary.

The sun rose fully into the sky, and in the first rays of morning light, she saw a glorious white flag rising on the main mast of the *Star of the Sea*, adorned with a golden outline of an angel bearing a fiery sword.

A roar of recognition went up from the ship behind them, and voices shouted. Although their words were lost in the distance and over the sea, she heard the high-pitched warble of the bosun's whistle.

Ahead of her, she saw that they had nearly arrived at a small cove. Slow minutes passed as they curved around a rocky outcropping and the ships were lost to sight. There was a loud boom, and she saw Tristan's jaw clench as his scales shimmered in rippling waves. Gods. It physically hurt to know that the warriors on the *Star* were fighting—Matt was fighting—for her. So that she could be queen.

The men on oars pulled heavily, and soon they were crunching onto the sandy shore and then piling out of the boat. Tor and Tristan pulled it high onto the beach, and they all worked quickly to dump piles of sand and salty, half-rotten seaweed over the boat, hiding it.

The sun had been over the horizon for less than an hour when Ramiel led them over the sand and then up a narrow track over the dunes. The dense tufts of spiky marram grass brushed at her legs, and her feet sank into the soft sand as the seagulls screeched overhead, but her thoughts were over the rough sea, desperate to know what was happening.

She stumbled on an old piece of driftwood, righting herself just before Tor reached her. After that, she kept her head down and focused. *One thing at a time*. First the crown.

They reached a hard track that allowed them to spread out and shift into an easy jog. Even Keely ran—despite still looking pale and wan—with Tor running beside her, watching her carefully. Although neither of them acknowledged the other.

A few weeks before, Lucilla would have struggled, but

not anymore. The ground disappeared beneath her feet as she focused on her breathing and did her best not to constantly imagine every horrific thing that could be happening to Matt and all the people they'd left behind on the *Star*.

It was midmorning when they crested a low hill and looked down to see the city spread out in front of them. It was vast; a massive array of people and buildings flanking the huge gray Tamasa river as it flowed down to the estuary and the sea.

She stared across the waters of the wide river mouth as they ran. Out in the distance, two ships sailed too close together. There were still two. Thank the gods. What was happening out there? They were too far away to see their colors, and she had no way to know.

She focused on running, placing each foot ahead of the other, and whispered a prayer to the gods in time with her footsteps; *let them be safe, let them be safe*.

"Your Majesty?" Tristan drew her attention as they all pulled to a dusty, panting stop. "We're here."

She looked up to see a sprawling gray stone building not far from the road, and they followed Ramiel to a heavy wooden door that opened at his touch.

Ramiel rang a small bell just inside the door, and within minutes there was a bustle of activity. Men and women with hair in shades from flaming red to deep auburn, all wearing white tunics, brought jugs of cold, clear water while the Nephilim spoke quietly, and Lucilla waited impatiently.

She, Nim, and Keely were led to a spacious waiting room with comfortable-looking seats covered in green cushions and a window overlooking a courtyard with a small fountain.

Nephilim acolytes followed them in carrying bowls of

warm water and washcloths, as well as trays of bread, cheese, and shining red apples. They took turns to wash their hands and faces and then all three of them began eating hungrily. Even Keely, who looked significantly better after a few slices of cheese and apple.

A short while later, a young woman arrived carrying a set of sumptuous-looking gowns in velvets and silks. There were deep blues and shimmering greens, even a buttery yellow. And among them was a heavy burgundy velvet dress shot through with strands of gold.

The acolyte dropped a stilted curtsey. "I hope these help, Your Majesty. They're the best we've got."

"They're beautiful, thank you." She gave the young woman a reassuring smile as she dropped another curtsey and left them to change.

Lucilla walked over and ran her fingers down the rich wine-red fabric. It was slightly too short for her, but otherwise, it was perfect. Burgundy and gold. She would go to her throne dressed in the colors of Matt's scales, in recognition of everything he'd given her. Everything he meant to her.

"And this," Nim said quietly, handing her the heavy folded fabric that Alanna had given her, and Tristan had insisted on carrying to the temple.

Lucilla took the folded bundle and shook it out, her breath catching as she realized what it was.

A banner. Deep midnight blue and beautifully embroidered in silver—with two fighting boars locked in battle.

Alanna, who had been so badly hurt by Ballanor and Geraint, had given her their family's crest. How many hours had she spent creating this gorgeous display of heraldry?

She had always hated those vicious boars, but Alanna

had seen something in them that she had captured for Lucilla. A sense of determination and grit. Nobility, even. And for the first time, she felt some kind of kinship with the boars that had stared at her for her entire life. They were fighting for survival.

And she would fight too. For survival—hers and her people's. For her crown. To be the queen her kingdom deserved.

And, when the time came, for the man she loved.

Chapter Twenty

MATHOS STOOD in a dark pool of shadow beside the fore-topmast, still close enough to see her clearly in the pool of golden lamplight. To see how she looked out across the deck, searching for him. Even after his goodbye.

She wanted him to join her in her final push to Kaerlud —to stand beside her as she took her throne—but there was no way that he could. If he rode into Kaerlud beside her, she would see it as a sign. As some sort of confirmation of their continuing… liaison? Affair? He didn't know what the word was for the mess of emotions churning through him.

This was better for everyone. Start as you mean to go on, his father used to say.

This is not what you started. And you hardly knew the man.

He took a step closer to her, driven by his beast, just in time to hear Nim speak in a gentle voice. "Mathos isn't coming back."

The words stopped him. It was done. She knew that they were over.

A piercing agony skewered through him, and he almost

fell to his knees. It took everything he had to stand still as his beast howled and roared in his belly.

Lucilla stared into the darkness, her chest heaving with repressed emotion, her denials still hovering in the air as his beast went into a frenzy of anguished violence within him.

Don't do this. Don't. Just… Go to her.

Mathos didn't want to hear any more. Couldn't bear to hear any more. Not from Lucy, not from Nim, and definitely not from his beast. He had to get away before he did something irrevocably stupid.

This is irrevocably stupid.

No. This was the only option he had.

He turned and walked away, following the shadows into the thick mass of warriors preparing for the coming confrontation, allowing himself to be swallowed up in the whooshing of the waves against the ship and the swift thudding of booted feet, in the rushing blood and excitement of battle.

"Hard-a-port! Evasive maneuvers!" Cassiel bellowed from the quarterdeck. "Keep them with us!"

Yes. This was what he needed. The one thing he was good at. The one thing that could take his mind off the look on Lucy's face.

He strode forward resolutely, past the rows of grim warriors and up the wooden steps to the quarterdeck to stand beside the captain and first mate at the helm.

Only then did he give in and turn to check. The rowboat was gone. Swallowed into the darkness.

Good. Now he could focus on keeping Dornar's attention and giving her a chance to escape. He had promised her protection, and he would provide it. And then he could go somewhere far away, whether as a mercenary or wherever the Hawks would be deployed next, holding tight to his last vision of her, asleep and beautiful. That was how he would remember her. Not this last, pale glimpse as he said goodbye.

You're just lying to yourself. Anyway, the Hawks—

No—he cut off the beast's complaints—he wasn't lying to himself; everything was exactly as it should be.

It was bleak and terrible and exactly as it should be.

The pain in his belly burned as his beast thrashed and his scales hardened. He forced himself to ignore it all and focus on the battle ahead.

He stood with the ship's senior commanders as they flew through the dark sea, always keeping ahead of their pursuers, but not so far ahead that the ship following them might give up.

It was a long, tense wait as the darkness dissolved into gray. Lamps were doused, and the details of the deck grew clearer with every passing second. And then the sun peeped over the horizon, a fiery ball between the dark slate of the water and the vibrant peach-and-gold outlining the clouds above.

Tendrils of light spread out from the magnificent golden sunrise as Cassiel faced the deck and bellowed, "Raise the colors!"

A member of the crew leaped forward to haul the flag up the mainmast. The snowy white banner adorned with the gleaming golden outline of the Nephilim warrior angel whipped and fluttered in the dawn light. And then a second flag was raised. The Royal Standard—the queen's colors of midnight blue and silver—flying proudly beside the gold and white. Tangible demonstration of the newly reaffirmed alliance between the crown and the Nephilim.

A roar went up from the ship pursuing them, there was no hiding now.

The bosun piped a sharp low-high blast, and the captain roared, "Raise the gunports!"

The wooden shutters crashed open, sparking a wild rush of exhilaration. He'd heard of the new Nephilim "flying fire," but he'd never seen it in action before.

"Ready the guns!"

"Aye, Captain."

Beneath him, he could feel a low rumble, presumably of the heavy cannon rolling forward as the two ships turned in a slow dance. They were close enough now to make out the grim faces and blue coats of the ranked soldiers, standing resolute as the rough crew swarmed anxiously around them. The two groups seemed uncoordinated, the crew working around the soldiers, not with them.

He looked closer at their pursuers. The crew wore loose trousers and dark gray woolen jackets, many of them had beards over deep tans.

Gods. Now that he could see properly, he could see the truth. This was no navy ship; this was a merchant brigantine, designed to be swift and maneuverable. No wonder it had caught them despite their hours of lead. But what in the Abyss were they doing? They could never hope to defeat a Nephilim man-o'-war.

He could see it on their stony expressions—they had not realized the power they were up against. Had no doubt expected a trading ship only too glad to hand over a troublesome pair of stowaways. Instead, they had picked a fight with the Nephilim. And they were regretting it.

He turned to Cassiel, who nodded decisively even before he spoke. "Yes, I see it."

The captain raised his voice. "Prepare to deliver a warning shot!"

"Aye, Captain!"

"Helmsman. Bring us about."

Eloa swung the wheel, and the *Star* turned slowly broadside.

"Fire at will!"

There was a loud boom and then a sharp crack as the cannonball flew over the brigantine's deck to splash loudly into the sea. Louder and more violent than he'd even imagined. And far more powerful than the opposing crew had considered, judging by their horrified reactions.

The pursuing ship's crew flew over the rigging as the ships drew inexorably closer, the Blues standing in ranks over their main deck. This could so easily be a bloodbath. And so unnecessary.

Mathos stepped up to the quarterdeck rail and shouted loudly, "Stand to and surrender!"

There was a rumble of disagreement from the Blues. But he couldn't let this happen. If the *Star* fired those cannonballs at the deck, all of them would die. These were once his men. Were still the queen's men. And they would be slaughtered for nothing.

"Where is Lord High Chancellor Dornar? Send him to negotiate your surrender."

The Blues parted, and Dornar stepped forward to the rail, the two ships so close now that only a few feet of churning gray water separated them.

Dornar widened his stance, hands behind his back. "I see you survived, Sergeant Mathos."

"I lived for you, Dornar." He clasped his hand to his chest in mock romance. "I knew that we would meet again."

Dornar's face remained set, but copper scales flickered up his forearms in an unusual display of agitation.

Mathos chuckled for the first time in two days. Gods, he loved enraging superior officers; it had made him feel better about his life since those first dark days when he had joined the army fresh from his mother's side, and it was no different now as his grief and loss churned inside him.

And he owed Dornar—the pain he'd caused Mathos was only the smallest part. He owed him for the pain he'd given Lucy.

"Where is she, Mathos?" Dornar demanded.

Mathos spread his arms wide, encompassing the *Star of the Sea*, and forced himself to grin. "Not here."

Dornar's fists clenched at his side as those telling scales fluttered higher.

"Why don't you come over here and take a look?" Mathos taunted. "I'll give you a tour on the way to the brig."

Dornar didn't bother to respond. He simply drew his sword, the men behind him following his lead.

"No!" Mathos ignored Dornar and turned to the men. "You are Blues! This is the queen's ship. The Nephilim are the queen's allies—just look at her flag. If you fight now, it will be treason. And you must know that you can't win."

There was an unhappy rumble from the men, quickly quelled as Dornar glared back at the Blues. "*We* are fighting for the queen," he told them.

"That is a lie." Jeremiel called from beside Cassiel. "I'm the truth seeker on this vessel, and I'm telling you that we support the true queen, Lucilla, daughter of Geraint, the son of Bar-Aloys, who on her coronation will be Lucilla the First, Defender of Brythoria."

The Blues shuffled, discomfited, but Dornar ignored them completely and strode back to take position on the brigantine's quarterdeck, calling loudly, "Grappling hooks... fire!"

Mathos didn't know what Dornar was thinking. His bid

to brazen it out made no sense. But he had no time to consider it in the storm of flying ropes and the loud, grinding crunch as the two ships collided.

Within seconds, they were swarmed, the Blues flooding over the side of the ship only to crash uselessly against the lethal discipline of the Nephilim.

The thunder of battle surrounded him. Swords clanged, crossbow bolts flew, men and women screamed and died as the deck grew slippery with blood.

He fought one and then two desperate Blues as the ships ground closer together in a haze of splintering wood and shrapnel. He knocked the first unconscious with a vicious backhand with his sword pommel and then beat the other to his knees with a flurry of brutal slashes as his beast poured out his rage and loss.

And then, almost as quickly as it started, it was over. He had a new cut bleeding down his cheek and a Blue kneeling dazedly in front of him.

It wasn't nearly enough.

He needed the fight. Needed to roar and bleed and lose himself in battle. Needed to utterly exhaust himself. But everywhere the Blues were laying down their arms.

He breathed hard, forcing the beast back down. Forcing himself to accept that the fight was over. Forcing himself to take stock.

It was a victory. But he couldn't see the Lord High Chancellor.

"Find Dornar!" He sped frantically, searching through the slowly clearing dust. Checking the faces of the dead and the captured Blues.

Nothing.

He leaped across the narrow gap onto the brigantine to see the tremulous captain kneeling and begging, hurrying to explain that he was not responsible for chasing them down. That his ship had been requisitioned by the Lord High Chancellor. That he would never have even followed them if he'd had a choice.

But where was Dornar? Fuck. His beast rolled over heavily. Something was wrong.

Mathos started to run, Jeremiel and Val catching up behind him, and together they searched the ship. Soon they were joined by a squad of Nephilim who helped them pull it apart as the captain moaned and complained bitterly at the damage to his ship and the loss of life around him.

Mathos hunted through cabins and in the galley, looking in storage and behind trunks as his heart beat heavily in his ears. Forcing himself to slow. To search thoroughly and carefully.

One by one, the cabins were cleared. And slowly he had to face what he already knew. Dornar had attacked them—sacrificing his men and the ship he'd taken—as a distraction.

By the time they returned to the deck, the two ships were sailing side by side through the estuary toward Kaerlud under Cassiel's stern command. But Dornar was gone.

The Lord High Chancellor hadn't been making one last desperate stand. No, he had betrayed the men under his command to their deaths so that he could escape.

Mathos had sent Lucy away. And now Dornar was free to follow her.

He had to warn her. Warn Tristan. Thank the gods she would be in the palace soon. She would be surrounded by guards; they would keep her safe.

His beast growled viciously at the idea of other guards watching over her, but for once it didn't bother to comment.

Chapter Twenty-One

THEY FLEW DOWN the hill at a gallop, Lucilla's long dress streaming out behind her as the proud stallions thundered toward Kaerlud. Warriors carried rippling banners of Nephilim white and gold and Brythorian midnight blue, flying side by side.

People came out of their homes to watch, at first silent and suspicious, but slowly gaining interest.

Lucilla's heart lifted as she saw them. Children and old people, young couples, working men and women. These were her people. They were the people that she would take up the throne for. The people she would spend her life trying to be worthy of.

She missed Mathos with a steady ache, and she wished that it was Penelope that she was riding, but she couldn't help the grin spreading over her face.

This was freedom. The freedom to be who she truly was.

They clattered up toward the city gates, slowing as the road grew busy. The stone walls of Kaerlud rose to either side of them, and around them throngs of people of every race made their way into the city. Some with red-and-black tattoos on their arms like hers, others with wings, or scales, occasional red-haired Nephilim, and she felt her heart swelling with love for them. The people of Brythoria.

The alarm went up with a loud bugle call and squads of guards rushed forward to cluster together in rough formation near the gates, their hands resting on their sword hilts.

The crowd fell away anxiously, pulling back from the menace in the air to press against the city walls and drag their children off the road, away from danger.

Damn. These were her people. But they did not look happy.

Lucilla had to force herself to hold her smile as they trotted forward onto the wide, dusty space in front of the gates.

Tristan urged his stallion forward. He was wearing a blinding white-and-gold tunic emblazoned with the Nephilim warrior angel, but he had added a swirling deep blue cloak, embroidered with the royal fighting boars. His scales flickered over his clenched jaw, and his horse danced nervously, unsettled by the unfamiliar beast on its back.

He lifted his chin and roared, "Open for Queen Lucilla!"

A sweating soldier in a green infantry uniform stepped forward. He opened his mouth, perhaps to argue, but then his gaze settled on Lucilla, and he closed it again. For the first time ever, she didn't regret that she looked just like her brother.

He looked behind him, to the group of rough-looking soldiers, and then turned back to the party in front of him.

Two squads of Nephilim warriors, the Hawks, three women dressed in velvet and silk, and all flying the royal colors.

There was a moment of tense silence. And then he turned and waved them through.

Tristan grunted as if he had never expected anything different, but his hand was still clenched firmly over the hilt of his sword. She let out a breath that shook more than she liked and then followed him into Kaerlud.

It was astonishing. So many people. So many homes, so close together. Children running down pavements, reminding her viscerally of Alis darting down the dusty path through the fields, despite the entirely different surroundings.

The city was frantically busy, noisy, smelling in turns of spicy food and rotting waste. Storefronts with brightly colored awnings lined the road while open squares were filled with hawkers and costermongers calling their wares. She had never imagined such seething masses of people or the strange frenetic vibrancy of such a huge city. But under the layer of noise and commerce, she could see a darker undercurrent. Children in threadbare clothes with no shoes, beggars on the street corners, women in tattered dresses, and haggard men wearing dusty uniforms, many with pinned sleeves and trousers where limbs were missing. The human cost of war.

The news of their arrival spread ahead of them, and huge crowds gathered to watch them pass, blocking out her view of the city with their bodies. The throngs stood with clenched jaws and heavy scowls, dark and suspicious. Bruised by their treatment under Ballanor and Geraint before him.

There was a low rumble through the crowds; exactly

what emotion it reflected it was impossible to tell... anger, mistrust, bitterness... perhaps all three.

Her shoulders bunched under the weight of those hard, assessing stares, but she lifted her chin and urged her stallion forward. They had the right to their cynicism.

They turned a corner and entered a space that made her throat close in horror. It looked like a battle had taken place, destroying buildings and leaving piles of broken bricks and old wood to litter the square. A gold filigreed astronomical clock was littered with embedded crossbow bolts and arrows. But worst of all, opposite the clocktower stood a huge wooden platform, and on it a massive gallows.

Gods. This was where her brother had tried to execute Alanna.

The crowd surged through the square, a beast in its own right, voices rising at the visceral reminder of Ballanor's rule and the lies he'd perpetrated. The justice they'd wanted and believed themselves to have been denied. Hatred for Alanna and Val, but also Ballanor.

She wished she could turn away and deal with it when she was better prepared, when she knew what to say, or how to fix the disaster Ballanor and Geraint had created. But everyone was watching, waiting to see what she would do. Would she allow the devastation that her family had perpetuated to stand? Would she ignore the rumbling misery of the people in her capital? Or would she act?

There was only one answer. She was the queen, and this couldn't wait.

She looked across at the huge, untidy structure of stones and bricks that made up the outer wall of the palace. There was a row of guards standing, resolute, side by side, blocking the entrance. She ignored them.

Instead, she turned to Tristan beside her, leaning over to

speak with him privately as she gestured toward the gallows. "How difficult would it be for me to tear that down? Right now."

Tristan's eyes gleamed; one side of his mouth even twitched in what, for Tristan, was a huge display of emotion. He bowed his head briefly and then pushed forward into the middle of the square, addressing the crowds that had followed them. "Queen Lucilla requests an ax. Can anyone help?"

There was a shuffling of feet and confusion, disbelief, a rising current of anger. The atmosphere in the square grew ripe with the threat of violence. They only had Geraint and Ballanor to judge her by. Geraint who had sent them to war, year after year, willingly paying the price in his own people's deaths. Ballanor who had torn up their city, filled it with violence and corruption, and then done everything in his power to continue that war, all while blaming his wife.

Her small group of Hawks and Nephilim were caught between the infantry and the crowds, neither of whom trusted or accepted her. They were balanced on the edge.

Lucilla clicked to her stallion and nudged him forward to meet Tristan. "Give me your sword."

Tristan's eyebrows clashed together in a deep frown, but he slid out his sword and handed it to her, hilt first. The watching crowd rumbled uncertainly.

She clasped the heavy broadsword tightly as she clattered over the cobbles, forcing a narrow path through the crowds as they parted reluctantly, Tristan and the others close behind.

Slowly, knowing it could be a fatal mistake, she slid down from her horse and stood among them.

No one moved.

A deathly silence fell over the square as Lucilla climbed

the gallows steps, all her nerves screaming as the array of eyes followed her. Gods. Her heart broke at the thought of Alanna walking up those same wooden stairs—in chains and expecting to die—so very vulnerable and alone.

She stepped forward to the edge of the wooden platform and looked out. Arrayed across the square were soldiers in uniform, ordinary people dressed for work and daily life, children, her own small company.

Nim stood at the foot of the platform, Tristan frowning beside her. Tor, a steady presence behind them; beside him, the pale-faced Keely. Jos, Rafe, Haniel, and Ramiel too. The Nephilim warriors blocked the access to the platform and watched the crowds carefully. Her new friends. And her people.

Sweat dripped down her back and she wished she could wipe her damp palms, but she was still holding the massive broadsword.

She cleared her throat and started to speak, her voice rough, but clear in the silent square. "People of Brythoria, I am Lucilla. I could tell you that I am the sister of Ballanor and the daughter of Geraint, but I'm guessing that you want to forget that about as much as I do."

There was a hiss of shocked laughter, quickly repressed.

Someone from the back of the crowd shouted loudly, "We can see who you are!"

Lucilla swallowed against the catch in her throat. "I may look like Ballanor, but I'm not like him in any other way. I'm not here for power or riches. I'm here to stop a war. I'm here for you."

There were several loud boos and hisses as the crowd laughed skeptically. Her hands shook where she clenched the massive hilt of Tristan's sword, but she didn't let go.

She looked out across the mass of angry faces. "You

don't have to believe me yet, and I don't blame you. My brother has told you so many lies, all while ripping your homes out from under you."

She took a breath, let it out again. "All I'm asking for is a chance. Without me, you can guarantee another war, but this time not one on the northern border. One right here, in your homes, as our kingdom gets ripped apart by those who would take the throne.

"I promise to do everything I can to keep our kingdom safe. To rebuild the trust that was broken. And this is where I start—here, with my brother's biggest lie. It was never Alanna that betrayed us; it was Ballanor."

Then, standing there in front of her people, the cold breeze tangling her hair, and her back damp from fear, she passed the sword from hand to hand to wipe her hands down her skirt, then lifted it as high as she could and brought it smashing down on the wooden post beside her.

The crowd watched, stunned, then opened their mouths and roared as she lifted the sword again and smashed it down on the post once more. And again.

Nephilim warriors appeared beside her, lashing coils of rope around the post. Nim called her name, and then, when she turned, pressed an ax into her hands, replacing Tristan's sword.

Then Nim stepped back, and everyone watched as Lucilla hacked away at that ugly post, which had somehow come to represent all the evil that had been in her family. The people who should have loved her and should have loved their kingdom, but never did. She crashed the ax back down, losing herself in violent catharsis.

"Step back, please, Your Majesty." Tristan's voice called her back, and she stepped away, letting the ax drag down, suddenly exhausted.

The post gave with a loud groan, pulled safely away by the ropes to fall, smashing to the platform in a cloud of dust and splinters.

There was a moment of breathtaking silence, and then the crowd screamed its approval.

Ramiel stepped forward, tall and authoritative, his voice booming over the noise. "People of Brythoria…" He waited until the crowd settled. "I am the Supreme Justice of the Truth."

The crowd rippled with astonishment. It was very rare for the Supreme Justice to journey away from the Temple at Eshcol, but his stature, his white-and-gold breastplate, and his fiery hair were unmistakable.

"The archangels and the gods are watching. They see our hearts and our truth."

A cold breeze whipped through the now silent square, and Lucilla shivered as the sweat dried on her back.

Ramiel continued, "Lucilla is our true queen and our only chance for peace. The Nephilim recognize her claim." And then, there on the platform, surrounded by the broken pieces of the gallows that she had destroyed, he sank slowly to one knee and bowed his head.

The squads of Nephilim and the Hawks followed instantly. And then, slowly at first, but in a spreading wave, one by one, the people in the square followed. The ache in her throat intensified as their commitment to her took her breath away.

Only once everyone had knelt did Ramiel stand once more, raising his powerful voice. "The king is dead. Long live Queen Lucilla!"

The chant was taken up all around them as her people came back to their feet. "Long live the queen! Long live the queen!"

Lucilla stood, panting and disheveled, her stomach swirling, but with her back straight and her heart full to overflowing.

She handed the ax to Nim and stepped forward, waiting a moment until all eyes were on her once more, and then slowly rolled up her sleeves to show her tattoos. Then she dipped her head and brought her closed fist to her heart, recognizing the people before her as family.

There was a roar of approval from the crowd as a wave of fists met hearts, and she had to swallow hard to hold back the flood of emotion; joy and love and relief.

Thank the gods.

She knew the reprieve was temporary. There was a huge amount of work to be done to undo the damage that Ballanor and Geraint had done and to truly restore the kingdom—and her people's trust—but it was a start.

They returned to their horses and rode toward the gates amidst the cheering crowds. The soldiers, faced with the chanting mob and the hard-faced guards at her back, wisely stood back and let them enter.

They crossed a low bridge, flanked by tall wrought iron lamps, passing over a deep moat of dark, still water. The bridge ended at a long line of scaffolding and piled stones forming an unfinished inner wall where a cluster of attentive soldiers in black uniforms hesitated.

Tristan called loudly, "Make way for the queen!"

They looked at each other nervously but didn't move. A heavyset Apollyon wearing a captain's sigil and a stern frown stepped forward. "You are not cleared to enter."

Tristan laughed. Loudly. "Are you saying that Lord Dornar said nothing about bringing the queen back to the palace?"

"No," the captain admitted, "he did make preparations

for the queen. But I don't see the Lord High Chancellor with you."

Tristan narrowed his eyes. "No, you idiot. You see Her Majesty, Queen Lucilla herself."

The captain looked across to Lucilla, recognition clear in his face.

Gods. After the intensity of the square, the long flight from the ship, the heartache of the morning, she was completely drained, and she wanted to go inside. "Captain, you know who I am. And you knew I was coming. You have three seconds to decide whether your loyalty is to the *former*"—she stressed the word—"Lord High Chancellor, or to me."

The captain took a hurried step back, signaling his men to allow them to pass.

They pushed their mounts down a short path and through a wide arch into a cobbled courtyard dominated by a massive three-tiered marble fountain formed by a trio of rearing winged horses, their forelegs raised as if they might leap from the falling water.

On either side of the courtyard were long covered walkways, accessed by rows of pointed gothic arches, and at the far side, a pair of heavy wooden doors set with iron bands stood open. A cluster of men, all Apollyon, in expensive robes and adorned with heavy gold chains of office, poured through the doors into the courtyard.

Damn, she was tired. She wanted this over. She wanted to sit down and drink something cold. She wanted Matt to say something ridiculous and make her laugh. She did not want to deal with her brother's council.

She was so very tempted to let her face fall back into her practiced "dealing with authority" blankness and fold her hands politely to avoid this confrontation. But then the lead councilor, a heavyset man with a pronounced belly, gray hair, and cold, dark eyes, began to speak. "What is the meaning of this?"

She put on her haughtiest stare, ignoring her exhaustion as she pushed her stallion forward with Tristan at her side. "Is that how you speak to your queen? Is that how you spoke to my father, Geraint? Or my brother, Ballanor?"

The man took another step forward, soldiers in blue tunics flanking him. All Apollyon. All, no doubt, from ancient families. His hands clenched by his side as his nostrils flared.

"I don't know who you think you are——" he started but stopped as Ramiel boomed, "That is a lie."

The councilor folded his arms over his chest. "What? How dare you!"

Ramiel slid from his horse and strode forward, glittering in his white armor. "I am Justice of the Truth. The *Supreme* Justice. Here in support of the true queen. And you just lied."

The councilor's ears turned red, but he didn't back down. "The Lord High Chancellor is bringing the queen back, and as he is not here, I have to question whether this… ah… young lady could possibly be——"

Ramiel stalked forward. "Lie."

The councilor stepped back, almost into the men arrayed behind him. "Wh-What?"

"You lied again. You know exactly who she is. We can all see it just by looking at her."

The councilor shook his head, mouth slack. "No. We don't accept——"

Lucilla had had enough. "You knew I would be coming back, and here I am. I'm not with Dornar nor under his control. I don't answer to him nor any of you."

She swept the councilors with a long stare, taking in their looks of mingled outrage and conviction that they would soon be rid of her. These were Ballanor's cronies, men who had supported Dornar because he promised to maintain their status and power. They would never accept her. Instead, they would do everything they could to undermine her at every turn.

She turned to Tristan and spoke loudly, ensuring everyone could hear. "Will you accept the position of Supreme Commander of the Blacks and Blues and join my new council?"

"Yes, Your Majesty," he agreed without hesitation, but then flicked a tiny glance back toward Nim, his brow furrowed.

Lucilla patted his arm. "With Nim and the Hawks, of course."

He gave a curt nod. "Thank you, Your Majesty. It will be an honor."

She turned back to the huddle of Ballanor's councilors. "Gentlemen, you are dismissed, and this council is disbanded. The kingdom thanks you for your service, but you are no longer needed here. Please return your chains of office and vacate your rooms by the end of the day."

"What? No!" There were howls of outrage as they all began shouting and pushing forward at once.

"Supreme Commander Tristan, please take the Blues in hand and escort these men and their families from my palace."

Tristan called a command, and the Blues who had been standing uncertainly at the door stepped forward to form a threatening ring around the councilors.

Lucilla turned to the powerful Nephilim beside her. "Supreme Justice Ramiel, will you join my new council? I need good people at my side. And I believe our people have spent too long apart. I would like us to work together."

Ramiel's face softened as he agreed. "Thank you, Your Majesty. It will be a privilege."

"It will mean staying here for some time, would that be possible?"

Ramiel dipped his chin. "Yes. I have spent too long at Eshcol, and I too would like to see our kingdom reunited." He smiled softly. "And I am proud to stand beside you, Queen Lucilla."

She reached out and clasped his hand, hoping that no one else could hear the tremor in her voice. "Thank you."

Tristan ordered the Blues to escort the former councilors back to their rooms to pack, allocating two Nephilim guards to join each group, as much to keep watch on the Blues as to watch the councilors.

She watched them leave, wishing she had rooms of her own prepared. Damn, it would be good to take a bath, change into a dress that wasn't damp with sweat, and have something to eat.

But that would have to wait.

She straightened her shoulders. First, she needed to take control of the palace. Then she desperately needed an update on the warriors on board the *Star of the Sea*. And Matt. Gods, she hoped that they were all okay.

She needed an immediate session with her fledgling council. They urgently needed more members and to start prioritizing tasks.

They needed to determine how best to haul the guards and soldiers back into an honorable force after months of Ballanor's, Grendel's, and Dornar's rule. And after that, start looking to reshape their military force into something much more like what she'd seen on board the *Star*. And she urgently needed to deal with the breakdown in talks with Verturia and ensure that they were not about to enter into a war that she'd promised to prevent.

The multitude of tasks to be done rose ahead of her like a vast wall of responsibility. But somehow, she felt certain that they could do it if they worked together.

She had made it this far; she just had to keep on going. One thing at a time.

Chapter Twenty-Two

DORNAR LAY on his back in the long grasses listening to the shouts of the men searching for him.

Longboats had trawled through the waves and even up on to the beach, but no one had made it as far as the rolling dunes. And he knew better than to stand and give them a lovely clear silhouette.

Instead, he lay in the swaying yellow and green grasses, well camouflaged by his copper-colored scales, and watched the skies slowly lighten. The heavy clouds that had followed them for the last few days were moving away, clustered in a dark band along the horizon while above him the sky was the pale, white-streaked blue of the encroaching winter.

He was bitterly cold despite his scales, the wind icy on his wet uniform, but it had been well worth swimming the last hundred feet so that he could leave the boat floating on the current. And it wasn't the first time that he had hidden in the grass.

He had spent many hours lying, staring up at the sky much like this as a child. Planning.

He had always known, even as a child, that he was different. Better than everyone else. Especially the pitiful excuse for a man who he called father. His mother had always told him so.

She had told him he would be as rich and powerful as he was handsome and clever, and that he would leave the wretched farmhouse and its relentless back-breaking chores far behind. And he had never doubted it.

And he had done it. He had risen faster, higher than anyone could have imagined. Discipline. Focus. Charm. And, mostly, a keen understanding of exactly what made people behave in the way they did.

He had learned how to motivate people early. Encourage them to his way of thinking. A nudge here, a nudge there. And, if they refused, well, he had spent his teen years learning the exact effects of every single available poison. And a few that were distinctly unavailable.

His useless father had watched him with that ever-deepening frown, as if trying to understand, trying to see a truth that he would never understand, when yet another village dog went missing, or the rats suddenly overflowed from the grain store because the cats were gone.

Father hadn't understood, but Mother had. If you want to know how something works, you have to be prepared to take it apart.

Gods, it had been a relief to get away. When Mother started to cough, he had begun to wonder. When the coughing turned bloody, he knew.

He took his set of highly honed skills and joined the army, where he flew through the ranks of the Blacks and then the Blues, all the way to Grendel. Gods, that man had disgusted him. Ballanor too. Both of them so wrapped up in their own primitive wants. Their lusts and thirsts. But it had made them supremely easy to manipulate.

And he had made it. From the boy expected to feed the cows, all the way to Lord High Chancellor. Almost, almost, to prince consort. Ruling over, and through, his inexperienced new wife. So close he could still taste it.

And yet, here he was, having come the full circle. Back to lying in the fucking grass.

And he knew exactly who to blame. Mathos.

Sure, he knew the others had played a part. But it was Mathos who had humiliated him in the palace when the Hawks came to free Nim. Fucking whistling in his face like a dockworker.

Mathos who had kept him away from Alanna when he so nearly had the perfect distraction to ensure that Val died. Ballanor had taken the blade instead, ending his life far sooner than planned. Creating the opening for Alanna to reject the throne and choose Val. Who could have predicted she would do something so stupid?

And then, when he managed to turn even that debacle to his advantage, it was fucking Mathos who snuck in and stole Lucilla. He should have drugged his soon-to-be fiancée to sleep again instead of relying on those idiot guards. She was so naïve. So desperate for approval. So very easily led. She was going to be perfect.

And then Mathos had taken her and ruined it all. Again.

His rage had been incandescent. That fuckwit Cerdic was, even now, mucking out stalls. A task that he was no doubt finding difficult after the whipping he'd had. Cerdic and all the other Blues who had been guarding her. The only one who had gotten off lightly was the one Mathos had already killed. Even Claudius was reconsidering his life choices, having been woken up just in time to see his men tied to the whipping posts before being demoted to kitchen duty.

They had deserved exactly what they got. Next time, they would know better than to fail. As would every other man under his command.

The bigger problem was that his fury had made Dornar lose focus just for a moment, for the first time in his life.

He had mobilized both the cavalry and infantry, pulling men from every barracks within a hundred miles and closed all the roads to the north, and then sent his men to flush Mathos and Lucilla south. He had riddled all the coastal towns within reach of the Derrow with soldiers, certain that they would try for the ports. He had even predicted that they would aim for Darant. And he had put men onto every single ship in the harbor.

But it had never occurred to him that when the captain of the *Star of the Sea* refused to allow his men on board, the assholes would drag their heels in reporting back.

They had seen the skin whipped off the backs of their officers; surely that should have made them quicker, not slower? Surely, they would have done anything to avoid the same fate?

But no. Instead, they had delayed. And the hours that they cost him had allowed the ship to sail.

That was his first mistake.

The second was in underestimating the Star of the Sea.

He'd known in his gut that she was more than the merchant ship she pretended to be. Otherwise, she would have accepted his guards. Would not have sailed at the first opportunity.

But he had been convinced that the Nephilim would stay out of this. That they would do anything to avoid a war between the church and the state, despite the bluster they'd given Ballanor.

Every action they had taken supported the idea that they were lying low and letting the Hawks try to contact the princess in secret and sneak her back to Eshcol. None of them wanted a civil war.

Which was why he hadn't realized that the *Star* was a Nephilim ship. He had thought that she genuinely was a well-fortified merchant ship, sailing because Mathos and Lucilla had bribed the captain.

He had wanted Mathos and Lucilla back so badly that he had done the one thing he had always despised—let his emotions sway him. He had let his rage fuel his decision to chase them down instead of riding night and day and beating them back to the palace, and then descending on them with all the might of the Blacks and Blues under his command.

He had been utterly focused on killing Mathos, dumping his body in the sea, and taking back his prize. And now they had escaped once more, finally destroying any chance of him becoming consort. Or even returning as Lord High Chancellor.

Damn them both straight to the Abyss.

But they hadn't caught him. And it wasn't over. He still had one more play to make. A play that would solve almost all his problems, at the same time as achieving the one thing he wanted more than anything else in the world; to punish Mathos.

The voices of the men hunting for him faded into the distance. Now, all he had to do was make his way back to the palace and the small storage area he'd built into the back wall of the head gardener's shed.

Chapter Twenty-Three

MATHOS STRODE down the long corridor. His footsteps were muffled by the thick blue carpet, but his heart was thumping loudly in his ears.

Lamps glowed in their sconces, even though wintery light still spilled through wide windows, illuminating the set of stairs that led up to the royal sleeping quarters.

Lucilla would have her rooms up there. She would walk those stairs each night to bed and every morning when she rose. One day, her husband would walk there with her, and their children....

He had thought he could avoid all of this. He'd planned to leave Val to update the queen—he'd reminded him multiple times to warn her about Dornar—while he went straight to the barracks to find himself a quiet room and a bottle of something strong while he waited for the Hawks to be deployed. But a message had been waiting for him at the gates. Tristan had demanded that he report back in person.

His chest ached, the healed wound in his shoulder

cramping and spasming, and he rubbed it slowly, trying to relieve the spreading pain.

That's not your shoulder, you idiot, that's your heart.

Shut up.

He walked past the staircase, following the Nephilim warrior who had met them at the gate down the plush corridor. Past heavy wooden doors inlaid with silver— official chambers, libraries, and studies.

Alanna and Val walked beside him, looking like they wanted to be ill at having to be back in the palace, and he felt much the same. Jeremiel and Garet brought up the rear. All of them vigilant, hands on their weapons, despite how easily they had been whisked through past the guards. Despite how jubilant and celebratory the mood in the city had been.

He wished he could think of something amusing to break the tension, but for the first time in his life, he had nothing.

Nothing except the torturous knowledge that Lucy was ahead of them, now queen in reality, and he would have to look her in the eye and act as if he wasn't slowly disintegrating.

His only hope was to find Tristan, report on the battle with Dornar, and find out the Hawks' plans. Maybe he could request a short absence from the squad and head out early, leave them to mop up in Kaerlud and meet them in a few weeks at Eshcol or wherever they were going next.

I keep trying to tell you that—

He snarled at his beast and it shut up. Thankfully.

Ahead of them, Mathos saw a familiar shape in a doorway and the tension in his shoulders eased slightly. If Tor was guarding the door, Lucy was safe, at least.

He reached out to his friend and then stopped, his hand hanging in midair. "What the fuck are you wearing?"

Tor's usually stoic face broke into a rough grin. "Back in the Blue, brother. Tristan is fucking Supreme Commander. We've got a new council. Half the palace has been tossed out. Queen Lucilla gave a speech, standing on the platform where she'd just hacked down the gallows with a sword. You can hear the people outside celebrating as we speak."

Tor gestured at the door behind him. "They're in there right now, deciding which title to bestow on Val so that he and Princess Alanna can act as Brythorian emissaries to Verturia to save the peace treaty. She's promised no more war."

Beside him, Mathos heard Alanna's soft gasp of relief. Even Val smiled. Jeremiel and Garet congratulated each other with a rough hug, and the Nephilim guard who had been leading them smiled broadly.

She had done so much already. All that grit and determination was now focused on her kingdom, just as he'd known it would be.

He should have been pleased. Excited about the massive progress in such a ridiculously short time. Delighted to be back, restored to the Blues as the Hawks had once dreamed.

It should have been obvious that she would reinstate them, but somehow, he had not imagined it.

I tried to tell you.

Gods. It didn't make any difference now. Now, all he could think of was that there was no swift exit. He couldn't give his report quietly to Tristan and leave. He would be stuck in the palace. A Blue Guard. Watching Lucy from a distance.

For the rest of his fucking miserable existence.

Tor opened the door, and they filed into the sumptuous council room. Ancient tapestries lined one wall while the other displayed a set of gleaming swords, each hilt more heavily bejeweled than the last.

A massive, polished table was littered with the scattered remains of a meal, plates pushed to the middle to make way for papers and pens, open books of heraldry. Maps. His heart turned over. So many maps. He had never given her the map she wanted, and now she had her own.

And standing beside it all, the queen. Everyone was there, but he hardly noticed them. All he saw was Lucy.

She had carelessly pushed up the sleeves of her rich burgundy dress, showing off the twining red-and-black tattoos around her arms. His beast turned over, noticing his colors now joined with hers. Her ebony hair was pulled up into a rough knot behind her head, but a riot of tendrils had escaped, framing her heart-shaped face. Her plump lips were curled up at the sides, and when she looked up, her dark eyes were bright despite the purple smudges beneath them.

She was everything he had never imagined possible. A beautiful, determined, powerful woman. She was magnificent. And she wasn't his.

She looked up, saw him, and smiled, a massive, joyful beam. "Oh, Matt." She stood and started around the table. "I'm so glad you're here. The messenger said you were all safe, but I needed to see you!"

He dipped his chin, keeping a tight rein on the beast snarling and howling inside him. Wishing that his scales hadn't covered his arms and neck, almost up to his eyes.

Fuck. He had said goodbye. He had walked away. But here she was still looking at him like he meant something. Like they meant something.

He had to work to keep his voice smooth, but he managed. "Thank you, Your Majesty."

Lucy stopped, eyes wide as the color slowly leached from her cheeks. She turned to look at Nim, who rose to her feet, some unspoken message passing between them.

Gods. Whatever hell this was, he wanted no part of it. He wanted this over. He wanted to warn them about Dornar and then escape. Far, far away. Somewhere with a barrel of alcohol where he could drown his grief and loss.

He wanted Lucilla to accept that this was over, not make it so much harder. He wanted to lash out at Tristan, who had put him in this awful fucking position in the first place.

He turned to Nim and gave her his most charming smile as he forced out the words, "Afternoon, darlin'."

Out of the corner of his eye, he saw Lucy reach for the back of a chair and grip it tightly.

Nim didn't reply, and nor did anyone else.

Eventually, Lucilla spoke softly. "Thank you, everyone. Please, can we adjourn here. I'd be grateful for a moment with Matt."

They rose silently from their chairs and began filing from the room, faces carefully blank. No one made eye contact with him, not even Nim. Mathos wished that he could leave too, but his feet were rooted to the ground as, one by one, they walked away.

The last person past was Tristan, and Matt put out his hand to stop him. "Talk to Val about Dornar. He escaped."

Tristan grunted, but Mathos knew he would take the threat seriously, and then Tristan was gone too.

Mathos folded his arms over his chest and looked up. The ceiling was decorated with a vibrant painting of swirling white clouds on a blue sky. But it wasn't the real thing. Somehow it didn't give him any of the reassurance he needed.

"What's going on, Matt?" Lucilla asked quietly.

How could he possibly explain? He had thought that she was a spoiled princess, when in reality she was a goddess. And then, when he'd finally understood, he'd had to face just how far below her he really was; he was a mercenary, and she was a queen.

But more than that, he had failed at every relationship he had ever had, while she was already making friends. He had run his father's estates into bankruptcy, and she had started bringing Kaerlud back to life in just one day. He had robbed her of her dreams, and she would hate him for it eventually.

He loved her. And his love would never, ever be enough. She would send him away, and it would kill him. He had tried to say goodbye, but she hadn't listened. Now it was up to him to end this charade.

"I told you that I don't have relationships."

Lucy let go of her death grip on the chair and walked slowly to stand in front of him. Her face was pale as she laid a soft hand on his arm, her dark eyes beseeching. "Matt, you must know how I feel about you. I thought—"

Gods. He couldn't bear to hear it.

He forced himself to sneer as he interrupted. "What? You thought you were different? So did every woman I've ever fucked… darlin'."

He saw the blow land, her eyes widening in shocked pain. Felt it as if he had landed it in his own gut. Gods, what was he doing?

And it was a lie anyway. Of the women he'd spent the night with, not a single one of them had ever wanted more.

He could feel her hand trembling on his sleeve, but she didn't back down. "I believe in you, Matt. I don't think you mean the hurtful things you're saying. I think, maybe, you're trying to push me away to protect yourself. Let's just talk about this—"

Fuck it all. He had expected her to walk away. To already be moving on. But instead, she was fighting for him. And it made it infinitely worse.

He ripped his arm back. He couldn't do this. Not for one more second. He whirled around and flung the door open, stalked through, and let it slam behind him.

"Guard her," he snarled to Tor and the Nephilim warrior flanking the doorway as he strode, almost running, down the long corridor.

"Where is Tristan?" he barked at a young Blue, who flinched and then hesitantly pointed toward the library.

Mathos ripped the door open, leaving it hanging wide as he stormed into the opulent room. His heart was broken, and his beast had gone insane. It thrashed and railed inside him so forcefully that it was all he could do to put one foot in front of the other.

His friend was standing alone in the massive, book-lined room, looking out through the large bay windows toward the grassy lawns that had once led to formal gardens and now led to the lapping edges of the moat. Tristan turned to look at Mathos, his own beast rumbling loudly.

"What the fuck have you done?" Mathos gritted out, trying to stay in some semblance of control.

Tristan took two massive strides forward until he was close enough to reach. Close enough to punch. Close enough for him to hear Tristan growl low and menacingly as he replied, "Be careful, Sergeant."

All the grief, all the confusion, that hideous feeling of being completely out of control, focused itself into fiery hot rage. He clenched his fists, ready for the fight. Ready to take off the head of the man he loved like a brother.

A brother! Can't you hear yourself? That's a fucking relationship.

He shook his head to clear it. He had followed Tristan unhesitatingly into battle a hundred times. He would have followed him anywhere. Except in this.

Tristan was now the man who had committed Mathos to a lifetime of pain, stuck in the palace with Lucy. "How could you do this to me?"

"Do what, Sergeant?" Tristan's face was a mask of cold green scales surrounding eyes that glittered with fury. "Is it that I rode beside Lucilla as she stood up for herself and this kingdom for the first time, taking the place that could —*should*—have been yours?"

Tristan looked him up and down with a sneer. "Are you genuinely refusing your duty as a Hawk, or is it really that you can't bear to face the truth of your own feelings and you think we should all be punished for your behavior along with you?"

Mathos snarled, only vaguely aware that his scales were flickering and sliding in confused turmoil. "How could you move us here without discussing it first? How could you force me to live… here?"

"I don't have to discuss anything with you, Sergeant. I follow my queen's orders, and you follow mine."

"I don't want—"

Tristan cut him off with a mocking laugh. "You don't want—gods, can you hear yourself? Who is spoiled now, Sergeant?"

"No, Commander." A quiet voice spoke behind him. Her voice. Lucy had followed him. Despite everything he'd said, how badly he had hurt her, she had still followed.

Mathos felt as if the world paused. Like that moment before battle, when all you could hear was your own beating heart and the knowledge, deep in your soul, that you might not last the next ten minutes.

He turned to look at her, her full robes rippling around her in a waterfall of dark red velvet shot through with golden thread. The knot in her hair had come loose, and thick waves fell around her pale face. She had never looked so regal, or so vulnerable.

Her voice was quiet but clear as she turned those deep, dark eyes onto Tristan. "I would like to hear this."

And then she looked at him. "What is it, exactly, Sergeant, that you don't want?"

Not Matt. Not even Mathos. No, he was merely "Sergeant" once more. His beast roiled in his belly as his scales flickered in slow waves up his arms and over his shoulders.

There's still time to fix this. Fall to your knees and apologize. Tell her that none of what you've just said was true. Tell her that you love her.

No. He was not made for this. The pain was already unbearable. He didn't want it.

You do want it, you stupid asshole. It's worth it for her.

He didn't. He wouldn't.

He was not ever taking that risk again. He would never be sent away again. This time, he was going to walk out before it got worse.

"I don't want to stay here." He swallowed, looked her in the eye, and forced himself to say it. "I don't want to stay with you."

She didn't say anything for long moments. The room

was so quiet that he heard the shudder in her breath as she inhaled and then slowly exhaled.

She reached out and took his hand, and for one agonizing moment, he thought she would refuse his stupid, hurtful words once more. But she didn't.

She lifted his hand, palm up, and opened her other hand above it. Hard, cold metal filled his palm. A ring, a sapphire, a few pearls, small gold coins.

She gently closed his fingers over the small treasure. Her escape plan. Fuck.

Then she took a small step back. She took another step back as her face settled into a polite, emotionless mask—the one she'd worn when they first met. All princess. Queen, now.

He remembered believing that disdainful look. Believing that she was a spoilt, coddled prima donna. But he knew better now. He knew that it was her protection—the only one she had had for so many years—but even that was failing her. A slow tear tracked down her face. She ignored it. Or maybe she hadn't noticed.

In all the time they'd spent together, she had never, ever cried. Until now.

She tipped her chin up and waved her hand. "You're released from service, Sergeant. Commander Tristan can see to your discharge. Go with the gods."

And then she turned and walked away.

To anyone else, it might have seemed the regal walk of a queen, but he knew the truth. There was nothing regal in those slow, considered movements. They were the aching steps of someone who was pouring every molecule of concentration into putting one foot in front of the other and not falling to the ground.

You did that.

His hands throbbed, his fists were clenched so tightly, and he slowly forced them open. They hurt like hell.

He looked down to see blood streaking his palms. What? He turned his hands over in shock. He had claws. Long, sharp fucking claws.

"Are you happy now?" The voice was Tristan's, but it sounded just like his beast.

Chapter Twenty-Four

DORNAR TIED the reins of the horse he'd stolen to the broken wood of the gallows platform, pulling the stinking woolen cloak more closely over his head.

Fucking gods-forsaken farms. The thick, shambling mare and the onion-reeking woolen cloak scratching his skin and no doubt rife with lice were exactly what he had left behind.

Around him there was a curious sense of celebration, Queen Lucilla's name on everyone's lips. Most with skepticism and rough humor, but more than a few with the beginnings of hope.

They didn't trust her, not yet, but they liked her. And they trusted the Supreme Justice standing behind her. Exactly where Dornar should have been.

He sidled up to a barrel fire and warmed his hands, listening to the flow of speculation around him. A rumor was spreading that she had dismissed her entire council and was, even now, clearing out the Blues.

If he wasn't so fucking angry, he would have been

impressed. He honestly hadn't thought she had it in her.

He slowed his breathing and calmed himself. It was too late to try to control her now; she was out of his grasp. What he needed was wealth, a lot of it, and small enough to carry. The kind of wealth that she would be able to access in the treasury.

And then he would find Mathos. Spend some time explaining exactly how he felt about their ongoing acquaintance. Starting with his other shoulder. And finishing with sharing the details of what he'd done with Lucilla. He'd seen how Mathos looked at her, killing her would hurt him. A lot.

Dornar slipped away from the fire and through the crowds toward the rough wall leading up to Court Gate. It was heavily guarded, with both cavalry Black Guards and Nephilim, each watching the other with suspicion. No entry there.

He walked slowly down the long wall until he found a deeper indentation in the stone. Above him he could hear the guards calling to each other, whistling out their positions. There seemed more of them than when he had created their schedule, but there were still breaks in their perimeter. Moments when the stretch of wall above him was empty. He silently removed his cloak, dropping it into the darkness.

Boots clumped past on the new fortifications, and then a second set close behind. As soon as they passed, he levered himself up the stone, hauling and pulling, digging his fingers into the tiny cracks between the stones as he quickly scaled the wall and heaved himself over the crenelations onto the narrow walkway. Without pausing, he slipped across and over the other side, hanging for just a moment and then letting go, to drop into the deep black water.

The water closed over his head in a freezing, burning wave, and he kicked upward. It took everything he had not to gasp as he breached the surface and turned to cling to the slimy rocks of the outer wall.

"What was that?"

"What?" Deep voices convened along the walkway.

"Something splashed."

"Here, pass me the torch."

Light flickered along the inky water, playing over the rocks and even the sides of the wall. Dornar froze, gripping the base of the wall, almost entirely submerged.

If he'd been king, the water would have been filled with something flesh-eating and truly nasty, but Ballanor was too much of an idiot to think of something so strategic, and he simply hadn't had the time to correct his former king's stupidity. It was probably a good thing, given his current position.

His beast rumbled at the cold, irritated and impatient. They'd never seen eye to eye, but they could work together, powerful primal abilities and cold, sharp intellect combining for their greater good.

"Give it a few minutes," a soldier commanded. "If there's something there, it'll move."

Long moments passed as the cold slowly seeped all the way into his bones.

"There's nothing there. Maybe it was a fish."

"Maybe...." The first voice sounded uncertain.

Another minute passed.

"Okay, back to patrol."

Boots thudded. Someone whistled out confirmation of their position. The soldiers settled back into their routine.

Dornar took a long breath and then dipped into the frigid water and started to swim.

Chapter Twenty-Five

MATHOS FOUND himself out of the palace and stumbling down the streets of Kaerlud, his discharge papers in his pocket, before he could properly grasp what had happened.

It had been so fast, like an explosion had gone off in his life. His head was ringing, his body was broken, and he had absolutely no idea of where to go or what he was going to do.

Even his beast had stopped commenting. Or moving.

They had been so closely entwined for his entire life that he had never imagined what it would be like to be so alone. The only remnants of their bond were the scales covering his arms and neck and the vicious claws piercing his fingers. Claws that would not retract.

He'd finally broken. And he'd smashed up everything around him on the way.

He stood in a small side street and looked up to the sky. It was entirely dark, misty clouds obscuring the stars, and it held no answers.

He had left the Hawks. Left his brothers and his friends. Left her. There were no answers.

His feet took him through the city, past the closing storefronts and the small homes stacked one on top of the other. Yellow light spilled through shutters as lamps were lit. Well-fed children skipped their last hopscotch before shouting their goodbyes and running home. Poorer ones gathered up their wares and trudged away.

He rubbed at his shoulder, trying to relieve the throbbing ache, but nothing helped.

Somehow, he found himself standing outside The Cup, the inn they'd stayed in when they came to rescue Val. Hard to believe that so little time had passed, just a few short months. He had been with his brothers, delighted to tease Tristan as he lost his mind over a woman. Gods. A shaft of pain radiated down from his shoulder across his chest.

Now it was almost winter; dry leaves rattled along the edges of the street as a cold wind pierced through his jacket.

Maybe it wasn't surprising that he had found himself back somewhere familiar when he needed to pause and lick his wounds.

He pushed through the door to the familiar shining tables and clean floor, nodding to the innkeeper as he looked over from behind the bar.

The rich smell of beef stew filled the air as Mathos found himself a table against the wall. A few locals sat enjoying the food, and in the darkest corner, a man in a heavy cloak lay slumped over the table.

The innkeeper arrived a few moments later. Apparently, he hadn't yet lost the habit of wringing his hands through his apron.

Mathos opened his coin pouch, struggling with the bloody claws, and then froze. He had forgotten that he'd stored her jewels in it. Fuck. He pushed them out the way and pulled out enough groats to pay for his dinner. "I'll have the stew and bread, with a tankard of ale, please."

The innkeeper's brows drew together, and he tipped his head to the side. "You're here for food?"

Mathos looked around him. Plenty of people were eating. "Ah… yes. Please."

"Oh. Okay."

The innkeeper turned to go, but Mathos called him back. "What did you think I was here for?"

He held out a wiry thumb and gestured back over his shoulder to the man now snoring in the corner. "Thought you were here for him."

"Why in the kingdom would I be here for him?" Mathos asked.

The innkeeper shrugged. "Thought you were a friend. Not a problem either way. I'll get you that stew."

Mathos sat back in his chair, determined not to get involved. A minute dragged by, and then another, his mind filled with Lucy. Lucy smiling. Lucy gripping the back of the chair. Lucy turning away, that one tear tracking down her cheek.

His beast said nothing at all, and the silence pressed heavily down on him, suffocating him.

Fuck, he had to do something, anything, to make some noise.

He pushed his chair back and strode to the corner, wondering how the hell he got into these situations.

Before he even got there, he knew. He hadn't seen it from further away, that ring of tarnished indigo scales, but now he was closer, he couldn't miss it. And he knew exactly who it was.

He bent down, right to the man's ear, and then shouted in his best parade voice, "Attention! To the front… Salute!"

Reece was out of his chair, his right-hand forefinger almost to his eye, when he fully woke up and realized where he was. He stumbled back, and Mathos put a hand out to stabilize him, but Reece pulled his arm back with a vicious snarl. "What the fuck, Mathos?"

Mathos snorted grimly. "Expecting someone else?"

Reece looked him up and down and then glared at the smirking men around them before sinking back into his seat. "Why are you here?"

"Same as you."

"What?" Reece's voice dripped with sarcasm. "You fucked the wrong woman, she turned out to be a vicious harpy, you single-handedly almost caused the death of everyone in your squad and, just to round it off, insulted the Princess of Verturia?"

"No." Mathos sank into the chair next to him. "Far worse than that. Nothing you did was your fault. I've told you that about a hundred times. Well, except for insulting Alanna, and she forgave you for that."

He lifted his hand to rub his eyes and then dropped it again when he remembered his claws. "I, however…." Gods. Where to even start.

Reece raised skeptical eyebrows over his puffy, reddened eyes. "Oh please. Mr. Charm himself. What did you do? Flirt with Nim? Kiss Keely in front of Tor? Or did Tristan get sick of your never-ending disregard for his orders?"

He could tell a joke, say something amusing, and Reece would drop it. But what was the point?

"I was supposed to keep the queen safe, but instead I got her caught by Dornar. I eventually helped her escape and took her into the woods, where I seduced her. Then I told her to be the queen when I knew it was the last thing she wanted. When we got back, I—" His voice cracked. "I broke her heart, blamed Tristan, and was discharged from the Blues."

"Fuck," Reece whispered, wiping the back of his hand over his blurry eyes.

"Yes. Fuck."

The innkeeper bustled over with the stew and ale. Mathos fished out another coin, studiously ignoring the other contents of his pouch. And his claws. "And a meal for my friend, please. No ale."

"Fuck you," Reece snarled, and then closed his mouth when he saw the claws. But he took the stew when it was delivered. The two of them sat side by side in silence as they ate, each alone with his thoughts.

Mathos pushed his empty bowl away. "Why are you here?"

"Nowhere else to go. Kaerlud still feels more like home than anywhere else. And then this was the last place…."

"Yeah." Mathos knew exactly what he meant.

"What are you going to do now?" Reece asked.

"Don't know." Mathos shrugged. "I guess I'll have to find a job." The very thought made him want to vomit. What did he know, other than how to fail spectacularly at estate management and being a soldier?

"You could go back home. At least you have one."

Mathos hid a wince. Reece had grown up with nothing, in the worst parts of Kaerlud, while his father was at sea and his mother sold flowers and mended clothes, desperate to keep them fed. His father had never come back, and when his mother had died, he had lived on the streets until he was old enough to join the army.

What had happened to Mathos was nothing like that.

But his former life was long gone, nonetheless. "I can't go back."

"Why not? Aren't you some la-di-da noble with a title and everything?"

Technically, he was a baron. But it had never meant shit. Hadn't saved him when the time came.

"They told me to leave, Reece. My mother kicked me out while my sisters looked away."

"Yeah, yeah. Poor little rich boy." Reece rolled his red eyes. "And you just walked away and never went back. So, who do you think really left who?"

His gut turned over, half with rage at Reece and just how little he understood, half with a sudden horror.

His mother had sent him away. His sisters had watched him go. It had never even occurred to him that they might expect him to go back.

Reece leaned back in his chair, his hands laced behind his head. "I'm so sick of this story. If you wanted to go and see them, you could've. You had a home and a family, Mathos. People who loved you."

Reece narrowed his eyes and glared. "So, they handed you a debt-ridden estate, and then, when it inevitably failed, they chose to accept the protection of a man who cared for them. Someone who promised to keep them safe and fed. Whose only crime was that he didn't want an arrogant little shit with a complete inability to handle authority fucking with his household. What would you rather they did? Walk barefoot to Kaerlud and live together in one room, sharing a bed while they sold flowers for pennies? Or, when that failed, sell their bodies down on the docks? Gods, you're an asshole."

Mathos sat, stunned, unable to think of any kind of reply.

He was the one who had never gone back. And he had been running ever since. Yes, they'd treated him badly. His stepfather was an asshole, and his mother should have done much more to help him. But she had also been in a spectacularly difficult position. And if he was being completely honest, she probably hadn't expected him to pack his bags and leave within hours of her decision.

For the first time, he looked past his own hurt, and recognized that her choice had had very little to do with him, and yet he had allowed it to influence his behavior for years.

And now he had destroyed what he'd had with Lucy. And with it, any chance of happiness he might have had.

For what? For nothing.

Even worse than that, all this time, he'd been certain she would hate him for convincing her to take the throne instead of stepping up and helping her. He could have stayed and made sure she had the adventures she wanted. Instead, he'd left her all alone. Just like all the other assholes in her life.

"You're right." His voice caught on the dry lump in his throat.

Gods. What had he done?

Reece's shoulders slumped exhaustedly, as if he'd used the last of whatever spirit he'd had to berate Mathos and now he was done.

"You could go back, you know, Reece," Mathos said in a rough voice. "The Hawks will take you."

"Nah. No one in their right mind wants me back."

Mathos leaned forward. "They do. Everybody misses you, Reece." He looked his friend in the eye. "And Queen Lucilla, she has an incredible heart. She would give you a place in the Blues; I'm sure of it."

"And if you're so sure of that, why don't you go back?"

Mathos froze. He had lost years with his family because of his stubbornness. Did he have to lose more years? Was there any possible way Lucilla could forgive him for what he'd done?

He sat quietly, waiting for a comment. A thought. Anything, from his beast.

Still nothing. Just the glaring, empty quiet. For the first time in his life, he had to make a decision alone.

He didn't deserve forgiveness. Maybe she would never trust him again, never want him near her again. But he could still try. He could still tell her the truth. Tell her that he loved her, that he would always love her. He would know that he had done everything he could. That he hadn't walked away because of his own failures.

He would beg Tristan, on his knees if he had to, to take him back. And if he had to stand guard and watch her make a life without him, watch her take a husband up those stairs and love children that weren't his, that would be his punishment.

He would take it. So long as she was happy.

He would stand guard as she fulfilled her destiny and be grateful for every day that he could watch over her and keep her safe.

Chapter Twenty-Six

LUCILLA SAT on the floor on a pile of soft cushions, leaning back against the post of her sumptuous, canopied bed as gold-and-orange firelight flickered around her.

She was finally, blissfully clean, and wearing a delicate cotton shift that was infinitely more comfortable than the poorly fitted dress she'd worn all day. She had pulled the bright comforters to the floor along with an array of cushions to make a soft place to sit while she stared out of the window at the moon and tried to make some kind of sense of her life.

The part that she couldn't quite get her head around was the three other women sitting on the floor with her.

Nim had been the first to arrive, carrying a flask of what she promised was the best honey liqueur from the kitchens. Tristan had arrived with her and quietly sent Jos and Garet away to take a break, promising to guard them himself just as Alanna and Keely turned down the corridor, Val behind them.

All of them were wearing their shifts, covered with blankets. And their boots. The boots had made her giggle as they poured into her room and closed the door, leaving Val and Tristan standing watch outside.

But then the giggles turned to sobs. And she didn't know what to do. She had spent her life perfecting her ability to show no emotion whatsoever, and somehow over the last weeks, she had lost that control.

Strangely, no one had seemed shocked. Nim had wrapped her in the warmest hug she might have ever had, other than from Mathos—who she was not going to think about—and then passed her a handkerchief as she led her back to the cushions on the floor.

Alanna had pulled a set of small wooden cups from her pocket, and Nim quickly filled them with the syrupy liquor before handing one to each of them.

"Ladies, we need a toast," Alanna said, completely ignoring Lucilla's puffy face and red nose.

"To new friends," Nim said immediately, but Keely rolled her eyes and replied, "To kicking ass."

"To ass-kicking new friends," Lucilla agreed as the women tossed their cups back. Gods. She'd never imagined it. These incredible, strong women supporting each other. Supporting her.

She loved the fiery burn sliding down her throat and the way her eyes were watering. If nothing else, it hid the tears.

Keely, however, spluttered and spat hers back in the cup. "Oh gods, what have you given me? It's off."

Alanna poured herself another cupful and sniffed it delicately. "Mine smells fine. Do you want a clean cup?"

Keely wrinkled her nose in disgust. "Bard, no. You drink it. I think my stomach is still unsettled from that bastard ship. I swear, nothing you say or do could ever get me back onto the sea again."

"Not even if Tor was on board, flexing his manly arms?" Alanna asked, fluttering her eyelashes as she poured another drink for Nim and Lucilla.

"Especially not then," Keely replied with a grimace.

The other women laughed, and they all settled back onto their cushions.

Lucilla took a slow sip of her drink, trying to decide whether she was allowed to ask. She raised her eyes to see them all watching her and quickly looked back down.

"You can ask," Keely said quietly.

"I wondered what happened between you. I heard Matt tell Tor that he should apologize to you, although at the time Tor was being so kind, I couldn't imagine what he might have done." She paused and took another sip. "Now, I guess, I realize that even someone you think would never…. Well, I guess anyone can do hurtful things."

Damn, she hated how rough her voice got as she spoke and how close she was to crying again.

"By the Bard." Alanna put her drink down. "He really fucked up, didn't he?"

"Yes," Keely and Lucilla both said at the same time, and they all chuckled softly.

"It's not the same," Keely said. "I didn't fall for Tor." But she kept her eyes down as she said it, her fingers twisting and untwisting the tassels on the cushion she was sitting on. And, somehow, Lucilla knew she was lying.

"Well, I did fall for Mathos," Lucilla admitted, "and I fought for him. I really did. But he threw it all back in my face."

"I'm so sorry," Nim murmured.

Lucilla gave a sharp shake of her head. "No, your advice was good. I'm glad I fought for him. I'm glad I told him how I feel. For the rest of my life, I'll know that I did everything I could. Honestly, I think it's better for me to know the truth now."

For the first time that day, something settled in her heart. Yes, it was smashed into a thousand tiny pieces. Yes, her dream of having Matt at her side was gone. But she had these amazing new friends. And even if they left, she knew she could do this. She could be the queen her kingdom needed.

Matt had given her the shove she needed to leap out of the nest, and now she would fly without him.

She would be the best ruler she could be. She would do what she could to make the kingdom whole again. And maybe, one day, the broken pieces inside her would start to heal. One day she would forget how much she'd loved a man who didn't care for her at all.

She settled back quietly into her cushions, suddenly exhausted, as Nim and Alanna bickered good-naturedly over the best way to introduce more women into the Blues. It was strangely soothing to sit quietly, listening to them chatting, without anyone expecting her to say or do anything. She didn't have to hide or pretend; they accepted her as she was.

Keely was also quiet, and looked just about ready to drop too, her pretty green eyes closing in her wan face. Whatever she might say, her fight with Tor was hurting her as much as it was hurting him.

Eventually, the cups were empty, the moon long past the window, and the fire burning low. Nim and Alanna gathered Keely up, and they all said their goodnights and made plans to meet early the next morning as Tristan and Val made way for Jos and Garet outside her door.

Lucilla cleaned her teeth and then sank gratefully into her soft mattress. She'd chosen a wing of empty rooms on the far side of the palace and the suites had been aired and cleaned and quickly filled with cushions and bedding. None of them had wanted to use Alanna or Ballanor's old rooms, and this way Nim, Alanna and Keely could all stay on the same corridor with her.

Until the Blues had been thoroughly vetted and retrained, only the Hawks would be guarding this wing, and both Tristan and Val would be sleeping on this corridor anyway. Tristan had doubled the external guard after hearing Dornar had escaped, mixing Nephilim into all the patrols. She was safe. Yet somehow, she couldn't make herself feel it.

She stretched her arm out across the empty space next to her in the bed, remembering the cramped, dirty shelters that she'd slept in with Matt and how much happier she'd been then, compared to lying all alone on the clean, soft sheets of her lonely new bed.

She didn't want to remember the last words he'd spoken to her. The closed-down look on his face.

He was gone forever, so why not choose her favorite memory? She brought to mind his burgundy scales, the way his arm had lain, so big and hard, over her pale skin as they curled together in their forest shelters, and drifted off to sleep remembering how he'd told her she was beautiful, brave, and smart. How he'd made her believe that it was true.

She came awake an hour or two later, with the fire burnt low and her room dark. She yawned, trying to orient herself. Trying to understand the deep, muffled voices arguing outside her door.

"No. Absolutely not." Was that Garet's voice? He was always so reserved and quiet that to hear him sounding so furious made her sit up in her bed and listen.

"Please, Garet, I have to speak to her. I...." Whatever else he said was too low to hear. But she knew that voice. She would know it anywhere. Even if she'd never expected to hear it again.

A door opened and then slammed shut, ending the murmured rumble of discussion.

"What the fuck is this?" Tristan's irritable growl was unmistakable.

She slipped out of the bed and crept over to the door, pressing her ear against the wood to hear better.

"I need to speak to Lucy... to Queen Lucilla. Please."

"Do you know what fucking time it is? How did you even get in here?"

"I let him in." That was almost certainly Tor.

"Come on, Tristan, I need—"

"Need. Want. I'm fucking sick of this. What you need, Mathos, is to leave."

Mathos's voice rose. "Oh, like how we made you leave after you hurt Nim—"

"Don't you dare compare your behavior with mine—"

There was a grunt and a scuffle and then Nim's clear voice. "What the hell is wrong with you people?"

There was a heavy silence and then a rush of whisper-shouting, which Nim spoke over. "The only person who can decide if she wants to see him is Lucilla. And since you're guaranteed to have woken her, you might as well knock on the bloody door."

Lucilla wanted to climb back in her bed and pull the

cover over her head and go back to pretending that they had never left the woods. But she was the queen now, hiding was no longer an option.

She swung the door open to step into the corridor, blinking in the lamplight after the darkness of her room. Gods, everyone was there. Val, Alanna, the Hawks.

They all turned to look at her and she was suddenly acutely aware of the delicacy of her shift clinging to her body, her wild hair falling loose down her back.

"Take this, Your Majesty, before you get cold." Jos passed her the dark blue cape he had been wearing over his formal tunic, and she took it gratefully.

She breathed in and out again slowly, hoping that her voice would be steady when she spoke. Then she lifted her eyes and looked directly at him. "What do you want, Sergeant Mathos?"

"Not a sergeant anymore," Tristan rumbled grumpily.

"Right. All of you"—Nim glared at Tristan and the others—"go back to bed. Jos, Garet, spread out and give them some privacy."

Slowly the corridor emptied and the doors around them closed. Jos and Garet moved to opposite ends of the corridor and studiously looked away.

She spent the time watching Matt. His dark blond hair was sticking to his head in places, standing in unruly tufts in others, as if he'd repeatedly run his fingers through it. His hazel eyes were almost entirely overrun by a thick band of gold, with dark smudges beneath them, and his scales were heavy and unmoving. His face was grim and his jaw so tightly clenched she could see the muscle jumping. He looked terrible. Even worse than when Dornar had stabbed him and they were on the run.

He put out his hand as if to touch her, but she stepped back, out of his reach, and he let his hand fall.

"Please can I come in and talk to you?" he asked in a low voice.

She shivered despite the cape and wrapped her arms around herself. He'd made the break he wanted, and she didn't have the strength to go through that again. "I don't think that's a good idea. If you have something to say that was so urgent that it couldn't wait, you can say it here."

Mathos dragged his hand down his face exhaustedly and then folded his arms protectively over his chest. "I'm so sorry, Lucy. I made a terrible, awful mistake."

What was she supposed to say to that? That he had almost destroyed her? That she didn't think she would ever fully recover? That she had told him he was making a mistake while he was busy doing it?

"Yes, you did," she agreed softly.

"I know that I fucked everything up," he continued, speaking slowly, as if he was choosing his words carefully. "I know that I hurt you and I'm sorry. More sorry than I can begin to explain. Please will you consider forgiving me?"

Her eyes burned with the prickle of more tears, but she held them back, determined to finish this hellish conversation and escape. "And if I forgive you, what then?"

His voice was low with conviction as he replied, "Please give me another chance. I don't know exactly what's between us, where we're going, but... I know that I want to be with you. Any way that you'll have me."

Gods. She would have given a limb to hear those words just a few hours ago. But now? Now, she couldn't trust them. What would happen when he changed his mind again? What would he do when he suddenly realized he could get hurt and decided to hurt her first? She didn't know if she could bear it.

He had pushed her out of the nest, and it no longer felt safe to fly back.

She tightened her hands into fists, striving for control. "But you do know what's between us, Matt. It's just the same as what you felt for all the other women you've fucked —all those other women who also thought that they were different."

He closed his eyes against her words, leaning back against the wall as if he needed the support as he replied, "That was a stupid, terrible thing to say." He opened his eyes and looked at her, his irises completely gold. "And it wasn't true."

She sighed and scraped at her eyes with the back of her hands. "That's exactly my point. How am I supposed to know what's true and what isn't?"

"That was the only time I've ever lied to you. I wanted to get away, I was… overwhelmed. But I'm back now. I'll never lie to you again. Not ever."

"Gods, Matt. Can you hear yourself? Were you so desperate to get away from me?"

And then it hit her—the true depth of what he'd done —and the words spilled out of her. "Damn. I was so hurt, so… it never dawned on me until now… you were so frantic to get away from me that you were prepared to sacrifice not only your career, but the Hawks, your brothers, everything."

"No." He shook his head roughly. "It wasn't like that. It nearly broke me to walk away. I think it did break me."

He held up his hands, and for the first time, she saw the lethal curved claws and the streaks of dried blood from where they'd broken through the skin.

The tears came then. Hot and out of control, burning her throat as the final broken shards of her heart shattered.

"That's even worse, Matt." She gestured toward his hands, tasting salt. "You were prepared to do that to yourself rather than be with me."

She was done. She hadn't realized that she could hurt any more, but she could. He had opened a bottomless pit of pain inside her.

She let her tears fall freely down her face as she stepped back into her room and closed her door.

She could hear him calling her name, but she ignored him as she collapsed back against the wood, her whole body shaking with grief. But also anger.

He had hurt her more deeply than anyone ever before him. But he'd also broken her out of the prison she'd been holding herself in. For the first time, she saw that he had walked away because of his demons, not because she wasn't worthy.

Cerdic, Ballanor, even her father, they had all abandoned her because of their own failings, not hers.

She had survived them all. And she would survive this.

The door thudded heavily behind her, as if he had fallen against it, mirroring her on the other side.

His voice cracked as he spoke through the barrier between them. "I'm not giving up. I'm not leaving you. You can put me to washing dishes, and I will. You can have me cleaning latrines in the Constables Tower, and I'll do it. If I have to stand back and watch you make a life with someone else…." He paused for a long moment. "I'll do that too. I'll still stay, as close as you'll allow, for as long as you'll allow it."

She brought up her knees, wrapping her arms around them, and let her head fall back, listening to the soft words, wishing that she could escape them but unable to tear herself away as the hot flare of rage slowly ebbed.

Perhaps he heard the soft scrape across the wood. Perhaps he would have kept talking no matter what she did. "I realized something important tonight, Lucy. Well, two things. The first is that I've been running away my whole life, and it's time to stop. And the other—"

He cleared his throat, and she found herself sliding down to press her ear against the crack where the door met the frame, even as she wiped fresh tears away with the back of her hand.

"The other is that I love you."

She couldn't help her quiet sob. Or the way her fingers crept to the door that separated them.

"Please don't cry, Lucy. Gods, I can't bear it." His voice was almost too rough to hear. "This is the hardest thing I've ever done, and listening to you cry is killing me."

She swallowed the next sob, trying to be silent.

"I know that you're right about everything, and I know I don't deserve it, but I'm asking you to forgive me for the awful things I've done. Please."

She sat quietly, frozen.

"Please, Lucy."

She stood slowly and faced the door.

He had left. And he had broken her heart. But he had also come back.

In all her life, he was the only person who had ever come back for her. But so much more than that, he was the only person who saw her exactly as she was and loved her for it. And she could see him exactly as he was. Loyal, honorable, dedicated. Hurt, and lost.

The man who had brought sunshine to her world and who desperately needed to feel the warmth on his own face.

She had known that he was lying when he had pushed her away. Just as she knew he was telling the truth when he said he loved her.

Could she forgive him? Or was she better off letting him go? Both options could end with her hurt. But only one had a chance of saving them both.

She opened the door.

Chapter Twenty-Seven

THE DOOR suddenly opened behind him, and he almost fell backward.

Gods. She had opened it. He hadn't thought she would. But he had heard her lean against the door—had hoped, desperately, that she could hear him—and he would have stayed there all night. Would have offered up his soul on a plate if she would keep listening. And now she'd opened the door.

He rolled onto his knees and looked up at her where she stood in front of him, still wrapped in Jos's cape. Her nose was red, eyes swollen and puffy, and her skin blotched. She was the most beautiful woman he'd ever seen.

He pushed himself to his feet and opened his arms, and, like a miracle, she walked into them. She wrapped her arms around his waist and rested her head against his chest, so soft and warm and vulnerable. With the biggest heart in the world.

He clung to her, his nose buried in her silky hair, telling himself that she was real, that he hadn't dreamed it and wouldn't soon awaken back in the hell he'd nearly sent himself into. Sent them both into. She turned her face upward, into his neck, and then he heard it. The low, contented rumble. His beast was back.

He pressed soft kisses onto the top of her head, feeling a depth of emotion that he hadn't known was possible. Relief and joy and grief for all the hurt he'd caused. But mostly love.

She leaned back and lifted her hands to wipe his cheeks, and he realized he had been crying too.

"Can I come inside?" he asked cautiously.

She gave him a wobbly smile and stepped back to let him in, closing the door gently behind him.

She took his hand and led him to the rumpled bed and then sat on the side, waiting while he pulled off his boots and dirty coat as well as his cotton shirt. But he settled for merely undoing the top button of his breeches. This moment was for holding her. Proving to her that she could trust him.

He crawled onto the bed and pulled her into his arms, her back against his chest, her knees spooned inside his, as they had that first day against the tree. She curled trustingly against him and closed her eyes as his beast rumbled softly, accepting the enormity of the gift that she was giving him.

With an aching slide, he felt his claws retract, and the sudden loss of pain spread like warmth through his body.

Lucy must have been exhausted, because she slipped almost instantly into a deep sleep as Mathos lay awake, stunned by her forgiveness, every sense filled with her.

He had no idea how they were going to make their relationship work. He was a mercenary—not even that anymore—and she was the queen. But he had promised that he would never leave again, and no matter what, he would never leave again.

You're not a mercenary, you ass. You're a baron—there's a fucking royal writ somewhere.

The idea filtered through him. For so many years he had rejected his childhood, to the point that it had never occurred to him to take back his heritage. But now it felt right. More than right. It gave him political standing and authority, a valid reason to stay at court and contribute. He would be able to support Lucy with more than just his protection.

He wanted to wake her to tell her, but she was fast asleep.

Instead, he closed his eyes and drifted, letting himself relax for the first time in days.

He woke before dawn, his stomach complaining loudly. No doubt Lucy was almost as hungry. He kissed her gently on the cheek and over her eyes until she stirred.

"Matt?" Her voice was thick with sleep.

"I'm going to get us some food."

"'kay." She rolled her face down into the pillow.

"I didn't want you to wake up and wonder where I was."

"'nks," she muttered from the depths of the pillow.

He kissed her again and then climbed out of the bed to pull his shirt and boots on. The fire was almost out, and he had to shuffle around the shadowy room, trying to find everything in the dim light without disturbing her.

Mathos pulled the door open as quietly as he could and slipped through it, straight into Jos and Garet, both wide awake and glaring, Jos's cheek still purple with the results of their shipboard scuffle.

He clicked the door gently closed behind him. It was on

the tip of his tongue to make a joke and hope they laughed. But he owed them more than that.

"I'm sorry for the things I did. And I'm sorry that I walked away from the Hawks."

Both men crossed their arms, their eyes narrowed. Neither of them replied. He expected that from Garet, the most taciturn and considered of all of them. But not from Jos, whose childhood with a collection of exuberant and slightly wild younger sisters had molded him into the Hawks' permanent big brother. Slow to anger, quick to defend.

And that was the problem, wasn't it? He let his arms drop to his sides. "You heard everything?"

"The things you said to Queen Lucilla. About all the other women. About how you lied to her and then left her. Yes, we did. And you're fucking lucky that she forgave you, because I don't think I would have," Jos snarled, his wings drawn back, battle-ready.

"I am fucking lucky," he agreed. "I don't deserve her, but I have promised to never leave again, and I meant it. I love her."

He'd thought it would be hard to say, but it wasn't. Now that it came to it, it was the easiest thing in the world.

The two men, his brothers, stared at him in silence. A long, slow judgment. And then Jos clapped him on his back, and Garet dipped his chin. Thank the gods.

"I'm going to the kitchens to get some food… but I'm guessing you don't need anything, since you're on duty and all?" Mathos grinned.

Yes, Lucilla would like pastries, with berries, she loves berries. And cream… lots of cream.

His grin widened. Damn, that was a good idea.

"Asshole," Jos muttered, and Mathos threw a mocking salute as he walked down the thick carpet of the corridor.

He was already on the stairs when his beast went insane, thrashing and howling in an inconsolable frenzy. He didn't hesitate; he spun back and started to run, already shouting, "Get in there! Now! Now!"

Jos reacted instantly, ripping the door open in time for Mathos to sprint through it and then slide to a scrambling halt as his brain tried to understand the horror of what he was seeing.

The bed was empty, sheets rumpled and pulled roughly to one side. On the far side of the room, the window was open. And, most horrifying of all, Dornar was straddling the casement.

In one hand, he was holding a vicious blade, the other, half-concealed outside the window, seemed to be wrapped in dark rope as he prepared to lever himself the rest of the way outside.

"Don't move," Garet called from the doorway, "or we'll shoot."

Dornar looked past Mathos to the men behind him and then lifted his head and laughed. It was a dark, malicious sound. Humor with no joy. "I don't think you're going to do anything of the sort. Not if you want your precious queen to survive."

"What have you done with her?" Mathos asked, a vicious snarl threading through his voice.

"She's right here. Aren't you, Your Majesty?"

"Matt?" Her frightened voice trembled through the open window.

"Come back up," Dornar commanded, lifting his outer hand, and for the first time, Mathos saw that it wasn't rope, but her dark hair wrapped tightly around Dornar's fist.

Her pale, terrified face appeared in the opening.

Dornar grinned. "I would put those crossbows away if I were you. This ladder has been sitting in the head gardener's shed for months, so who knows how stable it is. If you shoot me and I fall, well—"

He didn't need to finish. It was abundantly clear what would happen to Lucilla.

His beast churned and roared helplessly as Mathos took a step forward. "How the fuck did you find us?"

Dornar shrugged, his lips twisting up in a smug sneer. "It's actually surprisingly easy to find out where the queen's rooms are. All you have to do is stroll into the servants' quarters looking like you belong, and someone will tell you —they had to make the beds, after all—and no one seems to have remembered to let them know that I'm no longer Lord High Chancellor. The tricky bit was getting the ladder through the gardens unseen, but then I do have the advantage of having approved the guard rotation. Someone added extra patrols, but they didn't change the routes." He chuckled darkly. "Other priorities, I guess."

He focused his glare on Mathos. "I've got to admit though, I didn't expect you'd be in here too. Nearly fucked up my plans. Again."

Mathos took another step forward, Jos at his shoulder. His face was stiff with scales, his body armored from his long claws to his eyes, more beast than he had ever been before.

Dornar snarled. "Stop, or I'll drop her."

Mathos hesitated. "You can't drop her. If you do, Garet will shoot—and he never misses."

"Maybe I don't care. Maybe the look on your face would be worth it."

Mathos stopped. With Dornar, it was impossible to tell. "What do you want?"

"I want what I've earned," Dornar snarled. "Lucilla is going to take me to the vault and compensate me for all my… time."

Fuck. There was no way Dornar would release Lucy afterward. To escape, he would have to take her with him as a hostage. Was there even any chance she would survive his captivity? Almost certainly not. Without a chance at the crown, Lucy had nothing to offer him, and more than that, now he knew what killing Lucilla would do to Mathos, and he would do it just for that.

Mathos took another threatening step forward, letting his scales ripple menacingly, hoping to distract Dornar from Jos working his way forward beside him. "It'll never work. You've fucked up again, Dornar. Actually, now that I think of it, you're not nearly so clever as you imagine."

Dornar's face contorted. "If you take one more step, Mathos, my blade will be buried so far in your chest you can look for it between your shoulder blades. We both know that you're too far away to reach her before you die."

"Matt, stay back." Her voice was frightened but so determined, her eyes holding his over the sill. "He has two daggers and a crossbow on his back. I don't—"

"Shut up." Dornar shook her head brutally, and Lucy whimpered, trying to twist away but caught helplessly by his grip on her hair.

Mathos looked away from those beautiful dark eyes. He couldn't look at her and do what had to be done.

He let his most insolent grin spread over his face and took another step forward. "That's Right Honorable Baron Mathos to you, Dornar"—he spat the bastard's name—"or you can call me *my lord* if you prefer. Unlike you, I was born into this position."

A pulse was beating hard above Dornar's left eye. "Do you want her to die? Is that your plan?"

"Do you know what I think, you fucking asshole? I think you're betting that we'll let you drag her through the castle rather than risk her, when you have no intention of ever letting her go. I think you're going to kill her anyway."

Dornar laughed. "You would risk the queen's life on that guess?"

"No." Mathos looked left and met Jos's eyes. His friend gave a small nod, and together they took another step closer to the window. Behind him, he could hear running footsteps as more of the Hawks flooded into the room.

Mathos focused on Dornar. "No, I won't risk her life. I'll risk mine."

He let the beast take him, allowed his fury and fear and desperation to flood his veins as his scales set hard over his body and his claws lengthened impossibly further. And then he leaped.

A lifetime living in danger with his beast had built them into a weapon. A honed, ferocious unit, acting together almost entirely on instinct as he hurled himself at Dornar.

Dornar let the dagger fly and the blade struck Mathos with vicious power, slashing through his scales and sliding deep into his flesh below his ribs, scraping against bone. But he hardly felt it.

He met Dornar in the air, rolling and twisting to grab the former High Chancellor's head and pull him through the window. Holding him under his arm, with his forearm gripping Dornar's throat, legs braced against the wall.

Lucy screamed, pain and terror curdling in her voice,

but Jos was already through the window, the sound of his wings beating reassuringly against the wall.

He had to trust that his friend would hold her.

Dornar cursed and released her hair to push himself further into the room, grappling hard against Mathos's headlock. Surging up, he knocked the blade, driving it even deeper, and Mathos grunted in agony as he fought to hold his twisting, coiling opponent.

Dornar swiveled, snaking under his arm, but Mathos caught him, hauling him back. They both breathed hard, beasts rumbling savagely as they battled.

Mathos clenched his arm around Dornar's neck, ignoring the torture of the knife grinding between them, and squeezed.

Dornar flailed like a berserker, reaching desperately for his ankle and the knife that was guaranteed to be hidden there.

Mathos tightened his grip, using all the strength in his arms to crush the hard scales shielding Dornar's throat. The sides of his vision blurred and blackened, and something crashed heavily behind him. But all of his focus was on the thrashing man gripped in his arms.

Dornar reached his ankle, and the blade came free with a rasp. He started to lift it, swinging up, and Mathos used the momentum of Dornar's swing to haul him round, twisting brutally, throwing all his remaining strength and fury into that one devastating movement.

Dornar's neck broke with a crack, and he sagged limply, the knife falling uselessly to the carpet.

Mathos dropped him, unable to hold him, and sagged slowly to his knees, breathing heavily over the bloody corpse.

"Matt! Gods!"

He looked up to see Lucy running toward him. Her neck was bleeding and bruised, her white shift splattered with blood and her hair standing in rough clumps where it had been torn from her head.

"Oh, gods!" She flew into him, clutching him from the side, completely ignoring the butchery around them, entirely unconcerned by his beast, by the fact that he was fully battle-scaled and covered in gore, his long claws still extended.

"Lucy?" he asked in a gruff voice, terrified he might have frightened her. She lifted her head and pressed a rough, frantic kiss onto his mouth. "I thought he was going to…." Her small hand touched the knife, and he grunted in sudden agony.

She lifted her face, her hands fluttering over his shoulders as she screamed, "Rafael! Haniel! Help me!"

And then he felt the pain. The deep, burning torture. He groaned as she helped him lie back, the Hawks standing back to let Rafe and Haniel rush forward.

The two healers knelt beside him, working together to hold his wound, muttering about a perforated liver and shouting orders for boiled water and clear alcohol.

He shut his eyes, trying to breathe.

Someone pulled out the dagger, and he ground his teeth to hold in a rough scream. Firm hands held him down, warm drowsiness spreading up through his body.

Lucy's freezing fingers rested on his forehead and then took his hand in a tight grip as she hovered beside him anxiously, as darkness blotted across his vision.

There was a rough murmur, somewhere far away, that could only be Tristan, and frantic discussion about how Dornar had avoided the increased security.

People came and went while the healers worked. He

must have passed out briefly, but he awoke when they sat him up to wrap a bandage around his torso, Lucy still beside him.

Tristan and Rafe worked together to lift him onto the bed, and a flurry of guards cleaned the room and set a new fire as Haniel gripped his shoulder and a soothing warmth slid through his bones once more.

He forced his eyes open, found Tristan, and whispered, "Guards?"

"I've doubled the amount of time the patrols spend looking inward and put men on the roof. Val has gone to coordinate new patrol routes and all staff has been called to an emergency meeting in an hour. We found the weapons he'd hidden in the gardener's shed. As far as we can tell, no one's been in there, except Dornar, since the gardens were flooded."

Lucy curled up on the pillow next to him, still holding his hand as she murmured, "Thank you, Tristan."

Tristan nodded gravely. "It should never have happened. Please accept our deepest apologies, Your Majesty. If you feel, ah, if you would prefer a different Supreme Commander, I can help you find—"

"I've asked you several times to call me Lucilla," Lucy replied. "And no, I don't want a different commander."

Tristan bowed his head. "Thank you."

Mathos allowed himself an exhausted huff and opened his heavy eyes, just enough to focus on his friend. "Thank you, Tristan. For everything."

Tristan gave him a long, tired look, and then nodded. He turned to Lucy. "I've put three guards outside your door, and, obviously, my second-in-command is in here with you, even if he's not at his best right now."

His beast stirred tiredly in grateful relief. Tristan had forgiven him.

His old friend gave him another look as he opened the door to let himself out. "Next time you want some food, fucking send someone else to get it."

Lucy laughed, but Mathos just groaned. Laughing hurt.

He gritted his teeth and lifted the arm on his good side so that she could crawl underneath it and rest her head softly on his chest. She cuddled against him for long moments as he let his hazy thoughts drift.

He was almost asleep when he heard her broken voice whispering, "I thought I was going to lose you."

He tightened his arm. Gods. He had never imagined this life. Had never imagined finding someone so precious to him, so essential, that his own vulnerability, his own pain, was of no consequence.

"I thought I was going to lose you too," he admitted, pressing his lips to her hair. "Never again, okay? We're in this together now. Forever."

He could feel her smiling against his chest as she replied, "Yes, together. For all of it."

Chapter Twenty-Eight

LUCILLA STRODE THROUGH THE PALACE, Matt beside her.

The great hall was filled with bunting and silver-painted winter boughs and bright berries. It had been cleaned and polished, tapestries aired and ancient art rehung, ready for her coronation the next day.

Household staff and Blue Guards nodded as they passed. Although she still got occasional strange looks, they were growing accustomed to her chosen uniform of breeches, knee-high boots, soft leather bodice, and dark blue tunic embroidered with the royal fighting boars.

At some point, she would change the royal crest to the boars facing forward together, no longer fighting, but partners. Embodying the values they were striving to build within her new court: honor, courage, and perseverance. But she was leaving it as it was for the moment, keeping some stability among the sea of changes.

She glanced sideways at Matt—Baron Mathos now—the rock of support that she was building her new home on.

After days of constant care by Rafe and Haniel, fighting back the fever that had followed his stabbing, and regular healings of his wound, he was finally back on his feet. Keeping her amused with his usual disregard for authority and dirty jokes.

And wherever he went, he kept her small treasure in a pouch against his skin. The first day she'd seen it, he'd wrapped his arms around her and told her that he was holding it for her. That if she ever needed an escape, he would be ready to run with her.

Gods. How did he always know exactly what to say?

What he didn't know, what she hadn't yet told him, however, was that she had invited his family as special guests to attend the coronation. It was going to be a surprise. Damn, she hoped it went okay; it was going to be bloody awkward if it didn't.

At least Alanna, Nim, and Keely would be there to help her fix it if it all went horribly wrong. That's why she needed to bring them together now, before Alanna and Val traveled north to finally ratify the treaty, taking Keely with them.

Thank the gods they would only be gone for a few weeks. She needed her new friends.

They arrived at the stables, making their way through the buzz of activity as carpenters, bricklayers, and builders surveyed the nearby barracks. Tristan and Val had been so inspired by the Nephilim barracks that they had wanted to make a few changes, and Lucilla had agreed. It was a good way to start fresh. To clear out the bad and begin again.

If they managed to get the treaty signed in time, they might even drain the moat and look at restoring the gardens in the spring.

But that wasn't what they were here to see.

"Ah, there he is." She waved to Jos, who was emerging from the stable block. He saluted back and dipped his chin politely and then swung the big oak door open.

It was a huge block, housing the destriers and coursers of the warriors stationed at the palace, as well as the array of horses that served the royal household. They stepped inside the darkness of the cool building to find Haniel waiting for them, eyes twinkling.

"Your surprise," Lucilla announced, gesturing forward.

Matt looked over the wooden gate blocking the stall and grinned. "Heracles! He's back!" he looked over at the adjacent stall. "And Penelope too."

Yes, Penelope was back. And the knowledge that she was safe and home fitted the last missing piece back into Lucilla's heart. But that wasn't her surprise.

It was something else. Something that Matt had talked about repeatedly. Something he had been unable to do while he recovered and claimed his barony, then immediately started helping Tristan haul the Blues back into order, all while working with Val and Alanna to prepare for their trip and spending time with the council every day.

She tipped her head toward the stall. "Look closer."

Mathos gave her a curious look and then stepped up to the stall door. Heracles obliged by shifting to the side with a huff, and then they could all see the small figure dutifully brushing his rich coat.

She was clean, well dressed in a blue tunic, new breeches and shiny boots, blond hair neatly braided. Her face a little fuller. But still, unmistakably, Alis.

Mathos looked back at Lucilla over his shoulder, his eyes so full of love that it took her breath away as he silently mouthed, "Thank you."

He turned forward to lean on the stall door. "Hello, apple pip."

The girl grinned. "Hello, Mathos of the Hawks."

"What are you doing here?" Mathos asked, his voice casual, but Lucilla could hear the emotion beneath it.

Alis dropped an unsteady bow toward Lucilla, who couldn't help her lips twitching. Good, the girl was already learning to be a warrior.

"Queen Lucy got me a 'prenticeship with the Nephilim Clibanarii!" Her eyes sparkled as she danced from foot to foot. "My mum said yes, and I'm gonna go to the Temple at Eshcol with Mister Haniel when he goes back. To be in the cavalry and ride horses! But first I'm gonna be in the coronation. The actual coronation! I've even got my own room. And"—she lowered her voice—"Queen Lucy said I can eat whatever I want!"

Mathos tipped his head back and laughed, his beast rumbling pleasantly in a way that never failed to wrap itself around Lucilla's heart.

"Ah, apple pip, I'm glad to hear it." They chatted for a few moments more before leaving Alis to take care of Heracles under the Nephilim healer's protective eyes.

Mathos wrapped an arm around her shoulders as they walked back toward the palace, and she could feel the deep joy vibrating through him and his beast.

"Well, Mathos of the Hawks." Lucilla looked up at him from beneath her lashes. "I think the kingdom is safe for the next few hours. Can you possibly think of anything we can do to fill them?"

"Mm-hmm, Queen Lucy," Mathos agreed, gold spilling into the hazel of his eyes. "I've got a particularly good idea —one I've been waiting to share with you for some time now. We just need to stop off in the kitchens on the way back to our rooms."

She raised a quizzical eyebrow. "The kitchens?"

"Yes," he agreed, leaning down to murmur against her ear, "that's where they keep the cream."

Epilogue

KEELY STOOD on the tall battlements of the Old Tower, watching the slow drift of the dark Tamasa waters flowing past. The icy wind tugged at her, and she wrapped her cloak tighter, huddling into its heavy folds.

Alanna and Val would cross that cold expanse in the morning; pass through the sparse winter-gray woods on the distant shore, and join the Great North Road. They would be traveling on horseback, taking carts of supplies and gifts with them, as well as a covered carriage for if the weather grew particularly foul.

They would be in Verturia within six days. Seven, if you counted the final day of traveling from the border to the high mountain capital.

And she would be going with them.

When she'd left, she had never imagined returning. Never thought she'd see that great escarpment rising before her or climb through those high passes and emerge onto the windswept upland moors. Never expected to stand, once again, on the mountain-ringed battlements of Castle

Duneidyn and hear the clear chime of bells calling the prayers, or feel the drums beating in time with her pulse as she raised her voice and joined in the celebration songs, giving thanks to the Bard who sang life into the world.

And yet, it was the only thing she could think of doing. She was adrift—as loose and aimless as a water-scoured log floating on the Tamasa—and almost as lonely. And a deep need had overtaken her; the need to go home.

She took the letter out from the pocket in her cloak, gripping it tightly as the wind tried to snatch it away, and unfolded it; pressing it down on the cold stone to hold it flat while she read. Not that she needed to, she knew every word by heart.

She folded it back into a small square and returned it to her pocket. Bard. What was Tor going to say when he read it? What would he do?

For the hundredth time, she second guessed her decision. A part of her felt ashamed at the cowardice of writing a letter. Thought she should march up to him on the parade ground, or in the barracks, or wherever he was hiding from her today, and tell him everything.

But a bigger part, the part that still ached and grieved and wanted him to put his arms around her and hold her close, reminded her that she *had* tried. And he had been unable, or unwilling, to listen.

The letter was the best way. He would know everything, and then he could decide what he wanted to do. What choice he wanted to make.

And she wouldn't have to stand in front of him, waiting for her heart to be ripped apart by his decision—again—because she would be far, far away when he made it.

Thank you!

Thank you for reading *Mathos*, I hope you enjoyed his and Lucilla's story. It was a joy to write, and I can't wait to spend more time with my favorite squad's inner beasts!

Tor and Keely's story is coming next, and after that Reece is going to be looking for some redemption.

If you'd love to spend some more time in Brythoria (and possibly find out a little more about where the Mabin and the Tarasque came from (hint!)) please join my mailing list at www.jennielynnroberts.com.

I promise first looks, all the news, and bonus content including a free Hawks novella:

Kaden
He has to leave. He can't take her with him. And he needs to go *now*.

Kaden has always kept his true feelings for Ava hidden

—he couldn't give her hope when he knew there was none. He must walk away even if it breaks her heart and destroys him *and* his beast.

Ava can't let losing Kaden stop her; she has patients to care for and a secret of her own hiding in the icy northern mountains. But there's danger on those lonely slopes—danger that could cost them far more than broken hearts.

Will Kaden walk away like he's always planned? Or will he risk everything for a happily ever after with Ava—and trust her to save him back when the time comes?

Kaden is a prequel novella set six generations before the events in The Hawks series. It's a hundred page (fully resolved!) sexy, steamy, adult fantasy romance with a guaranteed happy ever after.

Sign up for my newsletter and download for free:

Get Kaden now!

Also by Jennie Lynn Roberts

Tristan (The Hawks - book 1)

His redemption might be *her* downfall...

Tristan has nothing left to lose. His best friend's betrayal cost him *everything*. Now, he's going to take it back. All he has to do to get the Hawks reinstated to their rightful position at the palace is track down the traitor's younger sister and turn her over for execution.

But Nim's not the girl Tristan left behind years ago; she's a stubborn, loyal, beautiful woman, and he can't stop himself from wanting her.

Nim fled with nothing when the king's favorite came for her. All she has left is the conviction that her brother is innocent—and her determination to free him. She'll do anything... even if it means convincing Tristan to help her. But the man he's become is a far cry from the boy she fell in love with so long ago. He's formidably stern and deeply untrusting. She'll just have to hope he still has a heart under that battle-scarred exterior.

When love and duty collide, will Tristan follow his orders or follow his heart?

Val (The Hawks - book 2)

He'll do anything to save her. And then he'll say goodbye...

Being framed for murder, captured, and tortured for weeks didn't break Val. But seeing Alanna every day, knowing she didn't love him as he loved her, surely would. So, he'll do whatever is necessary to stop the king from executing her...then he'll walk away. Forever.

Queen Alanna gave up everything—including her soul mate— to secure the treaty that would end the war. Now, her husband wants her dead and any chance she had for true happiness with Val is ruined.

The king's new guards are arrayed against them, the threat of war looms large, and their enemy has the upper hand. When all is said and done, will Alanna choose to sacrifice her own happiness to save her kingdom? Or will she risk it all for a second chance at happily ever after with Val?

Tor (The Hawks - book 4)

**What is it about her that makes him lose his mind?
Every. Damn. Time.**

Tor's world is falling apart. The king he'd sworn to guard? Dead.
The family he worked so hard for? They certainly wasted no time
disowning him. All he has left is the Hawks… and an intense
desire to win Keely's heart. It won't be easy—especially not after
the mistake he made when they were last together. But he has to
try, because the alternative, living without her, is unthinkable.

Losing someone you love leads to nothing but pain. Keely learned
that the hard way. But there was something about Tor that made
her wonder if loving him was worth the risk… until he opened his
mouth and ruined everything. Now her best option is to create a
new future on her own—no matter how much she might wish her
relationship with Tor could be different.

But all is not well in Brythoria. The treaty still isn't ratified, and
the mountain border is filled with enemies poised to destroy them.
Can Tor and Keely find their way back to each other? Or will
their second chance at happily ever after burn in the fires of
impending war?

About the Author

Jennie Lynn Roberts believes that every kickass heroine should have control of her own story, a swoony hero to fight beside her, and a guaranteed happily ever after. Because that doesn't always happen in real life, she began creating her own worlds that work just the way they should. And she hasn't looked back since.

Jennie would rather be writing than doing anything else—except for spending time with her gorgeous family, of course. But when she isn't building vibrant new worlds to get lost in, she can be found nattering with friends, baking up a storm, or strolling in the woods around her home in England.

If you want to talk books, romance or reluctant heroes with Jennie, feel free to contact her.

Printed in Great Britain
by Amazon